# "Death in S[ilver]"
# and
# "The Golden Peril"

## TWO CLASSIC ADVENTURES OF

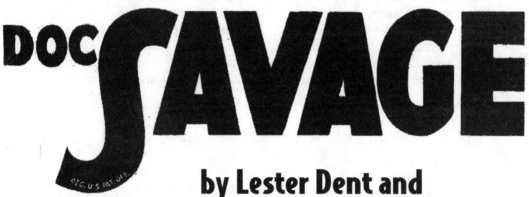

DOC **SAVAGE**

REG. U S PAT. OFF.

### by Lester Dent and
### Harold A. Davis writing as Kenneth Robeson

## with new historical essays
## by Will Murray

Published by Sanctum Productions for
# NOSTALGIA VENTURES, INC.
P.O. Box 231183; Encinitas, CA 92023-1183

This Nostalgia Ventures edition is an unabridged republication of the text and illustrations of two stories from *Doc Savage Magazine,* as originally published by Street & Smith Publications, Inc., N.Y.: *Death in Silver* from the October 1934 issue, and *The Golden Peril* from the December 1937 issue. Typographical errors have been tacitly corrected in this edition. This is a work of its time. Consequently, the text is reprinted intact in its original historical form, including occasional out-of-date ethnic and cultural stereotyping.

ISBN: 1-932806-26-7    13 Digit: 1-932806-26-1

First printing: January 2007

Series editor: Anthony Tollin
sanctumotr@earthlink.net

Consulting editor: Will Murray

Copy editor: Joseph Wrzos

Proofreader: Carl Gafford

The editors gratefully acknowledge the contributions of Tom Stephens and Scott Cranford in the preparation of this volume, and William T. Stolz of the Western Historical Manuscript Collection of the University of Missouri at Columbia for research assistance with the Lester Dent Collection.

Nostalgia Ventures, Inc.
P.O. Box 231183; Encinitas, CA 92023-1183

Visit Doc Savage at www.nostalgiatown.com

*Crime after crime, with the loot running into
millions—then the blowing up of a Wall
Street skyscraper finally involves
Doc Savage in a struggle with*

# DEATH IN SILVER

## A Complete Book-length Novel

# By KENNETH ROBESON

### Chapter I
### SILVER DEATH'S-HEADS

THERE was a frozen, stony expression on the tall man's face, and his dark eyes rolled and jerked with unease. His hands were drawn pale and hard at his sides.

These signs should have told an experienced observer that the man was worried and scared. But there were no experienced observers among the stenographers and clerks in the office of Seven Seas, so the glances they gave the tall man were merely the boot-licking smiles of employees who

had about as much spirit as rabbits.

A person with spunk did not work long with Seven Seas, because Paine L. Winthrop, the owner, was a cold-blooded driver of the old school, an industrial emperor who looked upon those under him as vassals. Had Paine L. Winthrop lived a hundred years earlier, he would have kept a retinue of slaves—and beaten them often.

Maybe Clarence Sparks had an inkling that something was awry. Clarence was a billing clerk for Seven Seas, which operated transatlantic freight boats and had no connection with Winthrop's Shipyards, which was also controlled by Paine L.

**Thrilling Tales and Features**

**DEATH IN SILVER by Lester Dent**
**(writing as "Kenneth Robeson")** ............................. 4

**INTERLUDE IN SILVER AND GOLD**
**by Will Murray** .......................................... 69

**THE GOLDEN PERIL by Harold A. Davis and**
**Lester Dent (writing as "Kenneth Robeson")** .......... 72

**POSTSCRIPT** ................................................. 128

**Cover paintings by Robert Harris**
**and Walter M. Baumhofer**

**Interior illustrations by Paul Orban**

Winthrop, and which built freight steamers. Clarence was a rabbit, like the rest of those who worked for Seven Seas. But Clarence also had sharp wits.

"Good afternoon, Commodore Winthrop," said Clarence.

Winthrop's only claim to the designation of commodore was that he held such an office in an exclusive yacht club, but he liked the title and the canny Clarence knew it.

Winthrop seemed not to hear. He walked stiffly, mechanically, from the corridor door to his private office, and his face was rigid, his eyes busy, his hands hard and gray.

"The old wolf!" grunted Clarence. "Some day somebody is going to give Winthrop what he has coming to him."

Clarence was a prophet, a great deal more of a prophet than he knew.

Paine L. Winthrop entered his office, turned the key in the door, then tried the knob to make sure it was locked. He stuffed a corner of a silk handkerchief into the keyhole, using a match for the purpose. He pulled off his topcoat and laid it along the bottom of the door. After these two precautions, he seemed to feel that no one would eavesdrop.

Striding stiffly to the window, he looked down at the street forty floors below. Pedestrians there resembled ants. Paine L. Winthrop ordinarily got a thrill out of the view, because he liked to think of other people as ants. But now the view made him shiver.

One of New York's frequent fogs was mushroomed over the city, especially thick out over the nearby East River, but less dense here in the Wall Street sector. Winthrop shivered again and jerked a cord which closed the slats of the Venetian blind.

Seating himself at his desk, he hugged a telephone close and dialed with a trembling forefinger. He missed his number the first time, through nervousness, but got it on the second attempt.

Before speaking, he drew out a costly watch and noted that it lacked only a few minutes of being four in the afternoon. Evidently he recognized the voice which answered at the other end of the wire, for no names were exchanged.

"Your t-time is almost up," he said shakily.

THE other did not respond immediately, and Paine L. Winthrop seemed on the verge of repeating his warning. Then a coarse, angry whisper came over the line.

"Winthrop, you are passing up a chance of becoming one of the richest men alive," said the distant speaker.

"I am passing up a chance of landing in the electric chair," Winthrop snapped.

"Listen, Winthrop," the other said earnestly. "I have explained to you very—"

"There is no object in arguing," said the shipping magnate. "I may be a hard businessman, and I may be a skinflint and a slave driver, as some people have called me; but I stay within the law. Early in my youth, I learned that was the best policy."

The distant whispering voice took on a menacing quality.

"You are already too deep in this to back out, Winthrop," it pointed out. "We have used your shipyard."

Winthrop flinched as if he had been seized with an inner chill in the region of his spine, but his forbidding face remained set and determined.

"I was deceived," he grated. "I thought the thing being built in my shipyard was for a foreign government. I think I can convince the authorities of that."

"It seems that I made a mistake in taking you into my confidence," said the whisper.

Winthrop snapped, "You certainly did!"

"I should have turned the matter over to the Silver Death's-Heads, as the newspapers so dramatically term them," retorted the other.

The mention of Silver Death's-Heads had the effect of nearly causing Winthrop to drop the receiver. The man peered about as if fearing some grisly menace might be in the room with him. Then he got a grip on himself.

"There is no more to be said," he stated grimly. "I have given you a chance to disband the Silver Death's-Heads and destroy the—the thing that was built in my shipyard. You refuse. Therefore, I shall now call the police."

His voice, charged with desperate excitement, had risen to a yell that had considerable volume. The sound penetrated through the door of the private office, despite the precautions which Winthrop had taken in stuffing the keyhole and covering the crack at the bottom of the door.

Clarence Sparks, at his desk outside, heard. He hesitated, eyeing the door, longing to listen. Then, summoning his nerve, he shuffled over to the water cooler, which was beside the door of the private office. He could listen from there.

Inside the office, Winthrop screamed, "I am going to call the police and tell them all about the Silver Death's-Heads! I am going to tell who is apparently their chief, and I am going to tell whose devilish brain is actually behind all of this!"

The coarse whisper over the telephone said, "I can promise that you will not live long enough to do that, Winthrop!"

Winthrop was squirming, perspiring. He shouted, "Killing me will not help! I have a blueprint showing some of your working methods. I have given it to my secretary. And I have told her the whole story."

"You are bluffing, Winthrop," snarled the whispering one.

"I am not!" Winthrop barked. "My secretary will give the whole story to the police if anything happens to me. Now, will you give this all up, or do I call the police?"

"Call them if you dare," suggested the other.

"I will!" Winthrop banged the receiver up.

Shaky and pallid, Clarence Sparks backed from the door. He had overheard too much for his peace of mind. He was in the same boat with the young man who was fishing for minnows and caught a shark.

The fact that Clarence Sparks was backing away from the door undoubtedly saved his life.

There was a cataclysmic crash. The door of Winthrop's private office exploded into fragments. The whole partition wall caved. Part of the ceiling came thundering down.

FORTY stories below, on the street, an ear-splitting crack of sound caused people to look up. It was like the lash of a stupendous thunderbolt. After one glance upward, the pedestrians cried out in terror and began to run.

A cloud of bricks, mortar and twisted steel was falling down the side of the skyscraper, giving at first the impression that the whole great building was coming to pieces. A moment later, to those farther up the street, it was evident that a great cavity had been blown in the side of the fog-piercing edifice.

Debris fell to the sidewalk with a great uproar. Three parked cars, fortunately unoccupied, were crushed, and a prowling taxicab was partially wrecked. The driver of the hack, slightly cut and bruised, got out and ran, squawling that there had been an earthquake.

Following the fall of the debris, there was a brittle jangling of dropping glass all over the neighborhood, for windows had been blown out by the blast. Numerous people were cut; others had narrow escapes.

Then came several moments of almost complete silence. The quiet was so complete that the droning of an airplane over the nearby river could be heard. Then, as the plane swept away, there was the sound of a motor boat, also on the river.

The presence of the plane and the motor boat on the river at that particular instant came to the attention of a number of persons, and was later to become a fact of significance.

The tension following the explosion snapped. Women screeched and had hysterics. More stoic souls peered up in the fog and observed the yawning hole in the side of the skyscraper where the private office of Paine L. Winthrop had been. Policemen came running, and ambulance sirens wailed. Bedlam reigned.

## Chapter II
## THE ARCHER IN SILVER

THE building housing Paine L. Winthrop's shipping company, the Seven Seas, was not the most imposing in the Wall Street sector, but it narrowly missed that designation. Penthouses ornamented the tops of most of the skyscrapers in the district, and this one was no exception.

The penthouse on this building was a pretentious affair with numerous glass walls which afforded the occupant full sunlight. Most of the glass had been shattered by the blast below. In fact, it was a miracle that the whole structure had not gone down, with a resultant vast loss of life.

One of the penthouse rooms contained many work benches, and these supported racks holding innumerable test tubes, retorts, microscopes, mixing trays, pestles and bottled chemicals. That the benches *had* supported this array would be more correct, for most of the stuff was now on the floor. Several small chemical fires had started.

A remarkable-looking man was picking himself up from the mess of glass and liquids. He jumped up and down and emitted a roar, for he had been slightly burned by a vial of acid.

The roar and the way the fellow bounced about gave the impression of a great, angry ape. The man's appearance did little to detract from the impression. He had practically no forehead; his thick, muscle-gnarled arms were longer than his legs, and his skin was leathery and covered with bristles which resembled rusty nails. His mouth was so unnaturally large that it looked as if there had been an accident in the assembling of his pleasantly ugly face.

"Habeas!" the apish man bellowed.

A pig came galloping into view, squealing excitedly—an almost incredibly grotesque specimen of the porker family, as homely in his way as was the man who had called him. The shote had long, dog-like legs, a scrawny body, an inquisitive snout, and ears almost large enough to serve as wings.

"Dang it, Habeas," the homely chemist grinned, "I was afraid that dude lawyer had thrown a grenade at you."

Someone seemed to be trying to open a near-by door. Loud kicks sounded, wood crunched, and the door fell inward.

The man who came through was slender, waspish, and attired to the height of sartorial perfection. He had a high forehead, the mobile mouth of an orator. In one hand he gripped a thin black cane which was slightly separated at a joint near the handle, thus disclosing the object to be a sword cane with a razor-sharp blade.

The well-dressed man glared at the homely chemist, his expression that of a gentleman who had just found a toad on his breakfast table.

## HABEAS CORPUS

Habeas Corpus is an Arabian hog who is not very big, but makes up for his size in other ways.

Habeas's master, Monk, got him in Arabia. Monk's story is that Habeas Corpus's former owner, an Arab, had sold the pig because Habeas had been making a nuisance of himself by catching hyenas and dragging their carcasses up to the house. It was possible that either Monk or the Arab exaggerated, of course.

But Habeas Corpus is unique among shoats, although it seems he was permanently stunted in youth. Monk has spent many long hours training Habeas, and the result is that the pig possesses a brain which is remarkable. Habeas also knows certain signals, conveyed by movements of the hands, or even a winking of the eye, and will do all of the things which he has been taught the signals mean he is to do. These secret signals of Monk's account for some of Habeas's seemingly human intelligence.

When not otherwise engaged, Habeas Corpus can usually be found annoying Ham in some manner.

---

"Monk, I always did know you would blow us up with some of your idiotical chemical experiments," he snapped.

This was nothing if not libel. The apish man, "Monk," was Lieut. Col. Andrew Blodgett Mayfair, and conceded by those who knew to be one of the greatest of living chemists. His head, which did not look as if it had room for a thimbleful of brains, harbored a fabulous amount of chemical and electrochemical lore.

Monk glared at the dapper newcomer.

"The shyster lawyer heard from," he growled.

That was another libel. The dressy gentleman was Brig. Gen. Theodore Marley Brooks, better known as "Ham," one of the most astute lawyers ever to get his sheepskin from Harvard.

A strange pair, these two. They were always together, yet no one could remember either one having spoken a civil word to the other. Those who knew, however, could cite a number of instances when each had risked his life to save the other.

Men far-famed in their professions, both of them. Yet they were known to the comers of the earth for another reason—known as two members of a group of five who were assistants to a man who was probably the most famed adventurer of all time.

Monk and Ham were aides of Doc Savage, the man of bronze, the man of mystery, the being of fabulous accomplishments, who was almost a legend to the general public, but who was the synonym for terror and justice to those who preyed upon their fellow men.

HAM flourished his sword cane. "What was that—that quake?"

"Search me," said Monk, whose voice, in repose, was remarkably small and querulously childlike.

Seizing a fire extinguisher, Monk went to work on the chemical blazes. He resented this damage to his laboratory, for it was one of the most complete in existence, exceeded only by those maintained by the man of bronze, Doc Savage, who was himself a greater chemist than Monk.

Habeas Corpus, Monk's pet pig, backed away from the flames, saw he was getting near Ham, and hastily shied off. Habeas and Ham did not get along together. Ham had repeatedly threatened to make breakfast bacon out of Habeas.

The fires doused, Monk cast aside the extinguisher.

"Let's find out what happened," he said.

"A good idea coming from a strange source," Ham stated unkindly, and they went out. The pig, Habeas, they left behind.

The elevators were not operating, probably due to the damage wrought by the blast, and they had to walk down. It did not take them long to reach the scene of the detonation.

They were efficient, these two—men accustomed to scenes of violence through their long association with Doc Savage. Doc seemed to exist always in the shadow of peril and destruction.

Without delay, they went to work to ascertain the cause of the explosion. And there, they ran up against a profound puzzle, as well as a gruesome scene.

Paine L. Winthrop was dead. No doubt of that, as it was necessary for the ambulance surgeons to assemble the scattered parts of his body on a stretcher before it could be carried away.

Several of the Seven Seas office employees had been injured. A broken arm, received by a stenographer as she was knocked over her desk, was the most serious. Others were only lacerated and bruised.

Monk and Ham put quick inquiries about the cause of the blast. No one could give a reply of value except Paine L. Winthrop's head clerk, who was quite sure there had been no bomb, since she had left the private office only shortly before the arrival of her boss.

Before Monk and Ham could locate fragments of whatever had caused the detonation, a swarm of policemen and newspaper reporters arrived. The officers herded everyone to an office one floor below, it having been decided that the skyscraper was in no danger of falling.

The office in which those who had been on the explosion scene were concentrated was the headquarters of a firm dealing in imported antiques and art works. Adjoining the office were numerous stock rooms holding pictures, armor, pieces of ancient furniture, weapons, costumes and like articles. These were all antiques.

The newspaper reporters descended upon Monk and Ham. Both were high-pressure copy, for it was known that they were members of Doc Savage's group of aides, and Doc was front-page news all seven days of the week.

"Is Doc working on this?" a journalist connected with a tabloid demanded.

"No," said Monk, irked because the locust swarm of scribes were keeping Ham and himself from investigating. "Keep Doc out of it."

The tabloid reporter ran to a telephone and informed his city editor, "Two of the famous Doc Savage's men are on the spot and working on the mystery explosion. They deny that Doc himself is interested, but we don't need to mention that. Doc's name in this will make it all the bigger."

"Our pals," Monk growled.

Modern newspapers function with breathtaking speed, and while the reporters were still harassing Monk and Ham, extra editions of their sheets arrived.

Monk snatched one of these and retired with Ham to a stock room, the walls of which were hung with the work of old masters, to see how much Doc had been brought into the affair.

THEY expected to see the blast story occupying a whole page of the tabloid, but to their surprise, it divided honors with another yarn.

"I say," said Ham, who affected a pronounced Harvard accent whenever he thought of it. "Those Silver Death's-Head beggars have been acting again."

They read the big black headlines and the news story below them. The thing was almost childishly dramatic, as written.

## SILVER DEATH'S-HEADS STRIKE; MYSTERY MEN ROB ARMORED CAR

### Get a Quarter Million In Loot
### Vanish As Usual

The terror in silver is with New York again. At three o'clock this afternoon, these frightful men of mystery shot down the drivers and guard of an armored truck in the streets of Manhattan and took $250,000.00 in cash.

Accounts of the number of robbers vary. Some spectators say there were twenty; others claim only five or six. The robbers escaped in a fast car and evaded police pursuit in the waterfront section of the East River.

The thieves wore silver-colored suits and weird silver hoods which made their heads resemble skulls. This description tallies with the gang which has committed other robberies and murders and which is known to the police as the Silver Death's-Heads.

The last crime committed by the Silver Death's-Heads was the cold-blooded sinking of the liner *Avallancia*, pride of the Transatlantic Company, in New York Harbor.

Bedford Burgess Gardner, president of the Transatlantic Company, has not been able to explain what motive could have been behind the sinking of the *Avallancia*.

"Wild stuff," commented Monk.

"Typical newspaper sensationalism," Ham clipped, agreeing with Monk because he still resented being questioned by the reporters. "Silver Death's-Heads! Imagine that! What rot!"

"Too melodramatic to have much foundation in truth," Monk added. "I doubt if there are really any men called the Silver Death's-Heads. This particular tabloid colors its news to beat the band."

The two men had been making no effort to pitch their voices low, and a number of the Seven Seas office employees huddled in the room of the antique dealer overheard what was being said. Among those who could not help but catch the words was Clarence Sparks.

Mention of the Silver Death's-Heads caused Clarence to stiffen visibly, then look undecided. He hesitated, mustering up his nerve. As yet, he had not told anyone of what he had overheard outside the door of Paine L. Winthrop's private office, but hearing Monk state his belief that there were no such individuals as Silver Death's-Heads apparently moved Clarence to speak. He sidled over to Monk and Ham.

"You—you gentlemen are mistaken," he said hesitantly.

MONK squinted at the receding chin and the none-too-robust physique of Sparks.

"You know something?" he asked.

Clarence Sparks moistened his lips nervously.

"I—I hope this won't get me into trouble," he muttered.

Monk and Ham were both intensely interested.

"Spill it," Monk directed.

The Seven Seas billing clerk swelled his thin chest with a full breath of resolution.

"I was eavesdropping outside Paine L. Winthrop's door," he said in a voice which excitement made loud. "I heard him make the telephone call which was directly responsible for his death."

"Blazes!" Monk exploded. "Then it was a murder, huh?"

Clarence Sparks clenched his fists and said, "It certainly was!"

"Who was Winthrop talkin' to?" Monk demanded.

"To the secret mastermind of the Silver Death's-Heads," Clarence gulped.

"For the love of mud!" said Monk. "What was his name?"

Clarence Sparks almost yelled, "I heard Winthrop say over the telephone that it was—"

That was the last word Clarence Sparks spoke, although not the last sound he made, for his mouth suddenly flew open to its widest and let a terrific scream rip out. It was as if the scream had burst out, destroying his vocal cords; the yell rasped and was unnatural.

Clarence Sparks put his arms stiffly above his head in the manner of an aboriginal saluting the sun. Then he turned slowly, trembling and on tiptoe. When he had his back to Monk and Ham, they could see the feathered shaft of the arrow which protruded from his back.

Because Clarence Sparks was thin and poorly, his body made a clattering sound as it fell to the floor. After he fell the stiffness seemed to go out of his thin frame, his head rolled over slackly until his cheek pressed the floor, and with a bubbling rush, scarlet came from his mouth and nostrils.

But Monk and Ham were not watching the phenomena incidental to death. They were staring at the archer who had discharged the arrow, an archer in silver, a being so grotesque of appearance that they were held stunned.

## Chapter III
### THE ARCHER QUEST

THE archer was not a large man—if he was a man. He was shorter than Ham, who was not tall, and he was also scrawny, with thin arms and gnarled legs.

His garb was the strange, the gripping thing. It was silver. The cloth was of the metallic stuff such as is used to make the stage costumes of show girls, and it was cut in one garment—a coverall.

There was a hood over the head, also of silver, elastic and tight fitting. Because eye and mouth openings were dark against the shiny metallic hood, the affair had the aspect of a death's-head, a silver skull. A costly wrist watch adorned one of his pipestem arms.

The silver archer stood in the door of an adjacent office, holding a heavy medieval bow, evidently one of the antiques which filled the rooms. He dropped the bow, it thumping loudly as it fell; then he leaped backward.

The movement snapped Monk and Ham out of their trance. They dived headlong in pursuit. But the killer slammed the door; a key clinked among the tumblers. Doc Savage's two aides, flinging against the panel, found it solidly resistant.

"So there isn't any such thing as the Silver Death's-Heads!" Ham snapped.

Monk knotted an enormous, bristle-covered fist and grated, "You were the first one to get that idea, you nitwit shyster."

Then Monk grimaced and hit the door panel with his fist. The wood splintered, gave a trifle; it splintered more extensively under a second blow, then collapsed, making a hole large enough to pass the apish chemist's hairy hand. Standing well clear of the door, Monk groped for the key, found it in place, and unlocked the panel. He shoved it open.

Ham started through, sword cane in hand.

"Wait, stupid," Monk growled, and shoved the dapper lawyer back.

From a holster, so cleverly padded under an armpit that it was unnoticeable, Monk drew a weapon bearing close resemblance to an overgrown automatic pistol. But it was no automatic.

It was a supermachine pistol, the product of Doc Savage's mechanical genius, a weapon which fired at an incredible speed, discharging—instead of regulation lead slugs—thin-walled composition bullets which carried an anaesthetic compound producing quick, harmless unconsciousness.

Machine pistol in hand, Monk jumped through the door. Considering that a murderer had just entered the room, his act might have seemed reckless. But Monk wore a bulletproof vest which protected his entire body, and he knew gunmen of the modern type do not often shoot at a man's head.

Ham trailed the homely chemist. He, too, wore one of the bulletproof vests which were so light and thin as to be unnoticeable under their clothing, and was not at all uncomfortable. These vests were also a product of Doc Savage's mechanical skill.

Both men jerked up inside the room. Their jaws sagged; their eyes, roving, widened in amazement.

"Well, I'm a camel's uncle!" Monk breathed. "Where'd he go?"

Ham shook his head slowly and turned his sword cane in his hands, for their quarry was nowhere in the room. Both the outer windows were down, and the lawyer knew that this skyscraper had a wall sheer and smooth, impossible for even a so-called "human fly" to scale by ordinary methods.

MONK, charging around the room, jerked a rectangle of expensive tapestry from the wall, scowled when he saw there was no aperture back of it, and flipped the carpet up. Nowhere was there a trapdoor.

"The windows are unlocked," Ham pointed out.

"But that bird in silver couldn't have—" Monk swallowed the rest, ran to a window and wrenched it up. He looked out, seemed stunned, but said nothing.

Ham leaped to his side. Together they peered down.

"We must be getting very dumb," Ham said disgustedly.

"Speak for yourself," Monk growled, then placed a hand on the window sill and vaulted through the opening, out into space.

Without hesitating, Ham followed, instinctively using care not to disrupt the neat hang of his garments. It was a rare occasion when Ham forgot his clothing.

Perhaps six feet below the window was a wide ledge. For the moment, the two men had forgotten that the skyscraper was set back, pyramid fashion, at intervals, and that one of these setbacks was at the level of the Seven Seas offices. The killer must have fled by this route, after closing the window behind him to confuse his pursuers.

Monk pointed, "He went this way!"

City grime was smeared on the roof of the set-back, soot and dust which retained footprints plainly. The two men followed the tracks around the skyscraper. They disappeared into a window on the opposite side.

Monk and Ham clambered through the window and found themselves among mops, buckets and window-washing paraphernalia; the room was

HAM

obviously one used by janitors. There was no trace of the weirdly garbed slayer.

A corridor was beyond the store room, this being deserted for the moment. Not until Monk emitted an angry roar did any one appear, then two policemen popped out of the offices of Seven Seas.

"What's going on here?" snapped an officer.

"Where'd that killer go?" Monk demanded.

The cop gulped. "Killer! Say, what're you talking about?"

And that was the first inkling the police had of the slaying of unfortunate Clarence Sparks, for the meek-spirited billing clerk was dead, the arrow having punctured his heart. They found that out when they examined him.

Where the killer had gone remained a mystery through the course of the next fifteen minutes. Then an excited call came up from the basement regions. A fireman had been found knocked senseless in the basement.

Monk and Ham hurried down.

The fireman had thick blond hair, and that had possibly preserved his life, for the blow he had received over the head, judging by the bruise, had been terrific. A policeman was waiting for a doctor to revive the fellow.

"Let me do it," said Ham. "I have an infallible system."

Ham unsheathed his sword cane, and the onlookers say that the tip was coated for a few inches with a brownish substance which was slightly sticky. This was a drug mixture which produced senselessness when a victim was pricked.

With a fingertip, Ham removed a bit of the drug from the sword and applied it to the tongue of the unconscious fireman. The stuff in small quantities was a stimulant, but if administered in quantity produced senselessness.

The fireman revived almost at once.

"What happened to you?" Ham demanded.

"Aye not bane know," mumbled the fireman, feeling his blond head.

"Who hit you?" Ham persisted.

"He bane a feller all dressed up in shiny suit," was the reply. "Aye just see him—then *bop!* He hit me with gun."

The room where they stood was a concrete inferno far below the street, where the great oil-burning boilers roared, generating steam for the radiators and hot water for the washrooms.

Moved by a thought—he was sharp in spite of Monk's habit of terming him a nitwit shyster—Ham went over and peered into one of the fire boxes. He started violently, moved to use his sword to probe in the heat, then changed his mind and employed a cleaning bar.

Out of the fire box Ham brought a crinkled mass that had once been silver metallic cloth.

"The suit the murderer was wearing," he declared.

"Then it is someone in the building," Monk growled. "The fellow burned his rig because the police have the doors blocked and are not letting anyone out."

UNNOTICED, a man was standing in the background near the door. He was a scrawny fellow, bedecked with grease stains and dirt, garbed in the green coveralls which the janitors of the building wore. It was because he was one of the janitors that he was receiving no attention.

He deserved attention. No hint of the fact showed on his features, but he was catching every word that was being said. He had a stupid face, anyway; it was almost without a jaw, being round, with small features, and having a sickly gray color. His whole head was very much like an old, white rubber ball which had been handled with grimy fingers. He wore a costly wrist watch.

The fellow glanced over his shoulder, as if anxious to get out of the boiler room. Shortly, he did leave, but he took his time so that no suspicion was attached to his departure.

Finding his way to a telephone, he called a number. A voice—a coarse, whispering voice, obviously disguised—answered.

"This ain't goin' so hot," said the man in janitor regalia.

"What is wrong, Bugs?" asked the whispering voice.

"Two of Doc Savage's men are snooping around," reported "Bugs," his round, pale face close to the transmitter.

The whispering one swore. "I saw that in an extra edition of a tabloid newspaper. What on earth got those two involved in the affair?"

"One of them, named Monk, has a chemical laboratory on top of the building," Bugs advised.

This called forth more sibilant profanity.

"If I had known one of Doc Savage's men had a place on the building, we would have used other methods on old Winthrop," grated the distant whisper. "Doc Savage is the last man on earth we want on our necks at this stage of the game. Savage is almost inhuman. He is a mechanical wizard, a scientific genius, and a man as strong as Hercules; and he applies all of his abilities to helping other people out of trouble. He goes in for big stuff. Something like we are pulling would be his meat."

"Boss," Bugs muttered, "there's somethin' else."

"What?"

"A clerk must've been listenin' outside old Winthrop's door when—well, you know—and he overheard stuff. I don't know how much, because I croaked him before he could tell it all to Doc Savage's two men."

MONK

"You damned fool!" snarled the other. "There was nothing said in that telephone talk which would give me away."

"How was I to know that?" Bugs whined. "I was afraid he had a line on us. I had my silver outfit on, and I got hold of an old bow and arrow and let him have it."

"Oh, you idiot!" the whispering man groaned. "Right in front of two men who are as brainy as they come. Doc Savage does not have any mental blanks working for him—like I seem to have."

"Aw," Bugs mumbled. "I got away, banged a fireman over the head and burned my silver outfit so they couldn't find any fingerprints or where it was made or maybe trace the cloth."

SEVERAL seconds of silence followed this; the distant mastermind seemed to be giving deep thought to the affair. Bugs, impatient at the delay, began speaking.

"If we just hadn't bumped old Winthrop," he said. "That was—"

"That was necessary!" the distant voice finished for him. "Winthrop was a man who would not hesitate to swindle an orphan, if it could be done legally. That fooled me. The old nut had his own screwy idea of honor. Or maybe he was afraid of the law. Anyway, he was going to tell the police all about us. And he knew plenty, especially about the job we had done in his shipyard."

"Well, Savage's two men are snooping," Bugs muttered. "What're we gonna do about that? Let it ride, huh? They ain't got a line to go on."

"They'll get a line, don't worry," grated the whisperer. "Doc Savage's men are wizards, and that fellow Savage himself is positively inhuman. We must do something."

"What?" Bugs wanted to know.

After a pause, the other said, "Listen to this."

Following that, there was a chain of rapid

commands, Bugs mumbling frequently that he understood. An expression of evil pleasure overspread his unhealthy moon of a face as he heard the plans unfolded. He consulted his remarkably high-priced wrist watch.

"That oughta fix 'em," he grinned finally.

Hanging up, he made his way back through the corridor labyrinths of the great building until he located Monk and Ham. Lurking in the background, unnoticed, he kept an eye on Doc Savage's two aides.

Bugs was waiting for something, and he eyed the watch often.

As for Monk and Ham, they had given up all hope of the blond fireman furnishing any valuable information. The fellow had seen only a grotesque figure in silver. The ashes of the silver garment, a shapeless sediment of metal and cinders, furnished no clue.

"Even Doc couldn't learn anything from this," Monk complained, indicating the garment.

Ham started to nod, then refrained, since agreeing with Monk on any subject was against his policy.

"We're killing time," snapped the dapper lawyer. "Why don't we go upstairs and look over the explosion scene."

"The police have done that," Monk grunted.

"They have not found what caused the blast," Ham pointed out.

That seemed to settle the question, and they started mounting stairs, the elevators not yet being in working order.

The skyscraper had not one basement, but three, one below the other, and the boilers were in the lowermost level, deep in the solid bedrock of Manhattan Island and probably below the surface of the nearby East River, which at this point was very wide, actually a neck of New York Harbor.

The two men reached the second basement and encountered a police officer. The cop had the rank of lieutenant, but he was deferential, for Monk and Ham held honorary police stations far above his own. Doc Savage and all of his men held these honorary commissions, issued out of gratitude for past services in aiding the law enforcement agencies of the city.

"We have learned something," reported the lieutenant. "I knew you gentlemen would want all information as quickly as we got it."

"Shoot," Monk invited.

THE police officer explained rapidly: "We are entirely mystified as to the cause of the explosion which killed Winthrop, although a more intensive search may turn up some clue. We are overlooking no bets. The blast might have been a bomb, launched in some manner from a plane. In checking up, we learned that a plane was flying over the river, very near the building at the time of the explosion. Too, there was a man on the river in a motorboat."

No one paid attention to Bugs, who was loitering within earshot.

"Any way of identifying the plane?" Monk asked the policeman.

"You would be surprised how people notice things like that when something grabs their attention," replied the officer. "I suppose some persons wondered if the plane had dropped a bomb. Anyway, we have several witnesses who got the number on the lower wing surface of the plane."

"Great!" grunted Monk. "You're checking?"

"You bet. And, moreover, two or three dock workers identified the motor boat which was on the river. There was one man in the boat, and he may have seen the plane drop a bomb."

"It's pretty foggy," Monk pointed out.

The officer nodded, fumbled in a uniform pocket and produced a notebook. He thumbed through the leaves.

"Gilbert Stiles is the owner of the plane, according to the check we made on the numbers," he said. "Stiles keeps the plane for his personal pleasure. The man in the boat was a fisherman named"—he stumbled over the pronunciation "—named Gugillello Bellondi, or something like that. The flier lives on Eighty-fifth Street in Jackson Heights, and the fisherman on Sand Street in Brooklyn."

Bugs, who had overheard all of this, turned surreptitiously, fumbled out a sheet of paper and a pencil stub and put down the name of Gilbert Stiles and Gugillello Bellondi. He added data on their residences. Bugs did not put much trust in his memory.

MONK and Ham, accompanied by the police lieutenant, mounted the stairs into the topmost basement.

"We had better ring Doc in on this," Monk suggested, eyeing Ham.

Ham said, "I had the same idea before you did."

In the skyscraper lobby were a number of telephone booths. Monk entered one of these, found the outside connections undisturbed by the blast, and called the number of Doc Savage's headquarters.

The headquarters was a strange aërie on the eighty-sixth floor of the most impressive skyscraper in uptown New York, and the bronze man spent much of his leisure there. Actually, Doc Savage allowed himself no leisure in the accepted sense, all of his time being spent in research, in experiments, in study. There was a fabulously equipped library and laboratory in the headquarters.

"Doc?" asked Monk.

The question was unnecessary—Doc Savage had a remarkable voice, one which was powerful, yet controlled, modulated, giving the impression of almost eerie strength. Unmistakable, that voice.

"I just saw an extra edition of the newspaper," said Doc Savage. "Was your laboratory damaged by the explosion?"

"Some," Monk admitted. "But that isn't what I called about, Doc. There is something underhanded going on down here."

"We do not involve ourselves in anything the police can handle," Doc reminded.

"I figured you'd be interested," Monk explained. "You see, it's a queer business all along. First, there's nothing to show what caused the explosion— or if there is, they haven't found it yet. Then a guy in silver murdered Clarence Sparks, a Winthrop employee."

"What is this?" Doc asked sharply.

"A bird dressed up in a sort of silver coverall suit and a silver mask shot Sparks with a bow and arrow just as we were about to question the fellow. Sparks seemed to know something."

"Did the killer resemble the strange silver-clothed figures who have recently committed a series of big robberies and who also sunk the Transatlantic Company's liner, *Avallancia?*" Doc questioned.

"Sure," said Monk. "I think he was one of the gang."

Doc Savage was silent a moment, as if engaged in thought, then a weird and most unusual sound came from the telephone receiver. It was a sound defying description. It was a most unmusical trilling, a whistle and yet not a whistle. Possessing a throaty, exotic quality, it ran up and down the musical scale, but without adhering to a definite tune.

It might have been a wind whistling with ghostly quality through a ship's rigging, or it might have been the song of some strange jungle bird.

Monk stiffened as he heard the sound; he had heard the eerie note many times before. It was the sound of Doc Savage, the small unconscious thing which the bronze man did in moments of mental excitement. It usually came before some startling development; often it marked Doc's discovery of some obscure fact which was later to possess great significance.

"Monk," Doc said, "have you noticed anything queer about the robberies these so-called Silver Death's-Heads have been committing?"

Monk began, "Well, their silver disguises—"

"Not that," Doc told him. "There is one strange point about the robberies themselves. Have you noticed?"

"No," said Monk. "What is it?"

"A number of men have been killed in the course of the thefts," Doc stated.

"Sure, but men are often killed during robberies."

"In each case, these men were prominent," Doc explained patiently. "And on one or two occasions, the thefts during which they were shot down were of a trivial nature. I can give you one very good example."

"Let's have it," Monk requested.

"Two weeks ago a gang of the Silver Death's-Heads, seven of them to be exact, held up a small filling station on Long Island," Doc announced. "The filling station was very small and never had more than a few dollars on hand. But a limousine had just driven into the station to fill up with gas. It was occupied by a wealthy man named Kirkland Le Page. He was shot and killed. The filling station attendant was lying on the floor of his station at the time and did not see what provoked the shooting. Le Page was driving his car himself."

"I remember," said Monk.

"Kirkland Le Page was vice president of Transatlantic Company, owners of the liner *Avallancia*, which was later sunk by the Silver Death's-Heads," Doc stated.

"Blazes!" exploded Monk. "There's something big behind this!"

"Exactly," Doc agreed.

MONK stood silently in the telephone booth, mentally turning over what Doc Savage had just revealed. The homely chemist nodded slowly to himself. He would have been willing to bet that Doc had been on the verge of investigating the weird Silver Death's-Heads, even if this afternoon's explosion had not occurred.

Monk opened his mouth to speak further—but things began to happen.

There was a stifled yell from the lobby behind Monk, where Ham and the policeman stood. Feet pounded on the lobby floor. There was another yell. A shot banged.

Monk tried to turn. His shoulder spread was vast, the telephone booth small. At first he did not make it. He squirmed to get around.

The booth had glass windows. With a jangling crash, these caved in. Glass showered Monk. The homely chemist got a flash of a hand encased in a silver glove. The hand held a heavy automatic.

Silver glove and weighty gun were all that Monk saw. The weapon lashed for his head. He sought to duck. The booth was too small, and the automatic came down full on the top of his nubbin of a head.

Monk slumped and never felt the gun club down on his head twice again, the blows murderously vicious.

## Chapter IV
### TWO SILVER MURDERS

DOC SAVAGE heard the ugly sounds of the blows upon Monk's head, for there had been no time for the homely chemist to replace the telephone receiver, and telephones are sensitive.

Doc listened closely. The noise had been

distinct enough to tell what had happened. Over the wire came scuffling sounds, grunts which meant that Monk's bulk was being hauled from the booth. Then the telephone receiver in the booth must have been replaced; there was a *click*, with silence afterward.

Doc Savage had been bending over an expensively inlaid table as he conversed with Monk. He straightened, and his tremendous physical build was apparent to its fullest. The telephone, the massive table, seemed to shrink beside him; yet it was only in comparison to these objects that his full proportions were evident.

So symmetrically was his giant frame developed that, seen at a distance and away from objects to which his size might be compared, he appeared no larger than other men.

But he would never be mistaken for another, this Herculean figure. His bronze motif prevented that—his skin, remarkably fine of texture, had been turned a rich bronze hue by countless tropical suns, and his hair, straight and fitting like a metallic skull cap, was of a bronze color only slightly darker.

His face was regular, the lineaments having an unusual quality of handsomeness, but in no sense possessing the somewhat effeminate prettiness often found in very handsome men.

The most striking feature, however, was his eyes. They were slightly weird, like pools of flake-gold stirred continually by tiny whirlwinds. They held an almost hypnotic quality, a compelling power.

The room where this amazing bronze man stood was the outer office of his headquarters, and held only comfortable chairs and a massive safe. Adjacent was the library with its thousands of scientific volumes and the laboratory with an array of equipment nearly without equal.

Doc whipped into the corridor, his movements apparently unhurried, but his speed great. A special elevator, a fast lift installed for his own use, lowered him eighty-six floors to the skyscraper basement. There, he kept several automobiles, all of special construction, in a garage the existence of which was unknown to all but a few.

The bronze man's skyscraper establishment had cost a small fortune, yet its expense was scarcely a drop from his reservoir of wealth. Doc possessed an almost unlimited source of funds, a treasure trove as unusual as the bronze man himself.

Scarcely three minutes after disaster befell Monk, Doc Savage was on the street in an expensive but unostentacious roadster. He touched a dash button. Under the hood a siren began wailing. Traffic police heard and opened a way for him.

Doc went down Broadway, and for a long time the speedometer needle swayed above seventy miles an hour. He drove with an uncanny skill.

THE roadster was fitted with shortwave radio receiving-and-transmitting apparatus. Ordinarily, Doc Savage would have used this to get in touch with the other three members of his group of five assistants.

But three of his aides were not at present in New York. William Harper "Johnny" Littlejohn, the expert on archaeology and geology, was in London, filling a special lecture engagement at a famous university.

Major Thomas J. "Long Tom" Roberts, electrical wizard extraordinary, was in Europe, collaborating in experiments with another electrical expert on a device which was Long Tom's pet dream—an apparatus which, when perfected, could be used to kill insects with ultra-short sonic or electric waves. This would be an inestimable boon to farmers.

Colonel John "Renny" Renwick, famous engineer, was in South Africa, halfway around the world, overseeing construction of a particularly difficult hydro-electric plant, a project in which the engineer had a financial interest.

For the first time in many months, Doc Savage would have to go into action without the aid of three of his remarkable group of five men, each of whom was a master in some profession.

Several blocks from the scene of the strange explosion in the office building, Doc switched off the siren. A crowd milled in front of the building itself. There were signs of excitement.

Doc parked at the end of the block and hurried forward, intent on learning what had befallen Monk and Ham. He caught snatches of conversation from the crowd.

"They came in an armored truck!" gasped a man.

A woman was telling a friend, "Did you notice how they were dressed? Silver-colored suits!"

"Those silver masks on their faces!" gasped the friend. "Ugh! Hideous!"

Doc went on and heard a fat colored fellow in a busboy's uniform exclaim, "Dem silver lads done lit out of heah in the same truck dat dey came in!"

"Boy, did yoah see dem two men they was draggin' when they up an' left?" asked a brother bus boy.

"Yassuh," agreed the first. "Dem two was daid, if yoah asks me."

Doc Savage's remarkable bronze features did not change expression. That did not mean he was unconcerned, for he schooled himself until he possessed an uncanny control over his own emotions.

A lieutenant of police—the same individual to whom Monk and Ham had been talking—answered the question. Doc encountered the officer in front of the building. The cop saluted briskly.

"It was the Silver Death's-Heads," the policeman explained before Doc could put a query. "They drove right through the crowd in an armored car. Ran down two spectators. They rushed in, clubbed down the guard at the door, and seized Monk and Ham. It happened so quickly that we could do nothing, although I did manage to fire one shot."

"Did they harm Monk and Ham?" Doc demanded.

The lieutenant shivered slightly at the grim sound of the giant bronze man's voice.

"Both were clubbed over the head," he said thickly. "Ham was caught beside me. The silver devils came up behind us. Monk was in the telephone booth and did not get out in time."

"How badly were they clubbed?" Doc questioned.

The officer moistened his lips. "Pretty hard. I don't know—if they are alive. They were dragged away."

"What about the armored truck?" Doc asked. "Armored trucks are not extremely common on New York streets."

"This one was a steel payroll truck," the policeman replied. "It was stolen, we learned, from a company which makes a business of delivering payrolls. It was taken only a few minutes before the raid here."

"You assemble information very quickly," Doc told the officer. "Good work. Was the truck followed?"

The policeman grimaced. "I'm sorry to say that it got away completely. Of course, every radio patrol car in the city is now looking for it. We expect a report at any minute. It cannot escape."

DOC SAVAGE did not rush off on any wild chase of his own in search of the armored truck. He knew the efficiency of the metropolitan police; he had, in fact, served in a consulting capacity when the present radio car system was inaugurated. A vehicle as prominent as the armored truck would not get far before it was discovered.

The bronze man's first move was to examine the semi-molten silver mass which Monk and Ham had found in the basement fire box. A small bag was brought from Doc's roadster. With chemicals taken from the bag, Doc tested the silver.

"Coin silver," he announced.

"Eh?" The police lieutenant was puzzled.

"The cloth is interwoven with fine wire made from molten silver dollars," Doc explained.

"Does that prove anything?" the officer queried.

"Only that the criminals must be making the garments themselves, which indicates that some of them are highly skilled metalsmiths," said the bronze man. "If the disguises had been purchased, it is almost certain that a different grade of silver would have been used."

The policeman nodded, not greatly surprised, for he knew the amazing detective ability possessed by Doc Savage. He was slightly abashed, however, when Doc went upstairs to the explosion scene and almost at once turned up the cause of the blast.

Doc did not expend much time on the wreckage itself, except to apply chemical tests to some of the powder stains.

"The work of trinitrotoluene," he stated.

"Huh?" asked the officer.

"T.N.T.," Doc elaborated. "The famous World War explosive."

"Oh!"

The bronze man dug into the office walls, probing pits made by bits of wreckage, and brought out, after some work, several bits of steel. He assembled these, studied them.

"We found some of that metal and sent it to a specialist for an opinion," said the officer. "We hoped it would tell us what caused the blast—whether it was a bomb or not."

"It was a high-explosive three-inch shell," Doc said.

"Good night!" the lieutenant exploded. "You don't mean a cannon ball?"

"You might call it that," Doc assured him. "Except that this was a very modern demolition shell from a three-inch artillery piece."

"But where was it fired from?" yelled the officer.

THERE was an interruption while a sergeant came in with a report that the armored truck had been found. A radio car had come upon the truck, abandoned on the waterfront of the East River.

No trace of the sinister men in silver garments had been found in the vicinity of the truck. Nor were there fingerprints. No one could be found who had seen the truck being abandoned.

"Finding it doesn't help us a bit," the police lieutenant groaned.

"I would not say that," Doc told him.

"Yes?" the other queried. "But how is this going to help?"

"According to the newspapers, the men in silver robbed another armored truck earlier in the day and took a quarter of a million dollars in cash," Doc pointed out.

"Of course."

"Police followed them," Doc reminded.

"Yes, and lost them—" The officer did not finish, but swore and snapped his fingers violently.

"Exactly," Doc said. "The police lost trace of them around the waterfront of the East River—in the same vicinity in which this armored truck was found, to be exact."

The lieutenant shouted, "I'll have every square inch of that area combed!"

"Do it unobtrusively," Doc requested.

"Of course," the officer agreed. "We will use plainclothes officers, and put a flock of stool pigeons to work. We've got a swell lot of stool pigeons. They're in nearly every crook hangout in the city. You'd be surprised what they can turn up."

"Do you wager?" Doc asked.

"Bet? Sure—on sure things."

"Want to bet me that your stool pigeons won't turn up a thing?" the bronze man asked.

"What makes you think they won't?" the cop demanded.

"These are not ordinary crooks," Doc told him. "And I doubt very much if robberies, such as the armored truck holdup this afternoon, are the real motive behind the organization of men who use the silver disguises."

The police lieutenant considered, then said, "I'll bet you fifty that the stool pigeons turn up something."

"The winner to contribute the fifty to the police Death Benefit Fund," Doc said.

"Sure."

A police messenger ran into the room. He was animated, breathless.

"Gugillello Bellondi was just murdered by a guy in silver!" he yelled.

DOC SAVAGE demanded, "Who is Gugillello Bellondi?"

"A fisherman who was in a boat in the river at the time of the explosion," said the police lieutenant. "We thought he might have seen the plane flying overhead drop a bomb, and we sent a man over to talk to him."

"And our man found him dead," said the messenger. "A woman saw a fellow in a silver suit run out of Gugillello Bellondi's room just before the cop got there."

"The killer got away?" the lieutenant wailed.

"So far, he has," the messenger admitted ruefully.

**WHERE DOES DOC SAVAGE GET HIS MONEY?**

Doc possesses a fabulous hoard of gold. The treasure trove lies in a lost valley in the remote mountain vastness of a Central American republic. Descendants of the ancient Mayan race live in this valley and mine the treasure.

When Doc Savage is in need of funds, he has merely to step into a powerful radio station at a certain hour on a certain day of each week and broadcast a few words in the Mayan language. This is picked up by a sensitive receiver in the lost valley. A few days later, a burro train laden with gold will appear in the capital of the Central American republic. These gold cargoes are always deposited to Doc's credit in a bank. It is a slim trip when one of the burro trains does not bring out a treasure of four or five million dollars.

Only Doc and his men know the location of the lost valley of the golden trove and the Mayans.

Doc Savage put in, "Any line on the plane?"

"Yes. I forgot to tell you." The lieutenant pulled out his notebook. "The flier was Gilbert Stiles, who lives on Eighty-fifth Street in Jackson Heights."

"What house number?" Doc asked.

The policeman furnished that information, started to ask a question, but did not—Doc Savage was already whipping for the door.

The bronze man reached his roadster. Once again traffic police opened a lane, and the trip north to the Queensboro Bridge, thence along Northern Boulevard to Jackson Heights was made in astounding time.

Jackson Heights was an apartment residential suburb near the north shore of Long Island, not far out. There were grass plots around some of the apartments, a few trees in the parkways down the center of a street or two.

Doc did not stop directly in front of Gilbert Stiles' home, but parked in an adjacent side street, under the lazy droop of a weeping willow. He swung along the sidewalk, reached the corner, made a move at turning, but instead of doing so, continued on with long steps—and stopped when he was sheltered behind a parked car.

Doc's move was urged by discovery of a man standing beside a shiny blue sedan down the street, near where Gilbert Stiles lived. The man was scrawny, with traces of grease stain on his bands and face. His face was a sickly gray hue, resembling a white ball which had been mauled in unclean hands.

During the past, Doc Savage had visited Monk's skyscraper chemical laboratory frequently, and in doing so had occasionally seen members of the janitorial force. The bronze man never forgot a face. The man down the street was one of the janitors of Monk's skyscraper.

Doc had no way of knowing the individual was Bugs, murderer of Clarence Sparks.

After watching Bugs for a moment, unobserved, Doc concluded something was not resting easily on the fellow's mind.

Bugs squirmed. He smoked innumerable cigarettes. He walked about, and he glanced frequently at a tall brick apartment building before which the blue sedan stood. He even got into the sedan, but remained only a moment and climbed out again.

Bugs stood scowling at the apartment house. Then his pasty face took on an expression of resolve, and he went inside.

Doc Savage whipped back to his roadster. The rumble seat jumped open at his touch upon a button, and he dipped in a hand, withdrew a small box to which stout spring clamps were secured; then he ran to the blue car.

Employing the spring clamps on the box, Doc clipped the container to the chassis of the car in a spot where it was not likely to be noticed. Then he followed Bugs into the apartment house.

THERE was a Spanish-type lobby, with ornate columns, fake iron balconies, and a rather threadbare carpet. Bugs was nowhere in sight. Nor was there a directory of the tenants to be seen.

The elevator was automatic. You got in and pushed a button marked with the floor to which you wished to be lifted. Doc listened. The lift was running.

These apartment buildings were all similar in construction. Doc leaped around a comer, found stairs which ran to the basement, descended them, and located the master electric fuse board. He could still hear the low whine of the elevator. The sound stopped.

Doc took out the fuse in the power circuit. The cage would remain where it was, now. The bronze man ran up flight after flight of stairs.

The elevator car was on the sixth floor, which happened to be the top story. A long hallway was lined with numbered doors. Doc stood perfectly still, listening.

The bronze man possessed remarkable hearing. He used a special scientific device giving forth sound waves above and below the usual audible ranges to develop his aural organs. This was a part of a daily two-hour routine of intensive exercise which he had not neglected since childhood. The exercises were responsible for his physical development, for there reposed in his great bronze frame a strength that to many seemed incredible.

Down the corridor, a doorknob rattled. Doc whipped back. A niche—it probably housed an incinerator door—offered concealment. He pressed into that.

He heard the door open. Feet scuffed. Doc counted at least six persons, all men. The clicking of women's high heels are distinctive, and there were none of those. One man walked far in the lead of the others. An instant later, the fellow appeared.

It was Bugs. He saw Doc Savage. He could not very well help it. His eyes flew wide; stark horror contorted his face.

"Savage!" he bawled. "Watch out!"

Then Bugs clawed at his clothing for a gun.

Doc moved with dazzling suddenness. Flashing out of the niche, he drove a fist. So that there would be no lasting damage, he struck lightly. But the blow slammed Bugs back against the wall, knocking him instantly unconscious. The gun he had tried to get into action skidded over the floor tiling.

Doc now faced down the corridor—faced weird, inhuman figures, forms garbed in grotesque silver garments. The footstep count had been good. There were five of them.

Bugs' yell had warned them. Three had drawn guns. The weapons gushed flame and raised ear-splitting thunder in the corridor.

THERE was a touch of the unearthly in the speed with which Doc Savage got back into the niche. Only fabulous muscles, carefully conditioned, could manage such blinding motion. The bullets, missing him, gouged plaster off the walls and knocked glass from a window at the corridor end.

"Rush him!" a man in silver squawled.

"T'hell with that, Ull!" another growled.

Shots almost drowned the words, and it was doubtful if the man in charge realized his name had been called—Ull. But Doc caught it and filed it mentally for future investigation—should he escape.

He was in a tight spot. It was his policy never to carry a gun, and he had none now. But he did have some of the scientific devices which he used. One of these he employed now.

A hand dipped into a pocket and came out with what might have been mistaken for a glass marble. This was actually a thin-walled glass globe, and the liquid inside was a chemical concoction which vaporized instantly into an anaesthetic gas.

The gas was unique in that its effects were immediate, and it became ineffective within less than a minute, so that Doc, holding his breath, could escape the potent stuff, while the unwary, breathing it, were rendered senseless.

Doc threw the anaesthetic ball.

Rarely had these gas balls failed to catch foes by surprise. But this was an exception. Doc waited, holding his breath to escape the vapor. But his enemies gave no sign of succumbing. They did not, however, call out again, and the clatter of their feet retreated. A door slammed. They had fled ahead of the gas.

Doc knew from past experience just how quickly a man can shoot at an unexpected target, and knew he could get a fleeting glimpse of the corridor without great danger of being shot. He looked out.

The hallway was empty. The silver men had gone back into an apartment. Doc stepped out into the hall.

An instant later, he flashed backward into the niche, for a door had opened and a metal object slightly smaller than a baseball had sailed through. No doubt the silver man who hurled it intended for it to stop beside Doc. But the thing had too much momentum. It clattered past. Then it exploded.

The concussion almost disrupted the bronze man's eardrums. Clouds of plaster gushed. The big apartment house trembled. The ceiling lifted, split, and came down with a thundering clamor. The floor collapsed for some distance.

Doc, secure in the niche, unhit, was enveloped in a cloud of smoke, plaster particles and splinters.

The grenade had been powerful. Directly in front of him, the floor was gone, fallen down into the hall below. Bugs' body had been blown back out of sight.

Toward the end of the uproar, the door down the hall opened again.

"Get him?" asked the voice which belonged to Ull—it was a shrill, querulously whanging tone. Ull was not the one looking into the corridor.

"It fixed 'im," said another voice. "The whole damn corridor is blown to pieces!"

At that point, a loud, agonized groan sounded.

"Who's that?" asked Ull.

"Bugs," said the other. "He's butchered up some."

"Let me take care of that," Ull suggested.

A moment later there was a single deliberate shot, and after that the groans no longer ground out.

"He's taken care of," said Ull.

"What next?" grunted the other.

"Down the fire escape—all of you," ordered Ull. "We've got to beat the cops away from here."

DOC SAVAGE gave Ull and his sinister silver aides a few minutes to be on their way. The bronze man did not want any more of those grenades thrown. Women were screaming, children crying, in the apartment below, although it was unlikely that any had been hurt.

When he considered sufficient time had elapsed, Doc stepped out of the niche.

Bugs was a slack figure, torn a little by the blast and with a bullet hole drilling his head just above the ears. Ull had made a cold, accurate shot in ascertaining that his followers did not live to talk. Evidently Ull had not wanted a wounded man on his hands during the getaway.

Doc shoved open the door through which the grenade had been hurled. He stood just inside, strange flake-gold eyes resting on the deep leather chair in the center of the apartment living room.

There was a man in the chair, but not a living man, for his body was stiffly erect, probably held that way by the blade of the long knife which had gone through his chest and well into the chair back.

A book had fallen to the floor beside the dead man and was open at the fly leaf, so that the name written there could be deciphered.

"Gilbert Stiles," the name read.

### Chapter V
### RAPID PACE

DOC SAVAGE rested a hand on the man's wrist where there should have been a pulse—had he been alive—but there was no throb.

This aviator had been flying over the river when the explosion occurred in Paine L. Winthrop's office. He must have seen something. The fisherman in the boat on the river must have seen the same thing. And both had been killed before they could talk, or be questioned.

How had the silver fiends gotten their names? Doc had a suspicion—he had no way of knowing how right it was—that Bugs was responsible for this. But Bugs had paid for his part.

Motor roar came up from the street, throbbed, then receded. Doc Savage did not look out. They might see him, and it was just as well if they thought him dead, for they might become careless.

The blue car had vanished when the bronze man did glance through the window. He stepped out on the fire escape and ran down, lightly, swiftly, and made for his roadster. He did not waste time, but there was no wild haste in his movements.

The sudden life in the oil gauge and ammeter was almost all that told when the roadster engine started, so silently did it operate. The car moved at a touch on the accelerator; it was equipped with the most modern of automatic clutches.

Doc touched one of innumerable buttons on the dash. Then he turned a knurled knob. Static noises came from a radio speaker under the dash, these became terrific as a street car was passed, and, as Doc continued to adjust the knob, snatches of voice and telegraph were heard. A radio fan would have realized that the bronze man was fishing through the ultra-shortwave bands, seeking some particular transmitter.

After a time, regular buzzes—short dashes repeated at three-second intervals—whizzed from the speaker. They were not unlike train signals, except more widely spaced, and they kept coming steadily.

Doc turned the knob to the right. The signals faded. He turned back to the left and they faded again. Setting the knob at the loudest point, he eyed a dial above, which bore close likeness to a compass card. A pointer on this indicated almost due west.

Doc Savage drove west. The apparatus he had just employed was a radio compass, the tiny loop of which was in the roadster rear and operated from the knob by remote control.

This compact radio directional device was one which Doc employed for many uses. For instance, his five men, when working with him, used cars which also had transmitters, and these were left on at all times. By simply turning the directional compass knob, Doc could locate the nearest of these cars.

The radio compass had another use, as well. Doc Savage had perfected tiny mechanical shortwave transmitters which, batteries self-contained, were little larger than a cigar box. These sent out a series of buzzing sounds. Attached to the containers were clamps by which they could be affixed to various convenient objects.

Doc had, as a matter of precaution, attached one

**The concussion almost disrupted the bronze man's eardrums.**

of the transmitters to the azure sedan. The bronze man overlooked few chances. In the perilous life he led, chances could not be overlooked.

From time to time, a twist of the directional knob, as the buzzing signals faded, brought the sounds in loud again and gave a check on the direction being taken by the blue machine.

The chase led to Manhattan Island, downtown to the vehicular tunnel under the Hudson, thence along the elevated roadway and, after a few miles, down into a manufacturing district. It ended close to the waterfront when Doc Savage sighted the sedan, empty now, parked before an imposing, massive steel gate.

The gate was not of steel bars, but of riveted plates; it looked forbidding. There was a square aperture in the gate for a watchman to peer through. Above the gate, a sign read:

WINTHROP'S SHIPYARDS
PAINE L. WINTHROP, President

Doc Savage advanced swiftly and put an eye to the square opening in the gate. The shipyard was beyond, grotesque in the fog, with its cranes, material piles and moving booms. There seemed to be no work under way.

Just inside the gate, a man was sprawled on his back, one arm angled across his face in an attitude of grisly slumber. The shoulder of his rough suit was sodden with crimson leakage from his head.

Doc gave the door a shove. It was unlocked, swung back quietly, and let him in. He examined the man.

The fellow was old, work-stooped, gray-haired, and on his breast was a watchman's badge. Doc felt his wrist, although he could see that the man still breathed. Some type of bludgeon, perhaps a revolver barrel, had beaten the watchman down.

He would be unconscious some time, judging from the nature of the wound, but was in no immediate danger.

Doc advanced into the shipyard. There was some breeze here; the fog eddied, swept past in nebulous streamers like marching ghosts. Moisture had been deposited on the packed earth, and this slime bore tracks.

Reasoning that the freshest prints were those of the sinister men in silver garb, Doc followed them. The tracks progressed in a direct manner which indicated a definite objective. They ended at the door of a massive brick building, evidently housing the offices.

Doc waited outside, listening. Gray fog swirling about made his great frame seem larger, more formidable. The gloom of early evening was pressing down, bringing the clammy murk of a water-logged catacomb.

A trial of the door showed it locked, but a moment's work with a thin steel probe tripped the tumblers. A professional locksmith would have been slightly stunned at the swiftness with which the lock was solved.

Inside was denser murk; mingled with it the faint heat from radiators which bubbled against the fog chill. There was a desk, telephone and hard, wooden waiting benches. A fly-specked calendar was crooked on the wall.

Doc advanced, passed through an open door, and found worn wooden steps which led upward. But he did not mount immediately. Instead, he dipped a hand into a pocket and brought out what might have been mistaken for a handful of black clover seed. He strewed some of this on the floor of the outer office. Then he went up the stairs.

At the first landing he found a door, open. Beyond was an office, fitted up more luxuriously. The desk drawers were open, the papers within littered up as if they had been gone through hastily.

A curl of smoke arose from a metal smoking stand which stood beside the desk.

Doc went over to it. The smouldering objects were old cigar and cigarette stubs which had been ignited by bits of burning paper dropped into the stand. The bronze man examined the charred paper fragments.

Blueprints, he decided. The print had been torn into fractional sections, each burned separately, and the ash crushed. Even his consummate skill was unequal to telling what nature of diagram had been on the blueprints.

The burning had been done within the last few minutes, however. And the care with which it had been done indicated sinister motives.

Doc dropped the ashes. He stood very still, listening.

From below came a loud report. It was like a shot. Three more followed. There was a cry—strangled, inarticulate.

DOC SAVAGE did not go back down the stairs, but whipped, instead, to a window. He managed to get it up without noise that could be heard downstairs. From inside his clothing came an object he always carried—a thin, stout silk cord, affixed to the end of which was a folding grapple of lightness and strength.

The grapple, hooked to the inner edge of the window sill, held his weight as he slid outside and down the silk line. He went slowly, supported by the incredible strength in his metallic hands.

A few feet to the left of the spot where he touched the ground, there was a window. It allowed a look into the reception room.

The glass pane was grimy. That, with the fog and darkness, made vision difficult, the outlines inside hazy. But there was one point cleaner than the other sections of the glass.

Through the clear section, Doc could distinguish—his flake-gold eyes peered closely—a small, flat automatic pistol, a vest pocket .25 caliber gun. A thin hand encased in a suede glove held it.

Doc brought out a handkerchief, doubled it, spread it over his knuckles, but did not wrap it around so that it would interfere with his fingers. He struck. Glass splintered. The cloth protected his knuckles, but did not interfere when his arm went through the window and his corded fingers gripped the gun hand.

Coat fabric over the bronze man's arm bulged slightly as great muscles exerted tension. Inside, a shriek piped out. The gun fell from a hand made nerveless by the steel pinch of Doc's fingers.

Doc knocked more glass out of the window, found the lock, twisted it, then released his victim long enough to get the sash up and bound inside.

The victim was on all fours, clawing for the

dropped automatic. Doc nudged the weapon away with a toe.

The woman on the floor—not until he had seized her gun arm had Doc been sure it was a woman—looked up angrily and gritted, "Why didn't you just shoot me? That's what you tried before!"

She was a vision in suede. Not only were her gloves suede, but her pumps and the pert, saucy riding béret topping a wealth of brown hair. Her frock was almost the gray of the suede, making, with her gray bag, an ensemble studied, yet extremely striking.

The garments set off some intriguing curves, and the picture was aided by a pair of exquisite eyes, a nose bordering on the retroussé, and rosebud lips, which trembled a little with rage and fear.

Doc gave the beauty an impersonal eye. Then he glanced at the floor.

On the boards of the floor lay the numerous particles which resembled black clover seed, just as Doc had left them—except in four spots, where there were scorched spots. It looked as if firecrackers had gone off on the floor.

The entrancing young woman got to her feet. In doing so she stepped on one of the clover seeds. There was a loud report as it exploded. She jumped and glared at Doc.

"What are those things?" she snapped, and put a hand up to adjust her luxuriant brown hair.

"Just a precaution to warn if any one was following me," Doc told her.

The girl fingered in her hair, thrusting in her fingers, patting. Suddenly she took her hand down. She pointed it at Doc.

The hand held the twin to the small automatic which Doc had caused her to drop.

"Your precaution," she said, "is not going to do you much good."

THE girl's arm was out rigid, the gun pointed at about the middle button of Doc's vest, and because her arm was tense, her gray sleeve was drawn off a white-gold wrist watch. He could hear the animated clicking of the watch, tiny as the sound was.

"This may be a mistake," Doc told her.

"It will be a mistake if you make any move that I don't order," she informed him.

Doc asked, "There has been a previous attempt to kill you? And you think I had a part in it?"

The girl seemed fascinated by the eerie quality of the bronze man's eyes.

"I can't prove it was you," she said.

"Why not?"

"The man who shot at me had some kind of a silver-colored suit on," she answered. "He had a silver mask, too."

"When did this happen?"

"The attempt to shoot me? Yesterday. Yesterday evening about this time." She moved her gun meaningly, but it still pointed at the center of Doc's vest. "I went right out and bought me two guns. And don't get the idea I can't use them. I was born and raised in Montana."

"Why," Doc asked her, "should a man in silver try to kill you?"

Her gun remained steady. "That is what I would like to know."

Doc Savage studied her, as if trying to read her mind. Then, slowly, but firmly, he walked forward.

"I'll shoot!" the girl shrilled.

But Doc came on and she did not fire, but retreated, biting her lips in vexation, until she was against the wall. The bronze man reached out and removed the gun from her hand without difficulty.

"You fool!" she flared. "You don't know how near I came to killing you!"

"Your pea-shooter," Doc advised her, "would not have dented my bulletproof vest."

She had tucked her bag high under an arm, so that it had not fallen throughout the encounter. She did not resist when he took the bag. There was a folder of business cards inside. They read:

MISS LORNA ZANE
Private Secretary to Paine L. Winthrop

"Lorna?" Doc asked.

"Miss Zane to you!" she snapped.

Silently, Doc extended the bag, after noting there was nothing else in it other than a metal powder box, almost full.

The girl took the bag, absently opened it—then apparently got a big idea. She flipped the powder case open and dashed the cosmetic flakes at Doc's eye.

But she had not counted on the blinding speed with which the bronze man could move. He ducked and the powder, shooting over his shoulder, spread in a cloud over the room.

The girl tried to flee. Doc grasped her arm. She screamed from fright, since he could not have been hurting her.

From behind Doc came a loud report as a black pellet on the floor exploded. There was a second bang, a third.

Doc whirled.

TURNING, the bronze man saw first the chair, big and heavy. It clubbed in a whining arc for his head. Doc threw head and shoulders back through the air, turned sidewise.

The chair missed him, snapped buttons off his vest, such was its speed, and broke itself into fragments on the floor.

"Blast me, you're lightning in chains!" rapped the man who had swung the chair. "Blast me, lightning in chains!"

The man gave the impression of something operated by electricity. His words actually gobbled, such was their high pressure speed. His arms moved as if driven by a clockwork which had lost its governor.

He stabbed a hand at his coat pocket. The weighty hang of his coat on that side indicated a gun.

Doc lunged. He was fast, but this other man had speed, too. He brought his left fist up in a terrific blow. It landed flush on Doc's jaw.

The other waited expectantly. His mouth fell open and his eyes flew wide when Doc did not drop. He looked scared, but desperate.

"Incredible!" he exploded. "Incredible! Yes it is!"

He started another blow. But he was not as fortunate this time. Doc's left hand drifted out, pushed, and the fellow upset. As he went down, Doc's other hand grasped his coat pocket and wrenched. Half of the man's coat was torn off, with it the pocket and the gun which it held.

"I'll be damned!" the man exclaimed with staccato rapidity. "I'll be damned! Yes, I will. Damned!"

Doc ignored him, for the girl was running to get the automatic which she had first held. When Doc swept across the floor and got the weapon first, she grimaced angrily and backed into a corner.

The man of staccato speech came up from the floor like a suddenly awakened cat. He bounced backward warily, as if apprehensive of encountering Doc again. His hands and lower lip trembled.

"Who are you?" he clipped. "Who are you? That's what I want to know!"

"Doc Savage," the bronze man said.

"That explains it," gulped the other. "It sure does!"

Doc glanced at the girl. "Who is this fellow?" he asked.

"Harry Pace is the name," answered the man for himself. "Yes, sir, Pace. People call me 'Rapid.' Rapid Pace. Get it? Efficiency, that's Pace. You bet. Efficiency."

"He," the girl said dryly, "is Paine L. Winthrop's efficiency expert."

The young woman had undergone a marked change. She wore a somewhat sheepish expression.

"So you are Doc Savage," she added. "I have heard so much about you that I began to think you were a legend."

"Yes, sir, you're almost a legend, Mr. Savage," said "Rapid" Pace. "Yes, sir, a legend."

"Why did you try to club me with that chair?" Doc asked him.

"A mistake," Pace clattered. "All a mistake. You see, I was protecting Lorna. Efficiency on all occasions, that is me."

Doc's flake-gold eyes probed. "Have you seen any Silver Death's-Heads around the shipyard?" he asked.

"Good night!" Rapid Pace stuttered. "What are you talking about?"

The floor seemed to jump a little under their feet. A loud thump accompanied this phenomenon. Several windows in the building evidently broke; they could hear the glass jangling.

"BLESS me!" gulped Rapid Pace. "What was that?"

"Stay here," Doc rapped, and whipped for the stairs.

Rapid Pace started after him, stepped on one of the explosive particles on the floor, gave a wild jump, and trembled furiously.

"Dear me!" he choked. "My nerves aren't going to stand this! No, sir!"

"Stay with Miss Zane!" Doc directed. Then the bronze man vanished up the stairs, his going as silent and swift as the progress of a gale-swept tendril of fog.

Rapid Pace eyed Lorna Zane and said hurriedly, "Lorna, I'm worried. What is this all about?"

"I do not know," said the girl grimly.

"If anything would happen to you, I think I—I'd die," Pace said earnestly.

The young woman studied him. "I doubt it," she said dryly.

"Now don't joke, Lorna," Pace pleaded. "You know I'm crazy about you. Yes, sir, crazy! Why don't you like me?"

"You get scared too easy," said Lorna. "You go off half cocked."

"I can't help it," Pace groaned.

"And you talk too much," Lorna continued. "You say everything twice, and you could get along with half as much conversation."

"I'm trying to stop that, too," Pace assured her.

"Well, we'll see how you improve," Lorna told him.

They strained their ears, but did not hear Doc Savage, for the bronze man was moving with an uncanny quiet through the upper floors of the building. He swung down a corridor, angled right, and found the building was much larger than it had seemed: there were numerous hallways. In fact, the place was a labyrinth.

Doc came unexpectedly to a room which was very large. There were rows of desks, many—judging from the lack of wastebaskets and absence of other paraphernalia—not at present in use. Others were seeing service. Evidently the Winthrop Shipyards had once done more business than at present.

Across the room was a safe, huge and battered, with flakes of the black paint scaled off by long usage. But there was more wrong with the safe than scuffed paint.

The door of the strong box was off and reposed on the floor. Papers, the former contents of the safe, were scattered about. A bilious-looking cloud of smoke eddied above the wreckage, and there was the itching tang of burned nitro in the air.

The safe being blown open was undoubtedly what they had heard downstairs.

## Chapter VI
### MYSTERIOUS BLUEPRINTS

DOC SAVAGE did not expend time examining the safe, but whipped to the left, found a door open, and went through. The hallway beyond led him several yards and turned, conveying him back the way he had come, toward the stairs and the front door.

An excited, staccato yell sounded. Rapid Pace's voice! A gun made an ugly roar. Lorna Zane shrilled something unintelligible.

Doc changed his course, found a window and got it up as silently as was consistent with slashing speed. More than a dozen feet, that drop below. He made it easily, tremendous leg muscles cushioning his landing.

An instant later, he was at a corner—it chanced to be the one nearest the gate.

Lorna Zane and Rapid Pace were running across the shipyard, striving to reach the shelter of a pile of steel ship frames. Neither looked back, but gave all attention to sprinting.

A gun whacked.

"I'm hit!" Pace grabbed his arm. "I'm hit!"

But he did not glance back, and both he and the girl dived behind the frames. Another shot slammed; the lead made a belling noise on the steel frames.

"Get that damned girl!" yelled the voice of the Silver Death's-Head member called Ull.

Feet pounded. Doc stepped from his concealment. The group in the weird silver garments and masks, which he had followed here, were running for the frame pile, guns ready.

Over the thin cloth of woven alloy metal which protected his body, Doc Savage wore a most unusual vest, a garment of many pockets, compartments rather, padded so that they were unnoticeable. From one of these, he extracted a metal vial, the padded interior of which held metallic objects about the size of cherries. He flung one of these ahead of the charging silver killers.

It struck. There was a blinding flash, a terrific crack of a noise which left ears ringing. Two silver men were upset by the blast.

Ull—he was prudently not leading the charge—yelled, "The girl must have grenades! Get her!"

In the gloom, it was impossible to tell from where the thrown object had come. They renewed the charge.

There was a second flash, and a rapping crash. This one knocked fully half of the group down. Even Ull was upset, and a bundle he was carrying flipped from his arms.

The bundle was long, round, azure-tinted at the edges, tied with cord and sealed with wax. A bundle of blueprints, undoubtedly.

Ull scrambled after the prints as if they meant his very life. Their merely getting out of his hands seemed to change his whole plan.

"Let the girl go!" he howled. "The big boss said to get these prints, and that's our job. We do not want to lose them, after all the trouble we had getting them out of that safe. Back, men! We'll leave here before someone calls the police."

The silver men retreated, firing freely at the pile of massive steel frames. Scrambling over the keel of a partially completed small vessel, they made for the gate, working around a tractor, a mobile derrick and other machinery. One produced a flashlight and employed it to aid their flight.

They reached the gate. It was locked.

"Hell!" snarled Ull, and glared at the watchman, who was still unconscious. "I thought we left this unlocked!"

The fastening of the solid metal sheet was a bar affair, and this was jammed very tightly, but they got it back and shoved out into the waterfront street. With frantic haste, they piled into their blue sedan.

"We'll go to Gardner's home next," barked Ull.

The car engine backfired, came to life, and the machine wailed its tires on the fog-damp pavement, then rocketed away.

THERE were shadows close to the wall outside the gate, very dark shadows, and the men in the silver regalia had neglected to examine them. Thereby, they had missed an important discovery.

The layer of damp murk seemed to swell, then condense and materialize into a bronze figure of giant size. This occurred at a point no more than fifteen feet from where the sedan had been parked.

Doc, taking advantage of the night and the fog, had beaten the silver men to the gate, gotten through, jammed the lock by the handle outside, and concealed himself.

Ull's bark, "We'll go to Gardner's home next," had reached his ears.

Doc had taken a good deal of trouble to avoid showing himself, for it was well that the silver men continue thinking they had killed him at the apartment of the unfortunate flier, Gilbert Stiles.

Finding his two men, Monk and Ham—rescuing them if they were still alive; punishing their murderers if they were dead—was Doc's immediate task. Eventually these silver men probably would lead him to his objective.

Once again, he could follow them by the radio directional device.

Doc did not take up the chase immediately. He ran back into the shipyard.

Lorna Zane came cautiously from behind the steel pile. Rapid Pace, once sure the coast was clear, bounded out like an excited cricket. He waved his arms and began to talk like a phonograph which had lost its governor, indicating a mere scratch on his shoulder.

"An outrage!" he yelled. "Yes, sir, an outrage! A mystery, too! A very black mystery! A most confounding affair—"

Doc ignored him, and asked the girl, "Do you know what was in that large safe upstairs?"

"I should know," she replied. "I am the only one who has the combination."

Doc gestured, "Come on!"

As they ran into the brick office building, Lorna Zane said angrily, "I do not understand this! Why should those men try to kill me?"

"What position do you hold here?" Doc asked her.

"I really manage the shipyard," she explained, "although I am only secretary to Paine L. Winthrop."

"That might explain it," said Doc.

The young woman glanced sharply at the bronze man, a strange light in her entrancing eyes. "What do you mean?"

Doc Savage seemed not to have heard the question, and they soon reached the large room where the safe had been blown open.

"Will you see what is missing," the bronze man requested, and indicated the rifled strong box.

Lorna Zane went through the strewn contents of the safe, picking up packages, dropping them, inspecting letters. The inventory did not take her long.

"Only one thing is missing," she decided.

Doc watched her closely. "What is it?"

"A sealed roll, a blueprint which Paine L. Winthrop gave me nearly four months ago to lock in this safe for him," said the attractive young woman.

"Blueprint of what?"

The girl hesitated. "There was something strange about that. I got explicit orders not to look at it, and it was sealed so no snooper could open it without that fact being apparent. I have no idea what it was."

Doc nodded. "The blueprint seems to have a sinister importance."

Lorna Zane bit her lip uncertainly, then said, "There was another strange thing. Last spring, Mr. Winthrop gave all his regular employees a five-months vacation with pay. That was queer, because he usually did not give vacations with pay. I came back four months ago."

"When you came back, did you notice anything?" Doc asked.

"There had been a great deal of work done in the shipyard," the girl replied. "But when I got back, whatever had been built was gone, and no workmen remained."

"Come on," Doc directed. "We'll talk as we ride."

"I wonder if the vacations could have anything to do with this," Rapid Pace mumbled. "You know, I got one, too. Yes, it was swell!"

THEY retired to the bronze man's roadster; all three occupied the commodious front seat, and the machine lunged away. The buzzing radio directional device gave them a line on the blue sedan.

Doc drove swiftly, silently for a time, so as to decrease the lead of the sedan. The radio transmitter under the car of the silver men would only carry a few miles.

"Did Winthrop have the combination of the safe which held the mysterious blueprint?" Doc asked.

The girl shook her head. "No."

"Why is that?"

"That is what I was wondering," said Rapid Pace. "Yes, I was wondering."

In the gloom—it was much darker now—the girl's rather inviting lips compressed into an angry line.

"I virtually manage the shipyard," she snapped. "There are many details to which Paine L. Winthrop does not give close attention. The combination of that safe happens to be one of them."

The tires on the roadster were designed with a tread which prevented, as much as possible, the usual wail present at high speed. The engine was still silent, although turning at high speed. Sway and pitch of the car, the blur of lighted buildings on their side, told of their true momentum.

Doc Savage said suddenly, "Paine L. Winthrop is dead. Did you know that?"

The girl became very quiet in her corner of the seat. She separated her lips as if to speak, seemed to reconsider, and closed them. Slender hands tangled and untangled on her lap.

Rapid Pace started up in the seat at the words, groped for expression, and burst out, "The old boy's heart, eh? His heart. Sure, I knew it would get him sooner or later."

"It was not his heart," Doc corrected. "It was a three-inch high-explosive shell, fired from a spot as yet not definitely determined."

For once Rapid Pace did not repeat himself. "This is very mystifying," he muttered.

"Do either of you have any idea of what is behind it all?" Doc asked.

"Not I," said Rapid Pace.

"Nor I," murmured the girl.

Doc adjusted the directional apparatus knob. The procession of buzzing was louder. Doc's metallic features showed no trace of concern, but he did not resume the questioning.

He slowed the roadster, for the increasing loudness of the signals indicated he was coming up rapidly on the sender. Then he turned sharply to the right, the roadster pitching over ruts, muddy water flying from puddles. He stopped.

They were on a side road. Brush walled them in. The headlights glinted on blue. Doc slackened speed, rolled up windows, especially designed in the doors of the roadster, and which were of bullet-proof glass. The car body, engine hood, radiator, were all protected by armor plate.

The machine ahead was the blue sedan, empty.

Using a flashlight, Doc located tracks. It seemed that the silver men had gone back along the road afoot. Following the trail closely, Doc progressed to the main thoroughfare and down that—footprints were faint in the fog damp on the pavement—to a drug store before which there was a taxi stand.

As a matter of precaution, the silver men had abandoned their easily recognized sedan.

Doc Savage secured, from the drug store clerk, a description of the taxi driver who frequented that stand. The driver was an elderly man, distinctive because of a great drooping white mustache.

The clerk had not seen the men who had taken the taxi, although he had heard the hack depart only a few minutes before.

THIRTY minutes later, Doc Savage pulled the roadster to a stop before an elaborately modernistic building on the more elite section of Park

Avenue. Instead of one doorman, there were two, and they were caparisoned in uniforms somewhat more distinctive than doormen elsewhere on this, possibly the most expensive street in the world.

"What now," Lorna Zane asked curiously, eyeing the imposing structure.

"I am going to leave you here," Doc told her.

Lorna nipped her lower lip with white teeth. "Haven't I anything to say about that?"

"Your life is in danger," Doc told her. "You will be safe here."

"What about me?" Rapid Pace clattered. "Yes, what about me?"

"You stay in the car," Doc directed.

The bronze man escorted Lorna Zane into the building. They received much attention, the doormen collaborating efficiently in ushering them inside. There was a waiting room, a bewildering resplendence of chromium, enamel and colored rugs.

A stately, exquisitely formed young woman ushered them to comfortable chairs. She was a blonde.

A redhead, equally as shapely, brought them a tray of iced drinks. A young lady with black tresses popped up with the most fashionable magazines.

*"Whew!"* said Lorna. "What is this, anyway?"

Doc did not answer, but watched another young woman who was approaching. The attendants who had waited upon Doc and Lorna were striking, but they were completely overshadowed by the new-comer. This entrancing Venus had bronze hair of a hue remarkably like Doc's.

"Hello, Pat," Doc greeted the bronze-haired beauty. "This is Lorna Zane. Lorna, this is Pat Savage, my cousin."

Pat shook hands with Lorna, then waved an airy hand.

"This is the first time you have been here, Doc," she said. "I want to show you the gymnasium upstairs. It's a knockout. And I have over thirty beauty operators at work, all highly skilled. I already have all the fashion leaders on my list, waiting to have their youthful figures restored. How I am going to reduce some of those heavyweights is a mystery to me, but they pay me in advance."

"Busy?" Doc asked.

"Busy?" Pat laughed. "Say, this business of running a combination beauty salon and gymnasium is no joke. You bet I'm busy."

At this point, a customer departed—a fat man whose countenance was still flushed from a facial, and whose sparse hair had undoubtedly been curled.

"Men on my clientele, too," Pat smiled. "But I do not know whether they come to have their looks improved, or to flirt with my snappy assistants."

"Want to help me, Pat?" Doc asked.

"Help *you?*" Pat said cheerfully. "Do I want to fly the Atlantic? Do I want to stand up and get shot at? Do I want to go in for parachute jumping? All of those are safer than helping you."

"Do you want to help?" Doc repeated.

"Sure," Pat laughed. "Who is trying to kill you now?"

"Miss Lorna Zane, here, is the one in danger this time," Doc explained, and briefly outlined what had occurred.

Pat Savage listened with profound interest. Pat liked excitement, and had aided Doc on other occasions. She had even tried to join Doc's group of assistants, had been turned down because Doc considered it no life for the so-called gentler sex, and had started this elaborate beauty establishment to keep herself occupied.

Rapid Pace was walking rapidly back and forth beside the roadster when Doc joined him down in the street.

"I am puzzled," clipped the high-pressure efficiency expert. "Yes, deeply puzzled. What I want to know is this: How are we going to find those silver devils?"

"Through an order their leader, Ull, gave," Doc said.

"What was the order?" Pace questioned swiftly.

"Something about going to an individual named Gardner," Doc told him.

"Oh, oh!" gulped Pace. "Gardner? Bedford Burgess Gardner, did you say?"

"Who is Bedford Burgess Gardner?" Doc countered.

"Gardner is owner of Transatlantic Lines, the ocean line which was Paine L. Winthrop's chief rival until lately, when there has been talk of the two companies merging," said Pace, using what for him was an extraordinarily long sentence. "Gardner is—"

"We will go to Gardner's home," Doc said briskly.

"I happen to know where he lives," said Pace. "Yes, I know. He has a lolapaloosa of a place. A lolapaloosa!"

THE "lolapaloosa" was a cluster of white buildings which stood like big dice atop a green hill that shouldered up impressively from the Hudson's tranquil blue ribbon some miles north of New York City.

The mansion itself was palatial, modeled after the lines of Mount Vernon, with tall white columns. Nearby were smaller buildings in imitation of old slave huts. The stables were large, and back of them a private race track looped around a private flying field on which stood a hangar, also ingeniously Colonial.

The river edge at the foot of the hill boasted boat houses and a seaplane hangar, also Colonial.

There was no fog this far north—it seemed to be present only along the sea—and the sky was comparatively free of clouds, so that moonlight spilled down, giving Doc Savage and Rapid Pace sufficient illumination to look over the ground.

Pace said, "A lolapaloosa! Didn't I tell you? Yes, sir, a—"

"Quiet," said Doc, who was getting tired of the efficiency expert's repetitive manner of speaking.

They had left the roadster a short distance from the palatial estate and they were approaching on foot. They were on a driveway which was banked on either side by black, ominous brush.

A small red point of light appeared ahead. They used more caution, came close and perceived a taxi. The tail light illuminated the license—a New Jersey plate.

"Probably the machine the silver men took when they abandoned their sedan in New Jersey," Doc imparted.

Doc rounded the cab, saw it was empty, and they advanced through the shrubbery until they came to a stretch of lawn which was close-cropped and somewhat glassy with dew. Beyond was the house—ample, impressive, almost unnaturally white.

"Makes me think of a bone," Pace shivered. "Yes, sir, a white bone."

"What do you know about Bedford Burgess Gardner?" Doc asked.

"A mysterious person," said Pace. "A very mysterious person."

"What do you mean?"

"He rarely gets out," Pace explained. "Offhand, I cannot recall anyone who has seen him. He does not keep offices downtown, and all his business is transacted by telephone. They say he is a strange person who does not like anyone around him. They even say his servants do not live here—that he makes them leave every evening before dark."

"Wealthy?" Doc queried.

"Within the last year his company has merged with other shipping concerns until he is the most powerful shipping magnate in America, unless I am mistaken," said Pace."

"Ever see him?" Doc asked.

"No, sir," said Pace. "Didn't I just tell you that very few people have ever seen the old codger?"

"Old?"

"An old wreck, from what I hear," said Pace. "They say—"

What "they said" never did come out, however. From the white house exploded a shout—hollow because it was inside; guttural with fright.

The cry repeated. A door banged open, spilling white light. It had opened on a small balcony, some fifteen feet up on the side of the mansion.

A figure reeled through the door. It was a man who made a grotesque form against the glitter from within. His age must have been near forty, and his face, even from that distance, radiated terror. He wore the uniform of a taxi driver.

The man was fleeing, obviously. He endeavored to get over the balcony railing.

Then a gun banged hollowly inside the house. Bullet impact kicked the taxi driver around so that he fell across the balcony rail, teetered a moment, then was carried over by momentum. There was a concrete sidewalk below and the driver struck that squarely on top of his head—which would have killed him, had the bullet not done so already.

## Chapter VII
## THE INDIAN'S HEAD

DOC SAVAGE heard a fluttering sound beside him, looked around and saw that Rapid Pace seemed to be in the grip of a violent chill. His shaking was oscillating a bough of the bush against which they stood. Suddenly, Pace dived for the nearest cover, disappearing like a frightened rabbit.

Doc ran for the house, angling to the right, keeping low so that he could not be glimpsed by the gunman inside the balcony door. The house seemed to grow in proportions as he came near it; the structure was very large.

A side door which he approached was locked, but Doc's thin metal probe gave him silent, quick admission. The darkness inside swallowed him.

A few feet inside, he turned into a room where the carpet was thick, soft. He caught breathing sounds, uneasy, jerking. After a few seconds, feet shuffled on the carpet.

Doc moved like a wraith; his tendon-wrapped bands lashed out and closed on arms. The struggle was brief. There was a soft thump, evidently of a gun falling. Doc released his captive, leaped back, got the gun, then found a light switch and clicked it on.

He studied the individual who was revealed in the brilliant flood.

It was a man, a weird figure, stooped almost double. The man had a black beard, slightly larger than a Vandyke, which made his lower face a dark bundle of fur. The eyes were squinted to the thinnest of slits; not even the color of the orbs were distinguishable.

The bent, bearded figure scuttled back, stooped over, almost falling, but managed to pick up a heavy cane which leaned against a chair. Then he glared at Doc from his slitted eyes.

Silence persisted for a few seconds. Then the thick beard bobbed as the other nodded.

"Doc Savage," he said in a coarse, quavering voice. "I've seen you somewhere before. Or maybe it was your picture."

Doc ejected cartridges from the gun—it was an automatic. None of the shells had been fired. He threw the cartridges out of an open window and placed the weapon on a stand near a telephone. Doc never employed a gun, although he was a skilled marksman if need arose.

"What's going on here?" he asked. "Who are you?"

The bearded man answered the last question first. "I am Gardner."

"What happened?" Doc repeated.

The coarse voice quavered, "I shall tell that to the police."

"I," Doc pointed out, "have a police commission."

"This is Westchester County," Bedford Burgess Gardner growled. "You may have a New York commission, but it will do you no good here."

"It is a State Trooper commission," Doc advised.

Gardner thought that over, while the cane trembled a little under his nervous weight.

"You go to hell!" he suggested finally. "And also clear out of here! I do not like people around me at night."

There was noise outside, footsteps, and Rapid Pace's voice called out nervously. When Doc answered him, Pace came in.

Gardner pointed a shaking hand at Pace and grated, "You get out, too!"

Pace asked, "Who killed the taxi driver?"

Doc eyed Gardner. "Who did?"

"I don't know," Gardner wailed. "I don't know anything about it!"

"That's going to make it tough for you," said Pace. "Yes, sir!"

Gardner lifted his cane and started for Pace. Pace leaped back, and Doc was forced to move aside to get out of his way.

Changing his course suddenly, Gardner moved for the door.

Nerves overwrought at what he considered an intrusion of his home, he left the room in haste.

DOC, disappointed at the results of the inquiry, started for the hallway, followed by Pace.

There was no sign of Gardner now—until they heard sounds from above, scuffing, scraping sounds.

They ran up a flight of stairs. Doc had his flashlight out. A moment later they dived through a door into the room that faced on the balcony.

On the floor lay the cane Gardner had carried. Near it were wet crimson spots. A chair was upset.

"Been a fight," said Pace. "A fight, sure! But was it the taxi driver, or was Gardner being seized? Is this Gardner's blood, or the taxi driver's? That's the question."

Doc Savage lunged forward, swooped, and picked up a shiny limp fragment from the floor. It was a bit of silver cloth, ragged, as if torn from one of the weird garments of the mysterious silver men.

"They got Gardner," Pace muttered. "Or did they?"

Doc Savage glided to the nearest door, opened it and went through.

Pace, slow in following, reached the door and seemed frightened by the darkness beyond. He squirmed uncertainly, his habitual nervousness even more pronounced.

The upshot of his hesitancy was that Pace, instead of following Doc, went back upstairs and got the gun which Doc had taken from Gardner.

Then Pace eased from the room and through the darkened house, the automatic ready in his hand, a grim expression on his features.

SOME moments later, in the murk beside one of the imitation slave houses which stood near the white mansion, a sinister meeting occurred. There was an elaborate garden about the slave cabins, with tall flowering plants arrayed in neat rows. These formed an ideal concealment for furtive comings and goings.

Two silver men were just being joined by a third.

"Ull?" one of the two whispered suspiciously, drawing a gun.

"Yes, it's me—Ull," hissed the newcomer.

"Did you see who was breaking them doors down?" asked the other, replacing his gun in its holster.

"It's Doc Savage," grated Ull.

"But I thought—"

"I know," Ull snarled. "He must have avoided that grenade at the flier's apartment. He is not dead."

The first man swore quietly, briefly. "Then what are we going to do? If we hadn't shot that taxi driver when he tried to run—"

Ull considered, a harridan figure in his all-enveloping disguise of silver which shimmered slightly in the moonlight.

"Everything else has turned out all right," he said finally. "The safest thing for us to do is leave here. The rest of our party went on ahead, did they not?"

"They did," said the first.

Ull gave the fellow a shove. "Then get a move on. We will join them."

The three furtive figures had taken scarcely a step when they were brought up by a voice. It came from the slave hut window.

"You fools!" said this new speaker. "You are overlooking a chance."

Two of the silver men started violently and wrenched out weapons. Ull, grabbing at their arms, swore in an angry whisper.

"This is the master!" he grated.

The other two obviously had never heard the voice before, but at Ull's words, they seemed profoundly impressed.

"You mean—the big shot who is behind all this?" one stuttered.

Ull ignored him and addressed the window behind which the unseen speaker lurked. "You say we are overlooking a chance? What is it? And what are you doing here?"

"An opportunity to get rid of Doc Savage," said the voice from the window murk. "And never mind what I am doing here."

"But it is too risky to rush him," Ull protested. "The man is a walking storehouse of scientific weapons. Twice as many men as I have could not overcome him."

The tone of the concealed mastermind took on an edge. "You do not underrate an enemy, do you?"

"Not if I can help it," said Ull. "And I have seen this fellow work. To rush him would be too dangerous."

"I am going to throw you a package," said the voice inside the cabin. "Catch it!"

An instant later, a small packet sailed out into the moonlight and Ull cupped it successfully in a silver-gloved palm. The parcel seemed to be a bottle, carefully wrapped, for it gurgled as it hit Ull's hand.

"Come close under the window," the unseen chief directed. "I want to give you explicit directions."

Ull crept near, and their voices dropped so that even the two who waited near by in the garden, the two who had been with Ull, could not hear what was said.

These two kept eyes avidly on the window, for they had never seen this mysterious chief, this sinister one of great ingenuity, who was their real leader. Nor did they see him now. The fellow did not show himself.

INSIDE the big white house, Doc Savage was pushing his search for some sign of Gardner or the silver men. Doc did not use undue haste, for that, in the perilous career which he led, was synonymous with risking sudden death.

He heard sounds after a time—someone moving. He waited. The prowler seemed to be coming from outdoors. The bronze man used his sensitive ears to their fullest, noting particularly the number of nervous moves which the skulker made. This identified the man.

"Pace," he said quietly.

Rapid Pace emitted a loud gasp, and struck a match. He seemed relieved at sight of Doc.

"I have been looking for you," he gulped. "Yes, sir, looking for you. I was outside."

"Where did you get the gun?" Doc questioned.

Pace glanced down at his weapon. "It is the one Gardner had. I got it. It had no cartridges, of course, but just holding the gun kind of makes me feel more—well, brave."

"Hear anything of Gardner?" Doc asked.

Pace denied this, and they continued their hunt in company. The efficiency expert seemed never to run out of conversation, and he began whispering his personal opinion in the darkness until Doc reminded him that the noise would make an excellent target.

"I think Gardner is behind all this," Pace breathed, and fell silent.

They moved outdoors, kept to the shadow-banked side of the house and moved to the right, toward the spot where the body of the murdered taxi driver had fallen. Doc peered around a corner.

For an instant, the bronze man's weird trilling note came into being. Hardly audible, it trailed up and down the musical scale, fantastic in its vague similitude to the cadence of an exotic tropical bird. It had been brought forth by surprise.

Over the prone form of the slain cab driver crouched a second silver figure. This individual held a glass bottle; he was sprinkling the contents on the clothing of the corpse.

Doc stepped into view. The silver man looked up, bleated and threw the bottle. Doc whipped back to let it go past. A few drops of liquid, showering from the bottle as it gyrated, spilled on the bronze man's coat.

Doc promptly wrenched the coat off, lunging for the silver figure as he did so.

The silver man ran. But his pace was wild with haste, his metallic garment slightly clumsy, and he stumbled. Down on all fours he slapped. Twisting his head over his shoulder, he saw that Doc was almost upon him.

Beside the silver man was a low basement window. Without thought of glass cuts, he rolled into the window, knocked the sash out with head and shoulders and vanished within.

DOC SAVAGE flung his coat aside and rapped at Pace, "Keep away from that coat. Don't touch the body, either!"

Pace barked, "But what—"

"Contact poison!" Doc shouted. "An acid and some sort of toxic in solution. A trick to kill whoever touched the corpse!"

The last words were lost in a crashing noise as Doc kicked the basement sash out and dived inside. He hit the concrete floor lightly, let the rebound carry him to one side.

Flame plunged through the basement murk, a yard-long tongue; powder bellow accompanied it. The bullet made a hammering sound against the wall.

Doc, seeing darkness with his hands, found a chair with one leg missing. He shied it at the gun flame source, but got only the noise of the chair striking. The gunman had shifted position.

Came a dull *pat-pat-pat* noise and Doc, looking up through the window, saw Rapid Pace's head and shoulders recede in the moonlight. The efficiency expert was living up to his name—he was fleeing across the lawn. The situation had gotten the best of his nerves.

Doc advanced under cover of the sound. He passed the spot where the powder fumes were thickest, and made for the opposite side of the basement. The quarry would be over there somewhere.

Bending low, Doc drifted a hand over the concrete floor. Like most basements, this one was covered with a film of gritty dust. The stuff did not grind audibly under Doc's shoe soles, because they were of rubber—not ordinary rubber, but the soft sponge variety. But the grit would make sound under ordinary shoes, even rubber heels of the prosaic type.

As Doc had hoped, the grit gave the silver man away. Doc heard the fellow drift slowly nearer through the gloom. When the man was near, the bronze giant leaped.

Doc did not flail blows or try to hold the man. He simply found the fellow's neck and grasped the back of it with corded fingers.

Doc Savage was skilled in many lines, but easily his greatest knowledge was in the field of surgery, of human anatomy. He knew the location of certain nerve centers on which pressure, properly applied, produced a temporary paralysis.

The silver man went limp under Doc's fingers.

DOC called through the smashed window, "Pace! Everything is all right!"

It was not a desire for Pace's company that moved Doc to call. The efficiency expert, with his aggravating habit of repeating half of what he said, was as tiresome a companion as Doc could recall encountering. Pace was shy on nerve, as well.

But Doc wanted to keep all threads of this weird mystery of the silver man as closely at hand as possible. And Pace might be one of the threads.

Rapid Pace appeared at the basement window, after giving the poisoned corpse a wide berth. Another man might have been sheepish over the recent show of cowardice, but not Pace.

"I was looking for another weapon," said Pace. "You know, a club or something."

Doc said nothing, but used his flashlight to locate a switch which filled the basement with light. Then he went to the man in silver and stripped off the hooded mask.

A rather square, stupid face was revealed. The eyes were ugly, the mouth twisted in a perpetual sneer.

"A typical crook," said Rapid Pace. "Yes, typical."

Doc searched the fellow, but found nothing to indicate the man's name. The fellow, unable to move or speak because of the weird paralysis, could only glare.

Doc turned him over, adjusted the thick neck and exerted pressure with skilled finger tips. The results were amazing. The victim began to squirm in an endeavor to sit up.

"Lemme go!" he snarled. Fear rasped in his coarse voice, and he stared at Doc's hands, at the sinews that were like bundled cables.

"There are two things I want to know," Doc told him quietly.

"T'hell wit' yer!" snarled the thug.

"What happened to my two aides, Monk and Ham? Where are they now?" Doc spoke slowly, and the ominous undertones of his great voice caused the listener on the floor to cringe involuntarily. "That is the first thing I want to know. The second is: What is behind all of this melodramatic business of the silver disguises?"

The evil-faced man wet his lip nervously, hesitated, then snarled, "I dunno a t'ing, s'help me!"

"Hit him, Mr. Savage," suggested Rapid Pace. "His type cannot stand physical pain."

"Yer been takin' in de movies," sneered the other. "I can take all yer got."

"Hold him, Mr. Savage," Pace urged. "I'll try busting him one on the nose. Hey—what—"

Doc, lashing out an arm, upset Pace. Simultaneously, the basement quaked with gun sound. A shot had been fired from the window—not at Pace, but at Doc himself.

The slug smashed against Doc's bulletproof vest. Despite his great physique, air was driven from his lungs and he was half turned.

A long lunge carried him to the shelter of a cellar pillar. Rapid Pace was safe where he had been propelled by Doc's shove.

There was movement at the window. A pistol came gyrating through the air and landed on the lap of the man Doc had been questioning. No words were spoken. None were needed. The fellow clutched the gun avidly and wheeled in Doc's direction.

The bronze man seemed, for a moment, caught between two fires. If he left the shelter of the pillar, he would be in range from the window—and the marksman would be intelligent enough to shoot at his head this time.

The thug on the floor heaved up for a deliberate aim.

Doc flattened closer to the pillar. His right hand seemed to vanish, so swiftly did it move. It dipped into his vest and came out with the only weapon at hand—the collapsible grappling hook with its silken cord. The cord was wound tightly around the hook, adding weight to it.

Doc threw the device, threw it with all the violence he could muster from tremendous thews. The gunman's hand was not a difficult target; any baseball pitcher of ability should have been able to hit it.

The thug howled. His gun, knocked from his hand, skittered toward Rapid Pace.

THE man on the floor peered abruptly at his hands. It was as if he were surprised by something he had discovered on the somewhat grimy paws. Then he began to scream. His voice held terror.

Pace reached for the gun which had been tossed to the thug.

"Don't!" Doc rapped—and Pace jerked his hand back, stared stupidly at Doc, then at the thug on the floor, and his eyes flew wide with horror.

The thug was becoming mottled of face. He made gagging sounds. A hideous foam came to his lips, and he twisted with a convulsive violence.

"That gun—stuff off corpse—on handle!" he choked.

Doc took a chance, leaped and broke the one electric light bulb with a snap of his hand. Darkness descended. There was no shooting from the window, the person outside evidently having departed.

Doc wheeled back and seized the stricken man, then moved him to the shelter of the pillar.

"Your chance to get back at them," Doc said rapidly. "The grip of the gun that was tossed to you was smeared with some of the poison you were putting on the body. It was a trick to kill you, to shut you up, just on the chance that you would fail to get me."

"Damn—damn Ull!" the groveling man choked. "What you—want know?"

"Where are my two assistants, Monk and Ham?" Doc rapped.

"Indian's Head," mumbled the man.

"Where?" Doc asked.

The stricken one was having difficulty with his words. The strange poison seemed to work with uncanny speed.

"The Indian Head—both there," he labored.

"What is this Indian Head?" Doc demanded.

But the man seemed not to hear.

"Ull—not brains—back of Silver Death's-Heads," he said, and the words seemed to come from a bag which had leaked almost empty.

"Who is the chief?" Doc snapped.

There was no answer.

The bronze man made a brief examination. He was careful not to touch the hands with which the other had gripped the gun tossed to him from the window.

"Dead," Doc said.

## Chapter VIII
### THE BIG MYSTERY

HEAVY silence hung in the gloomy basement. Outside, there was no sound but the faint shuffle of night breeze in the shrubbery. In the distance a dog moon-bayed mournfully, then, far up the Hudson, a boat whistle blew a deep note.

Doc Savage glided to the window, careful not to disturb the broken glass on the floor inside. He heard nothing. A quick glance showed him no one.

The bronze man did not go outside through the window, for that would be inviting a shot. Instead, he ascended stairs, worked through hallways and let himself out through a rear door. He began a search.

He found no one. The gunman who had fired through the window had disappeared—not a difficult task, since there had been time for him to flee.

Back in the house, Doc addressed Rapid Pace. "Do you want to stay here and watch things until the police arrive?"

Rapid Pace shuddered so violently that he almost fell down. "Stay with these two dead men?" he gulped. "Not me! No sir!"

Doc, however, had decided the efficiency expert was a liability.

"There will probably be much more violence before I find my two men, Monk and Ham," he pointed out.

Pace groaned, "I shall take my chances with you. Yes, with you. You seemed to bear a charmed life. Just being around you braces my—"

"Sh-h-h," admonished Doc. "Listen!"

The breeze made leaves flutter outside the basement window; the dog was still baying the moon in the far distance. Chunk! The sound was dull, as if soft dough had been dropped on a board. Chunk! It came again.

"The Silver Death's-Heads haven't g-gone!" Pace stuttered.

"Come!" Doc rapped, and swung up the stairs that led to the second floor.

They heard the sound again—more of a hollow thumping this time. It came from the front, from a bedroom. Doc swung into the chamber, across it, and opened a closet door.

A man fell out. He was bound and gagged, and had been making the noises by thumping the door with his head. Doc untied him and extracted the gag.

The man was a powerful, handsome fellow in his early thirties. His hair was dark and thick, a bit shiny with a pleasantly aromatic oil, and the sideburns in front of his ears were cut, not squarely across, but slanting. His complexion was as perfect as a woman's; his eyelashes were long. But his strapping physique kept him from seeming unnaturally pretty.

Rapid Pace took one look at the stranger and groaned, "Hugh McCoy, of all people!"

"You have seen him before?" Doc demanded.

"I have seen entirely too much of him," Pace said gloomily. "He has been hanging around the shipyard a lot lately. Er—Lorna Zane was the attraction. Yes, she was the attraction."

Hugh McCoy managed to get up on his feet, although his muscles apparently were cramped. He rubbed and kneaded himself briskly. It became apparent that his suit was of most expensive tailoring.

"What happened to you?" Doc asked him.

McCoy studied the bronze man briefly, then said, "Someone leaped onto me from behind and overpowered me."

"Who was it?" Doc asked.

"It must have been Bedford Burgess Gardner," McCoy snapped.

DOC indicated the door. "We will talk while moving. Two of my men have been seized by Silver Death's-Heads, and everything but their rescue is secondary."

"But you haven't got a clue to where your two men may be," Rapid Pace protested. "That man in the basement did gasp something about an Indian's head, but I do not see how that is going to help you."

Doc ignored that, said, "Hurry!" and they clattered down the stairs and out into the night, swung boldly across the lawn and reached Doc's roadster without anything happening.

The machine chased the white funnels of its own headlights through the night, like a quiet black ghost hurtling after some lustrous siren.

"You saw Gardner attack you?" Doc queried of Hugh McCoy.

McCoy shook his head. "It was dark. I saw no one. But it must have been Gardner, because there was no one else in the house. The black-whiskered old devil!"

"Any idea why you were attacked?"

"To get me out of the way," McCoy said, and shrugged. "I know of no other reason."

"I wonder," Pace put in.

McCoy stared coldly at the efficiency expert. Pace returned the frosty look with interest. It was apparent that no love existed between these two.

"Just what are you driving at?" McCoy asked harshly.

Rapid Pace snapped, "Your story sounds fishy to me! Yes, fishy!"

McCoy's features darkened in the back glow of the car headlights. He made one hand into a hard square fist and drew it back wrathfully.

"I'll cave your face in!" Then he lowered the fist. "No, I won't either. You're just a sorehead. Peeved because Miss Zane has gone out with me a few times, aren't you?"

"Let's not bring Miss Zane into it," Pace suggested stiffly.

Doc nursed the roadster over a bridge, where their speed caused the machine to travel a score of feet with all wheels off the ground.

"Drop the personalities," he suggested. "McCoy, what were you doing at Gardner's house tonight?"

"I am a financial relations counsel, by profession," McCoy began. "I—"

"A general four-flusher would be more like it," Rapid Pace sneered.

"Shut up or I'll crown you!" McCoy snapped. "Mr. Savage, I am a financial relations counsel."

"Just what does that mean?" Doc interposed.

"I give corporations and business concerns financial advice," explained McCoy. "Sometimes, I take charge of disputes between companies, serving as intermediary to get things settled amicably. For instance, take the currently discussed merger between Gardner's shipping company, and the steamship concern and shipyard owned by Paine L. Winthrop. Gardner called me in as consultant. I looked over the situation and advised the merger. Winthrop, however, opposed it. I was at Gardner's house tonight discussing the matter."

"Did you," Doc queried, "know that Paine L. Winthrop was murdered late this afternoon?"

"Hell, no!" Hugh McCoy said feelingly. "Who killed him?"

"The Silver Death's-Heads, undoubtedly," Doc answered.

McCoy shook his head slowly. "How was it done?"

"With a shell from a three-inch cannon," Doc replied.

"Listen," McCoy exploded. "Are you serious?"

"Do you," Doc asked, "know anything about this mystery?"

"Not a thing!" McCoy said vehemently.

Doc Savage seemed on the point of putting another question, but instead, he applied the brakes, bringing the roadster to a sharp stop. They were approaching one of the bridges which led over the Harlem River into Manhattan.

A squad of policemen with riot guns and tear-gas bombs was barring their way.

A BURLY sergeant advanced, recognized Doc Savage, stepped back hastily and motioned the car on. But Doc tarried to ask questions. He wanted to know what happened.

"Why the blockading party at the bridge, officer?" he queried.

"It's them blasted Silver Death's-Heads," said the cop. "We have all the bridges an' ferries an' the subways blocked. We'll get 'em."

"Have the silver men done anything since the murder of Paine L. Winthrop?" Doc questioned.

"Done anything!" the policeman exploded. "They've been running wild! They robbed a string of movie theaters, blew open a bank vault, and looted three jewelry stores. They worked like an army. They've got gas masks inside them Silver hoods they wear, and they've got bulletproof vests, machine guns and gas grenades. They're the worst thing this town has ever seen."

"Any trace of where they go to?" Doc asked.

"No—nor where they come from, either," groaned the officer. "Except maybe it must be somewhere in the East River waterfront district. After their jobs, they seem to flee in that direction."

Doc Savage drove on. Signs that the law enforcement agencies of the city were on edge was evident at point after point. Instead of one traffic cop on duty at a corner, there were two, or even three, and an unusual number of radio cars were prowling.

"But we have been chasing the silver men all evening," Rapid Pace remarked. "It does not seem possible that they could have committed the robberies the policeman told about. No sir."

"The organization must be large," Doc told him. "We have been following only a small portion of the gang."

"Where are we going?" Hugh McCoy asked abruptly.

Instead of replying, Doc Savage swung the roadster up before an all-night drug store which displayed a telephone sign, entered and thumbed through the directories.

Pace and McCoy, following him in, were interested observers.

In the directory, Doc found numerous concerns which used the name "Indian Head." He moved a metallic finger down the list.

"We will try this one," he said, and stopped his finger at:

Indian Head Club

Pace squinted, then asked, "But why this particular one?"

"Notice the address," Doc suggested. "It is in the Brooklyn waterfront district, across from the Manhattan side of the East River where the crooks have been disappearing. On Wallow Street, to be exact. After their crimes, they ferried in some manner across to the Brooklyn shore."

"Have you," Hugh McCoy asked abruptly, "any objection to my doing my bit to aid you? I have a personal interest in this matter."

Doc's flake-gold eyes were inscrutable. "Personal interest?" he queried.

"I am on Gardner's payroll," McCoy elaborated. "I do not like to have anything put over on me. Gardner has been acting uneasily of late, which leads me to think something is queer. If anything is wrong, I would be involved—in the minds of the public at least. If I have been working for a crook, I want to be known as one of those who helped put him behind bars."

"You think Gardner is a crook?" Doc asked sharply.

"Gardner might be the leader of the Silver Death's-Heads," McCoy reminded.

WALLOW Street was a narrow, teeming alley full of odors and gloom. The thoroughfare was less than half a dozen blocks long, with the first two blocks, the two up on the hill, lined with tenements of the lowest type. The other four blocks housed sail lofts, warerooms, and shops dealing in ship supplies.

Wallow Street ended at the waterfront, where piers bulked gloomily and the polluted water of the East River sloshed and eddied. At this hour, the section down by the water was deserted, while farther up in the tenement stretch, wretched inhabitants draped themselves on fire escapes and rooftops to escape the fog-soaked warmth.

Rapid Pace and Hugh McCoy were silent as Doc guided the roadster into Wallow Street. They were still showing a coldness toward each other, neither having addressed a word to the other since entering the city.

Doc pulled into a side street, stopped the roadster and motioned McCoy and Pace back when they moved to get out.

"You two stay here," he directed.

Then the smelly darkness seemed to absorb the bronze giant. There was no sound to indicate which way he had gone. Pace and McCoy watched the corners, where street lights were brilliant, expecting to see the bronze man. But, to their amazement, he did not appear.

They should have watched the roof line along the street. They might have seen Doc Savage poise for an instant against the fog-gorged sky, after he had climbed a heavy metal drain pipe.

There was no sign of life on the rooftops, but Doc went forward as warily as if he were stalking an abnormally alert sentinel. The roofs were level, except for one stretch a floor lower than the rest, an obstacle which Doc bridged by use of his grapple and silk line.

Advancing to the forward edge of the roof, he employed a thin periscope device to scrutinize the street. This apparatus functioned remarkably well in the darkness.

### INDIAN HEAD CLUB

The sign was almost below, the letters arrayed around a gaudy likeness of a redskin brave's head. The building was as devoid of lights as the black, sombre warehouses on either side.

Doc retreated. Buildings such as this usually had roof hatches. Doc searched and found one, and pressed an ear to it. He listened for a long time, but heard nothing from within.

Doc did not enter the hatch, but moved to the rear of the building, slid down his grapple cord with the hook affixed behind a chimney, and reached a window.

The glass pane in this was large. Doc's flashlight came out, protruded a beam little thicker than a lead pencil, and he examined the edge of the glass where it was puttied in. He dug very carefully with his penknife.

What he eventually found was so well concealed that it almost evaded his intent scrutiny. Affixed in the putty was a hair-fine wire of copper. Had he carelessly tried to remove the putty, the wire would have been broken, setting off an alarm somewhere.

The discovery was proof that his caution was not wasted. The roof hatch, of course, would be fitted with another alarm.

With a penknife, Doc went to work, carefully uncovering the fine wire, locating its terminals. He twisted them together, forming a short circuit that would keep the alarm system electromagnets energized. Without this short-circuiting, he would not have been able to remove the glass without actuating the ingenious device.

He now removed the glass.

Before entering, Doc clambered back up the roof. He ran boldly to the hatch, gave it a wrench, and it came open.

Doc whipped back to his grapple cord, slid down to the window he had operated upon, freed the grapple with a jerk, and rolled it up and pocketed it as he eased into the Indian Head Club.

He advanced silently, eased through a door— and found proof that his precautions were wise.

FOUR grim figures in silver crouched at the end of the hallway, scarcely discernible in the vague light which came down through the open hatch. Doc took a chance on the floor squeaking, and crept a bit closer.

"Be sure the silencers are on your guns," said a coarse whisper.

"Why don't the guy who opened that hatch come on down?" grated another.

Perhaps a minute of grim waiting ticked by.

"Two of you go back and watch Savage's two buddies," breathed the coarser whisper.

Two silver men detached from the group and eased along the hallway and down a flight of stairs. They did not see Doc Savage, for the bronze man was moving ahead of them.

Doc was doing a strange thing as he glided along; in one of his hands was a small can with a perforated top, not unlike the containers in which talcum powder is often sold. From time to time he sprinkled some of the contents on the floor behind him. The powder was dark, and did not show up in the darkness.

The two silver men reached a door, shoved it open and thumbed on flashlights. A glance within seemed to satisfy them.

"They'll never get away," said one. "Come on. Let's take a look at the back door. I don't like that business of the roof hatch opening. Somebody might've done that to cover up while they got inside some other way."

"Nobody could get in without setting off an alarm," the other snorted skeptically.

"We'll take a look, anyhow."

The two men retreated.

They were hardly around a corner when Doc appeared at the door, got it open and passed through. His flashlight traced its white thread.

Big, apish Monk and slender, dapper Ham were handcuffed, wrist and ankle. In addition, wrist shackles were linked to ankle manacles. Both their lips and eyes were taped, the strips almost concealing their features.

The manacle locks were simple. They surrendered quickly to Doc's metal probe. He got the gags off with quick jerks—the least painful method.

Monk, making a snarling sound, reached up and uncovered his eyes. He saw Doc, gulped and dropped the fist with which he was preparing to drive a blow.

"Glory be!" he grinned. "I knew it was only a question of time until you got here!"

The door snapped open. A silver-hooded head thrust in, attracted no doubt by the noise Monk had made. The observer let out an ear-splitting yell.

DOC scooped up a heavy handcuff and snapped it at the door. The head jerked back. The manacles struck the wood so hard that splinters were torn off. With a slam, the door was yanked shut.

From the hallway came a sound reminiscent of buckshot being poured on a taut bed sheet—a silenced machine gun. Its clamor was not as loud as the uproar made by the slugs tearing through the door.

**A silver-gloved hand thrust a machine gun inside. Monk threw a smoking stand.**

Monk was on his feet. Shoving, Doc propelled him to a corner. Ham was jerking at the tape over his eyes. Doc pitched him bodily after Monk, clear of the leaden storm. In the hallway, there was shouting and the pound of racing feet. The silver men were gathering to the attack.

The room which held Doc and his two men were fitted with easy chairs, tables and smoking stands. Doc heaved a chair at a window, and it went through with a great jangling of glass.

Three silenced rapid-firers were stuttering in the hall. But the weapons, firing cartridges of pistol caliber, could not penetrate the walls. The door, however, mangled by metal, toppled off its hinges.

A silver-gloved hand thrust a machine gun inside. Monk threw a smoking stand. It hit the hand; the owner screamed, and his gun skittered across the floor.

Monk started for the weapon, willing to chance being shot in order to get it.

"Wait!" Doc rapped.

The bronze man stripped off the light alloy metal mail which he wore to protect his torso from bullets. He spread this over a cheap, overstuffed chair, making a mobile shield. Using this, Monk scuttled across the floor.

The mail jumped and whipped under the impact of lead, and flattened bullets fell from it to the floor. But Monk got the rapid-firer. He loosened a brief burst of fire—and outside, a man squawked in agony.

"They're wearing bulletproof vests," Monk said grimly. "You've got to shoot at their legs or their heads. I got that one in the legs."

Monk's single burst had a remarkable effect, for the shooting outside suddenly ceased. Footsteps pounded, grew fainter. Monk promptly charged outside, holding Doc's bulletproof garment in front of his chest.

"Sounds like they're heading for the back!" he roared.

Doc and Ham followed. They could hear the running feet—until silence fell unexpectedly.

On the floor was a spattering of crimson which had come from the leg of the man Monk had shot. Doc followed the trail, but not for far. It ended, indicating the injured one had stemmed the scarlet flow, perhaps with a handkerchief.

"It's a cinch they didn't leave the place," Monk rumbled. "We'll find 'em."

"Watch the doors." Doc directed.

Monk raced to the front entrance, and almost at once there was a violent scuffle. It subsided quickly. "Doc, I've got one!" Monk called. "Caught him just inside!"

Doc Savage, running to the spot, found the homely chemist holding a very frightened young man speared on the muzzle of his gun.

The frightened individual was Rapid Pace.

"WE h-heard f-fighting," Rapid Pace stuttered. "We decided to h-have a look."

"Where is McCoy?" Doc demanded.

"He took the back way," said Pace. "Y-yes, the back way."

"Did you see anyone running from the club?"

"No," said Pace. "No, sir."

Doc studied Rapid Pace for a moment. It had taken quite a degree of nerve to enter the Indian Head Club as Pace had done. The efficiency expert was a puzzle; at times he exhibited plenty of nerve, at other times none at all.

Hugh McCoy, appearing from the rear door, put a halt to Doc's character appraisal. No one, asserted McCoy emphatically, had fled down the alley which ran past the back door.

"But they went somewhere," said Monk.

Monk had returned to his habitual tiny-voiced manner of speaking, in marked contrast to his gusty roaring when he was in action. Monk liked plenty of noise with his fights.

"We will," Doc stated, "pull this place apart if necessary, to find where those four silver men went. Monk, Ham—did you overhear anything to indicate who is behind this affair?"

"There is a mastermind," Ham offered crisply. "He is a fellow who remains in the background. He does not even mingle with his gang. Some of the gang do not even know him by sight. We did not

get his name, or overhear anything to indicate his identity."

"A bird named Ull is first lieutenant to this chief," Monk put in. "This Ull is no dunce himself. He is a scientist, from what I overheard. He has invented a lot of things these Silver Death's-Heads use—their disguises for instance, and bulletproof vests which are almost as efficient as our own. Too, he mixed up a poison which kills you when you touch it."

Doc's gaze, roving, eyed a telephone.

"Wait," he directed, and went to the instrument. Lifting the receiver, he found it alive. He dialed a number, then heard the ringer operate the distant phone twice before a receiver came up.

"Park Avenue Beautician," said a cultured feminine voice.

"Miss Savage," Doc requested.

A moment later another voice said, "Miss Patricia Savage speaking."

"Is Lorna Zane safe?" Doc asked.

"She is unless she succumbs from some of my beauty treatments," Pat advised. "I told her anything she wanted was free while she was with me. And did she take advantage of it! She started with my Special Egyptian Clay Pack Facial, and is going right down the list. Doc, do you know what I think?"

"Better put a guard over her," Doc suggested.

"Sure," Pat agreed. "Doc, I think she is setting her cap for you. She keeps wanting to know about you."

Doc said dryly, "Try to discourage her," and hung up.

## Chapter IX
## THE CAPTURE

PATRICIA SAVAGE smiled as she hung up, because she knew that Doc was as woman-proof as any man could be. Feminine attention only embarrassed Doc, and Pat, womanlike, enjoyed kidding him. More the pity, too, because there was no doubt but that Lorna Zane was actually entranced by the bronze giant, and Lorna was not only a beauty, but she had good sense and ability as well. No one without ability could run a shipyard.

"Poor Lorna," sighed Pat aloud. "She's bumping her head against a stone wall."

"And you, sister," said a cold voice, "are going to bump into some lead if you don't behave!"

Pat started violently and whirled. The windows of her private office were adorned with drapes which hung to the floor. From behind one of these, a man had stepped. At least, Pat decided he was a man, since the voice was too coarse to come from a feminine source. The fellow was garbed in one of the weird silver regalias.

"What," Pat demanded, "does this mean?"

"Never mind that," growled the silver man.

"Call that Zane dame in here."

The speaker moved his right hand, silver-gloved, to emphasize the presence of the pistol which he held.

Pat studied the gun. She was outwardly calm, and looked very chic in an evening gown from one of the city's finest designers.

"Get a jump on," advised the silver man.

"All right," Pat said, and picked up an interoffice telephone.

Leaping swiftly, the silver man wrenched the instrument from Pat's fingers and clapped it back on the hook.

"What in blazes are you tryin' to pull?" he grated.

"That phone connects to the operator who is now dressing Miss Zane's hair," Pat explained. "I was going to call her. If you don't believe me, call her yourself."

The other hesitated, thinking the matter over.

"You got some men working in this joint, ain't you?" he grunted.

"Of course," said Pat. "Very handsome men, too. The older society matrons like that."

"Yeah," the silver man leered. "Well, I'll take a chance on 'em thinking it's one of your men callin'."

He picked up the instrument, which was one of the cradle type—receiver and mouthpiece on one arm—and began: "I want to talk to the operator dressing Miss Zane's hair—"

That was as far as he got, because a popping noise interrupted him. He dropped the instrument and staggered back, gasping and blinking. He seemed to forget that he held a gun, and pawed at the eyeholes in his mask.

Pat lunged, seized his gun with both hands, wrenched and got it. She sprang back triumphantly. Because she helped Doc Savage occasionally, she was sometimes in danger, and she had taken precautions. This trick telephone was one of them.

It was not connected to anything; but the mouthpiece, when spoken into, ejected a tiny spray of tear gas. She had borrowed the device from Doc Savage, who had fashioned countless such trick contrivances.

"When you get around to it," Pat advised, "you can put up your hands."

The silver man snarled incoherently and kept on pawing at his masked features. The noises he made in his agony and rage were bubbling and babylike. They were loud enough to cover the sound, if any, as a second silver man appeared in the open door behind Pat and advanced swiftly, lifting a gun club-fashion.

The gun bludgeoned down heavily. Pat moaned and collapsed to her knees.

"A wise dame," said the newcomer. "But not wise enough."

WHILE still stunned, Pat was jerked up and slammed into a chair. The same gun which had clubbed her was shoved into her face.

"Don't think I'm finicky about usin' it on a dame, neither!" the man advised her. "We got too much at stake to take chances on the works bein' gummed."

Pat sat very still, and said thickly, "The last thing I would think of doing is gumming anybody's works."

"You take a lot of killin', don't you?" the other jeered, half admiringly. Then he snapped at his companion: "Get over in the corner to that water cooler and wash your eyes."

The blinded man stumbled to the water cooler, spilled water down the front of his clothing, but finally managed to bathe his eyes. By that time, the effects of the tear gas had started subsiding, and he was soon able to use his orbs. With gusto, he took over the task of guarding Pat.

"Pull a funny one on me, will you?" he gritted at the young woman. "I oughta hand you yours right here!"

"Nix," said the other. "This hank of hair goes with us. The big shot's orders."

"You mean," Pat demanded, "that I am going to be honored with your companionship?"

"You get the idea."

"Why?" Pat wanted to know.

The silver man squinted at her through the eyeholes in his mask. "This guy Doc Savage thinks a lot of you, don't he?"

"I suspect," said Pat, "that Doc sometimes wishes I had never been born. You would he surprised how much time he has to spend rescuing me from trouble."

The silver man laughed harshly. "O. K. Now he's gonna have another chance."

Pat snapped, "I fail to follow you."

"Live bait, sister," the other sneered. "Get it? We use you to pull the bronze guy into a trap."

"Is that why you kept Monk and Ham alive?" Pat asked.

Teeth made a gritting noise behind the silver mask. "So you know that Savage got 'em away from us, eh?"

Pat had not known this. Doc, with a reticence characteristic of himself, had neglected to tell her over the telephone. Pat smiled cheerfully into the gun muzzle.

"My feminine intuition or something tells me you fellows will be better off if you drop everything and hunt a nice hide-out in—let us say—Timbuktu," she advised.

"Your intuition had better show you when it's wise to pipe down," the other grated, and shoved his gun closer to her face.

"Can the chatter," said the second silver man, who was carefully examining the telephones on Pat's desk. He picked up one, held it gingerly, got the operator, and seemed satisfied there was no trick.

"Will you send Miss Zane to Miss Savage's offices," he requested, then put the instrument down, scowled at Pat and added, "You had better hope that scheme works."

THE scheme worked as perfectly as the two silver men could have wished. Lorna Zane, unsuspicious, freshened and more entrancingly pretty than ever, came swinging in. She was an advertisement for the effectiveness of Pat's beauticians.

The two men, stepping to her side as she came through the door, put guns to her side and chorused, "Do the wise thing, sister!"

Lorna Zane looked at the two men, then at Pat.

"Sorry," said Pat. "I did all I could."

"I could scream," Lorna stated grimly. "But they would probably shoot us both."

"You're damn right we would," she was assured.

"We're walking you out," advised the second of the two men in the metallic disguises. "Take the back way."

Lorna Zane did not move. She stared steadily at the two sinister figures in silver.

"What do you want with me?" she demanded. "Why did you try to kill me at the shipyard?"

"Don't kid us, sister," sneered the man. "You know why."

"I do not," Lorna insisted. "And that is the truth."

The vehemence in her tone seemed to penetrate the callous armor of the two men, convincing them that she was telling the truth.

"Let's get this straight," one growled. "Didn't you know what that blueprint was about?"

"You mean the print that your gang stole from the safe out at the shipyard?" Lorna demanded.

"Sure. You know what it was, didn't you?"

"No," said Lorna, "I did not."

The silver man whistled softly, as if amazed. "Didn't old Winthrop tell you what it was all about?"

"Emphatically not," Lorna snapped.

"Damned if I don't believe you," the man mumbled thoughtfully.

The second silver man emitted a gritting laugh. "Say, I see what happened! Remember when the big boss threatened Winthrop over the telephone? Winthrop was scared. He said this dame had the blueprint and knew the story, and would go to the cops if anything happened to Winthrop. We had been keepin' an eye on Winthrop and knew who had the blueprint—this dame, here."

"You think Winthrop stalled to save his neck for a while?" his companion questioned.

"It looks like it," the other admitted.

"Then you'll let me go?" Lorna asked hopefully.

"Watch us do that!" the man growled. "Get goin', both of you skirts! Out the back way."

Pat and Lorna walked meekly ahead of the two gunmen. There was nothing else for them to do.

INSTEAD of an alley at the back of the modernistic skyscraper which housed Pat's beauty establishment, there was a large tunnel of an affair, closed at the street by large steel doors. During the daylight hours, this was used by the trucks which had merchandise to deliver to the building, but at the present late hour, the tunnel was occupied only by an innocent-appearing truck.

The truck driver had his collar turned up and his hat was yanked over his eyes. This, coupled with the darkness, afforded him a complete disguise.

Pat and Lorna did not see his features as they were forced to get into the back of the truck, accompanied by their two captors. The doors were closed.

One silver man pressed his metallic mask to a slit in the van and spoke to the driver. "All set?"

"Sure," said the driver.

"And listen—did I get a message that was relayed from the big boss?" chuckled the other.

"Savage doesn't know it," the driver advised gleefully. "He's all set to get his within ten minutes, though. Everything is fixed. The big boss himself arranged it."

"Where is Savage now?" asked the silver man.

"In the Indian Head Club. He's frisking the joint."

The silver man swore violently. "Hell, if he ever finds—"

"Don't worry," snapped the driver. "He won't find anything but sudden death. It's all fixed, I tell you. Savage won't suspect a thing until—*blooie!* He'll be done for."

Pat heard each word. Desperation seized her, and she lunged at the nearest captor. It was a move doomed to defeat, because the fellow was alert. He simply stepped back and sideswiped Pat's head with the barrel of his heavy automatic, not hard enough to do violent damage, but forcibly enough to send her reeling back.

The van rolled out of the tunnel and into the traffic as the two men in the rear used tape to gag Pat and Lorna.

"You'll hear all about the party at the Indian Head Club."

## Chapter X
### DEATH BLASTS

THE Indian Head Club was outwardly quiet, but there was grim work underfoot inside. Doc and his party were searching.

"This place is more than a hide-out," Monk stated firmly. "There's some secret about it."

"What makes you think that?" Doc questioned.

"The way them silver mugs acted," Monk explained. "They were mighty careful. And I heard one of them remark that if you or the police found out what was here, the fat would be in the fire."

Ham, who was hauling clothing out of a closet, emitted a grunt of pleasure. He had found his sword cane.

"Our captors brought this along when they seized us," he said, flourishing the weapon. "They were curious about the chemical on the tip. I heard one of them remark that Ull might make use of it."

"Yeah," Monk admitted. "This Ull is a brainy cuss, from what they said."

Hugh McCoy, flushed and seemingly enjoying the excitement, put in, "Did either of you gentlemen hear a mention of Gardner while you were prisoners?"

"No," said Monk. "Who's Gardner?"

"A man who might conceivably be behind the Silver Death's-Heads," McCoy replied.

Rapid Pace snapped, "What makes you suspect Gardner? That is what I want to know? What makes you suspect him?"

"Have *you* any better suggestion?" McCoy asked coldly.

Rapid Pace merely glared at McCoy, then wheeled away.

"We are killing time," he snapped. "The thing to do is find where those four silver men went to."

"That will not be difficult," Doc assured him quietly. "Monk, you watch the rear door. McCoy, you take the front entrance."

The bronze man moved out into the street and ran toward the corner where his roadster stood. The streets were quiet, except that late-playing children made a little noise up in the tenement section. The fog seemed to be thicker.

From the rumble seat of the roadster, Doc got an object which might have been a press photographer's camera, but which was actually a lantern projecting light rays in the ultraviolet range of the spectrum.

The device was simple, merely being an electric bulb, battery operated, which gave off light closely akin to that of an arc, and a deep filter which cut out all the light but ultra-violet.

Doc went back to the house and to the stairway where he had sprinkled the powder from the shaker during the time that the silver men were unwittingly leading him to Monk and Ham. The silver men had walked through the powder without knowing it.

Doc extinguished all lights, turned on the ultra-violet lantern and pointed its dark lens at the floor. Scattered patches of glowing electric blue appeared wherever Doc bad sprinkled the powder—and where the silver men had walked through the powder, their feet had therefore left prints.

Doc followed the trail. It grew a bit fainter, for the powder would soon wear off the shoe soles of the quarry. The tracks progressed down into the basement.

The basement floor was of concrete. A large furnace stood in a corner, and insulated steam pipes stretched about like the tentacles of an octopus. There were barrels, boxes and a bin holding coal.

The glowing tracks led to a barrel which stood against one wall.

"Stand back," Doc warned, and moved the barrel.

At first, it seemed there was solid concrete below, but a closer scrutiny revealed a circular manhole, its lines intended to be concealed by the mark the barrel bottom had made on the floor.

With a heel, Doc put weight on various parts of the lid. It hinged up, uncovering a cavity so black that it resembled a puddle of drawing ink.

The thin flashlight beam showed a room below, with a ladder leading down. Walls and floor of the subterranean recess were lined with bricks. There was a table, chairs, a rack holding numerous silver garments, opened cases of sub-machine gun ammunition, and other boxes holding rapid-firers and hand grenades.

But there was no sign of the silver men.

Doc descended the ladder, after searching to make sure there were no trick triggers or death traps.

On the rack of silver garments, four metallic regalias lay askew, as if hastily cast there. Doc lifted them curiously.

One was crimson stained, still wet.

"Discarded by the man Monk shot in the leg," Doc decided.

He stood, hefting the silver cloaks curiously.

UPSTAIRS, Monk was shifting from one foot to the other as he watched the rear door. Monk believed there would be action below, and he hated to miss it. He peered into the alley, listened, then withdrew to the stairway that led down into the basement, and strained his ears.

He did not hear anything from the basement. Instead, he caught a faint sound from the direction of the front door, where Hugh McCoy was functioning as lookout. Monk hesitated.

"McCoy," he called softly.

There was no answer. Gripping his captured submachine gun, Monk eased toward the front. McCoy should have been just inside, but he was not there. Monk peered out into the street.

It was some seconds before he caught an indefinite blur moving away from the Indian Head Club, keeping in the shadow of the buildings. With a silence remarkable for a man of such bulk, Monk floated down the steps, glided a dozen yards, took a deliberate aim with his weapon and invited, "Whoever you are, stand still!"

The figure was silent so long that it seemed there was going to be no answer.

"Speak up!" Monk growled.

"You dope!" said McCoy's voice. "They'll hear you!"

"Who?"

"The four silver men," grated McCoy. "I just saw them sneaking up the street."

"Wait here," Monk grated. "Doc will want to know about this!"

The homely chemist whipped back into the Indian Head Club, went halfway down the basement stairs and barked, "Doc! McCoy just seen the four birds pulling a sneak!"

Monk saw Ham and Pace race for the stairs, saw Doc appear from the round hole in the basement floor. He waited for no more, but pitched back outside to aid McCoy.

McCoy was not where Monk had left him. Deciding the financial counselor had gone ahead, so as not to lose sight of the quarry, Monk scuttled up the street. He gained the corner and discerned no sign of McCoy.

Monk looked around to see if Doc and the others were following him—and saw the most stupendous display of pyrotechnics he had ever witnessed.

The ground seemed to sink several inches under Monk's feet, then jump straight up. Simultaneously, there was a sound as if a firecracker had gone off in each ear. Blood-red light flooded his eyes, blinding him.

Against the lurid glow, Monk saw Doc, Ham and Pace outlined. The trio were not running, but seemed to be flying through the air, carried by an invisible force from behind. Then the force of the explosion reached Monk, slapped him like an unseen Colossus, and he was knocked sprawling.

Dazed, unable to hear because the blast had temporarily deafened his ears, Monk managed to land on all fours. Peering upward, he saw copings toppling off buildings. Window glass was falling like brittle snow. Walls began to come down.

Down by the Indian Head Club—or rather, where it had been—a mound of flame and debris was climbing toward the sky.

Monk began to crawl. Then something happened to the top of his head; things turned very black in front of his eyes, and all noise of the uproar left him.

MONK'S next connection with the material world was a briskly calloused voice saying, "No ordinary brick could do anything to that head of Monk's. He'll be all right in a minute."

Monk, unable to think coherently, asked, "Where's Habeas?"

"There you are!" said Ham. "Thinking of that pet pig ahead of everybody else. We left the pig at your laboratory."

"Yeah?" Monk got his wits together. "I sure wasn't worrying about you, shyster. Say, what happened? The last I remember, Vesuvius seemed to turn loose."

"That was no more than a minute ago," Ham snapped. "Take a look at the Indian Head Club."

Monk, realizing he was facing away from the club, turned himself around with his hands, still in a seated position. A great glare caused him to close his eyes tightly.

Where the Indian Head Club had been there was a tower of flame that moaned and squirmed fully two hundred feet in the air. Waves of heat shoved against his face.

"Say, what could burn like that?" Monk gulped.

"Chemicals," Doc Savage said quietly. "There must have been a mine under the place, charged with an inflammable chemical in addition to explosives."

"Them four silver devils must have lit the fuse and were beating it when McCoy saw them." Monk reared up shakily. "Say, where did McCoy go?"

"No sign of him," Doc advised.

Rapid Pace, standing in the background dabbing at various minor cuts, snapped, "I do not trust that McCoy. No, sir. He is a very smooth man."

"If he hadn't discovered those silver lads skipping out, it would have been just too bad for us," Monk growled.

Down the street, a weaving figure appeared. It was a man. He was staggering, keeping both hands pressed to his head. His clothing was torn, and dust fell from him when he stumbled.

When he was close, they saw that it was Hugh McCoy.

"Where did the four silver men go?" Doc asked sharply.

McCoy looked at them painfully, still holding his head.

"How would I know?" he snapped. "Part of a wall fell on me. I've been unconscious."

THE flames from the Indian Head Club ruin seemed to be climbing higher; gory tongues of fire detached themselves and shot upward hundreds of feet. The howling bedlam of the blaze made conversation difficult.

To escape the searing heat, Doc and his men retreated. From all around them came the wail of fire sirens, but none of the apparatus was yet in sight.

Doc Savage, eyeing the flames, decided. "It will be a good many hours before we can get into that ruin to do any investigating. Come on. We have something to do besides watching the fireworks."

Monk peering at Doc, started slightly. He had just discovered that Doc carried, tucked obscurely under one arm, one of the strange metallic garments worn by the Silver Death's-Heads.

"Where'd you get that thing, Doc?" the homely chemist demanded.

"From the room under the Indian Head Club basement," Doc replied.

"Think it's a clue?" Monk questioned eagerly.

"No," Doc told him. "But there are pockets inside the garment, and the contents of one of those pockets is, I think, going to prove very valuable."

They were still retreating from the flames. A crowd sprang up rapidly about them, curious persons drawn by the terrific blast and the amazing fire. Howling fire trucks bored through the throng, followed by hose wagons, rescue squads and emergency police.

In the uproar, Doc Savage and his party attracted little attention.

They reached a drug store, windows of which had been broken by the detonation. It was unoccupied, the proprietor evidently having dashed off excitedly to the fire. Lights were burning inside—the first spot Doc and his party had encountered where there was illumination.

"Let's have a look at what was in the pocket of that silver suit," Monk requested.

Doc nodded, and they went in the drug store. Broken glass strewed the floor, for many bottles had been shaken off counters. The bronze man employed the marble top of the soda fountain as a table.

From the inner recesses of the silver suit, he extracted a long blue roll sealed with wax.

Rapid Pace took one look at them and exploded, "The blueprint that was taken from the shipyard safe!"

"You've seen it before?" Hugh McCoy asked sharply.

Pace scowled at his rival for the hand of Lorna Zane.

"No," he retorted. "But Miss Zane described it."

Doc unrolled the print—it was, it developed, the only one.

"Blazes," muttered Monk eyeing the lines traced whitely on the blue background. "A sketch of New York Harbor! Now, that ain't quite what I expected."

THE map—it was actually no more than that—of the harbor was not especially complete, but it showed certain prominent details, outstanding landmarks, and the depth of water was carefully gauged at numerous points. Compared with a regulation marine harbor chart, it would have been crude, yet it apparently had been traced from such a chart.

Doc dropped a finger on the blue expanse. "These four small stars seem to be the only especially-outstanding marks."

The stars with Doc indicated were situated in approximately the center of the East River—the first off the Wall Street section of Manhattan, the

next possibly a quarter of a mile south, and the others spaced at like intervals farther down.

"Maybe they're buoys," Ham suggested.

"No buoys at those points," Doc assured him. "And notice the position of the first, the northernmost one."

Ham looked again, then started.

"By Jove! It is almost directly opposite that Indian Head Club."

"Exactly," Doc agreed.

"You think that is significant?"

"I do."

"Will you explain, Doc?" Ham requested.

"Later," Doc told him.

The bronze man went to a telephone booth, took the receiver down, found the circuit intact, and dialed a number. He spoke quietly for some moments.

His metallic features did not alter expression. However, there was audible for a brief moment that unearthly trilling sound which was the bronze man's peculiar characteristic, the sound which he made unconsciously when some unusual danger threatened, or which marked some stark discovery, or which preceded some unusual course of action. Finally he replaced the receiver and left the booth.

"The Silver Death's-Heads," he said slowly, "have seized Pat and Lorna Zane. I just talked to Pat's establishment."

## Chapter XI
### THE RIVER BED MYSTERY

IT was getting along toward dawn, and Father Knickerbocker, as New Yorkers like to dub their city as a whole, was for the most part asleep. It had been a hectic night.

No less than twenty major robberies had been committed by the weird Silver Death's-Heads during the early part of the night.

New York had had her crime waves in the past; there had been nights which saw more robberies and nights when more loot had been annexed by thieves. But never had a crime wave possessed quite the spectacular qualities of this one. Never before had the thieves all affected the same fantastic costumes. That was the startling thing.

The tabloid newspapers ate it up; the radio broadcast it, and the police began to expect gray hairs when they next looked in mirrors.

The mayor was up all night walking the floor; the governor called twice to know whether the militia would help, and editorial writers sharpened their pencils to take digs at the city administration.

Almost a million dollars in loot had been taken, the largest haul being the armored truck earlier the previous afternoon. Robbery reports piled onto the city desks of newspapers so fast that the editors could not tell which was which.

The murder of Paine L. Winthrop, good for a front-page streamer on the first edition, was relegated to the back pages before the final edition went to bed.

Most amazing aspect of the whole thing, however, was the fact that New York's usually efficient policemen had not captured a single silver man. What was more, they had no idea where any one of the silver men could be found.

The sinister fellows in metallic disguises bobbed up, committed a robbery, shot down any one who resisted, and fled. Maybe the police chased them a few blocks. Then, without exception, the silver men disappeared.

Usually, they disappeared in the vicinity of the waterfront surrounding Manhattan Island. The police had noted this fact.

It was still foggy, and although dawn was more than an hour distant, there was still intense darkness. Ocean vessels were dropping anchor outside the Narrows, waiting for the soup to lift; such tugs as prowled the harbor nosed along with tooting horns and every spare man on lookout duty.

There was one boat on the river which was not making undue noise, however. It was a thin lance of a speed craft with motors which did not make sound proportionate to their great power, for they were scientifically muffled. With just a few alterations, that boat could well be a contender for the Harmsworth trophy. She was fast.

Doc Savage and Monk were alone in the speedboat, Monk handling the controls, Doc in the cockpit, donning a pair of heavy lead diving shoes.

From time to time, Monk lifted a boxlike device to his eyes and peered at, first, one shore of the river and then the other. Monk was getting bearings.

On the shore, Doc had placed projectors emitting strong infrared light, rays invisible to the unaided eye, but which had the power of penetrating fog and smoke to a remarkable degree. The boxlike apparatus rendered the infrared beacons visible. Merely an adaptation, this contrivance, of the signaling apparatus well known to naval technicians, and of principles with which alert photographers were familiar.

"The place is about a hundred feet upstream," Monk decided.

Doc paused in buckling on the lead shoes, and reached into a locker. He brought out a flashlight already tied to a float, and switched it on. This he tossed overboard, together with a long line to which was affixed an anchor weight.

The light bobbed astern, moored in place by the line and weight.

Monk took another bearing, then said: "We're right over the place where the first star was marked on that blueprint."

DOC SAVAGE stood up as the boat slackened speed. He lifted an apparatus which might have been mistaken for an oversized fish bowl, and put it over his head.

It was a diving hood of a transparent composition infinitely stronger than glass, and had the advantage of permitting vision on all sides. The helmet was a product of Doc's inventive genius, its composition vaguely akin to the common cellophane.

Inside the helmet was a receiver and microphone, these being connected to a tiny radio transmitter that was attached to a stout tool jacket which Doc now donned. The radio transmitter aerial was in one sleeve of the jacket, the receiving aërial in the other.

The receiving aërial was a loop, and by pointing the arm in various directions, the position of another diver using one of the transmitters could be ascertained.

Doc switched on the radio, which was waterproof, and twirled the wavelength knob. He got major broadcasting stations, amateurs, very shortwave stuff—then a sudden, ear-splitting moan.

He waited tensely. The moan came again.

The sound was the radio compass station operated by the Government. Doc searched on down until he found a clear band, then gave Monk the wavelength figure.

Monk, who had lifted another radio transmitter-receiver combination from a box, tuned to the same wave.

Doc stepped overside. The heavy lead shoes pulled him down with a gurgling rapidity.

"Cruise above this spot," Doc directed Monk. "Better shut off your motor, douse all lights and use the oars. You can hold your position with the oars alone."

"Sure," said Monk. "Keep me posted on what you find."

The two-way radio functioned perfectly, a fact that did not displease Doc, because this was the first time he had been able to test it and the transparent helmet under actual diving conditions.

Inset in the helmet side, low down where it did not interfere with vision, was a watch-shaped depth gauge calibrated in feet. It was marked with radiant paint. Doc watched the hand crawl around.

The pressure did not greatly hamper his powerful body, the water at this point being not excessively deep. Patent "lungs" of conventional type kept breathable air in the helmet.

When he was near the bottom, Doc switched on a powerful waterproof searchlight.

He hit bottom, and mud clouded up around him. By pointing the arm containing the receiver loop upward, he located Monk's transmitter. It was a bit upstream. Doc walked in that direction, sweeping the river bottom with his hand searchlight.

He almost missed it. The thing was drifted over with mud, and only the clank of the lead diving shoes against the metal cover disclosed its presence. Doc picked it up, washed it off and studied it.

He held in his arms a metal box something over a foot square. It had thickly soldered seams to render it waterproof.

"Lower a line," Doc directed Monk.

A moment later, a weighted line came snaking down. Doc grasped the end and was hauled upward.

"So you got it," Monk chuckled when they were both in the speedboat.

"Yes," Doc told him. "And I believe we have our hands on the whole secret."

The bronze man employed a screwdriver to thrust into one of the soldered seams. Prying, he gradually tore the metal box open. Inside was a soft black composition of the type used to fill automobile spark coils. Doc carefully dug into this.

He uncovered scattered wires, then a coil, and finally the rounded glass top of a vacuum tube.

Upstream, the light he had left afloat made a pale blur in the darkness. Doc worked low in the boat cockpit, his own light painstakingly sheltered. Down in the bay, two tugboats were hooting at each other. Their own boat was drifting.

"What do you make of it?" Monk asked anxiously.

"Well," Doc began. "It seems—"

Monk had stood erect to look over Doc's shoulder. He flopped flat in the cockpit as a piercing whistle sounded overhead.

THERE was a flash; it seemed to come from some distance down the river. Another, much brighter flash followed it—that one from up the river. Then came two ear-splitting roars which blended, intermingling until they became one whooping tumult.

A great geyser of water lifted where Doc had left the floating light. Bilious water pushed away from the spot in a wall that boiled down upon the speedboat.

The craft was caught broadside. It lifted, and turned completely over.

Doc and Monk, clutching life lines, remained with the boat—and the craft, because of its design, came upright again.

Everything loose, including the mysterious box on which Doc had been working, was gone from the cockpit. A full six inches of water sloshed in the bottom of the boat.

Doc lunged for the instrument panel, thumbed a button, and the big motors in their waterproof compartment moaned into life. A stroke of a lever set pumps to work emptying the shallow cockpit. No

ordinary boat, this, but one with such peculiar qualities of efficiency that the naval experts were considering its design for creating a fleet of light coastal defense speedsters.

"That was a shell!" Monk gulped. "Boy, I've heard too many of them things whistle to be mistaken."

Doc said grimly, "Fired from downstream, too. The sound from the gun reached us just before the shell detonated. It was aimed at that decoy light we left floating."

Doc had the speedboat controls now. The craft lifted its snout out of the water and knifed downstream.

Clambering forward, Monk wrenched at a hatch and a mechanical tripod lifted a gun into view. The weapon fired shells no more than an inch in diameter, but they were armor-piercing and high-explosive slugs which could sink a destroyer if carefully placed.

Monk hunkered behind the piece, waiting.

The homely chemist had no idea what manner of craft they might encounter, but any antagonist armed with a cannon was formidable. He wondered how it happened that they had not heard the motors of the enemy.

Monk found cause for fresh wonder when they passed over the spot from which the gun flash of the foe had come—and found nothing.

Doc curved the fast boat in a narrow circle. Still, there was nothing. He described a wider circuit, with the same negative results. Twice more, he went around. Then he cut the motors and both he and Monk listened.

The only sound was the noise of a loud motor upstream, and a bit later a siren wail from the same source. This identified an approaching police boat.

Monk squinted in Doc's direction, moistened his lips, then growled, "Well, only one thing can explain it."

"Yes," Doc agreed. "That shell was fired from a submarine, fantastic as the idea seems."

RAPID PACE and Hugh McCoy leaped to their feet when Doc Savage and Monk entered the reception room of Doc's skyscraper headquarters.

"Any word of Lorna—Miss Zane?" McCoy asked anxiously.

"Yes," Pace echoed. "Any word?"

"No," Doc said. "Is Ham back?"

Pace nodded at the library door. "In there. He told us to stay out. Said he did not want to be bothered."

Doc and Monk waved McCoy and Pace back when the pair would have followed them into the laboratory.

Ham gave them a well-bred frown when he saw their dripping garments.

"I knew I would miss out on some excitement," he said peevishly.

Doc questioned, "Did you have any luck with your end?"

"I followed the orders you gave before you and Monk started out in the speedboat," Ham replied. "A fine job I had, too, digging up old sanitation maps of the city at that hour of the night."

"What did you learn?" Doc demanded.

Ham picked up a rolled map which reposed on the writing desk.

"You can see it on here," he said. "But I can tell you just as well. Up until fifteen years ago, a large drainage pipe ran under the waterfront section of Brooklyn and emptied into the East River. It was abandoned fifteen years ago. Not taken up, mind you, because that was too expensive. It was merely abandoned."

Doc said, "It ran in the neighborhood of the Indian Head Club?"

"Right under the Indian Head Club, to be exact," Ham stated.

"Daggone!" Monk gulped. "This is beginning to shape up. The Silver Death's-Heads had opened a passage into that old pipe. That's why they blew up the Indian Head Club—to keep us from finding the pipe and the secret passage."

"But what did they use the abandoned drain pipe for?" Ham pondered aloud.

"To get to their submarine," Monk grunted.

Ham had secured a new sword cane from a supply of the unique weapons which he kept in his apartment at a fashionable club. He picked the weapon up, twirled it slowly, eyeing Monk the while.

"That brick which cracked you when the Indian Head Club blew up must have done some damage, after all," he said dryly. "You sound even crazier than usual. Submarine! Bosh!"

Monk scowled. "Listen, shyster, there was a submarine in the river tonight, or at least some craft that went under the water. What's more, whoever was running it took a potshot at us with what sounded like a three-inch cannon."

Ham absently unsheathed the blade of his sword cane a few inches, then clicked it back together. Amazement sat on his features.

"You are serious about this submarine business?" he asked earnestly.

"It may sound wild," said Monk. "But it is the truth."

Doc Savage put in, "You will recall that it was a three-inch shell which killed Paine L. Winthrop yesterday afternoon. Later, two men who were in a position to see the submarine were killed. I mean the fisherman and the aviator, of course."

"Murdered to keep the existence of the submarine a secret," Monk mumbled.

"I say," Ham queried sharply, "do you mean that these Silver Death's-Heads came into New York Harbor underwater, and reached the Indian Head Club through that abandoned drainage pipe?"

"That is not at all impossible," Doc assured him. "And now, Ham, did you learn anything about a scientist named Ull?"

HAM, drilling his sword cane with his eyes, said, "This fellow must he Don Ull, alias Ellis Nodham, alias Professor O'Donald, alias a flock of other names. He served a term in Sing Sing for manufacturing pineapples for gangsters. In the United States Patent Office he has over a dozen electrical inventions registered, some of them extremely clever.

"He was technician for a concern manufacturing poison gas during the war, which means he was a skillful chemist. He once designed a patent two-man submarine, and he is an expert on diving apparatus, having patented one of his creations. I talked to a dozen men who had known him in the past, and everyone said Ull was as crooked a snake as ever lived."

"Whew!" Monk exploded. "The fellow seems to be a jack-of-all-trades."

"Think what a clever rascal the mastermind behind Ull must be," Ham said.

Monk looked grim and stated, "That reminds me. How in blazes did the Silver Death's-Heads know we were going to be on the river?"

"Probably had men shadowing us," Ham retorted. "Now, what I want to know is: What did you find in the river?"

"A tin box," Monk told him. "A tin box soldered waterproof, and filled with black insulating compound, wires and vacuum tubes."

Ham demanded, "What was it?"

Instead of answering, Monk turned around and faced the door of the reception room. In there, the telephone buzzer was whining.

Doc leaped to the door. Rapid Pace was reaching for the phone.

"I'll take it," Doc said, and scooped up the instrument.

A voice remindful of a squealing rat said, "I wanta talk to a guy named Doc Savage."

"You have him now," Doc replied. "What is it?"

"A dame throwed a note out of a window," whined the rodent voice. "The note said some mugs had kidnaped her, and for me to call you for help and you'd pay me plenty to show you where she was bein' held."

"Was there a name signed to the note?" Doc questioned sharply.

"Yeah. It was 'Pat.'" The squeaking took on a more uneasy quality. "Listen, mister, step on it. I'm kinda worried. I dunno but what some guys are fol-lowin' me. I sorta thought they was, a time or two."

"Where are you?" Doc rapped.

"In an all-night drug store at the corner of Stein and Decker Streets. I'll wait here—" The ratty voice broke off sharply in an excited gasp.

There followed a tense dozen seconds of silence. When the squeaking tone resumed, it was stark with terror.

"Oh hell, mister, I'm on the spot!" it choked. "Them fellers that was followin' me just came in. They're them Silver Death's-Heads! They're runnin' for this phone booth—"

The rodent voice began to scream. Glass crashed and wood broke, as if the phone booth doors had been smashed in. Ugly thumps, coming over the wire, sounded like blows.

A voice that was unmistakably Ull's said, "It is fortunate that we saw this fellow loitering about the spot where we were holding the two women. I believe he was up to something."

"What's we do wit' 'im?" asked another voice.

"Take him to the place where the two women are," said Ull.

Then the distant telephone receiver was placed on its hook.

## Chapter XII
## THE TRICK

ULL glared at the receiver after he hung it up. In his all-enveloping silver garment, Ull made an ominous figure, and the heavy submarine gun in his left hand detracted no whit from his fierce aspect.

Behind Ull, two silver-cloaked men were pointing guns at a drug store clerk who was so frightened that he was on the point of fainting.

Two more silver men gripped a scrawny, pinch-faced fellow who was also badly scared.

"Lemme loose!" whined the prisoner in a rat-squeal voice. "I ain't done nothin'!"

"Lay off the jaw music," he was ordered harshly.

Ull directed loudly, "Everybody out!"

One of the pair guarding the clerk held up a hand, said, "Wait a minute, boss. I got a headache. Let's see if I can find something that's good for it."

"Hurry up, then," Ull snapped.

The silver man who claimed he had a headache began a rapid scrutiny of the drug store display shelves. He showed scant consideration for the stock, sweeping bottles off the shelves. He seemed to take an unholy joy in doing as much damage as he could.

He came to an array of vaseline in jars and tubes. These he upset. Then he trampled over the litter, and his weight forced the pale petroleum jelly from the tubes and jars and smeared the whole mess over his shoe soles.

The man left greasy tracks as he tore down more chemicals, and found his aspirin.

Then all the silver men moved for the door, dragging the fellow who had been in the telephone booth.

About to walk onto the street, Ull paused and snarled, "Maybe we had better shut this clerk up permanently."

The soda jerker paled, swayed, his lips moved without sound, and he fainted on his feet. Toppling forward, he fell on the fountain syrup pumps, pushing them down and squirting strings of chocolate, pineapple and strawberry.

Ull and his silver-masked companions cast alert gazes about them as they moved down the gloomy street. There was still fog over the city, thick stuff which deposited a slimy coat over every exposed object. This was a remote street, and at this early hour almost deserted.

The man who had stepped in the petroleum left greasy tracks for a time, but they grew fainter and soon were no longer discernible to the naked eye.

The man looked back at his tracks, scowled, then tried scuffing along to leave more pronounced prints.

"No," said Ull. "That might make him suspicious."

"How d'you mean?" the man growled.

"He can see from the way you scraped your feet that you deliberately tried to leave tracks," Ull told him.

"Hell!" said the man. "The guy ain't that sharp."

"Doc Savage is a mental genius," said Ull. "The trouble so far is that we have underrated the fellow."

They turned into an alley where it was almost as dark as night.

"Do you think Doc Savage will fall into it?" asked one of the weirdly garbed figures.

"Yes," said Ull. "It was perfect. The vaseline tracks, especially."

They now released the man with the ratty voice. One of the silver garments was produced and the rodent one donned it hurriedly. The suit was fitted with zipper fasteners, which facilitated getting into it.

"How about a bonus for me?" he chuckled.

"You did excellently," Ull told him with heartiness.

THE men were moving swiftly, as if aware that each moment upon the street was dangerous. The city was inflamed against them, because of the depredations committed the previous day and night. Mere sight of them in this section would be enough to create a turmoil.

"Hurry," Ull snapped.

"You figure Savage will come?" asked the ratty man.

"If your acting over that telephone was sufficiently convincing, he will," said Ull. "Did he sound as if he were being taken in?"

"He sure did," declared the rodent one.

"Then he must be on his way now." Ull

sounded vastly pleased. "He will search the drug store and, of course, he will find the vaseline which was so thoughtfully walked through."

"What if Savage ain't wise enough to know what we want him—I mean what we hope he'll do about the vaseline?"

"Forget it," snorted Ull. "He uses ultraviolet light a lot."

They clustered about a grimy doorway and Ull rapped a peculiar signal with his fingertips, playing a short, distinctive bit from a song popular at the moment. The fingertip aria could be recognized easily as such. The door opened.

Two men inside the building sighted grimly over machine guns. Safeties were off the weapons, and the eyes back of the mask holes were coldly grim. Both were garbed in the metallic disguises.

Ull stared at the gunmen, saying nothing.

"All right!" snarled one of the men. "You ain't foolin' nobody by wearin' them silver rigs! Get 'em off!"

Moving very slowly so as not to invite a bullet, Ull tugged one sleeve back and looked at an expensive, heavily protected wrist watch.

"Seventeen minutes and eleven seconds after," said Ull.

One of the machine gunners eyed his own watch, laughed and said, "O. K. How did I do?"

"Very well," said Ull. "Remember, we all wear watches timed to the exact second, all set together, but not at the correct time. At the present moment we are all two minutes and fifteen seconds fast."

"Sure," said the other. "It beats a password."

Ull and his party advanced down a gloomy corridor in complete darkness, reaching a room where other silver men waited. One of these men illuminated a flashlight briefly.

"What do we do now?" this man asked.

"We have set the trap for Doc Savage," Ull explained. "This building has been carefully prepared. There are many traps to kill him when he tries to enter."

"What about us?"

"We remain here to take a hand if the traps fail," said Ull. "There must be no slip this time."

A grotesque silver figure came in hurriedly, excitement in his walk.

"The big boss wants to talk to you," he said to Ull. "He sounds mad as hell!"

Ull emitted a startled ejaculation. "Is the chief *here?*"

"No," explained the other. "He is on the telephone. And he wants to talk to you."

AS Ull went into another room to the telephone, there was a trace of nervousness in his manner. He strode much more hurriedly than was his wont, and his hands made jerky gestures. Reaching the phone, he picked up the dangling receiver, put an ear to the instrument, got his mouth close to the transmitter and said, "Ull speaking."

A coarse, angry whisper said, "Damn you, Ull! You have just about bungled everything!"

Ull recognized that harsh sibilance. The rage it carried evidently impressed him as well, for before he spoke, his neck stiffened slightly, as if he were swallowing some trouble.

"But Chief," he murmured, "there has been no major misfortune. I consider that we have come off very luckily."

"Hell!" the other swore expressively.

Ull stammered in haste, "Of course, we have had backsets—such as losing the blueprint, and being forced to blow up the Indian Head Club, and a few other minor details. But in fighting a man the caliber of Doc Savage, we could not expect perfect sailing."

"Why, you—" The other tried to find a word bad enough.

But Ull, eager to plead his own case before this whispering mastermind of whom he stood in such awe, interrupted.

"Our situation is still very satisfactory," he pointed out. "Doc Savage does not suspect your identity. He has learned who I am, but that does not matter because I am already wanted by the police. We have Doc Savage's cousin and the girl, Lorna Zane. The two women are perfect bait with which to draw Doc Savage into a trap."

"Listen—"

"Doc Savage is now heading straight for a trap from which he cannot possibly escape," interpolated Ull. "We will get him out of the way. Then there will be no one to bar our path. We will repeat what we did last night. Why, chief, we got nearly a million, all told, from those robberies."

"You damned blathering idiot!" grated the distant master. "I did not order those robberies, except the first one—the armored truck holdup. You pulled the others on your own initiative. Ull, you went crazy. The city is in an uproar."

"They can't touch us," Ull said earnestly. "Not with the system we've got of making a getaway."

"And I thought you had brains!" the other snarled. "The governor will throw troops into the city. They will call on the navy. They will use naval submarine finders. Then how long do you think we will last?"

Ull mumbled, "Aw, maybe we can clean up first—"

"Damn you!" said the coarse whisper. "Why do you think I have been financing you? For the loot you could get from a few robberies? Not much. Why, the stuff you took last night won't repay a fraction of what I have invested in this thing! The money was in large bills and the banks have the numbers. The jewelry can be identified. Hell! By the time you dispose of last night's take, you will not have cleared two hundred thousand."

Ull seemed dazed. "Boss, do you mean there is something bigger behind this?"

"Yes," snarled the other.

Ull's confusion began to turn to anger. "You were using my brains and inventive ability, eh? Using it for your own benefit! Listen, I do not like—"

"Shut up!" gritted the whispering one. "I intended for you to pull a robbery now and then, like that armored truck job, to pay expenses. But the big money was not to come from that trivial stuff."

Ull snapped, "If you call what we got last night trivial—"

"Trivial alongside what I plan," interjected the master. "But we'll go into this later. Your job now is to get Doc Savage."

Ull stood perfectly still for some seconds, glaring at the telephone. He had thought he was fully in the confidence of this mysterious chieftain who kept in the background. He had just discovered that such was not the case. It made him mad.

"Doc Savage will be taken care of," Ull growled. "Then there's got to be a new deal on splits. I didn't know about this so-called big stuff you planned to pull. What is it?"

"I'll tell you after you get through with Savage," the other delayed.

And the telephone conversation ended with that.

## Chapter XIII
## THE PHANTOMS

DOC SAVAGE was giving orders as he drove through the early morning fog that hung like a stuffing of wet cotton in the New York streets. The bronze man was alone. The machine which he drove was not his roadster but a vehicle with an appearance totally foreign to his character.

The car was a slightly shabby laundry truck, with a noisy motor and a manner of jolting over cobbles in a manner which seemed most uncomfortable. The cab windows, being extraordinarily grimy, made it difficult for the driver to be observed.

The vehicle was deceptive. The noise was not actually in the motor, which was huge and powerful, but was created by a mechanical device. The cab and body were of armor steel, the windows thick and proof against anything less than a tank-rifle slug, and the machine could travel nearly a hundred miles an hour.

In giving commands, Doc Savage was utilizing a two-way radio apparatus. Just now, Monk's voice, small and disgusted, was coming from the speaker.

"Listen, Doc," Monk demanded. "What was the idea of leaving us behind?"

"I want you to do some work," Doc told him. "But first, I want you to ask Hugh McCoy and Rapid Pace if either of them left headquarters while you and I were out on the river bringing up that small metal box."

There ensued a brief pause while Monk relayed the question. There was sharp interest in the homely chemist's childlike voice when he spoke.

"Rapid Pace was out for a while right after we left," he declared. "He says he went to get some cigarettes."

"Have you seen him smoking?" Doc queried.

"No," Monk replied. "I asked him about that, and he said he had been too excited to smoke. Listen, Doc, I'm wondering."

"Wondering what?"

"Somebody must've tipped them damn silver men in their submarine that we were going to be on the river." Monk paused for dramatic effect. "Do you reckon Pace could have slipped out and given them the tip?"

Doc said, "From now on, watch Pace very closely."

"Will I!" Monk growled.

"Is Ham there?" Doc asked.

"Ham speaking," said Ham's voice over the radio.

Despite the outward noise of the laundry truck—the clattering, clanking and popping of the motor and the squeak of the spring—it was comparatively quiet inside the armored van. The radio operated through a loudspeaker, hence conversation could be carried on without great difficulty.

"Ham," Doc directed, "you will make a quick check on Bedford Burgess Gardner. Learn what you can of his character, his associates, his business career and that sort of thing."

"Certainly," said Ham's melodious orator's voice.

"Check up particularly on how it happens that Gardner's shipping company has become one of the largest in the business," Doc said pointedly. "Concentrate on learning the facts back of the mergers which made it one of the biggest companies."

"So you suspect Gardner," said Ham.

Doc did not comment on the swordcane-carrying lawyer's words.

"Get any available details, together with all suspicious circumstances in connection with the mergers," he directed.

"Righto," said Ham.

Doc clicked off the microphone button. He was driving on Decker Street, and Stein Street was directly ahead. The bronze man could see the drug store from which the rodent-voiced man had called.

There was a small crowd in front of the store, composed mostly of policemen.

DOC SAVAGE received courteous cooperation from the police, being told without delay that the soda clerk had, upon regaining consciousness, telephoned news of the raid of the silver men.

The clerk, knees still rubbery, stopping to swallow frequently, said the silver gang had entered, seized the individual who was telephoning, then one man had torn up a lot of stock while hunting some aspirin. By way of corroborating himself, the clerk indicated the smashed vaseline on the floor.

"We followed those greasy tracks," the police officer put in at this point. "But they played out very shortly."

Some moments later, Doc Savage departed. When the police would have accompanied him, he requested them to refrain from doing so. The cops looked disappointed. They had hoped to see this remarkable bronze man work.

Doc followed the greasy footprints until they were no longer visible to the unaided eye. This was a bit farther than the officers had been able to trace them. The bronze man was carrying a leather case, and this he now opened.

The portable ultraviolet light lantern came into view, together with another device which resembled welder's goggles, except that they were more bulky. Doc switched on the lantern and donned the goggles. The goggles simply made it easier to observe the fluorescing effect, by daylight, of substances in which the ultraviolet light caused the phenomena.

Vaseline being a substance which glows when exposed to ultraviolet light, Doc had little difficulty picking up the footprints which had become invisible to the naked eye. Microscopic quantities of vaseline showed up vaguely under the so-called "black light."

The trail led to the gloomy side street. Doc, canny, did not enter. Instead, he circled to the opposite end of the block, used his black light and, finding no tracks, knew that the quarry had entered a building somewhere in the block.

The bronze man considered. A boat was passing on the river, and it was near enough that the watery wash from its bows was audible. This evidence that the river was very near seemed to give Doc an idea.

He moved down the street, careful to keep clear of the street in which the vaseline trail ended, and the thick fog swallowed him.

Some minutes later, a creature with an appearance both grotesque and pitiable appeared in the street, and the grimy thoroughfare was filled with the whine of a hand organ.

The organ player was a beggar, a hideous cripple. His legs were drawn up and apparently useless, for the fellow dragged himself along by his hands. Judging from the enormous colored glasses under the brim of a shapeless hat, the fellow was also blind.

The hand organ jangled with a quality as macabre as the personality of the grisly beggar. From time to time, the mendicant lifted a face that was purple, lumpy and utterly repulsive.

The beggar moved slowly, cranking his organ, carefully feeling his way along the sidewalk. He stopped frequently to let the organ wail, and to clink some pennies in a tin cup.

Eventually he reached the house into which Ull and his silver men had gone. A few feet beyond it he stopped, put his organ down, drew from his ragged clothing a paper-wrapped sandwich and began to eat.

The slowness with which he ate indicated he would be some time at his dining. But it was not long before things began to happen.

A door opened.

"Get t'hell outa here, bum!" grated a harsh voice.

The beggar seized his organ and began to play his loudest. The street resounded with the discordant notes.

The man in the door cursed. Then he ran down the steps, across the walk and gave the beggar a resounding kick in the side.

"Beat it, I told yer," he snarled.

But the results were not as expected. The mendicant gave a convulsive jerk and fell over. He lay motionless, apparently in a dead faint.

The man who had done the kicking swore fiercely and seemed baffled as to what to do. He could not let the beggar lie. That would draw attention. He picked the fellow up and hauled him inside.

After he had the limp beggar through the door, the man dropped him, went back and scrutinized the street. The miserable avenue was deserted.

*"Whew!"* sighed the man. "I couldn't leave that bum layin' around for Doc Savage to see. It might make the big bronze guy suspicious."

He picked up a silver garment, which had been behind the door, and drew it on. Then he turned, intending to inspect the senseless beggar.

He got barely half around. His eyes flew wide; his jaw fell. For the erstwhile beggar had undergone a complete metamorphosis.

The mendicant had turned into a giant of a figure, legs uncoiling from their grotesque positions, back straightening, head lifting.

The silver man lashed out frantically with a fist. His knuckles skidded on purplish make-up, and the theatrical grease, rubbed aside, disclosed bronze skin beneath.

"Doc Sav—" The silver man did not get past the first syllable. A metallic fist under his jaw closed his mouth clickingly, and he slumped, knocked out.

**The beggar seized his organ and began to play his loudest.**
**The street resounded with the discordant notes.**

DOC SAVAGE let the fellow sag to the floor, breaking the fall enough to eliminate undue noise. He had not struck hard; the victim would be out only a few minutes. This was so that the man could be questioned, if necessary.

Doc listened. Then he whipped for the nearest shadows. The scuffle had been heard. The clatter of approaching footsteps told him that.

A door down the hallway came open with a smash. Silver figures appeared. They held flashlights which sprayed blinding luminance. The lights picked up Doc's form.

The bronze giant was a startling figure in the beggar make-up. The coat he wore—it went with one of several disguises which he carried in the delivery truck—was padded to feign deformities, and these padded portions protruded strangely, now that he was erect.

Curiosity gripped the silver men, held them long enough for Doc to move. He already had the implement he intended to use, had it in one hand. He lobbed it at the floor in front of the nearest silver man.

There was a roar! The floor splintered! The silver

man was knocked backwards, went end over end, then managed to gain his feet.

The other silver men backed away wildly, forgetting their guns in their haste. Then, as Doc lifted his arm with another explosive grenade, they pitched for the nearest door, got through, and hurled their weight against the panel in an endeavor to close it.

Doc tried to prevent the door from closing. The silver men strained and pushed, squeezing profanity through clenched teeth.

Except the floor, which was inadequate, there was no grip for Doc's feet. He was forced back; the door closed, and the lock clicked.

An instant later, machine-gun slugs began clouting splinter-edged holes in the panel.

Doc retreated, swabbing some of the make-up off his face with a sleeve. The stuff might get in his eyes in a hand-to-hand fight. He brought out a tiny, high-explosive grenade and lobbed it at the door.

Lightning seemed to strike inside the grimy building. Plaster fell off the walls; floor boards jumped up with a screeching of pulled nails. The door turned into a cloud of fragments.

The machine gun was silenced by the exploding grenade. After debris had ceased to fall, men began cursing. Then they ran away. From the dragging sounds, it seemed they were hauling one of their number, who was injured.

Doc Savage did not advance in pursuit. He held respect for these foes. They were cunning. Just how cunning was evident when there came a second terrific concussion, which caused the old building to rock, sent window glass sheeting out and loosened more plaster.

They had left one of their own grenades behind, the time fuse set for a long interval. Had Doc followed them, he might very well have been killed.

From the entrance to the building there came noise of a movement. That would be the silver man who had so unwisely kicked the pseudo beggar.

The reviving fellow floundered about a bit, then he ran outside. His feet made a rapid patter which receded down the street.

Doc Savage did not attempt to follow him.

THE bronze man waited, and it must have been fully two minutes later when he heard several shots which came from the direction the fleeing silver man had taken.

Doc did not try to ascertain what had happened.

The bronze man used a second high-explosive grenade to open a hole in the hallway wall, then whipped through the aperture while debris was still falling. He was now in a bare, litter-strewn room. Plaster dust seethed in choking clouds.

Doc produced a cuplike contrivance which fitted over his nostrils. A rubber tube ran from this to a compact arrangement of metal flasks. It was a gas mask; also a protection against smoke and dust. There were airtight goggles for his eyes.

The silver men were working toward the rear. Doc could hear their profanity. Then he saw distinct traces of a cloud other than plaster dust, and knew his foes had turned loose some type of gas.

Hoping they would think the gas had overcome him, Doc did not use more grenades. He worked toward the rear. Near the center of the building, he encountered a room which had windows opening on a ventilating shaft. Through these, light came.

On the floor, a large rat groveled, its antics madly agonized. As the bronze man observed, the rodent became still. The gas was poison.

Glass had been shattered out of the ventilating shaft windows. Looking out of one of these, Doc saw a fire-escape ladder leading upward. He swung out, but before he mounted he pulled another of the explosive grenades from a pocket.

This grenade, like all of its kind, was fitted with a time fuse, but this differed from the conventional type in that its explosion was capable of being delayed, by the turning of a tiny knob, so as to withhold detonation for as long as several seconds. Doc adjusted the turning knob and left it on the floor.

The fire escape was ancient, and groaned and shed rust under the bronze man's weight. But it furnished him the means of reaching the roof. Crouched on the roof edge in the fog, he could hear the caterwaul of police sirens headed for the spot.

As Doc had expected, there was another fire escape at the rear. He ran down that lightly and stood in an alley that was black, filthy. When he was very near the rear door, he could hear voices.

The silver men were grouped just inside, arguing.

"We gotta clear out of here," one was insisting. "Listen to the bull wagons howl. The place'll be runnin' over with law in a minute."

"Quiet!" commanded Ull's voice. "Savage may hear us."

At that instant, the grenade which Doc had left behind exploded deep inside the building.

"He's still blastin' around in there," a man said, voicing what Doc had hoped they would think.

Another growled, "Wonder if he's wise that the two women ain't here?"

The police sirens were getting very close.

"We shall have to leave," Ull snapped.

The rear door opened.

THE door, being heavy, opened but slowly. Ull's words had given Doc an instant of warning, too, and he was already in motion.

Forty feet away, up the alley, stood an ash can. Doc was behind it before Ull and his silver men stepped out into the alley.

The silver hoods were more bulky, due no doubt

to gas masks which Ull and his fellows had donned. The group ran in the direction of the nearby river. After one searching glance around, they did not look back, but gave all attention to getting away before the police arrived.

When they were out of the alley, Doc followed them. He kept undercover, using his greatest skill, for he wanted to follow these silver men to the spot where Pat and Lorna Zane were being held. The quarry made noise in their haste, and that simplified Doc's trailing them.

Warehouses shoved out of the fog, became dank, towering piles; there was the odor of polluted bay water, the sound of waves, and the noise of a disconsolate gull.

Doc quickened his pace. He caught sight of the silver men, still in their weird disguises. They rounded a warehouse and ran out on a wharf, where they were lost to view behind a tool house.

On the pier lay old machinery, piling, timbers. Doc worked through this, on hands and knees most of the time. A dozen feet from the tool house, he lay still and listened.

There was no sound.

The bronze man leaped up and lunged for the tool structure, a smoke bomb in one hand, a grenade in the other.

As soon as he was around the structure, all of his grim haste left him and his great muscles uncoiled from their tenseness, so that he seemed suddenly slack and weary. His motions as he pocketed the grenades were slow.

The gull that had been making the noise spun low overhead, then zoomed away, frightened by a fantastic note, an eerie, indefinable sound that might have been a spawn of the fog. The sound was trilling, melodious, yet devoid of tune, an eerie cadence which lasted only a moment, then came to an end as fantastic as its beginning.

Doc's lips did not move as he made the sound; such a quality of ventriloquism did it possess that a close bystander could not have told from whence it came, without previous knowledge.

The tool house was an open shed. There was no one in it, no one on the wharf, nor on the water which lunged, greasy and menacing, at the bronze man's feet.

Doc looked under the wharf. The silver men were not there. He listened for a long time. No boat could have taken them away in the fog so silently that he could not have heard their departure.

The silver men had vanished in a fashion as strange as their costumes.

THERE was a crowd of police about the ramshackle, grimy—and now half destroyed—building where the trap had been set for Doc. They asked questions of the giant bronze man who wore the grotesque, padded garb of a deformed beggar.

"A trap," Doc said simply, and got the hand organ which he had carried when playing the part of the mendicant.

The hand organ held, carefully concealed in its innards, the ultraviolet lantern. The big colored glasses Doc had worn while playing beggar had been the spectacles which helped in detecting, by daylight, the fluorescing of the black light. Thus he had traced the vague smears of vaseline to the building.

Doc started for his truck, but deviated to join a crowd at a nearby corner. There, police were keeping the crowd back from a body sprawled on the sidewalk.

An officer was removing an all-enveloping silver garment from it. The dead man was burly, evil of face, and his body had not spilled much scarlet, because he had been shot perfectly between the eyes. There was a gun near the corpse.

"I came around a corner and bumped into him, and he ups and ats me with his iron," explained one of the cops. "But he was a little slow."

Doc said nothing and did not change expression, although the death of the burly man closed a source of possible information, for the fellow was the one who had come out and kicked Doc when he was doing his beggar act.

"I will take the silver suit," Doc said.

The police passed it over without objection. They knew this bronze man, with his scientific skill, his daring which sometimes seemed madness, could probably accomplish more against the menace of the Silver Death's-Heads than the entire metropolitan police.

There was an expensive wrist watch on the dead man. Doc glanced at it, then at his own wrist watch. The other was exactly two minutes and fifteen seconds fast.

Doc Savage started away, only to pause and do what for him was a rare thing. He reconsidered. Then he came back and took the expensive wrist watch from the arm of the dead man.

He donned the watch and wore it in place of his own.

## Chapter XIV
### THE GREEN TRAIL

DOC SAVAGE had exchanged his armored delivery truck for a dark, somber sedan which, in its way, was as impregnable as the truck, and as deceptive. The change had been made at the skyscraper headquarters.

Ham and Rapid Pace occupied the commodious front seat with Doc. Monk and Hugh McCoy were wedged in the back with a large number of metal equipment cases. There had been no time out for explanations.

"Come on," Doc had directed, then rattled out a string of numbers. The numbers corresponded with the numerals inscribed on the equipment boxes, which Doc kept ready-packed in the skyscraper aërie.

But now the bronze man was finishing a brief synopsis of what had happened at the end of the vaseline trail.

"It was, of course, a trap," he said. "Now, Ham, what did you learn about Bedford Burgess Gardner? Or did you have time to learn anything?"

Ham rolled his sword cane between manicured fingers. He had changed his clothing and looked dapper, neat, not at all as if he had been in a mad whirl of death, destruction and mystery throughout the night.

"I learned enough," he said, and grimness crackled in his orator's voice.

"What do you mean by that?"

"One year ago, Bedford Burgess Gardner headed a second-rate shipping company," Ham stated. "Exactly one year ago negotiations were underway, involving the merger of Gardner's hack concern with a larger, sounder company. One man opposed the union—the president of the board of the other company. That night, the president was killed by a burglar whom he caught ransacking his house. The merger went through."

"This sounds bad," Rapid Pace gulped rapidly. "Yes, sir, it does sound bad!"

"Three months later, a second merger was under consideration, this one between Gardner's company and still another. Two men in the other outfit opposed the union. A private yacht blew up and killed them both. The merger went through."

"For cryin' out loud!" Hugh McCoy exploded, big-voiced, in the rear seat. "That was the merger between Gardner's concern and The Oriental Passenger-Freight Transport."

"Exactly," said Ham. "There was another merger a few weeks ago, and that one also had suspicious circumstances."

"Somebody else killed?" Monk demanded in his characteristic tiny voice.

"No," said Ham. "It was the sinking of the liner *Avallancia*."

"Hey," Monk barked. "We read about that in the paper yesterday. The newspaper story said the *Avallancia* belonged to Bedford Burgess Gardner's company."

"It did not at the time it was sunk," Ham corrected. "It belonged to the other company, a small concern, and its loss put them in such a bad financial predicament that they had to merge with Gardner's corporation. Gardner gave out that they had already merged. That was so Wall Street would not think the smaller company was financially embarrassed and try to beat down the price of its stock."

Doc Savage asked sharply, "Did financial manipulations in stock feature in these mergers?"

"All of them," Ham rapped. "And right here we haul the cat out of the bag."

"Listen," said Monk. "Use plain English, will you?"

"Bedford Burgess Gardner has made over a billion dollars during the last year," Ham said slowly and distinctly. "Does that sound like plain English?"

"It sounds like a blasted lot of money," Monk muttered.

THE conversation had not taken long, but the big sedan was traveling fast. They were now on the waterfront, gliding along before frowning phalanxes of pier warehouses.

"Stock ballooning?" Doc asked, without turning his head.

"Exactly," said Ham. "Recapitalization with each merger, and flotations of immense stock issues which were disseminated to the public."

"Again," said Monk, "will you use plain English."

"Here is a simple example," Ham snapped.

"Make it very simple," Monk told him sourly. "And don't make any cracks about me being ignorant."

"You own a boat worth a thousand dollars and I own a boat worth a thousand dollars," Ham explained. "We both carry passengers and freight. We are bitter business rivals. We do anything we can to cut each other's throat."

"I can see how *that* could be," Monk growled.

"As a result, neither of us makes much money," Ham continued. "I offer to merge, you refuse and I ruin the engine in your boat, so you've got to merge, which is another name for selling out to me."

"Very clear," Monk snorted.

"Now, I have two companies worth a thousand a piece," said Ham. "I issue stock—two thousand shares, of no par value—and offer it to the public. If the public has any sense, they won't pay over a dollar a share for the stock, because that is all my merged companies are worth."

"Hurry it up," Monk commanded impatiently.

"All right," said Ham. "I bid three dollars a share for the stock on the market, doing the bidding through a broker, so that no one knows my name, or even through a dummy purchaser. I jump the price to four dollars. The public gets excited, and begins to buy. Demand holds the price up, or possibly makes it go higher. The result, when all two thousand shares of stock are sold, is that I have cleaned up an extra thousand or two."

"Hm-m-m," Monk murmured, his homely features thoughtful.

"Then I find another company, make it merge with me, recapitalize, issue new stock to the holders of shares in the first merger concern, and do it all over again." Ham leaned back in the seat. "That is what Gardner did, fundamentally. Of course, the actual high finance was a bit more complicated than that. But he has cleaned up almost a billion within the last year."

Rapid Pace whipped around, glared at Hugh McCoy and clipped, "You work for Gardner. What do you know about this?"

McCoy returned the glare, his too perfectly handsome face turning scarlet.

"I have only been working for Gardner on the Paine L. Winthrop concern merger!" he yelled. "I did not know anything was wrong. And I dare you to show differently!"

"You mean you were so dumb you did not know you were working for the world's biggest crook?" Rapid Pace snapped.

"Gardner is a devil, a cunning devil!" McCoy shouted. "And don't you insinuate—"

"Pipe down, you birds, or I'll bob you both," Monk advised, his small voice turning into a rumble.

Doc pulled to a stop before an enormous building of brick and steel.

THE structure in front of which they had halted, for all of its size, differed little from other warehouses which stood on piers along the waterfront. A sign on the front read:

HIDALGO TRADING COMPANY

The building was Doc Savage's waterfront boathouse and seaplane hangar. Perhaps dock workers wondered why the place seemed deserted much of the time, but it was doubtful if any knew its true nature.

Doc touched a button on the dash. This operated an ultraviolet light projector on the front of the sedan, and the beam in turn actuated a photoelectric cell which caused the great door in the front of the warehouse hangar to slide open.

Doc drove into the enormous building and the door closed automatically behind them.

Rapid Pace and Hugh McCoy stared in gaping astonishment at the array of fast planes—they ranged from a tiny gyro to a great tri-motored speed ship which could carry two dozen passengers in excess of three hundred miles an hour.

"Hurry," Doc commanded.

The bronze man passed the planes, opened a door into another section of the building and switched on lights. If Pace and McCoy had been surprised by the planes, they were figuratively floored by what they saw now.

"A submarine!" McCoy gasped, and his manicured hand strayed up to his eyes as if to see if they were functioning correctly.

*Helldiver* was the name on the conning tower of the undersea craft.

The *Helldiver* was probably as unique a sub as man had ever constructed. The conning tower, as such, existed hardly at all, and from bow to stern ran great steel, sledlike runners, stoutly braced. The *Helldiver* had first been constructed for a trip under The North Polar ice.

Doc and his little group of aides had seen two great adventures aboard the *Helldiver*—the first under the Polar ice, and the second through an underground river into a fantastic phantom city in the Arabian desert.

After the Arabian trip, the submersible had lain idle, but carefully greased, the fuel tanks full. The craft was ready for quick service.

"Get the stuff aboard," Doc directed.

McCoy moistened his almost womanish lips. "Are we—are we going under the water?"

Doc studied him. "You do not like the idea?"

McCoy straightened his remarkably square shoulders. "I—I have never been down. But I shall go. I owe it to my reputation to help capture this devil Gardner."

Doc turned to Rapid Pace. "And you?"

Pace shuddered.

"I do not like the idea. I think I shall stay here." He shuddered again. "Yes, sir, I shall stay behind. No iron fish for mine."

Then Pace caught Monk's eye. Monk's eyes were small and normally pleasant, but now they were small and not pleasant, for Monk was thinking that Rapid Pace had gone out for cigarettes about the time he and Doc were in the East River diving for the mysterious metal box.

Monk was a blunt fellow, not given to suavity, and what he was thinking showed on his incredibly homely features.

Rapid Pace began to tremble.

"On second thought, I shall be glad to go," he gulped. "Yes, on second thought."

THE *Helldiver's* engines had been reconditioned since her Arabian jaunt. Diesels had new pistons, the electric motors new bearings. The electric motors were running now, and they made little noise.

Doc Savage and his four companions stood in the control room. The submarine was equipped so that one man could operate her if necessary, all controls centered in one spot.

The depth indicator read only twenty feet and the periscope was up above the surface, but Doc now turned a wheel and the steel cigar with the strange runners sank slowly. A touch of a button, and the periscope swished down into its well.

Rapid Pace moistened his lips, clenched his fists and cried uneasily, "But we're in New York Harbor! A ship may run into us!"

Monk, homely features placid, said, "We've

taken the *Helldiver* where icebergs were thicker than fleas, and never did hit anything."

"What saved you?" Pace demanded. "Yes, sir, what saved you?"

"The instruments," Monk shrugged. "There are sonic devices all over the hull. They tell us how deep the water is, and if anything larger than a rowboat comes near, we'll know it."

Monk indicated a bank of dials. These bore hands which were continually jumping slightly. Four of them were marked "North," "South," "East" and "West;" a fifth dial was labeled "Bottom Distance." The dial marked South abruptly began jumping.

"That means there is a boat to the south," said Monk.

Doc swung the steering controls slightly. After a bit, the jumping shifted to the West dial, then the North dial, which meant they had left the surface vessel astern.

"Remarkable!" Hugh McCoy murmured.

"You ain't seen nothing!" Monk snorted. "Doc has used this sub for testing out ideas. It's got more gadgets aboard than the average man sees in a lifetime."

Rapid Pace, shifting about nervously as was his habit, asked in a shrill voice, "But what are we out here in a submarine for?"

Monk scowled. "We're hunting silver men, of course."

"Whoever heard of a submarine hunting a submarine?" Pace said rapidly. "They use sub chasers, surface vessels for that."

"Listen, noisy, suppose you pipe down," Monk requested.

"Yes," McCoy told Pace. "You talk too much."

Rapid Pace glared at the handsome, well-knit figure of McCoy. His lips curled hatefully.

"You, of course, are large enough to whip me," he gritted. "Otherwise, I would hand you a poke on the jaw!"

"I'll tie one hand behind me, if it will encourage you any," McCoy jeered.

Monk said, "Cut it out—or I'll bump your heads."

Without taking his flake-gold eyes off the controls, Doc Savage announced, "Within not longer than two minutes, we shall know whether we have the slightest chance of finding the silver men."

THE electric motors had decreased their slight hum, and gear boxes made almost no noise, so that they could hear the bay water curling past the outer skin of the *Helldiver.*

"Where are we?" Monk asked.

Doc Savage dropped a sinew-wrapped bronze finger on the illuminated chart table, and said, "Here."

The gorillalike chemist hunched over the map board, blinked his small eyes and observed that they were navigating by the crude map which Doc had secured from the secret room in the Indian Head Club.

Their position, as indicated by Doc's finger, was near one of the four small stars, but not the star where the bronze man had dived and found the mysterious metal box.

"So we're gonna try to get another one of them boxes," Monk grunted.

"No," Doc corrected.

Monk squinted his small eyes. "Huh?"

"I saw enough of the first box, before losing it over the side of the launch when the submarine fired on us," Doc explained. "Those boxes are very clever radio buoys. They are nothing more than tiny transmitters."

"Radio transmitters!" Monk grunted.

"Very compact," Doc elaborated. "They are fitted with a form of the so-called air-cell battery, which delivers a small quantity of current over a long period of time. The transmitters in the boxes are of extremely small power, using a negligible amount of current."

Ham tapped the chart with his sword cane. "You say those stars mark the location of radio buoys? What do you mean—radio buoys?"

"I will illustrate," Doc answered.

The bronze man clicked switches, then turned a knob which controlled the *Helldiver's* radio compass. The latter did not differ greatly from the type in use on most naval and commercial vessels, except that it could function on extremely short wavelengths.

Manipulating the wavelength knob, Doc fished through the ether for the signal from the Silver Death's-Heads' radio buoy.

The others waited impatiently. The bronze man had decreased their speed even more, until the momentum was now barely enough to cause the planing effect of diving rudders to hold them off the bottom.

A faint popping came from the speaker. It loudened as Doc maneuvered the loop, a sound closely akin to static.

"There," he announced. "They did not use the regular dot-and-dash signals, but an arrangement of breaking contacts which creates a sound resembling static."

"Deuced clever," Ham murmured. "Anyone picking up that noise on their radio would think it was static and give it no more attention."

Doc moved levers. The *Helldiver* picked up speed and headed for the radio buoy; the sound got louder, then began to weaken as they passed over it and left it astern. Soon Doc picked up the sound of the next buoy.

Rapid Pace said abruptly, "I get it! Yes, I get it! These buoys are to guide the Silver Death's-Head submarine into the harbor. They must have a rendezvous somewhere outside the harbor."

There were thick glass windows in the submarine conning tower, and through these the men could see the vile green water of the bay curling past.

"The green trail," Ham said grimly. "I hope it leads us to something."

## Chapter XV
### HELL UNDER WATER

ALTHOUGH the *Helldiver* could be navigated by one man, it was considerable of a single-handed task. It kept Doc extremely busy moving levers, flipping switches. The tanks trimmed themselves through the medium of a robot apparatus—which helped.

Inset in the front wall of the control room was a large panel of frosted glass. There were similar panels in the side and rear walls, as well.

Monk, who was familiar with the *Helldiver's* intricate mechanism, adjusted dials which resulted in a remarkable thing happening to the frosted glass panels. They assumed a greenish hue. The glaucous tint seemed alive, moving.

Rapid Pace ogled the panels. But not until a bit of underwater driftage swirled past one did he realize he was seeing the watery depths outside the submarine.

"Marvelous!" he exploded. "Yes, sir, marvelous!"

"There are strong infrared searchlights recessed in the hull," Monk told him. "Infrared light penetrates water a little better than ordinary visible rays. Photo-electric eyes pick up the images and they are brought to these screens through common television apparatus."

Pace looked a little dizzy. "Why, this underseas boat is incredible. It must have cost a fortune!"

"It did," Monk told him calmly. "This iron fish was a whiz when it was first built, and it has been improved on ever since. I told you that when Doc invents something for a submarine, he tries it out on the *Helldiver.*"

Ham, eyeing his sword cane, put in. "And that reminds me of something: Where did these Silver Death's-Heads get *their* sub?"

Monk grunted, "I've been wondering about that, too."

"That may not be so mysterious," Doc offered.

"Eh?" Monk stared at the bronze giant.

"Do you recall my telling you that Lorna Zane said Paine L. Winthrop gave her five-months' vacation with pay last spring?" Doc queried.

"Sure," said Monk.

Rapid Pace exploded. "I was given a vacation at the same time! So were all of the regular employees

of the Winthrop Shipyards. It was very mysterious. When we got back to work, we found that the shipyard had been in operation during our absence. We never did find out what had been built."

"That," said Doc, "explains it."

"So the submarine was built in Winthrop's yard," Ham clipped grimly. "Winthrop was in on this. He got cold feet, or fell out with his partners or something, and they killed him with a shell fired from the submarine in the East River."

"Fantastic!" Rapid Pace murmured. "Utterly fantastic, yes, sir!"

The *Helldiver* had now passed the last of the radio buoys shown on the map which Doc had gotten from the Indian Head Club.

"What now?" Monk wondered aloud.

"We will keep on and hope the map did not show all of the radio guides," Doc said.

Sure enough, the directional apparatus picked up more of the bursts which had the sound of static. The buoys, it seemed, continued out toward the open sea.

Following the trail, always beneath the surface, they veered to the right, out of ship lanes. They were now heading down the Jersey coast, but a number of miles offshore.

"Pretty slick," Monk said. "Having a string of radio buoys to guide them right into New York Harbor. Boy, oh, boy! What a perfect getaway idea!"

"It required the expenditure of a lot of money," Ham pointed out.

Monk started to say something—and his mouth flew so very wide open that it seemed he was trying to yawn. His right arm jutted out like a bar, pointing.

"I'll be a whale's brother!" he choked. "Look!"

IN the stern-view screen had appeared an object which resembled a steel egg viewed from the front. It might have been a fish coming head-on, for they had seen other fish on the screens, but this was of a steely color and certain rudders and protuberances marked it for what it was.

"Submarine!" Ham ejaculated.

The other subseas craft was traveling more swiftly than the *Helldiver*, and therefore was gaining.

Doc Savage advanced the throttles. The *Helldiver* picked up speed. But so did the other ship. It continued to gain.

"This bus was not made for racing," Monk grumbled. "The ice-protector rails cut down the speed."

Rapid Pace cried anxiously, "How about torpedo tubes?"

"None aboard," Doc advised.

"What about depth bombs, then?"

Doc Savage shook a metallic head. "The *Helldiver* is not equipped for fighting. It is primarily a scientific experimental vessel."

The bronze man changed their course a trifle.

Monk was scowling at the screen. "One consolation—that other iron fish hasn't got torpedo tubes, either."

The pursuing sub swung slightly sidewise to follow the *Helldiver*, and they could observe the length of the craft. It was considerably smaller than the *Helldiver*, more slender, scientifically streamlined.

"Seems like I've seen that bus somewhere before!" Monk grunted. "Or maybe it was a picture."

"It was a picture," Doc told him.

Monk blinked little eyes. "I can't remember where I saw it. Do you?"

"Not long ago, United States newspapers carried a photograph of a small two-man submarine which the Japanese were testing," Doc advised. "It was a craft closely resembling that one. Probably the design of the Japanese submarine was copied in making this one."

The smaller underseas boat was now only a few yards behind. They could see, in the front of the conning tower, a round glass porthole.

Rapid Pace barked, "I wonder what they plan to do?"

Doc, not altering expression, said, "Nothing pleasant, you can rest assured."

Pace moistened his lips, then glanced down at his hands. He held them out in front of him. They were steady. This seemed to surprise him.

"Hurrah!" he shouted.

Hugh McCoy glared at him and snarled, "I don't see anything to be happy about!" McCoy's exquisitely handsome face was greasy with perspiration.

Rapid Pace grinned widely. "Gentlemen, I believe my association with you has ridded me of something which has hampered me all my life. I am speaking of my cowardice. I usually scare, get so frightened that I am positively a wreck. But now I feel like a daredevil. Positively, a daredevil."

McCoy groaned, "What are we going to do? Why don't we rise to the surface? We can't outrun them."

"See that streamlined hatch on the other sub?" Doc queried.

"Y-yes," McCoy stuttered.

"That undoubtedly covers the three-inch gun," Doc assured him. "They cannot fire it underwater. But wait—let us see if this helps."

The bronze man reached over and jerked a brass lever. The rear-view screen suddenly became black. But the viewing device had not failed. The blackness was from without—an inky cloud was pouring from receptacles in the skin of the submarine.

"Blazes!" Monk gulped. "This is a new one on me!"

DOC SAVAGE put the wheel hard over, then cut the motors to half-throttle.

"Remember when we went under the Polar ice in the *Helldiver?*" he asked.

"Do I?" grunted Monk. "I'll never forget!"

"We put tanks in the submarine skin to hold a chemical—a mixture you invented, incidentally—which would melt ice when released," Doc recalled. "That was to free us if we got trapped under the ice pack."

Monk nodded. "Sure."

"The chemical solution I just released from those tanks is my own invention," Doc told him. "It turns salt water black. The secret is now in the hands of the United States Government. It may come in handy should there be another war."

Doc now manipulated the sonic locators. These showed that the small submarine of the silver men was astern, wandering in its course, baffled by the sepia water.

Doc cut the motors of the *Helldiver* entirely. The craft lost headway, sank, and came to a rest on the bottom of the Atlantic which, at this point, was hard sand, according to the charts.

McCoy mopped perspiration from his too-handsome features and groaned, "I don't see where this is going to help us!"

Pace grinned at him. "We're alive, anyway."

Glaring, McCoy snapped, "You don't need to be so damned cheerful!"

Rapid Pace, in his new personality of a man who was not afraid, was a different individual from the nervous, rapid-talking efficiency expert. He even spoke more slowly, firmly, and did not repeat himself as much.

"From now on, you use a civil tongue when you speak to me," he told Hugh McCoy grimly. "Otherwise I am going to do my best to knock the hell out of you."

Monk growled, "For just about the last time, I'm telling you guys to cut that out!"

There came a loud, metallic clank. The rubber-ribbed floor tilted, throwing all but Doc Savage off balance. The bronze man's grip on the controls kept him erect.

McCoy wailed fearfully, and seemed on the point of bursting into tears.

"What was that?" he screamed.

Rapid Pace picked himself up, sneered at McCoy, then squinted at the window panels. These were black, due to the murky solution in the water without. But the ocean current had swept some of the sepia cloud away, and he could make out objects a few feet from the *Helldiver* hull.

"Look!" Pace barked. "That other submarine has fastened itself to our hull in some manner!"

DOC SAVAGE started the *Helldiver* motors. The sub began to move, but it was an erratic motion.

The resistance of the other vessel clinging to their hull—and the other craft did not dislodge—was sufficient to prevent them steering a straight course.

Manipulating valves, Doc caused the *Helldiver's* ballast tanks to blow. They lifted a few feet, then their rise stopped and they watched the depth gauge sink back until they jarred on the sandy ocean floor again. The *Helldiver*, an extremely heavy craft, did not have enough surplus buoyancy to lift the other submarine with its ballast tanks fully filled.

"Hell!" yelled Monk. "This beats anything I ever heard of! What's holdin' that iron fish to us?"

"That is the mystery," Doc said grimly. "And what puzzles me even more. How did it find us in the black water?"

There was quiet in the *Helldiver* now, except for the clicking of a gyro compass and the microscopic ticking of chronometers. They strained their ears. Hugh McCoy had changed color, not getting pale, but blue, as if he were being slowly smothered.

*Glub!* The sound was wet. *Glub, glub!* It repeated twice again.

"Bubbles from an escape hatch on the other sub!" Doc rapped. "They are sending divers outside!"

The bronze giant lashed a glance at the depth indicators. They read slightly below seventy feet. The depth was not excessive for diving work.

Doc ran to a locker which held diving equipment—flexible, mail-armored suits and some of the transparent hoods which vaguely resembled goldfish bowls. The locker held more than hall a dozen outfits. Doc hauled them out.

"Put them on!" he rapped.

Monk and Ham sprang to obey. They knew how the suits operated, having used them before. Rapid Pace joined them.

Hugh McCoy stood back, his exquisitely profiled face even more purple.

Monk picked up one of the suits and ran toward McCoy, intending to force the handsome man to put it on.

McCoy suddenly clawed at a pocket. He had a gun half out when Monk, lunging, wrenched the weapon from his fingers.

"What in blazes were you gonna do with that?" Monk yelled.

"I d-don't know," McCoy stuttered. "F-fight those devils, I guess. I don't want to go outside. I hate the water. I've never been in a diving suit, why, we're s-seventy feet down!"

Monk jammed McCoy's gun in his own pocket. "Yes, and we'll be down here permanently unless we do something about it."

McCoy, trembling, allowed himself to be helped into the diving suit and received instructions on its operation.

Rapid Pace, chest puffed with his new-found courage, said, "I'm not scared. I feel like a daredevil, positively. Damned if I understand it!"

## Chapter XVI
## UNDERWATER DEFEAT

THE *Helldiver* was not silent now. The men were breathing noisily from the exertion of getting into the suits; the suits themselves made clinkings against the metal parts of the submarine.

But there was other sound, a hideous sound. It was a series of resounding blows against the steel hull of the submarine. These came from forward, and from immediately overhead.

"They've found our hatches, and are trying to get them open to let the water in," Monk growled.

Then the homely chemist pulled the transparent helmet over his head, switched on the tiny two-way radio and added, "Let's get goin'. We gotta put a stop to that."

Doc Savage led the way aft. He opened an oval hatch which gave into a steel cubicle hardly more than six feet square. In the top of this was another hatch.

Doc closed the bulkhead through which they had come. He turned a lever. Machinery whined. The hatch overhead lifted and water came in, by strings at first, then with a smashing rush that jostled them about.

The bronze man let compressed air from the back tanks into his suit to compensate his buoyancy to approximately that of the surrounding sea. Then he leaped, floated upward, grasped the hatch edge and clambered out.

The others followed him—McCoy first, then Pace, then Monk and Ham.

Each man drew a sharp, long-bladed knife. These were holstered to the diving suit belts. Under water, knives were the most effective weapons.

It was lighter than they had expected outside. For one thing, the current had swept away the black cloud. And the silver men were carrying powerful portable torches.

Doc headed for the group about the main conning tower hatch. They were vague at first, like figures seen in a fog. Then they took on distinctness. There were four of them.

They wore self-contained diving suits—paraphernalia which did not require air hoses, oxygen being supplied by tanks worn on a back harness. Their helmets were not transparent, but of metal, with round grilled windows.

The diving equipment was of the sort which could be purchased at any supply house.

The silver men—there was not the slightest doubt but that they were Silver Death's-Heads—were working with wrenches and bars, and a cutting torch made a lurid spot of light and spewed bubbles through the water.

Doc ran toward them, leaning far forward. Probably the thump of his lead shoes on the sub hull warned the group about the conning tower hatch. They straightened. The one with the torch sidled ahead, waving the grisly flame before him.

It was a hideous weapon, that torch. It burned under water by grace of pure oxygen supplied from a portable tank, and it could slice through hard steel with no more difficulty than a finger is drawn through mud.

Monk lunged along at Doc's elbow. The pleasantly ugly chemist retained some of his apish aspect in a diving suit.

"We'll flank the man with the torch," Doc said into the radio.

The bronze man went to the right. Monk took the left.

The diver with the torch made a few erratic passes, then began to retreat. He had respect for the knives Doc and Monk carried. The body of his suit was of rubber and canvas composition, by no means proof against sharp steel.

Suddenly the silver men broke and fled. Resistance of the water made their movements grotesquely slow as they took flying leaps off the hull of the *Helldiver,* then churned for their own craft, which was attached slightly forward.

Doc and Monk, following, had a chance to observe how the other submarine managed to cling so tightly to the *Helldiver.*

Attached to the hull of the smaller U-boat was a succession of circular objects which might have been washtubs. It was these which were in contact with Doc's submarine.

"Electromagnets!" Monk yelled through the intercommunicating radio. "But what in blazes are electromagnets doing on their tub?"

The answer to that did not come until later, after unpleasant things had happened.

THE submarine of the silver men, while small in proportion to the *Helldiver,* was larger than it had first seemed when viewed through the lookout screen from within the *Helldiver.* It was no two-man craft. At least a dozen silver men in diving suits were outside.

They grouped to meet Doc and his party. Some of them held diver's knives. But others were doing something else, working at the escape hatch by which they had left their own submersible.

They drew out black rods some six feet or more in length, to the ends of which were attached what resembled black rubber hose. The men held these rods like lances, and advanced. The black line trailed out behind them and led into their own submarine.

One of them stumbled. He put the end of his rod down against the sandy bottom to maintain his balance. Where the rod touched, there was abrupt, sizzling blue flame, like an electric arc.

"The rods carry high-voltage current!" Doc warned his companions. "Pressure closes a contact. If they touch us with those things, we're finished!"

The silver men came on. Their features were grotesque inside the helmet windows, for they still wore the gruesome masks which had caused the tabloid newspapers to give them their designation of Silver Death's-Heads. The insulated high-voltage rods probed hungrily.

Doc halted, wheeled, saw that his four companions were behind him and waved them back.

"To fight them would be fatal," he warned. "Stay away from those rods. Circle around them. Keep them worried. I am going back into the *Helldiver.*"

The bronze man spun and sloped back for the escape hatch. His best speed was not as fast as a normal man could walk on land. Injecting extra buoyancy into his suit, he lifted himself up to the conning tower, compensated the buoyancy, then dropped back and let himself down into the hatch. Compressed air forced the sea water out.

A moment later, he was in the *Helldiver* control room.

A twist of a lever discharged a fresh quantity of the chemical which, due to its reaction with the saline content of the sea water, created a black smudge.

Next, the bronze man dug a cutting torch out of a locker. He did not ignite it. Then he passed through the escape hatch and emerged outside again.

"Everyone safe?" he asked.

Monk and Ham replied almost at once over the intercommunicating radio. McCoy was a bit slower.

"How about you, Pace?" Doc asked.

"I'm not a bit scared," said Rapid Pace. "I cannot understand it."

"SIMPLY stay clear of them," Doc directed. "Give me a chance to work on their electromagnets with this cutting torch."

The bronze man did not ignite the torch immediately, since its glow might betray his presence despite the black smear which now filled the sea. It was like working through ink as he crept along the hard, sandy bottom.

The silver men, he reasoned, would be worried by the black cloud and stick close to their own craft. Getting between the two tightly-clinging submersibles, Doc fended off with one hand, then puffed his suit with the air valve and sailed upward.

He found one of the electromagnets which were like washtubs. The cutting torch was fitted with an underwater igniter. With a mild explosion, it began to flame.

Doc Savage promptly clamped his transparent helmet to the steel side of the submarine. This would cause the clank of lead shoes, should any divers approach, to come to his attention before danger was too close.

Instead of holding the cutting torch in his hand, the bronze man placed it on the sub hull in such a position that the flame was held against the electromagnet covering without aid from his own hand. This was a matter of precaution. The torch might short-circuit through the coil and bring a death-dealing jolt of current.

Shortly, a flash of blue flame showed through the sepia void. That would be the burned-out coil wires arcing. Doc jerked the insulated lanyard attached to the torch and drew it to him.

He worked down the hull in the intensely dark, gently resisting void that was the sea, and found the next electromagnet. He repeated the process there, even to keeping his helmet pressed to the subhull.

And it was well that he did not neglect that last. He might have missed the clanking of rapid footsteps. Lead shoes were coming along the subdeck. From the jangling noises, other divers were striving to clamber up the hull.

Doc waited. The torch made a roaring that almost drowned out the footsteps, but it did not drown them quite as much as before. The divers were getting close.

Doc hauled the torch in, cut the flame and eased away. A few feet down the hull, he stepped out and let himself sink to the sand.

Before he got his balance, the ocean current carried him against the *Helldiver's* hull. He crept along it, feeling his way.

"Monk! Ham!" Doc called into the microphone. "Get in the *Helldiver* with Pace and McCoy."

Doc reached the escape hatch and a moment later, with a dull clanking and a bubbling of released air, his four companions also reached the hatch. In order not to get lost, they had linked themselves together with a line—a hank of stout cord was a part of each diving suit belt equipment.

Doc closed the escape chamber hatch, blew the water, then stepped into the *Helldiver.* He ran for the control room without removing the diving suit.

Motors wailed out at his touch of the starting switch, wailed and labored. Suddenly there was a great crashing of circuit breakers cutting current off from the motors. The breakers functioned automatically, to protect the motors from an overload.

Doc tried again. Unclutched from the propeller drive shafts, the motors turned over readily. But the shafts themselves refused to turn. The overload caused the breakers to bang open.

"What is it?" Monk asked anxiously.

"They seem to have wrapped chain around our propeller shafts," Doc told him.

THE bronze man now blew the *Helldiver's* ballast tanks to their fullest, in an endeavor to get the submarine to pull free from the electromagnets which still held it to the other underwater craft. Since some of the magnets had been rendered useless, Doc hoped the others would be insufficient to hold.

He was positive they could have gotten away had the *Helldiver's* motors been able to turn over the propellers. The submarines did not separate, however, but continued to repose on the sea bottom, magnetically glued together.

And now there was more noise at the hatches, as the silver men endeavored to force themselves inside the *Helldiver.*

Doc went back to the escape chamber, accompanied by the other four. They were grim, saying little. Enclosed in the chamber, they shut the inner door, then Doc touched the control which started opening the outer panel.

The door had opened but a few inches when he lunged for the controls and reversed them. A black rod had protruded through the opening. Its end was armored with the shiny copper of an electrode.

"One of them blasted electric lances!" Monk growled.

"Keep away from it!" Doc commanded grimly.

The lance had been caught in the closing door. The steel panel pinched shut, and a moment later cut through the lance insulation with a resultant explosion of blue flame.

The *Helldiver* was equipped with two escape hatches, so that divers could come and go. They had been intended for scientific exploration work underwater. The second hatch was located forward and was smaller.

"We'll try the other hatch," Doc decided.

They were in water well above their knees. When the inner door was open, this flooded into the *Helldiver* with them. But the automatic pumps would take care of it.

But they did not reach the other escape hatch, or pass through it to engage in combat.

They were abreast of the conning tower when there was a moaning roar, and water sheeted out of the control room. It came from the control room door, as if that aperture were the mouth of a great faucet which had been turned on suddenly.

Doc Savage, for all of his great strength, was tumbled about and smashed into bulkheads. The torrent jostled him down a passage, banged him into a steel support, and the transparent helmet he was wearing would have broken had it not been of very strong construction.

Monk and the others, lacking Doc's physical hardihood, were handled with greater roughness. McCoy yelled in pain as he smashed over a motor; there was terror in his voice also. Pace swore calmly.

Monk and Ham resisted the water with grim silence.

Had they all not worn diving suits, death would have come within the ensuing few minutes. As it was, they were jostled about, helpless to resist the tremendous force of the water, until the *Helldiver's* main compartment had filled.

Only the central section filled at the moment, however, for there were safety devices on the bulkhead doors, mechanical contrivances which closed and made the bulkheads watertight when water entered.

There were no air locks between the bulkheads, so that it was impossible to move from one compartment to the other, now that the central one was full.

Silver men in diving suits began dropping down the conning tower hatch.

THE sea water, due to the strong current, had cleared up again, the black cloud having been swept away. The first silver man to enter held one of the long dark lances, and close at his elbow came another man bearing a strong underwater searchlight. They advanced.

More sinister divers entered behind them. They floated down in an ominous procession, vague forms in the water, like spectral bodies from some Stygian domain. There was only the one electric lance. The others held diver's knives.

Doc and his men retreated. There was nothing else to do. The lance was deadly. It was the thing which had defeated them, the one weapon with which they were helpless to cope, having, as they did, no time to rig an insulated shield or other defense.

There was not even an insulated pole in the *Helldiver* which could be employed to fend off the electric lance.

Doc watched the lancer. The bronze man's remarkable features, plainly distinguishable inside his transparent helmet, showed no emotion.

Doc's attention—all of it—was on the lance. The clanking of lead shoes made a metallic mumble on the floor plates. That was why he did not hear the bulkhead door behind him open. It was a carefully-made, well-greased door.

Doc had no way of knowing that the other compartments had been opened and flooded. But they had. The work had been done with wrenches and cutting torches. And silver men had come from behind to flank Doc's party.

A second diver appeared in the bulkhead opening. Then came a third, a fourth and a fifth. They had no lance, but they all held knives. They lunged in to the attack.

Doc was not taken entirely unawares. He heard the flanking divers, wheeled, noted the absence of a lance, and lunged in fiercely to the attack.

The silver divers did not retreat. They must have felt they had safety in numbers.

It was a weirdly fantastic battle which was fought in the water-gorged entrails of the submarine. The fellow with the electrified lance made a few jabs, then the electric cord, leading to the power plant in his own underwater craft, became entangled and he had to abandon the unique weapon.

Doc Savage and his men, surrounded completely now, formed a tight ring, a circlet that bristled with the razor-sharp steel thorns of their knives. But they did not hold it for long.

Silver divers lunged in on the side defended by Pace and McCoy. They broke through. One man sagged back, bubbles pouring from a hole which Pace had knifed in his suit.

The fighting ring disintegrated. Four men seized Doc Savage. One lost interest in the fray and stumbled off for his own submarine, his suit streaming bubbles.

A man leeched upon Doc's arm. Doc endeavored to shake him off. In the open air it would have been a simple task, but underwater it was a Herculean job. The bronze man's second arm was trapped. A man tangled with his legs.

Doc was forced over sidewise. There was no purchase for footing, because his weight above the displaced water was negligible. The diving suit hampered him.

He felt someone at his back. He endeavored to spin, despite the men trying to hold him. But it was too late. There was a roar of escaping air. His oxygen apparatus had been wrenched away!

AS air pressure left the bronze man's helmet, water began to pour in. It sloshed cold upon his neck, his shoulders, spilled down in his suit, which had been pressed tightly to his great frame when the air escaped.

Water came up around his neck, his lips. Had he been erect, air pressure in the top of his helmet might have kept the water out for a few moments. But he was tilted over on the steel floor. The brine covered his nostrils, his eyes.

A few bubbles left his nostrils. Then the mad desperation of impending death seemed to seize the metallic giant. His great arms corded, convulsed, and the two silver divers who held him were carried together, head first. They dropped off his arms, stunned.

Doc stamped the other man free of his legs.

The fellow who had torn off the oxygen tank retreated, still holding the tank in one hand, a knife in the other.

Doc made a move as if to follow him. But a great weakness seemed to have seized him. He swayed, was moved about by the water currents within the swamped *Helldiver*. He sagged.

The current carried him backward and he disappeared into the gloom of the compartment from which the silver divers had come to stage the flank attack.

## Chapter XVII
### THE SUBSEAS RIDE

ULL himself had wrenched the oxygen apparatus from Doc Savage's suit. He was elated. He yelled once in unholy delight, as Doc vanished into the black tomb of the compartment. Then he lunged toward two men who held Rapid Pace, and jammed his helmet to one of theirs.

"Keep them alive!" he yelled.

Because their diving suits were not equipped with the ingenious radio inter-communicating sets, it was necessary to put helmets together when they wanted to talk. In that manner, vibration through the metal carried their voices.

"Hell's fire!" the man shouted back. "Why?"

"We'll pump them!" Ull bellowed. "We must know whether they told the police what they had learned about us!"

Ull moved rapidly to his other men and repeated the order. As a result, Monk and Ham were hauled to the conning tower hatch, not greatly damaged, except in spirit. Monk's diving suit was leaking on one leg, but that would not be serious as long as he kept upright. A knife had made a gash in it.

Rapid Pace and McCoy were also unharmed. They were dragged along behind.

To the homely Monk, the trip back to the submarine of the Silver Death's-Heads seemed to take an age. He struggled at first, then desisted at the very real threat of a knife point against his chest.

The air lock by which they were taken into the other subseas boat was of the conventional type, possibly a bit larger than usual. But Monk was not interested in structural details.

Forlorn grief contorted the chemist's pleasantly ugly features. He had seen what had happened to Doc Savage. The bronze giant, he was convinced, was now dead.

The thought appalled Monk. It weakened him, took his spirit, made him listless, not caring greatly what happened henceforward. The fact that Pat Savage and Lorna Zane were still prisoners of the Silver Death's-Heads, perhaps alive, was temporarily forgotten.

Monk's existence was tied up with Doc Savage, and had been for years; but Doc was dead now. Scientist, a being of superhuman physical powers,

master of incredible feats, the bronze man had perished in a tomb of steel sixty feet beneath the Atlantic.

Monk thought of that, and it put him in a mood where he could not see the need for carrying on.

Monk and Ham, under the guard of alert submachine guns, were placed together in a tiny compartment in the silver men's submarine. Their diving suits were removed.

They had to sit down, shoulder to shoulder, between two lockers. There was barely room for them. Nor was there headroom for even the shortest of their captors in the submarine.

The U-boat was incredibly cramped, and she had a big cargo of humanity aboard, if these men who wore the silver disguises could be classed as such.

Rapid Pace and McCoy were placed somewhere else. Monk and Ham did not see them after they entered the underseas craft.

The homely chemist and the dapper lawyer did see a large metal canister being passed through the air hatch. A clockwork device was attached to this, and they recognized it for what it was—a mine of the type used by the Coast Guard to destroy derelicts.

They could guess to what use the explosive was to be put.

The Silver Death's-Heads loaded aboard the submarine and took off their diving paraphernalia. They were a jubilant lot. Some removed their silver masks. The faces they revealed had one thing in common—there was viciousness about the eyes.

A switch was thrown, cutting current off from the electromagnets. The submarine lifted a little, but did not clear the surface, and traveled away.

By the sound of the motors, Monk and Ham knew the craft was making full speed. They knew why—the mine.

The mine went off after a few minutes, and the shock of it rolled the submarine and made her steel plates groan.

Ull came and leered down at Monk and Ham, and said, "That blew your submarine and the corpse of Doc Savage to where they belong!"

ULL removed his mask now, probably because it hampered his breathing. The fact that he did remove it promised an unpleasant future. He would not show his face to men whom he expected to live to identify him later in a court of law.

It was a surprise, this face of Ull's. It mirrored no evil, not even the eyes. It was a round, cherubic thing, the countenance of a matured cupid. The eyes were soft and brown and the fat, round chin had a cleft that was almost a dimple.

Ull stared peacefully at Monk and Ham.

"You see," he said dryly, "we were prepared for trouble under the water."

"Whatcha mean?" Monk asked thickly.

"The electric lances," Ull chuckled. "We have carried them aboard for a long time. You see, there was always a chance that we might be trapped underwater, and divers sent down to investigate. The lances were the most effective weapons I could devise."

Monk said nothing but tried not to think of Doc Savage and what had happened to him. His groping mind hit on another thing which was puzzling him, so he asked about it.

"The electromagnets?" he asked. "How come this—this thing was equipped with them?"

"We use them," Ull chuckled.

"How?" Monk questioned hoarsely.

Ull chuckled. If there was placidity and innocence on his cherubic face, it did not extend to his voice, for that was ugly in its very quietness. There was satanic evil also in his calm demeanor.

"The electromagnets enabled us to contact you in that black water," Ull offered. "We were lucky. We came close to you, and had sense enough to have the magnets switched on. Before we knew it, we were fastened to you. The magnets pulled us close. They are very powerful!"

"You didn't put them on for that purpose," Monk muttered. "They wouldn't operate over a distance of more than a few feet. What are they intended for?"

Ull smirked. "Before long, I think that will cease to puzzle you."

"Yeah," Monk growled; then, still trying to keep his thoughts off Doc Savage's fate, the homely chemist ejected another question: "Pat—is she all right?"

"She is alive," Ull told him. "I would not say she is all right. In fact, her position is very bad. So is that of the other young lady, Lorna Zane. To be quite clear, they are to be killed along with you— unless you tell us whether or not the police know of our method of getting into New York Harbor by the underwater route."

That last was an afterthought, plainly, and Monk did not honor it with an answer. They would be tortured, of course. Whether or not they talked would not make much difference—to them. They would be killed anyway.

Monk tried to clear up another mysterious point. "Is Bedford Burgess Gardner behind all this?" he asked.

Ull hesitated, put the end of a pink tongue between his teeth as he considered, then burst into an explosion of hollow laughter.

"Is Gardner the big brain?" he smiled. "You want to know that?"

"Yes," Monk grunted.

"Yes," said Ull.

THE submarine was traveling along at half throttle, and not making great speed. That was fortunate. Otherwise, Doc Savage might have been torn off.

True, he was lashed to a mooring ring on the deck. He could never have held on any other way, even with his fabulous muscles. Maybe he could have managed for a time, but the chances were against it, especially earlier, during the time when the underseas craft had charged full speed from the vicinity of the *Helldiver*, endeavoring to get clear before the mine exploded.

Doc's escape from death had been executed without great difficulty or impossible legerdemain. The water where the subsea fight had occurred was not so deep that its mere pressure produced extreme discomfort.

The bronze man had managed to get to a locker in the compartment into which he had disappeared after Ull had torn off the oxygen apparatus. This was not hard, for Doc knew the *Helldiver's* every rivet, and he could hold his breath, due to long practice, for a time an ordinary man would consider beyond human ability.

A pair of diving "lungs" had come out of the locker. These were merely the tubes and mouthpiece, purifier and oxygen tanks, minus the helmet and suit of an ordinary diving rig. Donning the diving lungs had entailed no greater problem than the swallowing of a quantity of salt water. Doc wore them now.

The bronze man had to keep his head down and his features protected with enwrapping arms. Otherwise, the diving lungs would have been torn out by the rush of the water. That was why it was well that he had lashed himself to the mooring ring.

Getting atop the submarine had not been difficult either, since the silver men thought him dead.

Not that the bronze man was having an easy time of it. The water tore at him with terrific force. The lashing line was gradually sawing into his great ligaments, and eventually he was certain to weaken and be battered into insensibility, or else to lose the diving lungs, which would be more disastrous.

He was unable to keep his eyes open against the tearing water, except for an occasional brief squint. The lighter hue of the water about him told him that the sub was not running far beneath the surface. No doubt it was following the radio guide buoys. The fact that they were not as deep indicated, conceivably, that they might be nearing shore.

Soon the shoreward course hypothesis became a certainty, for there was a grinding sound, and Doc, chancing a glance, saw the periscope rising. He could barely make it out through the sunlit waters.

The fog must have cleared up, judging by the illumination in the water.

The submotors became more silent. The water lost some of its tearing force. After a bit there was a soft jar, and mud billowed up around the sub.

It had touched bottom. Probably its keel was reenforced against just such contacts as this.

The sub was built almost as strongly as the practically indestructible *Helldiver*.

The U-boat lifted out of the mud and continued. With bare headway, it nosed forward. Everything indicated that the craft was nearing the secret base of the Silver Death's-Heads.

Doc could keep his eyes open. He saw the underwater searchlight on the bow of the submarine spout brilliance, although it was hardly necessary with the brightness of the sun.

A moment later, the bronze man began a mad wrenching at the lashings which held him to the mooring ring.

A mass—it resembled a gigantic log with the bark on, due to a profuse growth of barnacles—was looming overhead. He was in immediate danger of being crushed.

## Chapter XVIII
### THE BASE

DOC SAVAGE unlashed himself from the ring, then stroked down and seized the fin of a diving rudder. A watery rush from the propellers nearly tore him loose.

The sub was jockeying to get under the huge hulk above. The slow, tedious task the silver men made of it was nevertheless an expert job. Undoubtedly, they were guided by highly scientific soundwave projectors and receivers, or, possibly, beam radio apparatus which told them when they were directly under the mass overhead.

Ballast was slowly blown and the underseas boat lifted. There was a jar as it touched the barnacle-covered hulk. In some spots the barnacles had been sheared away by past contacts, and steel plates were disclosed.

The sub did not move after the contact. It was being held in place by the electromagnets.

The thing above was the bottom of a ship. It could be nothing else. No doubt there were other electromagnets inside the ship to keep the U-boat from changing position.

Machinery ground. A great turmoil of bubbles poured up from the direction of the air lock by which divers came and went from the U-boat.

Doc Savage hastily released the diving fin to which he clung, then stroked down and under the submarine. From there, he managed to get under the hull of the ship, where he would be comparatively safe from discovery.

The bronze man worked forward, swimming a little, using the more clustered patches of barnacles for fingertip purchase. The hull began to narrow as he approached the bow. It was not a large ship, it seemed.

He did not follow the bow up out of the water, but shoved himself free and swam to the right, keeping far beneath the surface. He prowled out there for a time, but found nothing. Then he tried the left side. There, he located the anchor cable, a procession of thick iron links.

Doc drew in all the air his lungs would comfortably contain, then removed the diving lungs and tied them to the anchor linkage by the straps which held the purifying mechanism to his back.

It was a precaution. If he got aboard the ship, was shot at and went overboard, not to come up, the Silver Death's-Heads would think him dead again, perhaps. He could reach the lungs, swimming underwater to don them.

The anchor chain ran down on the side opposite the point where the submarine had fastened itself—which was fortunate. But Doc broke the surface very cautiously, keeping under the anchor links, they being large enough to partially conceal his head. He stared upward.

The ship was a tramp, a rusty old hulk of a few thousand tons, one of the type which helped make up the Rum Row of prohibition days.

The Row still existed, for that matter, well outside the jurisdiction of the Coast Guard, and handled other things beside rum—perfumes, watch movements and other things on which there was a high duty. No doubt a few aliens were smuggled, too.

The tramp needed paint; her brasswork was almost beyond being helped by polish, and her one funnel leaned slightly askew.

Doc saw the funnel when he reached the anchor hawse hole and lifted himself by the strength of his great arms. The vessel had two crow's nests, that suspicious in itself; and in each, a lookout was on duty.

Doc watched the lookouts closely. They would sweep the horizon with binoculars, then give attention to their comrades, who were coming up from the submarine through the air lock.

It was while they were eyeing the sub that Doc whipped over the rail, flashed to the nearest open hatch and dropped down it.

No one saw him, because there was a commotion aft, along the rail.

THE commotion was of Monk's making. The homely chemist still thought Doc Savage dead; he had been benumbed by the fact, but now he was shedding the agonizing lethargy.

Monk topped the rail, dripping and sputtering; he had been forced to swim up from the air lock without benefit of a diving suit, and he was mad. He lashed out at the first convenient jaw. Bone crunched under his fist.

The man who had been hit caved as he went backward.

Someone tried to smash Monk over his bullet-like head with a revolver. Monk grabbed the short arm. He almost got it, but silver men, rushing in, clubbed him back. He was seized and handcuffed.

When Ham appeared, he and Monk were led below. They did not see Hugh McCoy or Rapid Pace. Nor had they seen the pair since the misfortune aboard the *Helldiver*.

"I wonder if they're alive?" Monk growled.

"Get below, gentlemen," suggested cherub-faced Ull.

Monk and Ham were convoyed below decks by a grim ring of gun snouts. They were halted before a metal door. Monk's wrists were decorated with an additional pair of manacles, and Ham was hand-cuffed. The door was opened and they were shoved inside.

Monk took one look at the two occupants of the rusty steel chamber and let out a loud grunt of relief.

"Pat!" he ejaculated. "So you are safe, after all!"

"Do you call this safe?" Pat demanded caustically. "Where's Doc?"

Patricia Savage, wrists ornamented with steel linkage, was far from being the immaculate person-ality who headed a successful swanky Park Avenue beauty establishment. She still wore her evening gown, but it was grimy, and she had torn it off above the ankles for greater freedom of movement.

Lorna Zane was with her, and she also showed traces of a rough evening and night. Her brown hair was disheveled; her ensemble of gray had lost its effectiveness; the gray béret and gray bag being missing, and a heel was gone from one gray pump.

"Where's Doc?" Pat repeated.

Monk turned around as if to look at Ham, but actually to hide the expression on his homely features.

"I dunno," he mumbled.

Pat, voice suddenly shrill, demanded, "Monk! Has something happened to Doc?"

Ull, laughing loudly from the door, said, "I will tell the broadminded world that something happened to him. He drowned! Then we blew his body to little pieces."

Pat became very pale and swiveled so that no one could see her face.

Lorna Zane bit her lower lip so furiously that it seemed certain her small white teeth would go through.

A silver man appeared behind Ull and said, "Listen, the big boy wants to see you. And he's as mad as hell!"

ULL scowled, his childishly round face suddenly ugly. He leveled an arm at the prisoners.

"I'll be back," he promised. "And you had better make up your minds to tell whether or not you spilled the dope on us to the police before you start-ed out in that submarine."

Then Ull stamped out and made his way up a companionway, then along a filthy passage. The old boat had once carried passengers, and Ull turned into what had been the lounge.

In the center of the lounge stood a large table. It was long and wide, but it was none too large for the use to which it was being put.

The table held the proceeds of the Silver Death's-Heads' robberies of the night before. There were stacks of currency, canvas bags of hard money, piles of necklaces, bracelets, and fully a bushel of rings. Almost a million dollars' worth of it, if sold at retail by the original owners.

At the head of the table stood an ominous figure. He waved an arm and snarled, in a coarse whispering voice, "I suppose you had this display arranged to impress me?"

The expression on Ull's cherubic features showed that he had done just that.

"There is a great deal of money here," he muttered.

The ominous one at the end of the table wore one of the silver cloaks. The whispering tone he used was obviously assumed to disguise his voice.

"You still think that the loot taken last night justifies the turmoil into which the robberies threw the New York police?" he asked sarcastically.

"They won't catch us," said Ull. "I'll order the anchor hoisted, and we shall cruise out to sea for a few days. No one will suspect us. The papers of this ship are in order, and there is a cargo of innocent wool and hides in the hold, by way of proving we are enroute from South America to Canada."

"You are avoiding!" rapped the whispering one.

"Avoiding what?" Ull asked with pretended innocence.

"The fact that you ordered those robberies on your own initiative," snapped the other. "You were to loot that first armored truck. You were to kill Paine L. Winthrop. And that was all, except for the work incidental to fighting Doc Savage."

Ull began, "We took nearly a million dollars—"

"And you endangered a scheme which has netted me a billion within the last year!" the silver mastermind hissed.

Ull's cleft chin sagged.

"What?" he choked. "A—how much?"

"A billion!" snarled the man at the head of the table.

Ull seemed dazed. "I do not understand this."

"Do you recall that at various times during the past year I have ordered certain men killed," queried the other grimly. "The killings were well done by yourself and your aides, I must admit. In no case were they traceable to an organized plot."

Ull wet his lips. "I thought they were just—enemies of yours, like you said."

"Enemies—business enemies," the other said hoarsely. "They were men who stood in the way of business mergers which I was engineering. It was necessary to get them out of the way."

"But what about the billion?" Ull gulped.

"That was made by recapitalizing the merged companies and selling the stock," he was informed. "The financial details are too complicated to consider here."

Ull eyed the loot on the table, and it did not seem to impress him as much as it had earlier.

"Was Paine L. Winthrop in the way of one of your mergers?" he asked.

"No," rasped the other. "Winthrop was working with me. As you know, he built our submarine in his shipyard a few months ago, when all of his regular employees were laid off, and we used our own men for the construction work. I was going to merge his company and give him a handsome cut of the profits. But he got cold feet. He had been told the submarine was for a foreign government. When he found out its true use, his nerve failed. I had to put him out of the way to keep him from going to the police."

"Oh," Ull said vaguely.

THE master in silver teetered on his heels. He even wore the silver gloves, but it was apparent that his hands were shaking slightly with rage.

The sinister one's anger began to get on Ull's nerves, as did the mask. He was uneasy. Here he realized, was a schemer of much greater magnitude than he had thought.

"You do not have to wear that disguise aboard," Ull mumbled.

"Most of your men do not know me," the other whispered hoarsely. "It is as well that they remain in ignorance. But let us not get away from the subject. You disobeyed my orders last night."

"That," Ull told him quietly, "is not entirely my fault."

"How do you figure that way?"

"Had I known of this billion business, do you think I would have been fool enough to endanger it?" Ull demanded.

The other seemed to think this over.

"In the future, my orders must be followed implicitly," he said.

"They will be," Ull replied earnestly.

The being in silver waved an arm at the treasure-laden table. "Divide this stuff among the men. I do not want a share. And you will get no share yourself. That is by way of punishment for overstepping your authority last night."

Ull looked as if he had been stuck with a pin, but said nothing.

"What about the prisoners?" he asked.

"Question them," commanded the other. "Then execute them."

Ull departed.

"Close the door behind you," he was directed. "And do not disturb me."

Ull closed the door of the treasure table room and walked away.

AFTER Ull had gone, the man in silver walked over to the table, gazed upon the jewels with an experienced eye and picked out the more valuable. He selected packets of bills. In less than a minute, he had annexed nearly a fourth of the loot.

The fellow now left the room, chuckling harshly. The passage into which he went was dark, but he strode blithely along it—until he suddenly fell on his face.

He never heard the blow which had struck him, for it had been delivered silently, with great force. Nor did he see the giant man of bronze who bent over him and searched him.

A bulky packet—not the loot from the table—was fastened inside the silver man's garment. Doc Savage took that.

Then Doc removed the silver garment.

It was very dark in the corridor and Doc did not make a light. Hence it was impossible for him to view the features of his victim, the chieftain of the Silver Death's-Heads. Nor did Doc risk striking a match.

He drew the silver cloak on over his own head, found that it was snug, but could be worn, then searched his victim again and found matches. He pocketed the matches.

Back to the treasure room, Doc walked. Under a light he opened the packet which had been inside the silver man's garment.

The package held a large, well-made black theatrical beard. Doc replaced the set of dark whiskers in his pocket.

The bronze man left the treasure room, stooping, bending his knees and hanging his head in order to make himself appear smaller.

He sighted a guard down the passage and made for the fellow. But before he reached the watchman, another silver figure appeared and attempted to pass.

The lookout challenged, snarling, "Get that rig off! I wanta see your face!"

Instead of complying with the command, the silver man held up an arm and exposed a wrist watch. The guard compared its reading with the expensive timepiece on his own wrist.

"Sure," he said. "Go ahead."

Doc paused, and for a brief moment his fantastic trilling sound was audible, but not loud enough to penetrate to the guard. Doc had just discovered the significance of the expensive wrist watches which all of the gang wore. They were used in place of passwords.

The bronze man still wore the wrist watch which he had taken from the man who had kicked the beggar in New York City—the man who had discovered his mistake and later fled, only to be shot to death by a policeman. Its underwater bath had evidently not hurt the watch.

Advancing, Doc was challenged. He showed the watch as the other had done. It got him past.

A few yards beyond the guard, he turned and in a voice greatly different from his own, a harsh, cruel tone, asked, "Where are the prisoners being held?"

"Right ahead of you," he was told. "You can't miss it."

Doc went on. He saw the room in which the prisoners were being questioned, but instead of pausing, went on as if he were uninterested.

He had seen that Monk, Ham and the two girls were safe for the time being. They would be safe until they talked, providing they did not hold out until Ull was exasperated.

Working deep into the old tramp steamer, Doc carefully avoided the engine rooms. The craft was an oil burner. He found the fuel tanks, got a cap unscrewed and learned they were almost full.

He left the cap off, scooped up oil in his hands and spilled it along the tanks and down the sides, thence to the nearest bulkhead door. He carried the trail beyond that for some distance.

At the end of the oil trail, he sank to a knee and felt through the pockets of the silver frock until he found the matches. With a quick scrape, he struck one, then dropped it.

The bronze man was running furiously when the match hit the fuel oil. There was a sizzling. The stuff did not burn like gasoline, but it flamed, nevertheless, and the fire ran along until it reached the bulkhead, passed through and went on.

That was all Doc saw. He was still running. He mounted a companionway.

There was a loud roar and a rush of superheated air as the fuel tank took fire. There had been enough gas inside it to explode and split the container.

## Chapter XIX
### DESTRUCTION

ULL was yelling threats at Monk and Ham when the explosion came. The cherub-faced man rocked on his feet, brought up against a bulkhead and looked very surprised.

"What the—" he began, then a mad shout apprised him of what was wrong.

"Fire! Fire!" was the yell.

Ull wheeled and plunged out of the steel cell, rapping over his shoulder, "Watch these prisoners!"

He disappeared down the passage. Other men, some in silver frocks and some in shirt sleeves, followed. They streamed past the door.

But one did not pass. He whipped into the cell. The guard stared wonderingly at him.

"I'm taking your place!" snapped the newcomer. "Give me your gun and go help fight that fire."

The guard hesitated, then passed over his weapon and plunged outside. He had little hankering to be left below on sentry duty where he might be trapped if the ship sank.

The replacement wrenched down his hood.

"Doc!" Monk squawked, and looked as if he were going to faint.

Doc Savage snapped, "Come on! We've got to get out of here fast!"

The bronze man replaced his hood, concealing his features, and waved his gun prominently as he herded Monk, Ham and the two girls down the passage. Other silver men, passing him, thought, if they took time to think at all, that he was merely one of their number moving the prisoners.

Doc stopped one of them.

"Where is the other captive?" he demanded.

The silver man pointed. "Third door," he said.

Doc ran to the designated panel, wrenched at the heavy hasp which secured it, got it open—and Rapid Pace came stumbling out. He lunged fiercely at Doc and tried to strike with his fists.

"Stop it!" Doc rapped.

"Bless me!" Pace gulped. "I thought you were dead. Yes, sir, I thought you were dead."

Doc herded his party on, still pretending to be escorting them to another prison cell.

They came to the room which held the treasure table.

Monk stared at the assembled wealth, then made a growling sound and plunged to the left. Sacks lay there, stout rubberized canvas bags in which the loot had no doubt been brought aboard. He seized upon some of the bags, and with sweeps of his great arms began stuffing the sacks.

"Gimme a hand!" he snapped at Ham. "I don't want to see these guys get away with this stuff!"

Ham leaped to aid. To expedite matters, Doc also lent a hand.

Rapid Pace dashed forward, opened a door, yelled over his shoulder, "I'm gonna see if the coast is clear," then disappeared. He had entered the passage in which Doc had overpowered the master of the Silver Death's-Heads.

A moment later were grunts, blows, painful exclamations.

Pace yelled, "Ouch! There's somebody on the floor here! Say, he's tying a handkerchief over his face!"

"Watch it!" Doc shouted. "He is the man behind all of this!"

Pace shouted. "Ouch!" again, after which there

were more blows. Heels kicked steel plates; grunts came from between clenched teeth. The thumping and tearing of clothing indicated a terrific fight.

Doc leaped forward and plunged into the passage. It was very dark.

The fight had worked farther down the corridor. The master of the Silver Death's-Heads seemed to be in flight, with Pace close on his heels.

"I licked 'im!" Pace howled. "But he's getting away!"

An instant later, Doc bumped into Pace. The efficiency expert stood in the brilliant sunlight outside. An open hatch nearby indicated where the quarry had gone.

Pace's face was blank. He tried to speak twice before he could manufacture words.

"T-that was the mastermind?" he stuttered.

"It was," Doc told him. "Did you see his face?"

"I s-sure d-did!" Pace gulped. "And am I s-surprised."

DOC gave Rapid Pace a shove. They headed for the nearest lifeboat, the two girls immediately behind, Monk and Ham, heavily burdened, bringing up the rear.

The lifeboat was an unusual craft for a tramp steamer of this sort—it was more of a fast seagoing launch. Evidently it was a provision against the necessity of a getaway sometime when the submarine was not at hand.

Doc wrenched the tarpaulin off, then he and Monk threw their weight against the levers which swung the davits out. Ham heaved sacks of loot into the craft. They loaded aboard.

A silver man in the crow's nest yelled and shot at them. The bullet dug splinters out of the boat. The second lookout had quitted his post—to assist in fighting the fire, no doubt.

Doc directed a single shot from his gun at the crow's nest. The man there screamed and dropped his weapon, then tried to get both hands down in the crow's nest bucket to squeeze the pain out of the leg which Doc's bullet had drilled.

It was one of the few times the bronze man had used a gun, but the shot was accurate; he might have been practicing with the weapon all of his life.

They ran the rope through the falls a bit more swiftly than was sane, but with alert eyes and husky muscles, Doc and Monk managed to keep the craft level. Ham had the engine going as they hit the water. It was perfect teamwork.

The shots on deck had spread an alarm. Men leaped to the rail.

"Get down!" Doc rapped.

The boat sides were thick enough to break the force of a revolver bullet and, flattened below the water level, it was unlikely that they would be hit at all.

The boat heaved its nose up, dug its stern down in a mass of propeller-stirred foam and scudded away from the tramp.

Lead smacked the hall, chewed a thwart and clanged off the engine. One slug opened a pair of holes in the gas tank, and Monk, crawling back, calmly planted a hairy finger over each aperture.

A few minutes put them out of bullet range.

Smoke was climbing from hatches and portholes of the tramp. It was very black oil smoke, and it indicated the silver men had not been successful in extinguishing the oil fire. That the flames were spreading rapidly was evident when men began diving overside. They fought each other to get over the rail.

"Trying to get in their sub," Monk grunted, lifting his head from his job of stoppering the gas tank.

"They'll have a job," Ham said grimly. "The sub won't hold a fifth of them."

Some of the silver men undoubtedly reached the submarine. Perhaps they entered through the air lock. But it did them no good.

The tanker suddenly blew up. Possibly it was the fuel tanks. In later discussion, Doc tended toward the theory that explosives were stored aboard, and these had let loose.

There was a great geyser of debris, smoke and flame. The ship came apart in the middle, separating, the two ends turning half around while men spilled off the decks, their bodies hardly distinguishable amid the flying wreckage.

A boiling inferno of oil poured out of the rent craft and spread, flaming on the sea, engulfing those men who were in the water, burning them to death, or forcing them down until their lungs took in water convulsively.

At that, the swimmers were no more unlucky than those in the submarine. The blast undoubtedly crushed the submersible, so that those within perished.

Doc said slowly, "It is too bad that they tried to fight the fire so long, and then wasted time in seeking to get into the submarine. They could have gotten off in the lifeboats. We did not take them all."

Ham offered. "Probably afraid they would get picked up in the boats and turned over to the police."

"Poor guy," Monk put in.

"Who?" Ham demanded.

"Hugh McCoy," said Monk. "We did not rescue him. That's tough."

Rapid Pace had been sitting as if in a stupor. Now he started and eyed Monk.

"It's not tough!" he snapped. "No, sir! It's not!"

Monk scowled. "Listen, that ain't no way to talk about a dead guy, even if you were all the time going to lick him."

"I did lick him!" Pace exclaimed triumphantly.

"I finally did! I don't understand how I had it in me."

"When?" Monk grunted. "When did this happen?"

"Just before we got off the boat," said Pace.

The significance of the words dawned on Monk. "Listen!" he exploded. "Say that again, will you?"

"Hugh McCoy was the brains behind all of this," Pace said grimly. "It was him that I fought in the corridor."

Monk swiveled on Doc. "Is that right?"

"McCoy was the chief of the Silver Death's-Heads," Doc said slowly. "That was finally evident when the silver men attacked our submarine when they could have used a depth bomb and destroyed us. Their chief was aboard. They did not want to kill him."

Monk waved hairy arms, the gas-tank leak forgotten. "But what about Gardner—Bedford Burgess Gardner?"

"The same person," Doc said.

"What?" Monk all but choked on the exclamation.

"Remember the black beard which Gardner wore?" Doc questioned. "You did not see him, but Pace and myself did, and I told you about it."

"Sure," Monk admitted.

Doc produced the packet which he had taken from the unconscious chief of the silver men. He tossed it over. Monk opened it.

The packet held the black theatrical beard.

Monk slowly put his thumbs back over the holes in the gas tank.

THERE was not much more they could do. The sea about the spot where the tramp had gone down was a flaming mass of oil; in it, no creature could live. But they cruised as near as possible, hoping to pick up any survivors.

Lorna Zane gave way and sobbed a little, and seemed quite willing for Pace, the efficiency expert who had improved his nerve so remarkably, to comfort her. Pace was radiant.

Pat looked wan, a little exhausted by the whole grisly episode.

Doc Savage and his men were relaxed, unconcerned, now that the trouble was over. They were accustomed to this sort of thing. They had been through it before.

They would go through it again, too—as much and more. For within the month, a fantastic, perilous series of adventures would befall them, although they had no way of foreseeing that.

Johnny—William Harper Littlejohn, the archaeologist and geologist who was now in England—was destined first to see King John's ghost, and from that grisly meeting would grow the whirl of peril and dangerous mystery that surrounded *The Sea Magician*.

Strange and terrible was this ghost of King John, ancient ruler of England, who roamed the marshlands of The Wash, that fantastic swamp on the eastern coast of England. And even more fearsome and mystifying was the thing behind the walking of King John's ghost.

When Johnny went to investigate King John's shade, he found much that he had not expected, and was placed in terrible jeopardy. And in aiding Johnny, Doc Savage was to tackle a mystery that seemed to have absolutely no explanation at all.

*The Sea Magician* was destined to be about as baffling a problem as Doc Savage and his men had ever encountered.

But Doc and his party, not being clairvoyants, were satisfied that the menace of the silver men was ended, and were unconcerned over the future. They cruised with the launch until there was no possible chance of survivors being found.

Then they turned toward the Jersey coast. There was sufficient fuel to make it, and the sea was not too rough for the launch.

In the stern, Rapid Pace had an arm around Lorna Zane's shoulders.

"You know, I've stopped getting scared," he told her. "I can't understand it. No, sir!"

THE END

# INTERLUDE IN SILVER AND GOLD
## by Will Murray

*Death in Silver* marked the 20th published Doc Savage novel, and a significant turning point in the long-running Street & Smith pulp series.

In the early years of *Doc Savage Magazine,* Lester Dent was obliged to include in the climax of each story a teaser for the next adventure—whether or not he had one outlined and approved.

At the end of 1934's *Fear Cay,* Dent dutifully looked ahead to the next issue, writing:

> In the meantime, things were to happen which caused them to forget all about [Fear Cay].... Forgotten, also, was the trouble they had met.... There came upon them a peril infinitely greater— a menace, not to themselves alone, but to thousands of others.
>
> A naval destroyer in the Brooklyn Navy Yard was about to sail. Suddenly, workmen in the yard threw off their overalls, revealing strange uniforms of silver, uniforms of no known country. They seized the destroyer, and as they sailed her out of the harbor, opened fire upon a certain skyscraper, destroying it. The stolen destroyer went on to sea and was never heard from again.
>
> Who were these men in silver? Why was the skyscraper destroyed, with the death of hundreds of innocent persons? That was what Doc Savage and his crew found themselves striving to learn.
>
> *Death in Silver* was to pitch them into danger such as they had never before encountered, was to throw them against a master of terror…

It's clear that Dent had yet to outline *Death in Silver,* since no such scene opened the novel. Nor did his formal outline call for such an audacious start. Instead, he changed it, emphasizing the element of destruction instead of violence.

Usually, *Doc Savage* editor John L. Nanovic caught Dent's false starts. Here, it slipped into print. No harm was done, and an insight into the workings of Lester Dent's creative thinking stands revealed.

With *Death in Silver,* the Doc Savage series shifted into its fundamental format. For one thing, it marks the third appearance of Doc's Canadian cousin, Patricia. Introduced in 1933's *Brand of the Werewolf,* Pat relocated to New York in novel *Fear Cay,* where she first displayed her knack for horning in on Doc's dangerous adventures. In this present story, Pat has gone into the physical culture business, and Lester Dent clearly signals that she's in town to stay. Whether the Man of Bronze likes it or not.

Feisty fighting females were not common in the 1930s. Pat was so unusual that around the Street & Smith offices she was nicknamed "Tarzana." Perhaps it was because she broke the mold so outrageously that John Nanovic suggested another line of work

when he read the following in Dent's outline: "Pat is now operating a private detective agency of her own, with head offices on swanky Park Avenue."

Dent usually improvised his yarns as he wrote them, freely abandoning pre-plotted characters and story elements if inspiration seized his fertile imagination. In the white heat of composition, sometimes he forgot to include interesting explanatory material.

The mysterious Ull and the rationale behind his Silver Death's-Heads never quite got into print. But here is the outline backstory:

> Don Ull [is] a half-cracked scientist who lost his fortune in the depression and thinks he is entitled to get it back by force.... Ull has his men dress in silver-colored uniforms with silver death-face masks, because it was in speculating in silver stocks that Ull lost his fortune.

Dent included an interesting autobiographical element in Chapter 4 of *Death in Silver.* While writing the first dozen Doc Savage novels, he had been living at 8904 34th Street in Jackson Heights, Queens, but even though he had moved into Manhattan at the beginning of 1934, he describes the apartment building he had just vacated.

*Death in Silver* represents a radical departure from the original Doc Savage formula. From the beginning, Lester Dent had to fit Doc and his five iron men into every novel. Managing all of those personalities and finding useful things for them to do every month became a strain.

At the time of this yarn—spring of 1934—Dent was also scripting the *Doc Savage* radio program for Don Lee's Golden West Network. There, he limited his cast to Doc, Monk and sometimes Ham. Perhaps this inspired Dent to whittle down his cumbersome collection of characters to a more manageable group.

As Dent points out in *Death in Silver,* this adventure marked the first time that the Man of Bronze was called into action without his Iron Crew. As the most popular aides, Monk and Ham were indispensable. Readers would have complained about their absence. But by having them fall into the hands of the Silver Death's-Heads early on, Dent cleared the way for Doc Savage to carry much of the story. Hence, *Death in Silver* is a showcase for the Man of Bronze at his most formidable. When Dent once wrote, "The violence of Doc Savage is in a category all its own," he was not exaggerating.

From this story on, Dent enjoyed the luxury of using only Doc aides whose professional skills fit a given story. It must have been a tremendous relief to him. Six protagonists made for quite a juggling act. Dent's had evolved strategies to cope with them all. Johnny, for example, often disappeared while investigating some faraway archeological mystery, and the search for his whereabouts started the action while keeping him out of the story until he was found. Renny, too, could be counted on to stumble across danger while plying his engineering trade in distant lands, but was sometimes relegated to his trademark door-smashing habit and favorite expression of "Holy cow!" Long Tom often simply faded into the background, overshadowed by his more colorful comrades.

In *Death in Silver,* Dent carefully detailed the whereabouts of the missing three. It was his plan for each one to stumble upon a new adventure in the next three issues, starting with Renny Renwick.

But those plans hit an unfortunate snag. When Dent was wrapping up *Death in Silver,* he found himself once again caught without an outline. But he did have an idea. Here is what he wrote:

> Doc and his men were relaxed, unconcerned, now that the trouble was over. They were accustomed to this sort of thing. They had been through it before.
>
> They would go through it again, too—as much and more. Within the month, a fantastic, perilous series of adventures would befall them, although they had no way of foreseeing that.
>
> Renny—Colonel John Renwick, an engineer who was now in South Africa—would be first to come in contact with the grisly mystery of that Lost Island. A man would come out of the jungle, a wasted, stumbling bundle of bones. He spoke to Renny. And the instant Renny heard that voice, he was condemned to mysterious death.
>
> For the words the man whispered had to do with a fantastic secret, a secret that was not of Africa, but of an incredible place in the vastness of the Indian Ocean. It was of Lost Island that he spoke, and of the unholy thing to be found there, a thing which no man understood; he spoke of a treasure, too, a treasure for which men killed and themselves, died.
>
> He wore weird garments, this man who came to Renny; he was a white man, yet his speech was

strange. But most ghastly of all was the thing that was wrong with him—the spell wrought by the sorcery of Lost Island.

> And because that strange fellow spoke to Renny, death was to strike, not only at Renny, but at Doc Savage, distant half around the world, in New York City.

When it came time to formally plot this adventure, the outline was shelved, forcing Dent to skip ahead to the next premise, the planned Johnny Littlejohn adventure called *The Sea Magician.* Dent wrote a new teaser blurb to replace the old. In the interest of textual completeness, we've included it too.

What happened to "Lost Island"? It was the only one of Dent's Doc Savage outlines to be unceremoniously abandoned. Yet it was not lost forever. But that's a story for another time....

Discovering lost civilizations was a Doc Savage specialty from the beginning, when the murder of his father led him to a strange Central American valley in the first Doc adventure. There, a lost tribe of Mayan Indians dwelled as they had in their golden age, unknown to the outer world, protecting a hoard of gold designated for a special purpose.

The Mayan race has enjoyed a recent resurgence of interest thanks to *Mel Gibson's Apocalypto* and *The Fountain.* Who were these strange people who simply vanished, having deserted their great cities long before the Spaniards arrived in America? Why did their sophisticated civilization collapse? Scholars are still trying to determine definitive answers.

This was a mystery that long fascinated Lester Dent. Some of his earlier pulp fiction delved into Mayan lore. And the Mayan background was one of his most significant contributions to the genesis of Doc Savage.

It's well established that Doc was created by committee. The idea originated with Street & Smith business manager Henry W. Ralston, and was inspired by a now-forgotten adventurer named Richard Henry Savage. A soldier, author, engineer, lawyer and diplomat, Savage was an astonishing

**Henry William Ralston**

**Lester Dent**

**John L. Nanovic**

figure of the 19th century. Ralston wanted to update Dick Savage as "a science-adventure guy" named Doc Savage.

According to *Doc Savage* editor John L. Nanovic, "...the beginning of Doc Savage was in the mind of Mr. Ralston. When he brought this up with me, one lunch, he had *all* the characters in mind, with names and descriptions. He also had the purpose of Doc Savage strongly in his mind, and passed all this on to me, and then to Lester Dent."

As explained early in the series, "Doc's father had trained him from the cradle for a certain goal in life. That goal was a life of service. To go from one end of the world to the other, looking for excitement and adventure, but always helping those who need help, punishing those who deserve it, that was Doc Savage's noble purpose in life. All his marvelous training was for that end."

"We grabbed him right out of thin air," Ralston later recalled. "We made him a surgeon and scientist, because we wanted him to know chemistry, philosophy, and all that stuff. We also made him immensely wealthy—he'd inherited a huge fortune from his father. He crusaded against crime of all kinds—plots against the United States, against industry, against society at large. He was very strong physically, a giant man of bronze with eyes whose pupils resembled pools of flake gold, always in gentle motion. You might say he was the poor man's Monte Cristo."

After months of planning, Ralston and Nanovic brought in Lester Dent, and invited him to contribute ideas of his own. Doc Savage needed a headquarters and Dent suggested the new Empire State Building. Doc also required a lot of money to pursue his life's work of traveling the world, righting wrongs, punishing the wicked and protecting humanity. How to fund that career? they wondered.

Dent had an unfinished outline he'd abandoned three years earlier about a soldier of fortune who stumbled upon a lost civilization in the wilds of Mexico. There, in what Dent dubbed the Valley of Eternity, a surviving Mayan enclave hid from the 20th century. Renamed the Valley of the Vanished, it became the plot basis for *The Man of Bronze.* Mayan gold would provide Doc Savage with the unparalleled wealth he would need to fulfill his mission in life.

Nanovic took everyone's ideas and distilled them into a story treatment he called "Doc Savage, Supreme Adventurer." Lester Dent was assigned to write *The Man of Bronze* from this document.

Doc Savage would return to the Valley of the Vanished twice more after his first adventure there. His second visit came in 1937, and we've chosen *The Golden Peril* to reintroduce 21st century readers to the roots of Doc Savage.

**Doc Savage and the Mayan Princess Monja were reunited in 1942's *They Died Twice.***

To appreciate this tale, all you need to know is contained in this passage cut from *Death in Silver:*

Deep in remote Central American mountains lay a lost valley, a chasm on the floor of which dwelled descendents of the ancient Mayan civilization, a people shut off from the world. In this valley was a fabulous deposit of gold, the greatest mine of the old Mayan civilization. Doc had befriended these people long ago. There was a radio receiving set in the valley. Doc had but to broadcast a few words in Mayan at a certain hour each seventh day, and a week or so later, a burro train of bullion would appear mysteriously from the mountain with funds to be deposited to his account in the national bank of the Central American republic.

As for the mystery of the Mayans, Lester Dent did some digging into that on his own. When fellow pulp writer J. Allan Dunn recommended Dent for membership in the Explorers Club, one of the accomplishments cited was Dent's investigations into Mayan pottery artifacts discovered in the Caribbean, and their historical significance. Dent speculated that they had found their way to this remote area via trade, and did not indicate a previously-unknown Caribbean Mayan outpost.

Lester Dent was inducted into the Explorers Club in 1938.

# THE GOLDEN PERIL

*Two fighting factions lock in a battle to the death on the scene of Doc Savage's first adventure!*

## By KENNETH ROBESON

### Complete Book-length Novel

### Chapter I
### THE AMBUSH

THE vultures knew a feast awaited them. They hung almost motionless in the gray, ominous sky. Their beady eyes stared greedily down into the deep canyon that lay beneath them.

The canyon was gloomy as a grave. Its walls rose sheer and straight for an interminable distance. Boulders and runty trees lined its sides. A small stream droned a mournful dirge in the center. Except for the dirge of that stream there was no sound.

But death waited there!

Only the vultures from above could have seen the men-vultures below. They were huddled behind boulders. The half darkness of the canyon combined with the khaki they wore to make them almost invisible. Fully two-score men were there.

They were of almost every race and nationality. But they were alike in the greed that shone in their eyes—and in the modern instruments of murder they carried.

A faint sound came from the far end of the canyon. The dim figure of a man appeared in the distance, stood motionless for a moment, then vanished.

There was a sudden tenseness among the hidden men. Weapons were moved cautiously.

"Be quiet. Do not move until I give the command."

The order was given softly, but there was a chill note in the voice that brought instant obedience. The man who had spoken was not large, but there was a look of utter ruthlessness on his copper-tinted features and in his glacier-cold eyes. His shoulders were broad, his frame powerful. He wore the insignia of a general.

The aide at his side spoke in a whisper: "The trap has been set well, my general."

"*Si*. Soon the jaws of that trap will close." The general's Spanish was guttural, as if he were speaking a language still partly unfamiliar to him. "But care must be taken. Those we await have keen eyes."

Even as he spoke, more figures came into view at the far end of the canyon. Their eyes searched the scene before them, then one raised an arm in signal. A donkey train moved around a bend.

Scouts were out ahead. Other tall men moved beside the heavily-loaded beasts of burden. Still others brought up the rear.

A faint fire kindled in the general's eyes, and his lips made sucking sounds.

"Soon that will be ours!" he breathed fiercely.

THE men escorting the donkey train were unusual in appearance. They were tall, with thick shoulders and powerful muscles. Almost copper-colored, they wore a short mantle over their shoulders, a network of leather which had projecting ends. They wore broad girdles of a dark blue and leggings fashioned like football shin guards.

Those in the lead carried modern rifles. The others were armed only with spears and short clubs bearing vicious, razor-edged flakes of stone.

Slowly, they advanced. A few were chanting a weird song, utterly unaware of the terror and death that soon was to strike.

"Another sun and we shall reach Blanco Grande," said one.

"Then we will have fulfilled another task for Doc Savage," his companion replied. "It has been long since we last saw the bronze man. I wish he would come again."

"He is busy, but he will visit us again some day. We shall see him if we are patient," rejoined the first speaker.

But he was wrong in at least part of his statement. None of those with the donkey train ever were to see Doc Savage again. At that moment, they were passing squarely between the khaki-clad men concealed on either side of the trail.

The general would bark only one word, but that word was to start a chain of circumstances that was to bring many deaths; that was to reach out to New York, where Doc Savage had his headquarters; that was to bring the bronze man's aides into the fray; that was to test to the utmost the skill of Doc Savage and his five friends, experienced as they were in battling evil and injustice.

"Fire!" roared the general.

Instantly, the quiet of the canyon was shattered by the murder-roar of guns. Khaki-clad men reared up from behind boulders with automatic rifles. A rain of lead poured from those rifles into the ranks of the guards with the donkey train.

The guards were brave. The leaders brought up their guns, tried to reply to the merciless hail of death. Then they went down, almost cut in two by lead.

The others hurled their spears and dived for the temporary safety of the rocks. The heavily-laden donkeys snorted, burst into a panicky run. Khaki-clad figures leaped toward the trail and barred their path.

Shrill, pain-stricken cries came from the doomed guards. One grunted with satisfaction as his spear drove through the body of an attacker, only to die a moment later with a bullet through his brain.

Crimson stained the cold waters of the creek. It became literally a river of blood. The crashing roar of high-powered guns filled the canyon with thunderous echoes.

"Let none escape! Kill them all!" roared the general. The glacier-cold of his eyes had melted. The orbs were now red with a killing lust.

His men needed no urging. Relentlessly, their bullets were hunting down fleeing figures. The guards were dropping on all sides.

"We are lost!" moaned one of these. It was he who had first spoken on the trail.

"Doc Savage should know," his companion said throatily. There was a terrible wound in his chest. Red-flecked foam was on his lips. Already, his eyes were glazing. "Y-you should try to get word to him, Zum. I—I—" He became limp.

HIS companion eased behind the rocks on his stomach. His skin was almost the color of those boulders. Bullets whined over him suddenly. Zum rolled over and lay still. The death blast moved behind him, caught a guard who had risen to his knees to hurl a knife.

Cautiously, Zum wiggled on a short distance. Again he lay still. Then he moved ahead once more.

Exultant cries of victory were coming from the sides of the canyon. Khaki-clad men were rising to their feet. The steady roar of guns had ceased. Now there was only an occasional shot from a revolver held close to some wounded guard's head.

Zum neared a turn in the canyon. He leaped to his feet. With the speed of a racing hare, he rounded that turn. An automatic rifle burst into life. Hot lead played a tattoo on rocks. Slugs ricocheted and howled. One nicked the running man's right shoulder just before he vanished from view.

"Get him! Don't let him escape!" the general shouted viciously.

Khaki-clad figures raced in pursuit. When they reached the bend in the canyon, Zum had disappeared. He was running with all his speed. His mighty lungs were drawing in great gulps of breath, his feet were pounding tirelessly.

"He escaped," reported the man who had fired the automatic rifle.

"Fool!" The general's face was livid. He swung a fist, knocked the man to the ground. "You know what happens to men who fail! You know what The Leader does!"

The man on the ground groveled. His face became a pasty color. His eyes rolled wildly. "The—the hand of death!" he half screamed. "Don't let it get me!"

The general's eyes were scornful. "You deserve to die. Too much is at stake to permit errors. But this time I shall let you live. I can stop that pig of a runner before he gets word to Doc Savage."

Bodies of the slain guards were lying on all sides. Some were horribly mutilated by lead. Of all who had been alive only five minutes before, only Zum still lived. The vultures were swooping low.

The general paid no attention to the bodies. Callously, he stepped on them, as he walked toward the still-trembling, frightened donkeys. His men, also, had leaped toward those donkeys. With anxious, feverish hands they were tearing loose the covering on the packs the donkeys carried.

"Gold!" one breathed softly.

"Much gold!" said a second.

"Retie those packs!" snapped the general. His lips were working with quick anger. "This is only a drop in the bucket compared with what we will have later."

UNWILLINGLY, the covers were restored. The khaki-clad men looked at the packs with greedy, cunning eyes.

"This must be taken to Blanco Grande. You shall be its escort. Do not try to escape with it!" the general went on harshly.

One of the men shivered slightly. Escape! That would be impossible! Well he remembered the scarred, evil shape of the mountainous country over which they had been flown to reach this point of ambush. And they had dropped from those planes by parachute. There was no way of returning except to walk. They could have walked to this destination, but that would have meant loss of time. Other troops of gold-hungry men would meet them when they left the mountains.

The men had to do as they were ordered.

"This will be a blow to Doc Savage," the general's aide said craftily. "Are you not afraid?"

The general sneered. "Why be afraid of him?"

"But I have heard of many marvelous exploits of his," said the aide. "He is dangerous to evildoers. He has done almost uncanny things."

For a moment, a faint flicker of worry passed over the general's hard face. Then it was gone. "Do not worry," he jeered. "The Leader knows how to handle him. Besides, Doc Savage will know nothing of this—until it is too late."

"And when will that be?" There was a cunning, shrewd look in the aide's eyes.

"When we have launched our plans. When the entire world is rocked. When power such as men seldom dreamed of—" The general broke off. One hand strayed to the heavy gun at one hip.

"It could not be that you desire too much information, that you are a spy, could it, *mi amigo?*" he queried softly.

The aide took a step back. "No—no!" he cried. "I am just naturally curious. That is all."

"Curious!" A peculiar expression flared in the general's glacier-cold eyes. The gun came to his hand, lifted. "We do not encourage curiosity in our ranks, *mi amigo.*"

The other jumped back, turned to run.

*Blam!*

The general's gun spoke once. A section of the other's skull vanished. He was dead.

"I think you were not a spy, and that you were just curious," the general said. "However"—he whirled on the other khaki-clad men—"let that be a warning. You will take my orders. You will be paid in gold—as long as you obey those orders. You will be paid in bullets if you become curious. In bullets by me, or paid by The Leader in another way."

The khaki-clad men were silent. They had heard how "The Leader" paid. Hard-bitten, vicious as they were, they showed fear.

"Now take the gold in. I have a plane waiting for me near here. I fly back to Blanco Grande. The man who escaped must be stopped at all costs. No word goes to Doc Savage."

ZUM didn't know about the plane. He did know that no one could catch him on foot. Through winding canyons and deep gorges he ran at a steady, tireless pace. His feet ate up the miles.

Zum's heart was sad. Many of his friends had died in that murderous ambush. Hope of seeing those murderers brought to justice was one of the things that spurred him on. For he knew Doc Savage would act.

The gold that had been stolen had been on its way to Doc Savage. The men who had been guarding it were Mayans. All the world knew of Doc Savage and his men, and of their unceasing fight on evil. Until now, few had known where the money came from that financed that fight.

It really was a legacy left Doc by his father. It came from the Valley of the Vanished, where the bronze man had found pure-blooded Mayans, long lost from the outside world.

When Doc had left the Valley of the Vanished, he had arranged with King Chaac, chief of the

Mayans, to listen in on a radio on every seventh day. When his funds ran low, Doc would send a call for gold. Mayans would take it to Blanco Grande, the capital of Hidalgo, where the president, Carlos Avispa, would see that it was sent on to Doc.

Dusk was falling as Zum came in sight of Blanco Grande. The mountains long since had been left behind. Zum's pace had slowed. He was weary. His face bore long lines of strain.

But steadily he went on, entered the narrow streets of the capital of Hidalgo. Zum had been there before with gold trains for Doc. He knew where the radio towers were. He knew that in some way it was possible to send messages from there that would reach Doc Savage. He turned that way.

Had he not been so weary, Zum might have noticed the unusual activity in the ordinarily sleepy Central American city. Many soldiers were about. They were fully armed and in small detachments, moving with evident purpose.

Zum did not notice. He had only one thought, only one driving motive: He alone was alive to let Doc Savage know what had occurred. He intended to fulfill that trust.

A LONE operator was on duty in the shack beneath the radio towers. He had difficulty in understanding what Zum was saying. The Mayan was breathing hard, his words came in gasps. His Spanish was not good.

"Señor Clark Savage!" Zum blurted at last.

The operator understood that. His eyes became wide. He had heard of Doc Savage.

"Gold stolen! Mayans killed!" Zum panted. "Send message!"

The operator stood as if paralyzed for a moment, his brain trying to digest what he had heard.

*Blam!*

A pistol shot came loudly. Zum fell to the floor, twitching. A short, heavyset man with glacier-cold eyes and wearing a general's uniform stepped into the radio shack, gun in hand.

"Don't send that message!" he ordered crisply.

"But—but—" The operator's mouth dropped. "It—it's to Doc Savage, general. I—I've got to send it."

His voice ended almost in a scream at what he saw in the general's face. He made a dive for the radio key.

The gun came up. Once again it spoke. The operator died, the radio key untouched.

A faint grin cut the general's face. He patted the gun in his hand.

"Unless Doc Savage is a clairvoyant, I do not think he will ever receive that message," he said dryly. "And he couldn't hear those shots in New York."

Two men came in then at the general's barked command and gathered up the dead bodies and wiped up the blood. Some might wonder what had happened to the radio operator that he should disappear. But none would ever know just what had taken place. It would remain a mystery.

## Chapter II
### A PLEA FOR HELP

FEW sounds penetrated to Doc Savage's office on the eighty-sixth floor of one of Manhattan's skyscrapers. That office might have been in a world by itself, far aloft, with view unhindered by surrounding structures. But there was a curious, strained tension in that office.

"You've got to help, Mr. Savage. No one but you can do so. For you to refuse may mean unreckoned tragedy."

The speaker's voice was urgent, pleading. A tall man, he was dressed entirely in black except for a brilliant, white shirt. His eyes and hair were black, but his thin, mobile face detracted from the somberness of his costume.

"Already there have been riots, some indication of what is afoot," he went on quickly. "I am sure the peace of the world is at stake, perhaps the fate of the world as well. You must act!"

His black eyes flashed entreatingly to the man seated behind the only desk in the room.

That man stirred slightly. He was a big man, but did not show it. He was so well put together that the impression was not of bigness, but of power. His face and hands were the color of golden bronze—a bronze that exactly matched the color of his hair.

But it was his eyes that held the attention of his visitor. They were like pools of flake gold. They were penetrating, with an almost hypnotic influence.

"What definite information have you that such a plot exists, Baron Vardon?" Doc Savage asked. His voice was low, but it had a peculiar timbre, one that made it carry clearly and distinctly.

The black-clad man sat more erect in his chair. His fingers toyed with his black felt hat.

"As I explained, I am on the League of Nations staff. We receive much information that is not made known to the general public—information that comes to us from all our member States. Recently, we have heard much of a mysterious man known only as The Leader. Who or what he is, we do not know. But of his actions we know much."

Baron Vardon paused, frowned as if collecting his thoughts.

"We know that a skeleton organization of well-trained fighting men is being organized in every country in the world. Already, there have been a few outbreaks. You remember the recent ones in China, Africa and South America. Those were merely tests of power. The big coup is still to come. It awaits some signal. What this signal is, we also do not know."

"And just what do you wish me to do?" the bronze man asked.

"We are convinced that the headquarters of this mysterious Leader is somewhere in Switzerland. As a League of Nations representative, I am empowered to ask you to go to Europe, find that man and block his plans."

"Seems like quite an undertaking to me," a third voice put in unexpectedly.

The speaker was sitting far back in one corner. A thin, not very tall man, he was pulling absently at an ear that was much too big. His complexion was sallow and unhealthy-looking. He appeared a physical weakling.

Only those who had tangled with Major Thomas J. Roberts, better known as "Long Tom," knew what an error that was. Nor did his appearance indicate that he really was one of the world's most famous electrical engineers.

DOC'S fingers played a rapid tattoo on the top of the desk. His flake gold eyes surveyed Baron Vardon.

"A coup of such magnitude as you suggest would be difficult," the bronze man said.

"Practically impossible, I'd say," drawled Long Tom. Still tugging at his ear, he came to his feet slowly and sauntered from the room.

"I assure you this is not only possible, but so," Baron Vardon said earnestly. "And whoever The Leader is, he rules by fear. We have had reports he kills by a hand of death. Men who have seen victims of the hand of death say bloody fingers and palm appear on the neck. The features contort, horribly—"

Doc lifted one hand suddenly. A faint red light had appeared on a big panel at one side of the room.

"Anyone know you came to New York, Baron Vardon?" the bronze man asked quietly.

His black-clad visitor started, his eyes receded in his thin face. "N-no. But why?"

"Several men are trying to break into this office," Doc responded softly.

"But they can't get in, can they? I'm safe, am I not?" Baron Vardon's voice was hoarse, his features twisted with quick fear.

"No, they cannot get in unless I wish them to," said Doc. "But I believe we should see whom we are opposing. Just sit quietly. I am going to release the doors." The bronze man moved a foot on one spot on the floor.

Five men were in the hallway. One was working on the lock of a door which bore the sign: "Clark Savage, Jr." The others carried businesslike automatics. Their faces were hard and weather-beaten.

"Speed it up! Get that door open!" one of them barked. The lock-picker snarled in reply.

Then an amazing thing happened!

The door opened of its own accord. On either side of it panels also slid open. A gap fully twenty feet wide was created in the office wall.

And inside, apparently rushing forward, appeared an entire company of armed men. They carried submachine guns. Their faces were horrible grimaces. They seemed to be leaping from behind shell-torn trees and out of huge shell-holes.

A yell of terror and horror came from the five attackers in the hall. One threw up his gun, fired, then turned to run. Three of his companions also started to take to their heels.

"Halt!" The leader roared the order. His own eyes were gazing wildly. He was making an apparent effort to keep his courage. Then his eyes became normal.

"Stop, you fools!" he bellowed. "It's a trick! There are no men there! See, they're not moving forward at all!"

The running gunmen stopped and looked back. Even as they looked, the scene changed.

The company of armed men faded. Gigantic seas took their place. Huge waves with white-topped spray appeared. The beat of surf came, low at first, then louder.

But no water splashed on the office floor.

The gunmen laughed, their nerves still jerking with their release from fear. Now they could all see it had been a trick. They did not know how they had been fooled; it was enough to know that they were not really facing a company of armed men. With cautious steps they moved into the room.

And now the waves began to disappear. The office itself came into view. At one side was seated a man dressed in black. Behind a desk sat Doc Savage.

"You wished to see me, gentlemen?" the bronze man asked.

Four pistols came up as one. Four bullets tore toward the bronze man. Doc Savage slumped. His head went down on his desk. Then those weapons were turned toward Baron Vardon. Again a hail of death poured out.

"Run! Run for your lives!"

The four gunmen turned with sudden fear. The cry had come from behind them, where their leader stood. The men took one look and then obeyed. They dived frantically backward.

For the door and the panels on either side were closing. Frantically, the gang chief threw his weight against one of those panels, tried to hold it back. The panel moved on.

Shrill screams of terror came from the four men inside. Desperately, they threw themselves through the opening. The shoe of one was caught. The heel was nipped off as neatly as if by a sharp knife.

"Let's get out of here, that was too close," their leader rasped. He was breathing heavily. "Another moment and we'd have been trapped in there. And even if we did get Doc Savage, his men are still alive. They would have killed us."

DOC SAVAGE lifted his head, smiled at Baron Vardon. "Professional soldiers of fortune from their appearance. Would you not say so, Baron Vardon?"

The baron's face was a startling white in contrast to his black clothes. Nervously, he pulled a handkerchief from a pocket, wiped his brow.

"I—I guess so," he breathed. "But—but, I still can't understand why we're still alive."

"It is too bad they discovered the doors closing so soon," the bronze man went on, apparently unheeding the other's remark. "Another moment and they would have been caught, then they could have been questioned at leisure."

"But—but they had guns. They surely would have killed us, had they remained," exclaimed Baron Vardon.

"No," Doc Savage corrected. "I do not believe they would. You see, they merely thought they saw us. When I pressed my foot on a certain spot on this floor, I opened the doors, and bulletproof mirrors dropped. You have seen the childish tricks with mirrors used at amusement parks, where a person would appear without a body. This was on the same order. In addition, the mirrors were of a type which permitted us to see through from this side, but prevented them from seeing us."

"And—and I—" Baron Vardon gulped. "I suppose they saw something that frightened them at first. That was it."

"Yes. Merely some motion pictures projected against the mirrors, with a few added sound effects. Sometimes the sight of those pictures suffice to frighten away intruders. These fellows were of sterner stuff."

Baron Vardon swallowed hard, and an admiring grin appeared on his face.

"It was wonderful," he said. Then his expression changed, became serious. "But you see, this attack alone proves that we are up against something desperate. It would have to be if hired gunmen were sent all the way from Switzerland to kill you, and just because I am asking your aid. You must help us!"

"I think it might be interesting at that, Doc."

Baron Vardon glanced up swiftly. Long Tom had returned to the room. His thin, unhealthy-appearing face was blank of all expression, but one big ear wiggled slightly as he looked at the bronze man.

Doc Savage's flake gold eyes looked long and hard at Baron Vardon. "We never refuse help where we may assist in any way to correct injustice, or to prevent evil," he said quietly. "We will undertake the task, Baron Vardon."

Emotion twisted the baron's mobile face. His features came alive. He leaped to his feet, raced forward and grabbed Doc's hand, shook it hard.

"I am delighted. I had hoped, of course, for your help. But to hear you give me your promise makes my trip really worth while. You will leave at once for Switzerland?"

"We will start our search for The Leader as soon as possible," the bronze man said.

"Good! Get in touch with me at my hotel if I may assist you in any way." The baron turned to leave, hesitated at the door, his face becoming solemn. "But be careful. I have heard much of this hand of death. I will not rest easily until I know you have succeeded."

The door closed behind Baron Vardon.

"He's O. K., Doc," Long Tom said. "I checked with Geneva. He's an accredited representative, and was sent here to contact you. Funny, I had him figured out as a phony."

The electrical wizard pulled one lobe of his oversized ear thoughtfully. "When you tapped that code in Mayan for me to check on him, I thought you believed him a fake, also," he added.

"I do not care to embarrass guests," the bronze man said. "Baron Vardon might have understood the code had it been in English."

Long Tom looked up sharply. "And by the way, Doc. Isn't it time to be hearing from Blanco Grande? Shouldn't another gold shipment be on its way?"

"I expect such a message at any time. Probably we—"

The bronze man broke off suddenly. A scream of dreadful agony, of pain and knowledge of death, penetrated the office walls. It was a thin cry, high-pitched. It came from the hallway.

LONG TOM moved fast. He appeared slow beside the bronze man. Almost before the electrical engineer had unlimbered his long legs, Doc Savage was out from behind his desk, had reached the door. He moved with the smooth, unbelievable speed of a man in the perfection of physical condition.

The office door came open. Doc Savage leaped

into the hallway, knelt beside a body that lay there. A low, trilling sound seemed to fill the air. It appeared to come from no one spot, yet from everywhere. It was a strange, eerie thing.

Long Tom hurtled over the bronze man. He understood what that trilling sound was. It came unconsciously from the lips of Doc Savage when he was either surprised or sounding a warning.

The thin electrical wizard did not halt. Whatever had happened to that limp figure on the floor, he knew Doc could take care of it much better than he could.

He glanced once at the elevator indicator, saw no change was within six floors of them, then his thin legs darted like pistons as he raced toward the end of the hallway and started down the stairs.

It was five minutes before Long Tom returned. His unhealthy-appearing face wore a look of chagrin. He was breathing heavily.

"No one in sight," he said, his tone filled with disappointment.

Doc was still kneeling beside the fallen figure. The bronze man had a physician's kit beside him.

"Adrenaline did not work. No restorative I had succeeded," the bronze man said.

Long Tom looked down. The fallen figure was that of a boy. He wore a messenger's outfit. His visored cap lay upside down on the floor. Inside it was a yellow envelope.

Then Long Tom's eyes opened and he whistled slightly. On the boy's neck, growing more clear with each passing instant, was the shape of a hand. It was a hand of blood—blood that came from the boy!

"The hand of death," Long Tom grated.

Doc Savage rose to his feet slowly. His flake gold eyes were sad. It was seldom that his astounding knowledge of medicine failed to save a life.

Carefully, he opened the envelope that had been in the messenger boy's cap. Again came that low, trilling sound.

"What is it?" Long Tom asked swiftly.

Silently, the bronze man handed him the message. It read:

GOLD HAS ARRIVED OKAY STOP WILL SHIP TO YOU TOMORROW  CARLOS AVISPA

## Chapter III
### DEATH STRIKES

DOC SAVAGE stood motionless, his eyes riveted on the message in his hand. Abruptly he turned, strode into the office.

Long Tom, his mushroom complexion a blank, followed him. Doc's silence had indicated there was something peculiar about that message. What it was the bronze man had seen, Long Tom didn't know. And he knew that he wouldn't find out until Doc had proved himself right or wrong.

The bronze giant went quickly to the laboratory. First, he treated the message and the envelope with his own development of Flemming's solution. He put it on an automatic drier and then dipped it in a square container of dye.

Long Tom knew Doc was using the most modern method of developing fingerprints. Prints undetectable under ordinary methods stood out like bold landmarks with this new treatment.

Doc placed the paper under an ultraviolet lamp. The body of the papers fluoresced with a brilliant, blue-green luminosity. Only two fingerprints were on it. They stood out stark and black.

"Those are mine," the bronze man clipped. "There is no other print on either the envelope or the message. And the boy did not have any gloves."

"Then—" Long Tom began.

"The message was switched." Doc said flatly. "Whatever *did* happen to that gold shipment, someone is trying to keep us from finding out."

Long Tom opened his mouth to speak. He stopped. A low whine and a *swish* of air told him that the private, high-speed elevator was soaring up from the basement garage.

No one but Doc and his aides were supposed to know the existence of that private lift. It could shoot upward, as if flung by a catapult, and dropped like a plummet. It took both experience and fortitude to ride in it at all.

No one else was supposed to know of it—but attacks on the bronze man and his aides came always from places least expected. Neither Doc nor Long Tom said a word.

They heard the automatic doors open. Then there was a crash of glass; a heavy body fell on the floor. Low, angry mutterings reached their ears; then there was silence. The only sound that came was a stealthy shuffling of footsteps.

LONG TOM reached quickly into a desk drawer and took out a weapon that looked like an oversized pistol. It was equipped with a large ammo drum. It was one of Doc's superfiring machine-pistols, twice as fast and deadlier than a machine gun.

Doc Savage did not move a muscle. His bronze face was expressionless.

Slowly, Long Tom approached the door to the corridor. Then he stopped; his jaw dropped, and a look of supreme disgust spread over his face.

He saw the immense back of the closest thing to a gorilla that could come in human form. Long, red-tufted arms dangled almost to the floor. The huge human swayed from side to side. A nubbin of a head was almost completely sunk in the huge shoulders. More red, simian hair came out from the head and neck.

A baffled, childlike muttering came from the huge man as he backed up. In front of him, one hand raised behind him, the other extended confidently with a vicious-looking sword, was an immaculately clad and dapper figure. With a handkerchief peeking from his breast pocket at just the proper angle, a spotless, pearl-gray hat on his head, the man danced forward with the agility of a fencer.

In spite of his slender, foppish attire, he gave every indication that he was about to commit a highly pleasurable murder.

"I'll tear that danged sword cane to pieces," the hairy one complained, in a voice that would have better befitted an immature youth, "then I'll tear you apart, you animated writ of hocus-pocus!"

"Try it, you hairy vacuum!" Brigadier General Theodore Marley Brooks advised the apelike one. "Destroy my choice presents, will you? I'll run this through your gullet and hang you up on the wall!"

"Cut it!" Long Tom's voice rapped out. "Things are happening."

The apelike one turned around. It was odd to see a face like his look so plaintive. It was probably one of the homeliest faces in existence. His little eyes were nearly invisible, so deeply were they sunk in their pits of gristle.

This was Lieutenant Colonel Andrew Blodgett Mayfair, probably one of the greatest living chemists in the world. He was a Houdini of the test tubes. His friends knew him as "Monk." No other name would have been fitting.

"That danged shyster bought a statue of an ape and had my name engraved on it," he complained. "Then he had the crust to make me a present of it. I smashed it right here. And I'm going to grind him into hamburger!"

Then Monk saw the body of the messenger boy. His expression changed. "Trouble," he exclaimed. "Do you suppose—"

The dapper figure, better known as "Ham," sheathed his sword cane with one quick motion. Together, they whirled and darted into the office.

Monk and Ham quarreled continually. No insult was quite enough for one to heap on the other. But either would have gladly given his life to save the other. And both would have died for Doc Savage.

Almost running, the two raced to the room where Doc Savage stood waiting for them. Monk breathed an inaudible sigh of relief at the sight of the bronze man.

Ham was less demonstrative. One of the shrewdest legal lights that ever came from Harvard, he was trained to hide his feelings.

Doc Savage smiled slightly. He had seen the tableau in the hallway from where he had stood inside. An intricate system of mirrors enabled him to watch almost every part of his domain from any other point, while hidden microphones enabled him to listen to the conversation.

"I am afraid great danger may be threatening Hidalgo," he said softly.

A howl of rage and excitement burst from Monk. He fairly danced up and down.

"What are we waiting for? Let's go!" he bellowed plaintively.

"Still thinking of that good-looking princess down there?" Ham asked sarcastically.

Monk blushed.

"We all know that without Hidalgo we couldn't carry on the work we've sworn to do," Doc went on calmly. "And not only that, but we owe a debt to both the citizens of the republic and the Mayans to protect them from trouble."

"Well, then—" Monk blinked.

"I have accepted another task," Doc explained quietly.

For an instant there was silence. Yet that silence was indicative of the respect his aides held for their bronze chief. Their looks were not questioning. They waited merely for orders.

In crisp tones, Doc explained to Monk and Ham what had happened, what Baron Vardon had told them.

"I don't like that guy's looks," Long Tom gulped. "Even if he is from the League of Nations, he looked phony to me. And he went out of here just before this messenger boy came in."

Bristles seemed to rise on the back of Monk's neck. The chemist even preferred fighting to annoying Ham. And that was saying a lot.

"Let's go get him!" he howled. "Any guy that would kill a kid like that—" He waved his arms and started for the door. Doc's low voice stopped him.

"We must know more than we do now before we throw suspicion on anyone," he admonished. "But I think we had all better call on the baron. He may have seen someone in the hall as he left here and can give us a clue to the murderer."

Swiftly, the four went toward the corridor. As they opened the door, elevators stopped at the far end of the hallway. A group of blue-clad policemen poured out.

"We heard a guy had been killed!" bellowed one in a captain's uniform. "What is it all about?"

Long Tom stepped forward, as if to explain. A bronze hand shot out, jerked him back.

"Look out! Duck for cover!" the bronze man cried.

His warning came just in time. For strange things were happening.

TO Doc's aides, the sudden arrival of an army of cops had not seemed suspicious. They had forgotten that no such force would be sent to investigate an ordinary murder. And they had forgotten, also, that the murder of the messenger boy had not been reported. No one knew of it except themselves— and the slayer.

The bronze man had not forgotten. His crisp order came just as the man in the captain's uniform made a grab for an object in a coat pocket. One hand went back, came forward with an overhand motion. What he threw looked like a tear-gas bomb.

Long Tom had already darted back inside the door. Monk and Ham instinctively grabbed handkerchiefs to place over their noses as they, too, jumped back.

But the keen, flake gold eyes of Doc Savage had seen something the others had missed.

Protruding from the body of the thing speeding through the air toward them were rows of tiny spikes. Those spikes made the object look something like a prickly pear.

Every one of those tiny spikes was a plunger. Should any one of the scores of spikes on the side of that bomb touch even the slightest projection, the plunger would set off a thermite compound that would tear a score of men to tiny bits!

And now that bomb was almost upon them, spinning and turning. The fake cops were racing backward down the hallway, evil grins of anticipation on their faces.

Doc Savage stood feet apart, one hand in the air. The thumb and middle finger were separated. It looked as if he were trying to talk the deaf and dumb language. Then those two fingers snapped onto the whistling bomb with a speed that defied detection.

The fingers closed *between* the tiny plungers!

But the body of the bomb was slippery; it had been greased just to prevent any such miraculous catching. Doc couldn't hold it steady. Already, it was slipping. If he reached with his other hand he would be sure to snap a spike, explode it in his fists.

So the bronze man did the only other thing he could do. He yelled a warning, hurled it from him, straight back where it had come from.

The phony cops had paused at the end of the hallway. They had stood rooted to watch the culmination of their evil work. But they didn't stand there after Doc let out that yell.

Scrambling, screaming, falling over each other in their frantic desire to get away, they poured down the stairs.

Then the thermite bomb landed. There was a blinding flash, a searing heat and a detonation that knocked Doc and his three aides flat on the ground.

Masonry had been torn from the floor and from the sides of the hallway. The entrance to the stairs was blocked. From far down those stairs yells could still be heard, as the fake cops raced for safety like they had never run before.

Doc picked himself up and looked at his aides. They were bruised a bit, but otherwise unhurt.

"The real police will now be here shortly. Stay here and explain to them," Doc instructed Long Tom. "Monk and Ham will come with me."

With swift strides, the bronze man led the way to his private, high-speed elevator.

THE Hotel Royale, where Baron Vardon was stopping, was one of the more pretentious of Manhattan's hostelries. It ran more to the ornate than suited the average visitor, but it was always filled.

Monk and Ham automatically dropped back a few paces and separated as they strode through the lobby. That was a matter of habit, a practiced system. If trouble occurred, they were less vulnerable, more ready for effective action than if they were packed together.

Monk and Ham scrutinized faces closely, mentally catalogued types, ran experienced eyes up and down figures for suspicious bulges in their clothing.

Two men stood together at one side, hands thrust into their pockets. One spoke out of a corner of his mouth to the other. Both looked hard at Doc and his aides.

At the desk, a seedy, long-haired man argued violently with the hotel clerk. His shiny frock coat was green with age. Under an arm, he held a battered violin case. In a foreign accent that somehow sounded counterfeit, he loudly insisted that there *must* be some mail for him.

It seemed to Ham that the two shifty-eyed men in the corner glanced at him and at the violin case. But Ham couldn't be sure. It might be his imagination.

Doc had the baron's suite number. He didn't bother with the clerk, but went straight to the elevator.

"Twelve," he clipped. The lift rose.

Baron Vardon's suite was 1208. Doc Savage knocked softly on the door. There was no reply. He knocked again. The door yielded under the slight vibration.

Monk's bulgy muscles swelled under his coat. Ham swung his sword cane swiftly. Doc opened the door wide.

A dim tablelamp gave the only light. Curtains in the room had been drawn. But that tablelamp was sufficient.

Directly before them, on the floor, were a pair of expensively shod feet. Above the feet came well-creased trousers and a dinner jacket, then the face of Baron Vardon.

The diplomat was twisted in an unnatural position on his back. His lips were contorted into a grimace of horror.

But it was the neck that held the attention of the three who had walked into the room.

Upon that neck was the red outline of a hand. It seemed to be growing brighter every instant.

"The hand of death!" Ham gasped. "It has struck again!"

## Chapter IV
## INTO A TRAP

DOC stepped quickly past the body on the floor, leaped to a door at one side of the room. He flung it open and found only an empty bathroom. He looked at the room's one large window, pulled back the shades.

Outside was a narrow airshaft court, scarcely twenty feet square. Another door gave onto the bedroom of the suite. Apparently no one was there.

Monk waddled about the room like some huge anthropoid, sniffing on a trail. The hairy man's eyes lighted on a great wardrobe trunk in one corner of the room. It was a bigger trunk than he had ever seen before. He moved toward it.

And the trunk erupted!

From a horizontal slit near the top of the trunk, a long, thin muzzle was jabbed. It swept the entire room.

*Br-r-r-r-r-r!*

The machine gun roared in a staccato crescendo of death; .45 caliber slugs sliced through the room like a solid metal knife, just above waist height.

That terrific blast should have killed everyone in the room. It didn't. The killer within the trunk thought at first he was dreaming. That dream slowly turned into an awful nightmare.

Growling, long arms outstretched, Monk walked straight into the hail of lead like an avenging Juggernaut. Fingers that could bend a silver dollar double gripped the edges of the trunk. The muzzle of the gun swung squarely toward his stomach.

With a bellow of rage, Monk tore the top of the trunk open. A mean, ratty face was there. But there was a horror and disbelief on it, now. The killer forgot all about his Tommy gun. Here was a man who absorbed Tommy slugs as casually as he would take a shower!

The killer screamed, leaped from his little fortress. Red eyes darted back and forth. Doc and Ham were between him and the door. Monk took one step forward, a look on his face that would have made a tiger shrink.

The thug's voice ended in a gurgle. He ran blindly, crashed into a window. The sill struck him just above the knees. Before he could stop he had soared on out into space. A cry that was scarcely human came from his lips. That cry ended abruptly as he hit the bottom of the airshaft, twelve stories below.

There was a moment of silence. Then a low, grating voice broke in.

"I will shoot for the head, my friends," it said. "I know you wear union suits of chain metal that will defy machinegun slugs. But the bones in your head are not that strong."

The three men whirled. There in the doorway crouched the musical-appearing fellow who had been shouting for his mail in the lobby downstairs.

There was no artistic expression on his face now. The wig of long hair was pushed askew on his forehead. A mirthless grin was on his face. A businesslike machine gun had emerged from the violin case.

That gun swung up, head high; a grimy finger tightened on the trigger.

And then Doc Savage moved. He moved like chain lightning. Like a bronze flash he dived across the room. His arms swept out.

The bronze man had been too far away to try and nail the gunner. He didn't try. His arms scooped up Ham and Monk, lifted each as if they were little children. In the same fraction of an instant he swung, head low, head away from the killer.

*Br-r-r-r-r-r!*

Slugs bounced off Doc's back as he covered the length of the room in two quick leaps. Crouched, holding his aides so their heads were out of the direct line of fire, he was safe for the moment from the deadly bullets.

But the room was small. It was an easy matter for the killer to maneuver into a better firing position.

And he did. But it didn't do him any good.

Without slackening his stride, his two aides held firmly, Doc Savage leaped through the window. On the concrete, far below them, lay the crushed body of the first killer.

THE homely face of Monk wore an expression of blissful unconcern as he felt himself catapulted into the airshaft. Ham, likewise, looked as if he were thinking about some abstruse point of law that he might argue before the Supreme Court.

Both of Doc's hands were occupied holding Monk and Ham. He doubled up like a contortionist in the air. His teeth closed on a tiny button on his vest. Then his head snapped erect. There was a *swish,* a sudden tugging, and their plunging drop was checked to a gentle fall.

Monk looked up above them critically. It was the first time he had seen this experiment. He had often thought of the possibilities of a special parachute built for an airshaft. There was no reason, he had figured, why one of the proper size and shape couldn't be just as effective in a short drop as the plunger in a pump. There was little space for the fugitive air to escape.

But Monk had only *thought* about such a parachute. It had remained for Doc Savage to construct one.

They drifted gently to the bottom. The gangster up above could have shot them during the last few seconds of the fall. But when he first looked out the window, he was too amazed to move. By the time he poked his gun over the sill, there was nothing but an expanse of silk for a target.

**Without slackening his stride, his two aides held firmly, Doc Savage
leaped through the window.**

Doc and his aides on arriving at the bottom dove
through a doorway into the cellar of the hotel.

"That parachute was good, but I don't think you
gave it a real test, Doc," Monk argued as they
reached the street.

"What do you mean?" Ham asked suspiciously.

"Why, your head is so full of hot air, we could

'a' floated down just hanging on to you," Monk
chuckled gleefully.

Ham whirled, waved his sword cane angrily.
"We shouldn't have taken you, anyway!" he yelped.
"An ape like you should have been made to climb
down!"

Monk chuckled. Things were back to normal.

He became serious. "That seems to wash up Long Tom's theory that the baron was in on this," he grunted. "That is, unless he was double-crossed."

"We still must do what the baron asked," Doc Savage said quietly. "I gave my promise. You and Ham go to the hangar. Fuel the plane for a three thousand mile non-stop flight. I need several things from the office, and will bring Long Tom."

"We head for Switzerland?" Ham asked.

"We take the danger trail," the bronze man promised.

IF Doc could have seen the electrical wizard right then, he would have realized that danger had already arrived for Long Tom.

Behind the impersonal, mushroom-complexioned face of Long Tom was hidden real sympathy for those in need. That sympathy had gotten him into trouble before. But he couldn't help being the soul of generosity. He could never resist the plaintive pleading of beggars.

If someone had knocked on the door of the office laboratory, he might have been suspicious. But Long Tom was standing in the hallway just after the coroner's men had taken away the body of the dead messenger boy.

An aged and infirm step came down the stairs that led from the observation tower of the skyscraper. That was not unusual. It was one way that peddlers could get down through the building and canvass the offices.

The man was white-haired. His face was pinched and drawn, as if life had dealt harshly with him. He might have had a family to support, and selling pencils is not usually considered a quick way to riches.

The pencils were in a square box. Around them was a band blazoning a well-known make.

"Please, mister," the ancient said haltingly, "couldn't you use a few pencils?"

Long Tom hesitated, thrust his hand into a pocket. Then he remembered his wallet was in his coat pocket back in the office. He didn't have any change.

"Just a minute," he said, and opened the door.

It was only two steps to where his coat was hanging. Long Tom was a little surprised to see that the man had followed him in. But there was still that apologetic, suppliant look on his face. Long Tom reached out to take some of the pencils.

*Pfffft!*

A hissing sound came from a dozen little nozzles. Every pencil was a tiny hose from which came a jet of tear gas. Long Tom staggered back, blinded. Too late he realized he had been tricked.

The bent old man straightened. Sharp orders tumbled from his lips. There was a rush of feet from outside. A dozen dark figures swarmed through the door.

Long Tom, blinded though he was, plunged forward. The men quickly understood that his unhealthy appearance was no catalogue of his fighting ability. Three men went down, moaned on the floor.

But twelve against one are too many, particularly when that one cannot see. Long Tom's sight was slowly returning, but even that wasn't enough.

He flung two foes from him, staggered back. Four more gangsters bored in. The electrical wizard was driven back against a wall. Then a mighty fist sent him sagging to the floor. He landed on his back, hands outstretched. One slammed against the desk's baseboard.

Groggy and helpless, he was bound hand and foot and gagged.

THE phone jangled sharply.

The white-haired man who was no longer old seized it. At first he imitated Long Tom's voice. It was a surprisingly good imitation. Then his voice dropped back to normal.

"O. K.," he rapped. "He's got away with a lot of things. I don't see how he got out of the hotel. But he can't get out of this trap. We'll fill him so full of lead they can use him for an anchor."

The man clicked the receiver back on the hook and turned to the gangsters.

"The bronze man is in the elevator," he rasped. "Go to the stations appointed. Shoot for the head only!"

There came the sound of the high-speed elevator. Its meteoric ascension forced air whistling through the cracks of the door.

The elevator outside clicked to a stop. The automatic doors opened. Footsteps came toward the door. The white-haired leader glanced quickly at Long Tom, smiled in satisfaction.

Long Tom's expression showed he had recognized that tread.

The footsteps reached the door. Guns were pointing that way from all directions.

The door swung open. Long Tom held his breath. The white-haired man stopped smiling.

For the footsteps walked right into the center of the room. But no one was there!

Hair rose on the necks of the gangsters. Eyes seemed almost to pop from their heads. Some moistened dry lips. Others could only gape stupidly.

And the sounds went on!

The chair behind Doc's huge desk scraped back. There was a sighing, as if a huge bulk had dropped into the soft leather cushion. The seat of the chair sank.

Sweat was pouring now from a dozen faces. One gangster whipped a little paper from a pocket, sniffed the powdered contents up his nostrils. But the drug didn't seem to have any effect. He was still scared to death.

The white-haired man broke the spell with an effort. "Shoot, you idiots!" he screamed. "Shoot at that chair!"

The roaring of the guns sounded like a stepped-up Niagara. Acrid smoke filled the air. The chair behind the desk seemed to disintegrate. Lead literally tore it apart.

The silence that followed that burst of firing was like that in a courtroom following a verdict of death. Long Tom lay wide-eyed and motionless.

Then there was a low cough. It came from right above the shattered chair!

Then a memo pad on the big desk was riffled back.

"Long Tom," came Doc's voice from the chair, "when these persons have gone, I would like to talk to you about our plans."

THE gangsters stood frozen. If they had been frightened before, now they were actually oozing fear. Their features were chalk-white, their entire bodies shaking.

Through the door to the library came the shrill voice of Monk.

"You danged shyster!" he shouted. "As soon as we clean out this nest of gangsters, I'm going to take you apart, injunction by injunction!"

"Ha!" Ham's voice came sarcastically. "You're not any tougher than those twelve babies out there."

Two pairs of footsteps clattered into the room. But no one was visible.

One of the coke-fiend gangsters let out a scream.

"I've got 'em, I've got 'em!" he yelled. "Lemme go! I'm goin' straight to Bellevue!"

He dropped his Tommy gun and dived toward the door. It was the signal for a stampede. Overtensed nerves could stand no more. Rat-faced figures fought each other to get to the hallway, the white-haired leader among them. In the space of seconds, the office was cleared.

Then the elevator doors opened again. Doc Savage stepped out.

## Chapter V
## A WARNING

LONG TOM'S jaw sagged as Doc untied him. His eyes held a vacant look. His fingers played with a lobe of one oversized ear.

"I've seen you pull a lot of stuff, Doc, but how was that done?" he asked weakly.

"I caught your signal when you pressed the baseboard," the bronze man explained. "So I went to the room below, looked into the panoramic television in the ceiling, and saw the gang.

"The desk was wired to turn over a page of the memo pad. And the chair seat was wired to sag when I wanted it to. The rest—the sound effects—was done by microwaves and ventriloquism."

"Oh!" Long Tom's expression cleared. Then his face showed admiration. An electrical genius of no mean ability himself, those few words had been sufficient explanation.

"That's something new. I've been working on it, but never got so far. In other words, the micro radio waves hit the diaphragm of the telephone in whatever room you aimed them at, and reverted into sound, and by ventriloquism you make it appear—"

Doc nodded. "What happened?" he interrupted.

Long Tom explained swiftly and somewhat shamefacedly.

"Our opponent, whoever he is, not only has money and an exceedingly alert organization, but he must also have imagination and brains," the bronze man commented. "I believe Vardon was right. The stakes are high."

"So much the more reason for us to get to Europe in a hurry," the electrical wizard said glumly. "I suppose we'll have to stick our necks out again for some rough gang to take a crack at. I—"

The door burst open with the bang of a cannon. Ham bolted into the room. His usually immaculate attire was disheveled. He showed unusual excitement. He was waving a newspaper in one hand.

"Look! Look!" His words were wheezing gasps.

Long Tom craned his neck and moved forward. "Now, Ham, take it easy. Excitement is bad for your heart."

Ham thrust the paper at Doc. "This extra just hit the streets. I grabbed it and came on up. Monk went on to get the plane ready. Read this!"

Across the front of the newspaper were big headlines:

BIG REVOLT IN HILDALGO!
TROOPS STORM PALACE!

Only a few lines of reading matter were under the headlines. Evidently but little information had been received when the extra had been put to press.

"Hidalgo!" breathed Long Tom. "That must mean old Carlos Avispa is in danger. But what about the gold? Is that lost?"

THE bell of a telephone sounded. Doc lifted the receiver.

"Mister Savage? I am speaking for the secretary of state." The voice was smooth, almost regretful.

"Yes?"

"I am afraid the news we have for you may already be in the papers, but we wished to verify it before calling you."

"Thank you," said Doc. "And the message?"

"There has been an uprising in Hidalgo. Knowing your interests there, the secretary of state asked me to give you what facts we have."

"And those are?"

"Few, very few, I am sorry to say. We do know

there was a sudden uprising, seemingly by a major- ity of President Avispa's troops. What caused it, or why, I do not know. An attack is believed to have been launched on the palace. But all communica- tion was severed after we had received but one short bulletin. Whether the government of Hidalgo has been overthrown or not, we do not know."

"I see. I wish to thank you for calling." The bronze man spoke slowly.

The speaker at the other end of the line coughed slightly. "I—we—er—we realize, Mister Savage, that this may be a blow to you. President Avispa, we know, is a personal friend of yours. And we under- stand you have big interests there. But, ah—ah—"

"Yes?" Doc's voice did not raise, but there was a sudden firmness in its tone.

"Ah—well, the secretary asked me to remind you not to get into any entanglements with Hidalgo. United States citizens must not participate in the quarrels of other countries." He paused, then added: "I am sorry, sir."

Doc Savage hung up the receiver slowly.

"A FINE pickle!" raged Ham, after the bronze man had related the phone conversation. He paced to and fro rapidly. "Avispa and our gold in danger, and we must stand by—helpless!"

"There are many things to consider," Doc Savage reminded quietly. "The fact remains that much trouble has been, and will be, avoided with other countries if United States citizens minded their own business."

"Yes, it is justified, undoubtedly; but not in this case." Ham straightened, became Brigadier General Theodore Marley Brooks. He spoke in his best courtroom manner:

"But this situation is different, your hon—par- don, I mean Doc. If we went to Hidalgo it would not be to embroil our country in a private war. We would go merely as friends of the duly constituted authorities, to lend our advice and counsel—"

"And to do a little scrapping, if necessary," Long Tom interposed, with a sly grin.

"For all we know, President Avispa may be dead," Ham continued, with a stern glance at Long Tom. "The country may be in the hands of rebels. Our friends, the Mayans, may be endangered. We owe them a debt we can never repay. Besides—" The lawyer hesitated. "Incidentally, Doc, we were not told definitely that we couldn't go, were we?"

The bronze man shook his head, said, "No. I was merely reminded not to interfere with anything that might drag the United States into trouble with Hidalgo. We would experience no trouble from the law if we went to Hidalgo, provided we left before our passports to Hidalgo are suspended."

"But—but," sputtered Long Tom. "You told Baron Vardon we would go to Switzerland, that we would leave at once! Even if our sympathies are with President Avispa in Hidalgo, we cannot go there until that job is taken care of."

"No," contradicted Doc softly. "I did not promise that we would go to Switzerland at once." Light flamed in his flake gold eyes. "What I did say was that we would undertake at once the task Baron Vardon suggested. We will do that. But now, we will go to Hidalgo. I believe the uprising there has a definite connection with the plot Baron Vardon mentioned."

Ham's face shone with delight. "The attorney for the plaintiff wins his case," he beamed. "Of course, I'm sorry we will be there just as advisers and can't get into the fighting, but—"

He danced about, using his sword cane to spar with an imaginary enemy.

"Always thinking of fighting," Long Tom said disgustedly.

"Ham, you go on down to the plane, help Monk load," the bronze man put in. "You know the equip- ment we should have."

The dapper lawyer minced toward the door, still sparring with his cane. A broad smile was on his face.

"Long Tom, here are your instructions." Doc Savage spoke for some length. A look of bewilder- ment on the electrical genius' face gradually faded; his expression became eager and intent.

"That's good," he gulped at last. "We can't take any munitions except, of course, weapons to defend ourselves; but with this stuff—"

"It may come in handy," Doc agreed dryly.

Long Tom went to one of the big laboratory rooms that were included in the office suite. Doc turned to the radio room. The bronze man sat down before a large panel. He threw a switch and watched tubes slowly become warm.

"Renny and Johnny!" he said, his mouth close to a small microphone. His voice was unraised.

MORE than three thousand miles away, that voice came clearly from a small radio. Huge moun- tains reared on all sides. There was a tremendous cut through one of those mountains. Steam shovels were panting as they dug up tons of earth.

An enormous man, fully six feet four inches in height, was watching those steam shovels through half-closed eyes. As he watched, he opened and closed fists that were bony monstrosities. They appeared big enough to break doors. In fact, break- ing doors with those fists was one of the favorite occupations of their owner.

His face was severe, the mouth thin and tightly compressed. Even though his eyes showed pleasure in the scene he was witnessing, his features had a puritanical look.

A small native, his clothes mud-covered, panted up.

"Señor Colonel Renwick," he wheezed. "The black box, it speak!"

The big man's look of indifference vanished. Long legs taking gigantic strides, he jumped over boulders, cleared a sixteen-foot stream with scarcely a break in his pace.

He halted before a big boxlike tent. A small radio was sitting outside that tent. Beside it was a portable sending set.

"Renny speaking," he said clearly.

As "Renny" spoke, another tall man came running into view. But where Renny was heavy, this man was thin. He looked almost half-starved. Glasses were perched on his nose. His features were studious and intellectual.

Known wherever geologists and archaeologists gathered as William Harper Littlejohn, one of the most famous in his field, he was called "Johnny" by his friends.

"And this is Johnny elucidating," he said into the microphone.

"There is trouble in Hidalgo," came Doc's clear tones.

Renny's big frame jerked erect. Forgotten in a moment was the engineering project he was directing. That project was one that would add to his fame, but additional renown meant nothing compared to a call to action.

"You two being in South America, are much closer to the scene than we are in New York," Doc's voice went on. "By leaving within an hour, you should be able to fly to Hidalgo before dawn. Keep in touch with me by radio, and help President Avispa in every way possible."

"Boy, this sounds like action!" Renny chortled exultantly. "It's great!"

"Positively stupendous," agreed Johnny.

In New York, Doc turned away from the radio.

"All set," called Long Tom. "Let's go. Too bad Johnny and Renny will beat us to the scene, but they may leave something for us to do."

Long Tom might not have felt so certain Johnny and Renny would arrive first, or that everything was all set, had he been able to see through the ceiling.

A SMALL, dwarflike man, an evil grin on his face, was rapidly coiling a strand of wire back into a small briefcase in the room above. The wire was almost invisible. The microphone at the end was no larger than a dime.

"A marvelous invention, this," he chuckled without sound. "So the great Doc Savage has decided to interfere in affairs in Hidalgo? That will prove very interesting to The Leader, I am sure."

He took earphones from his head, placed them on top of the wire and the batteries the briefcase contained.

"And the great Doc Savage must be worried. He is calling in all his men to help."

The dwarf snorted with disgust. "Seems to me I read about the project Colonel Renwick is directing in South America. Littlejohn is making some archaeological surveys at the same place. It will be easy to discover just where."

Once more that evil grin crossed his wrinkled features. He moved noiselessly toward the door.

"Who can withstand The Leader? His organization is perfect. I do not believe that Colonel Renwick or William Harper Littlejohn will ever arrive in Hidalgo."

## Chapter VI
### DEATH CALLS

JOHNNY and Renny were troubled by no such doubts. Their movements were swift and assured.

They wasted no time on the tent. Growling, his puritanical face more stern than before, Renny threw clothes recklessly into a suitcase.

Johnny worked more deliberately, but almost as fast. He looked at some of his archaeological specimens with regret, but did not bother to pack them.

A youth wearing high leather puttees, military trousers and tropical hat, came toward them. His face wore a look of dismay.

"Colonel Renwick, what is the matter? Where are you going?"

Renny looked up impatiently, snapped the clasps on his suitcase. "Come on, Johnny, what are you killing time for!" he snapped.

"But—but you can't do this! You can't leave!" the youth exclaimed excitedly.

"Who says I can't?" roared Renny. "I am, ain't I? You're supposed to be an engineer, aren't you? You take charge. I'll be back—when you see me."

One huge fist reached out, yanked Johnny to his feet. "Come on!"

"You're a domineering, despotic, dyspeptic martinet," wailed Johnny. But he went along.

Two slender steel threads led down the mountainside. They vanished in the mists of clouds that hung far below the top of the mountain. They appeared tiny and fragile. Yet an open car was suspended from the upper thread.

This primitive elevator was used to bring material and men from the plains thousands of feet below to the summit. The lower thread acted as a brake, to keep the elevator from descending too fast.

Johnny and Renny leaped into the car. Renny reached over and released the brake. The effect was like that of a sudden, steep dive on a roller-coaster. Only this dive didn't stop in a second or two. It seemed to continue indefinitely.

The car rocketed downward. Johnny's mouth opened and closed as he tried to speak against the wind. He motioned for Renny to use the brake, to slow the speed of the car.

Renny grinned broadly. "Doc asked for speed, didn't he?" the big man shouted.

Johnny looked over the side. One hand was holding tight to the glasses on his nose. The other gripped frantically at one side of the car. His face suddenly went a pale, pasty color. He gulped.

Renny's face lost its grin. He reached for the brake, applied it hard. The speed of the car did not slacken. It increased.

Hunching his huge frame, Renny looked over the side. His face, too, went ashen.

The bottom steel thread had vanished. Somewhere, it had either broken or been cut. There was no way to stop the terrific speed of the car. It was hurtling downward at ever-increasing speed. There still were thousands of feet to go.

When the car reached the bottom, there would be one tremendous crash. Only pieces would ever be found of car and occupants.

Renny groaned, but not from fear.

"When we don't get there, Doc sure will think we've disobeyed orders!" he shouted.

DOC was having troubles of his own just then.

Even Ham's features were streaked with perspiration as the last of a long series of boxes and provisions were stored aboard a huge amphibian.

The plane rested on a slide at the end of a long warehouse. The name "Hidalgo Trading Co." was painted on that warehouse. It was inconspicuous-appearing from the outside. Inside, it appeared more like a transportation exhibit at Grand Central Palace.

A submarine was there; both swift scout and heavier passenger planes and an autogyro were stored, ready for immediate use. And hovering close to the top of the warehouse was a speedy, modern dirigible.

"Too bad we can't use the dirigible," Monk groaned, with a look aloft. His simian countenance appeared pained. The dirigible would be easier riding than the amphibian, but the hairy chemist knew there was no chance of using it. Where they were going they would be buffeted by wind currents that would tear apart even the strongest airship.

"All loaded, Doc," panted Long Tom. His complexion was yellow-colored.

Doc nodded, swung through the door at the rear of the amphibian, made his way to the controls. A moment later and four motors burst into speech.

On the water, the plane was clumsy-appearing. Its nose reared up. It was huge, with the long wings that meant tremendous lift, but with wings so angled that they signified speed as well.

Monk cast off the mooring ropes as Long Tom and Ham clambered aboard. The roar of the motors increased in pitch.

Far down the river, a launch was approaching. Spray curled, destroyer-fashion, from its bow. It was headed directly toward the Hidalgo Trading Co. warehouse.

Ham eased into the co-pilot's seat beside the bronze man. A carefully applied handkerchief restored his usual appearance of freshness. He glanced down the river.

"Visitors on the way, Doc," he said laconically.

Doc Savage revved each motor in turn. The amphibian moved out slowly, drifting with the current.

"I expected them," the bronze man said quietly.

The launch was close now. A gun could be seen on its bow. It was an efficient-appearing gun, quite large enough to destroy an amphibian. A man appeared from the cabin, waved his hand frantically.

Monk's face appeared suddenly in the pilot's compartment. He wore a worried look.

"Step on it, Doc!" he howled hoarsely. "They'll be on us in a minute!" Behind him was Long Tom. The electrical wizard's features also showed strain.

The bronze man pushed forward on the wheel, drew back the throttle. The amphibian leaped like a race horse from a starting stall.

A yell of dismay came from the launch. It was close enough to make out the features of the men aboard. A police lieutenant held a megaphone, bawled a frantic order.

"Hold it, Doc Savage! You can't take off now!"

For answer, Doc smiled. Once more he pressed forward on the wheel, pulled back the throttle. The amphibian shot ahead, then rose into the air like a graceful bird, circled the police launch.

Down below there was much confusion. The police lieutenant yelled again through the megaphone.

"Stop!" he bellowed. "Where are you going?"

His voice carried to the plane, which wasn't so high up.

"To Hidalgo, of course, you mug!" bellowed Monk. A delighted grin creased his homely features. "They can't stop us now!"

"No?" Ham turned a look of withering scorn on the hairy chemist. "You think they can't, you baboon! They couldn't, probably, if you had kept your mouth shut. Now—"

"What did I do?" Monk howled belligerently.

"Oh, nothing!" Sarcasm blistered from Ham's tongue. "Just nothing at all. Here we are up against a clever opponent who found out someway that we were not headed to Europe, but to Hidalgo, and tipped off the state department to get us stopped. Then what do you do but bellow out the truth!"

"Well, what of it?" Monk looked hurt. "We're in the air, aren't we? They can't stop us."

Ham's shoulders lifted in a long sigh. "I don't suppose it ever occurred to that simian brain of yours that there is an air division of the Coast Guard, did it? If they really want to stop us, they'll send a fast plane after us as soon as that copper reports. We couldn't get away then without a fight, and you know we couldn't fight."

Monk's big frame suddenly seemed to shrink. He did his best to hide his head. "I—I didn't think of that," he admitted sheepishly. "But if we don't get there, at least Renny and Johnny will."

RENNY and Johnny didn't think they would reach any place safely.

The car elevator was moving downward so rapidly that trees and rocks were only a blur on either side. The pulley on the steel cable overhead whined and shrilled like a banshee.

Johnny's eyes watered even behind his glasses. His hat whipped off. When he opened his mouth to yell, the wind tore the sound away so swiftly it could not be heard.

Renny stood fully erect in the car. His huge figure seemed unaffected by the tremendous pressure of the wind. His enormous arms were outstretched, so that the long fingers of his powerful fists grasped each side of the car.

He was looking over the side, his gaze placid and unworried.

"Always wanted to make a trip this fast sometime!" he shouted.

Johnny caught the words only faintly. "Inexplicable exhibitionism of juvenile philosophy!" he screeched.

The car sagged dangerously close to high knolls at times. Again, it was a hundred feet in the air. Always there was the danger it would overturn, would spill its occupants to instant death.

And death could not be long delayed. The bottom of the mountain could not be far away.

Renny appeared to sigh deeply. He loosed the grip of one huge paw, reached down in the bottom of the car. He lifted up a small derrick hook. There was a rope attached to the hook.

The studious features of Johnny brightened as he saw Renny lean over a side of the car. The big engineer dropped the hook. His attitude was that of a man about to try for a trout.

The car dipped toward a knoll. Renny jerked on the rope. His face changed expression slightly as the car again rocketed high in the air.

"Missed!" he shouted.

Trees were bigger now, on each side. They grow bigger lower down on the mountains, where they can get more oxygen. And that meant the end of the elevator ride was very close.

Another knoll approached. Renny's features set hard. His thin mouth was more severe and grim than usual. It was compressed so tightly he seemed to have no lips at all.

Once more his enormous arms swung out, down, then up.

Johnny didn't need to hear his yell. He saw Renny's mouth open, saw the expression in his eyes.

Without hesitation, Johnny loosed his grip on the sides of the car, threw himself to the bottom.

A thin, piercing wail cut the air. It grew louder. It sounded as if thousands of saws were rasping against metal.

Renny's shirt split with the strain. Muscles knotted in big bunches. Perspiration poured from his face. A small, white streak of light came into view. It was a streak that cut across directly above the level of the car top. The derrick hook appeared to be holding that light in place.

Johnny's arms reached up, caught hold of the rope attached to the hook. He braced his feet against the side of the car, poured all his strength into holding that streak of light motionless.

A huge clasp was at the front of the car. It was used to hold the car in place at its terminal.

Now, Renny moved that clasp around, screwed it down slowly on the streak of light.

THE sound of buzz saws increased. Smoke curled up from about the clasp. The streak of light appeared to dance.

Then it became apparent what that streak of light was. It was the lower end of the two wires upon which the elevator depended—the wire that had been cut.

It was moving upward as fast as the car was traveling downward. Loose and uncontrolled, it would slice through a man's body easier than the keenest knife.

Johnny's eyes had a harried look behind his glasses. His arms were as rigid and immovable as steel. The slightest slip, the slightest slackening of pressure on the hook against the wire, would cause it to leap and whirl. Renny would be directly in its path.

The big engineer showed no indication of fear. His bony monstrosities of fists were slowly squeezing the clamp tighter against the wire.

The car pitched up on its nose. Instantly, Renny eased the pressure a trifle. As the car settled, he put that pressure back.

The car's speed was still that of a diving airplane, but even so it had slackened. Tightening of the clamp on the wire was acting as a brake.

Slowly, carefully, Renny increased that pressure. The car bucked like a rodeo bronco. The world gradually took on a more calm appearance.

Time seemed to stand still. Crimson showed in a long gash on one of Renny's arms where it had barely brushed the speeding wire. The car's pace slowed to that of a slow-moving auto.

"O. K., Johnny, get set!" Renny said quickly.

The car crashed. The two aides were hurled out. But they had landed with only minor bruises.

Near them lay another body. It was that of the watchman supposed to be on duty at all times at the bottom of the elevator. He had been shot neatly through the brain.

"Seems like someone didn't want us to go where we're going," Renny observed without humor.

"A platitudinous observation, but justifiable," Johnny agreed dryly.

Fifteen minutes later, they lifted their plane from a South American field and headed northward.

Neither spoke of the peril that was just past. Neither thought of the perils that might be ahead. It was just as well they did not know what was in store for them.

## Chapter VII
### A SPIDER STRIKES

WHITE, foamy clouds stretched for miles in either direction. They appeared solid, except where a shaft of sunlight drove through. Then it could be seen they were as filmy and intangible as a spider's web.

In the center of those white billows was a darker spot. It darted and circled rapidly, over and under, in and out of the white web, much as a spider does. But it emitted a deafening roar. It did not pounce noiselessly on helpless prey as does the spider.

Otherwise, the simile was quite correct. The plane that was seeking shelter in the clouds high over Florida not only resembled a spider with the clouds for its web, but its purpose was the same: it also was preparing to stalk prey.

Inside the plane there was little sound. Words of the men who sat there were quite audible.

"They should come soon," said one. His voice was thick, guttural. Heavy, protruding eyebrows masked small eyes in an aggressive face.

"Bah! They should not have been permitted to leave New York at all. The United States is too easy with Doc Savage," said a second.

Fingers of one hand twirled the ends of a tiny, waxed mustache. Shoulders shrugged expressively.

The third occupant of the cabin turned from the window. "What are the reports?" he asked.

His voice was flat, lifeless, without expression, but it brought an amazing change in his two companions.

"Just a moment, Leader," the heavyset man said excitedly. His aggressive face shone with eagerness.

"Permit me to get them, Leader," exclaimed his smaller companion. The ends of his mustache bobbed up and down rapidly.

"I have just come from the radio!" boomed the first.

"Me, I can answer the questions!" blurted the second.

"Quiet, Louie. Calmly, Henry." The man called The Leader did not raise his voice. It remained flat and lifeless. But a chill was there, suddenly. Louie and Henry stilled as swiftly as they had erupted.

THE LEADER swung his eyes slowly from one to the other. There was something malevolent about that look. It would have been hard to describe at first. Then the reason would have been clear.

The face was as lifeless as the voice. Only the eyes seemed alive. The nose, cheeks, lips and chin were not unhandsome, but they were devoid of all expression. Color was in the cheeks, the lips were pink. But that color appeared artificial.

It was almost as if rouge and lipstick had been used. The face might have belonged to a corpse. It seemed impossible that it belonged to a living man. Yet power was reflected there, and a ruthless will.

"You first, Louie," that cold, dead voice said.

"We have just heard from Blanco Grande," the big man said hurriedly. "Everything, it is going according to plan. The soldiers have revolted. The country is in an uproar."

"And President Avispa?"

"I—uh—I regret to say he has not yet surrendered." The big man appeared frightened, suddenly. Beads of perspiration appeared on his forehead. "It—it seems he was well loved by many of his people. Not all the troops revolted. The palace is still holding out, although it is only a matter of—"

The chill look in the other's eyes stopped him. Those eyes were as merciless now as his face.

"Do the men so soon forget the hand of death?" that cold, dead voice asked.

Louis' hands shook openly. He moistened his lips with a thick tongue. "No," he said hastily. "It is just a minor delay. They will be in command by the time we reach there."

"And your report, Henry?"

The small man twisted the ends of his mustache nervously. "All, it is well. The unit organizations in each country are progressing rapidly. From England, France, Germany, Russia and others, the reports come in. All wait the word from The Leader."

The hum of the plane's motors came but faintly. The ship twisted and turned through the sky.

"It is well," the dead-voiced man said at last. For just a moment a flash of hate lighted his eyes. "We should have headed directly for Hidalgo, but the men I sent to New York failed. The world is within my grasp. I will win, but it is necessary to eliminate

Doc Savage. Soon his plane will be coming by here. And then—"

Strange smiles lighted the faces of Louie and Henry. Their eyes dropped to a queer apparatus on the floor of the cabin.

"WE are making good time, Doc," Long Tom said laconically.

"We can't make too good time to suit me," Ham said anxiously. "I'll be glad when we leave the United States far behind."

"A shyster that can talk like you shouldn't be worried," Monk grumbled. "You're supposed to be able to talk your way out of anything." The hairy chemist sighed. "I wish Habeas was along. It would be a pleasure to look at a face that doesn't have law written all over it."

At the start of the trip Doc had requested that the pets be left behind because of the danger that they would meet, much to the chagrin of both Ham and Monk.

"That hog?" Ham sniffed contemptuously. "Now if Chemistry were here—"

"We are nearing the outer coast of Florida," Doc cut in quietly. "Soon we will be beyond the jurisdiction of the Coast Guard."

"And if we are stopped?" Ham asked.

"I am sure we can explain to the state department," the bronze man said. "That would take time, however. I trust that will not be necessary."

Clouds were moving in on the plane. Long Tom moved to the radio compartment. He placed a pair of headphones over his ears and twisted a dial. A startled expression crossed his face.

With one move, the thin electrical wizard yanked the headphones from his ears, raced toward the front of the plane.

"Another ship is nearby!" he shouted. "I heard the roar of her motors over the airphone!"

"I know. It is to our right, and above us," the bronze man said. He twisted the controls slightly, plunged the plane into a cloud bank to the left.

Long Tom's mouth dropped open. He knew Doc Savage had exceptional hearing, that the long, rigid training the bronze man had followed since childhood had made his ears super-keen, but even so Long Tom was surprised.

The airphone was tuned delicately. It was designed to pick up the slightest motor roar at the distance of several miles. Even so, the sound that had come to Long Tom's ears through the headset had been only moderately loud.

"The Coast Guard?" breathed Monk. A look of childish disappointment was on his homely face.

"There are numerous pleasure craft about here," Ham put in hopefully.

"The plane is drawing closer," Doc said quietly.

"In those clouds?" Monk asked incredulously.

His look of disappointment changed to one of acute dismay.

"Some of the Coast Guard planes use airphones, also, you hairy ape!" Ham said bitterly. "They use them to help locate smugglers who use planes. You would pop off and talk too much!"

Doc looked thoughtful.

"WE are drawing close to them," Louis said jubilantly. His eyes under their big eyebrows were shining wickedly. Headphones were over his ears.

"This—this Doc Savage, he is a tough man to go up against," Henry said hesitantly.

"Bah!" Anger flared in the malevolent eyes of The Leader. "Who is he? Just an adventurer who has been lucky. He will not escape me!"

"I—I wish we could use the hand of death," Henry muttered, half to himself.

The pale, ghastly white features of The Leader spun toward him.

"That's child's play," he said in that cold, dead voice. "And it would not work at any distance. The hand of death is only to impress and kill fools. Doc Savage, I'll admit, is no fool. But what we are going to do—" He broke off, turned toward the queer apparatus on the floor of the plane.

"The roar of the motors is much louder!" Louie yelled excitedly. "We must be almost up with them!"

The Leader glanced out a window. The clouds were thinning. The spot could not have been better chosen for an ambush. A swift drop, and then—

A signal was given the pilot. The plane turned up on one wing, dived downward. A second ship appeared below them. It was a big, four-motored amphibian.

"THEY'VE caught us," Ham said wearily.

Doc's flake gold eyes were looking upward. A plane was shooting down from above. On the sides of that plane were the insignia of the Coast Guard.

"I'm sorry," Monk said. For once his voice was quite humble.

"Can't you outrun them?" Long Tom broke in heatedly.

"We are carrying too heavy a load. The speed of our plane is not up to that of the one they are using," Doc said concisely.

The bronze man's eyes narrowed slightly.

The other plane had dropped until it was almost level with them. The helmeted head of the pilot could be seen through the side.

But no signal was being given them to land.

"Something queer about this," Ham breathed. A puzzled look passed over his features.

"Maybe," Monk began, "they're not goin'—"

He broke off. Doc had wrenched hard on the controls. The big amphibian went into a barrel roll, straightened out and dived.

Monk hit the top of the cabin, rolled and came up sputtering. Long Tom sprawled his length. Ham's features went white.

They all saw then what Doc had seen an instant before.

The plane bearing the Coast Guard insignia had turned toward them slightly, then its nose had gone up.

And as the nose went up, a long, dark shape hurtled from the bottom of that ship. It headed directly toward the amphibian.

"An aërial torpedo!" whispered Ham.

The fake Coast Guard plane pivoted, rose slightly, then leveled off. The aërial torpedo whizzed swiftly through the air.

Once more Doc whipped the big amphibian around. He looped, did tricks few pilots would ever have attempted with so large a ship. The plane should have been far removed from the course of the torpedo.

"It's following us!" howled Monk.

Long Tom's eyes were bulging. Ham was sitting upright, hands clenched.

Doc's eyes swept the scene. As he twisted and dodged, the torpedo went through the same motions.

Up above, the fake Coast Guard plane loafed easily.

"It's radio-controlled! We can't escape!" cried Long Tom. Doc was a master pilot. Under his hands the amphibian became as nimble as a pursuit ship. But in vain.

With every twist of the amphibian, the torpedo made a similar turn. A small screw behind it beat frantically. Short, stubby wings made it a flying engine—and a flying bomb.

And the aërial torpedo was fast. It was gaining. Slowly but surely, it was overtaking Doc's ship!

## Chapter VIII
### A TRAP CLOSES

A GRIM expression came over the face of the bronze man. The big plane was wide open. The throttle was pulled to the last notch. Her four giant motors seemed to be trying to tear their way from the wing sockets.

But escape that way was impossible.

Doc gave a faint signal. As Ham seized the controls, the bronze man slipped from the cabin. With Long Tom at his heels, he went into the tiny radio control room of the plane.

Monk slipped into the co-pilot seat. His features worked with futile rage.

"Daggonit," he howled, "if we could only get above that thing, I could drop down on top of it!"

"Try sticking your head out a window!" Ham blistered. "If it sees you, it'll probably get scared and run away."

The fact that Monk failed to reply to that one caused Ham to turn around. He could hardly see Monk for his mouth. It was open, wide. When the chemist did that, his head all but disappeared. Monk just pointed.

The dapper Ham stared. His eyes opened wide, his jaw dropped.

The aërial torpedo was no longer pursuing them!

As they watched, it appeared to hesitate. It wabbled and twisted. Then it spun, its nose going up as it turned.

The aërial torpedo headed back, directly toward the ship from which it had come!

ABOARD the other ship there was sudden confusion. The man called The Leader who had been watching with a frozen face, leaped to his feet, raced toward the radio room.

Henry was sputtering unintelligible words. His arms were waving wildly.

"It's turned around! It's coming for us! I can do nothing!"

The Leader's malevolent eyes became hard. "Get out," he said, in that cold, flat voice. "I can control this."

Louie's big form appeared behind him. The Leader worked keys rapidly. The aërial torpedo came on, twisting and dogging as the pilot of the fake Coast Guard plane went through maneuvers even as Doc had gone through them a few short seconds before.

Without change of expression, The Leader turned to Louie. He whispered a few words in the other's ear. The big man nodded, raced out of the radio room.

The Leader rose, motioned to Henry. "Take it. The torpedo is harmless now." Henry's eyes were fear-stricken, but he obeyed. The Leader's eyes narrowed slightly. He closed the door of the radio room behind him.

A moment later, and his air of calm had disappeared. The torpedo was gaining, it was coming closer with each passing instant. The frozen-faced man raced to the belly of the big ship.

Louie was already there, was pushing himself into a small opening. The Leader crammed himself in a similar one.

Louie looked up questioningly. The other nodded. With a heave of mighty muscles, the big man jerked down on a lever.

The next instant they were falling. A tiny plane had dropped away from the belly of the big ship. Wings shot out from its side. A motor roared.

The Leader scarcely looked around as the aërial torpedo hit the plane he had just deserted. Safe with Louie in a small, swift pursuit plane, he showed no concern over the fact that he had tricked the man that he had left behind. That he had died.

But his eyes were terrible in their anger. He had come to grips with Doc Savage. He had lost—this time. But next—

DOC'S big four-motored plane was more than a mile away when the fake Coast Guard plane appeared to dissolve in air. He swung the big amphibian toward the speeding dot of the pursuit ship.

It was useless. The tiny plane was merely a blur of motion. Even as he looked, it dived into a cloud bank and disappeared.

"That was unfortunate," the bronze man said. "But we can hardly be responsible for that."

Monk's breath came out in a slow sigh. His mouth closed like a big hinge. Eyes still staring, he surrendered his seat to Doc.

"Dang it," he complained, "I saw it, but I still don't believe it. Just what happened?"

"There are two types of aërial torpedoes," Doc said quietly. "One is radio-controlled at will. The other, like this one, was newer. The two planes, the sender and the object to be destroyed, complete a radio-wave circuit. The torpedo rides the beam. No matter what the direction the pursued ship takes, the torpedo will follow."

"But this one turned around!" Monk howled. "It destroyed the ship that fired it. How come?"

"The same principle as reversing a motor on an alternating current. We have stronger apparatus than they have. I merely reversed the beam."

"But two of them got away at that," Ham said regretfully.

"Yeah, and at the speed they were making, they'll get to Hidalgo long before we will," Long Tom put in dolefully.

"That may not be fatal," Ham said dryly. "Johnny and Renny are closer than we are. They should get there first. And they should be able to handle one pair, at least."

"If they get there," Monk said pessimistically.

As if in answer to his words, a light began to flash on and off on the switchboard at the radio controls. It showed that a message was coming in on the special micro-wavelength used by Doc and his aides.

Long Tom sprang to the board, pressed a switch.

"Conditions deemed meritorious for incursion of landing terrain," the emotionless voice of Johnny droned through the loudspeaker. "Propugnaculum of legions of Avispa seem in prepotency."

Long Tom looked quickly at Doc, then spoke into the small microphone.

"All right, then," he clipped. "If Avispa's soldiers are in control of the landing field, go on down. We'll be seeing you."

RENNY looked over a side of the plane. The little joystick was almost invisible in one huge hand. But those enormous fists that could smash a solid oak panel were as sensitive as a mother's touch on the stick. The plane wheeled slowly as he picked up wind direction and prepared to land.

Below them was scattered fighting through the streets of Blanco Grande. That Central American city looked far different than when Doc's aides had first seen it.

The presidential palace had been rebuilt. Now it was one of the wonder spots. There was a great modern hospital that Doc had ordered built. That building and its highly trained staff had practically banished disease from all Hidalgo.

Gold from the Valley of the Vanished had made that possible, just as the same gold had financed Doc in his fight on evildoers.

"Yeah, gold in proper hands can bring lots of good, but if the wrong guy had it—" Renny spoke almost to himself.

Soldiers in the uniform of the Republic of Hidalgo were putting dark, brown-clad men to rout all over the city. Bursts of smoke came from rifles, and brown-clad men fell in the streets. At the airport itself, a large contingent of soldiers stood on guard. They waved wildly to the approaching plane.

"Looks like they've got the beggars on the run," Renny said.

"We must get to Carlos Avispa before any untoward interposition by the criminals changes that tide," Johnny commented.

Renny moved forward the stick and the plane flattened into a glide, began to descend slowly. The soldiers were waving and shouting even more than before. It was as if they were hailing rescuers from the sky.

The big engineer frowned slightly as his eyes combed the crowd for sight of the distinguished figure of Avispa. If his soldiers had really been victorious, it was not unlikely that the white-haired president of Hidalgo would be at the flying field to greet them.

The motor roared as Renny gunned it, dropped one wing of the plane in a quick turn; then they were swooping down, and the wheels touched the ground gently in a perfect three-point landing.

Soldiers were rushing toward them from all parts of the field.

"*Viva! Viva!*" came the cries.

"*Viva*, nothing!" Renny growled. "I'll be durned glad to get my feet on the ground." He hoisted his big frame out of the cockpit. Johnny already had dropped from the ship.

"An extraordinary welcome—" Johnny began. Then he paused. The half-starved look on his face changed to one of incredulous wonder.

"Renny!" he yelled.

"Holy cow!" roared Renny.

Somewhere, a sharp voice had barked out an order. The soldiers stopped cheering. Bayoneted rifles swung up as they raced forward.

"Surrender!" came the harsh command.

JOHNNY and Renny already were several paces from their plane. The odds against them were overwhelming. With smiles wiped from their faces, Doc's two aides forgot all about the military strategy that says "do not fight a useless battle."

They went into action!

A strangled roar came from Renny as he leaped forward. His hamlike fists clubbed out like bludgeons. Two soldiers sank to the ground as if they had suddenly been mesmerized. Their uniforms were split, and beneath the colorful dress garb of the Hidalgo presidential guards, khaki uniform showed plainly.

Johnny dived to the plane, reached inside. He came out with his superfiring machine-pistol even as a soldier leaped for him. The starved-appearing geologist tripped his attacker, brought the pistol up. He was too busy even to use a big word.

The gun moaned in his hands. A wave of soldiers went down like wheat before a reaper.

The blast cleared the way so Renny could reach the plane and get his machine-pistol. He whirled, crouched low. His weapon, too, went into action with a bullfiddle moan. The phony guards went down like tenpins.

"We've got to get word to Doc!" Renny howled.

"Get word to him yourself!" came a bellow from Johnny. It had probably been years since he had used such simple words.

As their machine-pistols moaned and coughed, the uniformed men screamed, broke back.

*Blam! Blam!*

A rifle spoke sharply, twice. Lead pinged into the plane behind their backs. Johnny and Renny ducked, firing steadily. Only "mercy" bullets were in their weapons—bullets that brought quick unconsciousness, but not death; but their foes did not know that.

Then the tide of the battle turned. Behind the wave of retreating figures, a soldier set up a Lewis gun on a tripod. Sandbags were in front of him. A cruel leer was on his face.

The gun started with a deadly chatter, even before his own retreating confederates were past him. Three of them fell, filled with his machine-gun lead.

Doc's aides dropped, rolled. Dirt kicked up in front of them. They pressed themselves flat on the earth. There was a tiny rise in the ground between them and the machine-gunner. It made them more difficult targets.

But the machine-gunner chopped his gun down. The slugs tore off that little rise of ground, sent it flying away in a cloud of dust. Bullets tore through Renny's clothing. The deadly rain of lead came nearer—

A voice roared suddenly from a loudspeaker at the edge of the field.

"Do not kill them, fool! We must take them alive. Until Doc Savage is dead, they must live. By torturing them, we may bring the bronze man to terms."

The machine gun stopped chattering. Instantly, Johnny and Renny were on their feet. They turned, dashed toward their plane.

A veritable wave of men rushed around that plane toward them. A yellowish vapor was pouring from a large tank in the arms of the leading man.

Johnny coughed. Renny felt as if his muscles had suddenly gone powerless. The machine-pistol dropped from his hands. Figures wearing gas masks poured over him.

Arms flaying the air instinctively, his huge fists knocking down men right and left, the big engineer went on. His clawing hands caught a side of the plane. He felt as if his lungs were bursting. Arms caught him about the legs, tried to hold him back.

With the last ounce of his tremendous strength, Renny jerked himself forward, fell head down in the cockpit of the plane. His head collided with the radio switchboard. He tried to shout.

It was too late. He could not. He slumped down, unconscious.

## Chapter IX
### THE SKIES EXPLODE

FAR to the north, in Doc's big plane, the radio control board light flashed again. Once more, Long Tom tuned in on the microwave. A voice came in steadily.

It used none of Johnny's long words. It was a compact message, designed to pack the most meaning in the fewest words:

*"Overpowered by enemy. Too many to tackle. Turn back. Use other plans."*

Doc Savage's flake gold eyes opened slightly. His mouth tightened.

"They've been trapped!" Monk's voice was a moan.

"I don't see how—" Long Tom gulped.

"Evidently they mistook hostile forces for the loyal troops of President Avispa," the bronze man said crisply.

For a moment there was silence. Ham's brow was furrowed. He knew, as did the rest, that the very wording of the warning they had received indicated that Johnny and Renny had been overcome.

It was a warning designed to indicate that very thing.

Small, easily concealed dictographs were hidden just under the radio board on all the planes used by Doc's men. Pressure of a button was all that was necessary to broadcast one of several prepared messages. Renny had banged his head against the button that controlled the one he wanted to send.

"If no one saw Renny get that warning off, maybe we can surprise them," Ham exclaimed.

"More and more, we are having evidence that the man we are opposing is not only clever, but has sources of information that has enabled him to anticipate us," the bronze man said slowly.

Monk roared, thrust out his powerful arms. Monk always was a direct actionist. Trickery might be all right, but he preferred stronger methods.

"Let's go on and take 'em!" he howled. "We'll knock 'em clean to the Pacific!"

"One shot, if it struck this plane in the right place, and we'd be the ones who would be knocked clean to the Pacific," Long Tom commented dryly.

"Can't we let Monk get there somehow in any case?" Ham asked pleasantly. "They would think they had harmed us if they chopped him up, and that certainly would be fooling them."

"Why, you encyclopedia of reversed decisions!" Monk bellowed. "If I wasn't better than you, I'd take a parachute jump without the parachute!"

Ham pulled open a large window of the control cabin and smiled. "I think it's big enough," he said significantly.

"Turn east," Doc interrupted evenly. He turned the controls over to Ham. "Head for Havana. Give her all the speed she's got."

HAM obeyed unhesitatingly. Conversation quieted. Doc Savage had reached a decision. What it was, his aides did not know, nor did they ask. The bronze man seldom revealed what he had in his mind until it came time to put that plan into execution.

But they all knew that there must be a good reason, or Doc would not be turning off their course when Johnny and Renny were in danger.

For time and time again, they had all seen instances to show that Doc Savage's first concern was the safety of his men. The bronze giant would take terrific personal risks when his aides were in the clear. But when he was the only agent that could free them, he made sure they would be safe before he walked into almost certain death.

Vital supplies were aboard the big amphibian. Ham knew Doc would sacrifice those supplies willingly if it would aid Johnny and Renny. But if not, those supplies had to be saved.

Doc rose, went back into the cabin with Long Tom. The green foliage of Cuba appeared before them.

"Tilt the nose up," the bronze man instructed briefly.

The dapper lawyer obeyed. There was a faint jerk on the plane. An object hurtled downward. Then a huge, white mushroom appeared.

Long Tom had bailed out. He was landing in Cuba.

Doc watched Long Tom land, pick himself up and fold the chute. As the unhealthy-appearing electrical genius headed for a highway, the bronze man took the controls.

"Where to now?" Monk growled.

"Hidalgo," Doc answered briefly. "No stops until we get there."

Monk and Ham looked at each other questioningly. They would have liked to know what Long Tom was going to do, but they knew they would have to wait until Doc decided to tell them.

The bronze man looked straight ahead. Tiny flakes in his eyes looked like whirlwinds. His mouth was grim.

FAR ahead of the big four-motored ship, a smaller plane whipped along like a humming bird. It went so fast it was merely a blur in the sky.

The malevolent eyes of the man at the stick were inscrutable. His face was set and lifeless. It had no expression. Radio headphones were on his ears.

The little plane was high in the air. It had to be. The country below was rugged and wild. Just ahead was a mighty mountain peak. It was on one of the two great Central American ranges that wedge between them the Republic of Hidalgo.

The great area between the two giant ranges was traversed by half a dozen smaller but even more rugged groups of hills. The whole scene presented a perfect spot for guerrilla banditry.

It was almost impenetrable. The tiny ship topped the big peak and glided down into the valley. Nearly in the center of it was Blanco Grande.

The pilot, his malevolent eyes glowing, circled and spoke softly into the microphone slung before his mouth. Still swinging, he waited for his answer.

The view below him was one of beauty. Blanco Grande's crooked streets had been straightened. There were no squalid shacks, but only great parks. Crystal-clear water played from fountains. There was a great, white marble library that permitted the education of those Hidalgans who wished to partake of it. Gold had done that for Blanco Grande.

The vicious-eyed pilot saw, but was uninterested. He thought only of the gold that had made the beauty of Blanco Grande possible. The corners of his lifeless mouth lifted slightly. Gold!

If the world only knew what he intended to do with that gold, armies from every civilized nation would be sped by warships under forced draft to block him. But the world did not know. When it did learn, it would be too late.

"Gold has been used in many ways, but never as I intend to use it," The Leader assured himself.

The earphones crackled slightly. He listened, then turned to the big man in the tiny cockpit behind him. The slit that was his mouth straightened.

"The ones they call Renny and Johnny have been captured," he said in that flat, expressionless voice. "They are being held as hostages—or until I decree they must die."

Again the earphones crackled into life. The malevolent eyes of The Leader sparkled at what he heard.

"The bronze man went off his course to fly over Havana," he announced. "He circled and dropped the man known as Long Tom. Our men lost trace of Long Tom, but he is believed to have headed back for New York.

"Doc Savage is worried. He should be. I am almost glad we did not kill him in the clouds. I will be happy when he reach Hidalgo. For then—" A mirthless chuckle came from between his thin lips.

Louie shivered faintly; perspiration dampened his fists. The big man did not hesitate to kill. He feared little. But he did fear the lifeless-faced ruler who piloted the plane.

If The Leader said he was glad Doc Savage would reach Hidalgo, then it meant the brain behind those evil eyes had concocted some terrible scheme.

A GROUP of soldiers rushed out as the plane dropped to the landing field at Blanco Grande. Gone were the fake uniforms that had fooled Johnny and Renny. Now the soldiers of fortune were dressed in khaki.

At their head was a stocky, agate-eyed man in the uniform of a general. His shoulders were broad, his eyes set a little too close together. Copper-tinted features grave, he bowed low before the figure approaching from the plane.

When he raised his head, he endeavored to keep his features calm. But fear showed there. A silence fell.

Slowly, deliberately, The Leader raked him with his malevolent, repelling eyes. They started at the feet and moved slowly up to features that were turning ashen.

General Juan Glassell's mouth opened, then closed. He ran a tongue over dry lips.

"Glassell, you are a fool." The flat, lifeless tones of the other were not raised. They did not need to be. There was a chill in them like an icy blast.

The big man in the general's uniform tried to speak. The words would not come. His throat seemed glued.

"You were in command of the armed forces of Hidalgo," that dreadful voice went on. "You assured me you could seize control of this country within two hours. You failed."

The Leader took a step forward. His lifeless face jutted forward. Involuntarily, Glassell moved backward.

"I—I—" he half shrieked. "How did I know so many would remain loyal? How did I know we would have to kill so many?" He gulped rapidly. "But we are winning! We will soon be in control!"

The other looked at him for a long moment. "It must be that way, you must win before tomorrow. If not—"

"Not the hand of death, not that!" Glassell screamed.

"Blanco Grande must be in our hands. It is the only exit from the Valley of the Vanished. Unless we control that exit, we could be trapped." The Leader spoke as if to himself.

Some of Glassell's color returned. "It shall be done. We shall hold the city. There will be no attack on our rear when we push ahead. We can even start part of the advance tonight."

"You blundered also when you permitted this Doc Savage's men to send out word that they had been captured," the cold-voiced one went on.

General Glassell started with honest astonishment. "But—but that is impossible! I was here myself! They could not—"

The Leader held up a hand. "Enough. They did. But it is just as well. This bronze man will rush here to rescue them. That is what I want. Now here is what I want you to do—"

THE Hidalgo airport became the scene of great activity. Pursuit planes were rolled out, their motors warmed. Big bombers trundled from their hangars. Pilots and observers swarmed about them. At the edge of the field, antiaircraft guns were moved into position.

"His plane should be here in ten minutes." General Glassell spoke excitedly. His close-set eyes were gleaming wickedly. "Every report has been the same. It is the four-motored craft you described. The markings are such they could not be counterfeited."

Beside him the frozen-faced one nodded slightly. "There is no question of that." His eyes narrowed, then he shrugged. "It has taken him longer to reach here than I estimated, but that means nothing."

The pursuit planes took off. The bombers roared in the air behind them. Up and up they soared. The pursuit ships were only faint dots in the sky, the bombers far in the distance, when a huge amphibian showed in the clear mountain air. At first, it was many miles away. Then it was quite close.

Relief showed suddenly in The Leader's evil eyes. "It is the right ship," he breathed. "At first I feared a trick, but now—"

On and on came the amphibian. It circled the field, high and suspiciously.

The Leader lifted the microphone in front of him. He spoke into it.

Instantly, it seemed as if all hell had arrived. There was the terrific roar and moan of diving motors. Pursuit ships that had been hidden high above smashed down, motors wide open in desperate power dives. Machine guns rent the air like riveting hammers.

Doc's ship wheeled. It was clumsy by comparison with the hornetlike attackers. Its big bulk seemed to loom large, make a perfect target.

But machine-gun bullets bounced off it like rain.

"Armor-plated," The Leader sneered. "But wait!"

The big amphibian was dodging and twisting with amazing agility for so large a ship. Time and time again, it seemed to dart directly out from under a rain of steel that would have been fatal.

But gradually the attackers were closing in. Squadron after squadron zoomed close. The bombers were coming down, their observers firing fiercely.

Then a second contingent of battle planes drew near. Doc's plane was locked in a perfect circle of enemy ships. It had no way to escape. The pursuit planes drew aside to let the latest arrivals close.

Strange-looking weapons protruded from the sides of these ships. Gradually they jockeyed close.

Flame suddenly filled the air. Flame blasted with tons of pressure from the muzzles of those queer-looking weapons. That flame was white-hot. Even the watchers, far below, could see the armor plating on the big amphibian melting. The flame cut through the steel like an acetylene torch through a cheap boiler plate.

The lips on the frozen-faced one twitched. His grin was a horrible grimace.

Then that grin vanished. Stark dismay flamed in his malevolent eyes.

ONE instant the entire sky was filled with fighting ships. The next, and the sky was filled only with flames and flying pieces of things that had been ships and men.

The Leader had expected Doc's plane to be carrying explosives. He had counted on that to wipe out the bronze man and his aides. But he hadn't counted on the terrific destruction that occurred.

Doc's big ship vanished. It just wasn't there. But neither was the entire attacking fleet. The blast, when its concussion reached the earth, flattened hangars, hurled men to the ground.

Doc's plane was blown not to bits, but to fine powder. But with it every ship of that tremendous battle fleet was destroyed!

Hidalgo's entire fighting fleet had been destroyed. But—

The evil sparkle returned to the malevolent eyes

of The Leader. Once more those lifeless lips twisted. He turned to General Glassell.

"The price was high," came that flat, cold voice. "But it was worth it. Doc Savage was more dangerous to us than any ordinary army would be. Now he is dead. He and his aides. And I am happy that I watched him die."

## Chapter X
### VIVA THE LEADER

DARKNESS fell on Blanco Grande. But the night was red. Streets resembled an old-fashioned torchlight parade. And there was a revelry of victory such as no political celebration would have dreamed about.

Khaki-clad figures staggered drunkenly, waved half-empty bottles in the air. They repeated one monotonous victory chant:

"Doc Savage is dead! *Viva* The Leader! Doc Savage is dead! *Viva* The Leader!

Eyes stared wildly. Sometimes they glanced about nervously, only to start and continue their celebration. There could be no doubt about it. Doc Savage was dead!

That decision had not been reached at once even after the terrific explosion in the sky. Hundreds of men had been put to work. Carefully, they had picked up every piece of wreckage, every part of a human body they could find.

Enough pieces of the big amphibian had been found to identify it positively. There could be no mistake. It had been Doc's plane.

Identification of bodies had been more difficult. They had been torn into thousands of pieces. But one unanswerable clue had been found: among the shattered fragments that had been men, had been found a queer substance, several pieces of it, in fact. That substance had been tested. It was crimson-soaked underwear of the type only Doc and his men wore.

That had convinced even The Leader.

And as revelry reigned in the streets, the frozen-faced one and General Glassell sat comfortably in the traitor's well-furnished offices. As sound of the celebration penetrated those offices, Glassell smiled happily.

"With one stroke, you have insured victory," he complimented. "Even those who have stood with President Avispa will quail now. The bronze man was their only hope."

The frozen-faced one nodded slightly. His eyes darkened as the shrill echo of shots came to his ears.

"But those at the palace are stubborn. They still fight on." He shrugged, his lifeless face unchanging. "It does not matter. We can localize the fighting there. You have dispatched more troops toward the palace?"

"As you ordered. None can stand against the force I have dispatched. Every instrument of modern warfare is included in the equipment—everything but planes."

"The loss of those planes was regrettable, but need not concern us," the other said in cold, clipped tones. "More could be ordered, but we will not need them. Before they will have arrived, we will have conquered."

"And then?" There was a sly, shrewd look in Glassell's close-set eyes.

"Then I am ready." For the first time a note of hardness, a grim hint of implacable power and greed, broke through that flat voice. "Authority such as no man has ever had will be in my hands. Dictators, kings, emperors and czars of the past will be as nothing compared to me."

"But how—"

General Glassell's voice choked, his face paled. The other's repelling eyes had swept over him, once. That was enough.

"It is not well to ask too many questions," the frozen-faced one told him. "The secret of how that power is coming to me is known to me alone. No one else can guess, no one else will know—until it is too late."

From outside came that steady, monotonous shout:

"Doc Savage is dead! *Viva* The Leader! Doc Savage is dead. *Viva* The Leader!"

THE cries filtered dimly through a subterranean passage. They reverberated hollowly against walls of stone. The walls were damp, cold and clammy. But the two men leaning against them felt just as damp and just as clammy.

Sweat—the cold sweat of horror—oozed from the pores of Renny and Johnny.

"If Doc is gone, it doesn't matter much what happens to us," Renny said.

Johnny was slow in replying. His grief was heavy.

"Doc had to get it sometime, I suppose," he said in a low voice. Under stress of emotion he had returned to simple words. "But if he'd only had a chance to fight—"

The guards had told the two men all about it. They had told it with great glee. Their description had been complete. They had even revealed the fact that lookouts had been watching Doc and his men all the time, and that Long Tom had landed in Havana.

Renny shuddered. That chant of death came again through the cell window. "And Monk and Ham went with him. There were six of us. Now there are only three. Long Tom's the only one left, outside of us."

"And we are incapacitated by lack of locomotion," Johnny said crisply. His eyes narrowed behind their glasses. His half-starved features set.

Renny looked at him quickly. The big engineer's puritanical face became severe. His thin mouth compressed tightly.

"I see what you mean!" he snapped. "Doc wouldn't want us to quit, just because he is gone. He'd want us to carry on, to do what we were supposed to do."

His huge frame swung toward the door. His monstrosities of fists battered furiously. He was accustomed to smashing through doors with those fists. This one was different. Skin came from his knuckles. The door did not move. It was of iron.

Johnny gestured faintly toward one side of the dungeon. Renny looked that way and his eyes opened slightly, his features became even more thin and disapproving.

Mortar appeared chipped and flaky around one huge stone in one side of the cell. Some previous occupant had undoubtedly spent hours working away at that mortar, buoyed by undying hope.

Softly, despite his height, Johnny eased to the stone. His powerful fingers brushed the mortar away. Then those fingers jammed in hard, caught a firm grip.

Muscles rose in huge ridges on his back, perspiration broke from his face. The big stone creaked. Fine dust flew out. Renny moved over, caught Johnny about the waist, added his ponderous weight.

There was a dull, crunching sound. The huge stone came out.

In the corridor outside the cell, a guard laughed jeeringly. "Birds do not fly from this cage, señors," he called bitingly.

With disappointed eyes, Doc's two aides looked into the hole left by the huge stone. Behind that hole was another stone, equally as big. The cell was a veritable fortress. Escape was impossible.

"Maybe Avispa can win out without our help," Renny said. But his voice showed that he had no such hope.

NOR did President Avispa hold any such hope, either. Despair was written on a face that once had known only smiles. Harsh lines of worry had wiped out his look of kindliness.

Shoulders that once had been powerful, now were bowed with sorrow and disappointment. His head was cupped in strong, well-formed hands. His eyes had a look of grief and resignation.

Words dinned into his ears, words shouted by a drunken, boisterous mob of khaki-clad men that encircled the palace.

"Doc Savage is dead! *Viva* The Leader! Doc Savage is dead. *Viva* The Leader!"

A scattered volley of rifle shots sounded, near at hand. The monotonous chant broke off, but only for a moment. Soon it was resumed.

A small man slipped into the room. His face was bloody, his clothes torn.

Avispa's head came up. For a moment hope lighted his eyes; then that hope died as he saw the look on the other's features.

"It is so?" he asked needlessly.

"There is no doubt about it, my president," the little man said. "I myself saw the pieces of the plane and the—the other things that show the bronze man is dead."

For a moment President Avispa did not speak. He was thinking—thinking back into the past, as the old sometimes do. Clark Savage, Sr., had been his friend. Clark Savage Jr. had been his friend. Now both were gone. He had respected the elder Savage, but he had had an affection for Doc such as he had had for no other living man.

But Doc was gone. And enemies were pressing ever harder.

"What else did you learn?"

The man hesitated. It was as if he did not care to be the bearer of evil tidings.

"The two known as Renny and Johnny are captives," he mumbled at last. "They are held in the dungeon, where none can get at them. From words I heard dropped by liquor-loosened tongues, they are to be executed."

A sudden shout went up from outside the palace. A machine gun wrote rapidly. And the words it wrote were death. Rifles cracked.

"An attack!" the little man breathed.

Avispa grew old again. He slumped in his chair. "They are many. We are few. My men are loyal, but why should we fight a useless battle? Why shouldn't I surrender and at least save their lives?"

"No! No, my president!" The little man fairly spouted words. "That cannot be! I did not want to tell! But now I must!"

"There is worse to come?" Avispa asked incredulously.

The small man gulped, and nodded. "They are boasting in the streets of what they are to do," he said brokenly. "Those of us who are captured alive are to be tortured in ways that make the blood run cold. Never surrender. If you are not killed in the final fighting, then—"

Slowly, with hands that shook, President Avispa reached into a drawer, brought out a pistol. "I understand, *mi amigo*. One bullet I shall save for myself."

A second, then a third machine gun joined the riotous chorus of death beyond the palace walls. A pitiful line of defenders hunted cover, praying only that the end would be a merciful one.

THE men manning those machine guns outside the palace were angry. They alone had been kept on duty. While others drank and celebrated, they were forced to work.

"Let's get it over with!" a hardboiled sergeant snarled fiercely. "The quicker we wipe out that bunch of rats in there, the quicker we can have some fun ourselves!"

"They at least are a stubborn bunch of rats!" a corporal grated.

Sullen murmurs swept the ranks of the attackers. The monotonous chorus of the revelers brought only fierce swearing.

A tall figure came swaying down the street. He was dressed as a captain. Or he had been in a captain's uniform. Now that uniform was ripped and torn. A civilian's hat was pulled down tightly over his head. He held a bottle high in one hand.

"Doc Savage is dead! *Viva* The—"

"*Viva* hell!" bellowed the sergeant. He made a swipe for the bottle in the other's hand.

The big man toppled, but held onto the bottle. "Naughty, naughty," he said thickly. "Shish is mine. Why don't you get your own?"

"Yeah, why don't I?" the sergeant rasped bitterly. "By the time I get free, there won't be any left!"

The big man nodded his head sagely. "You shonow, I spect you're right. Shere isn't very much more."

Machine guns quieted. Eager, angry ears were cocked toward the speaker.

"You mean the supply is about gone?" the sergeant asked, with dangerous calm.

"Yes, shir. It's about gone." The big man swayed again, lifted the bottle to his lips, then wiped his mouth with a tattered sleeve. He coughed, the bottle almost fell from his hands.

The sergeant grabbed it, took a deep swallow. The anger faded from his face. "If we only didn't have to push on and take this place tonight—"

He hesitated a moment, and fear showed thinly on his features. "But it's no go. I only wish—"

The big man regained his balance with an effort, stared owlishly at the bottle in the sergeant's hand. He pawed for it awkwardly.

"Shay, that's mine."

"Scram!" snarled the sergeant. "I'm keeping this, and it's little enough as it is!"

"O.K." The big man turned, staggered off. "If you're goin' tuh be so—so unsociable about it. I got a bunch hidden I was goin' to give yuh, but not now."

The sergeant's mouth dropped open. He looked quickly at the corporal. The corporal nodded feverishly. Together they slipped off, behind the swaying figure. They did not see the men from the machine guns take in after them.

And soon they discovered they had lost the big man. He seemed to have vanished in thin air. For a moment the men swore, then they hurried back to their posts. A vacant spot had been left in the lines for a moment. But no one would know about that.

EVEN as they were warming up the machine guns a moment later, a tall figure eased into the palace grounds. A moment later and that figure had reached the palace itself.

President Avispa heard a faint tap on his window. He whirled, grabbing up the gun from the desk.

Peering in at him was a disheveled figure wearing what had been a captain's uniform. A civilian's hat was jammed tight over the head.

But Avispa did not notice the uniform or hat. He saw only a pair of eyes. Those eyes were of flake gold.

As he stared, momentarily paralyzed, the big figure eased quickly into the room.

"I came as swiftly as I could," said Doc Savage quietly.

Avispa found it hard to speak at all. Outside, he could still hear that monotonous chant:

"Doc Savage is dead! *Viva* The Leader!"

But Doc Savage was not dead.

## Chapter XI
### SEEING DOUBLE

PRESIDENT AVISPA seemed to grow younger with each passing second. Age dropped from him like a cloak. His features were lined, his hair white; but now his shoulders were erect, his head up.

"My—my friend," he said simply.

Doc wiped dark grease paint from his face. Bronze hair that closely matched the color of his skin showed as he pulled the hat from his head.

"You are safe. I thought you were dead." Avispa had difficulty in standing still. He seemed to want to hop up and down with joy. Then he sobered. "But I can't understand. You have had many narrow escapes. But this—" He gestured expressively. "Positive evidence was found that you were dead."

"Evidence that I hoped would be found," the bronze man said dryly.

"Then you really weren't in the plane?"

Doc smiled slightly. "Of course not, although I wanted The Leader and his men to think so. Long Tom dropped off the plane at Havana. In the disguise of a peasant, he purchased some supplies, then chartered a small, swift plane and followed us. We met over the Valley of the Vanished."

President Avispa nodded eagerly.

"I had supplies we could not afford to lose," the bronze man continued. "Those were the ones Long Tom purchased in Havana. Those supplies were dropped by parachute. Monk, Ham and Long Tom went with them, and I took over the small plane. Using radio control, I directed the big amphibian here."

"But when the attack came?"

"My plane was hidden in the clouds, even above the pursuit ships that were waiting for me. In the amphibian was thermite, in great quantity. Naturally, when the explosion came it was devastating, as you saw."

"But the bodies," protested Avispa. "How did you do that?"

"They were artificially created," the bronze man responded quietly. "I knew The Leader would demand more than an exploded plane to make sure I was dead."

Doc then told the white-haired president of the ruse he had used to get inside the palace grounds. Although he had pretended to drink, the bronze man hadn't touched a drop.

"Now the enemy thinks you are dead." The white-haired president grinned broadly. "What a surprise is in store for them when they discover their error, when they find that you have arrived and saved Hidalgo!"

"Hidalgo is far from saved," the bronze man cautioned. "The enemy we oppose is resourceful, he is dangerous."

Avispa sighed, sank back in his chair. He knew that Doc was right, that the battle had still to be won; but now that the bronze man had arrived, he felt his first ray of hope. And he was glad to shift his burden to another's shoulders.

"First, you will want to know what has happened. I will tell you," he began.

"The revolt is led by General Glassell. He was in charge of my army. He turned traitor. Why, I do not know. I do know that in the weeks just preceding the revolt, he enlisted many strangers in the army. They were of a type I did not think we would need: evil-faced, villainous-appearing. But he said they were fighters."

"They were renegade soldiers of fortune, men who came here solely to take part in this revolt," Doc said quietly.

Avispa nodded. "So I discovered. When the attack came, many of my men were loyal. But they were caught unprepared. A majority were killed. Only a few reached me here at the palace. They have done their best. They have repelled attack after attack. But it is only a question of time. They cannot hold out much longer."

"And Johnny and Renny?"

A shadow of pain flickered over the other's face. "They are prisoners. They are to be executed," he said.

DOC SAVAGE'S expression did not change. Only the gold flecks in his eyes appeared to move.

"Where are they held?" he clipped.

"In the dungeon," Avispa said apologetically. "I should have destroyed that dungeon. I did not. I kept it as a curiosity. It was built years ago by another ruler. In it are all the medieval instruments of torture ever devised. And it is impenetrable."

A shudder shook the white-haired president's frame.

"Johnny and Renny are there. They are fifty feet underground in a fortress that has walls twenty feet thick. The only entrance is a narrow passageway in stone. It is heavily guarded."

Guns sounded with renewed vigor outside the palace walls. A scream of pain came from an unlucky defender. Doc Savage's face hardened. His life had been dedicated to fighting injustice and evildoers. The screaming of dying men and the snarl of guns outside symbolized the worst type of injustice.

Directed by a man with an insatiable lust for power, revolt had been brought about in a peaceful country. Hundreds of innocent lives had been lost. And the trail of blood was not yet ended.

"The situation is bad," Avispa said doubtfully.

"Johnny and Renny are in peril," Doc said quietly. "They are prisoners because they obeyed my orders. My first task is to save them, if possible."

Avispa agreed slowly. Age seemed creeping back over him.

"Where does Glassell live, or have his offices?"

"They are combined." The white-haired president gave brief directions. "Perhaps if you could talk to him, you could persuade him to see the evil he has brought," he concluded wearily. "He did not appear bad to me. I thought once—" he gestured resignedly.

"I will be back," Doc interrupted swiftly. "Do not give up."

As swiftly as he had entered, the bronze man was gone. He melted into the shadow of the palace wall.

A machine-gunner thought he saw a dark shape move against that wall. He turned his gun that way, squeezed the trigger.

*Br-r-r-r-r-r-r-!*

Lead tore fragments of stone and dust from the wall. The dark shape had vanished.

The machine-gunner swore half-heartedly. He was beginning to be accustomed to ghosts. The captain who was going to lead the way to a liquor supply must have been one. Nothing else could have disappeared so fast.

A breath of air fanned the gunner's cheek suddenly. He spun, twisting his gun with him. Then he laughed nervously.

A tall figure appeared to have materialized beside him, coming out of the very ground. The figure was swaying. One hand passed a bottle to the gunner.

"Brought this to you," the big figure gulped.

The gunner grabbed it gratefully. It wasn't until much later that he recalled that his benefactor must have come from the palace wall. By that time the bottle in his hand was half empty. He no longer cared.

GUARDS almost encircled the home of General Glassell. They, too, were thirsty. But liquor would not have tempted them, even if they could have had it.

The Leader was in the office with Glassell. The very thought of that was enough to bring chills to otherwise hardened spines. They had heard of The Leader. They had heard more of the hand of death. So they walked their posts alertly, quick to challenge any who came too close.

But walking in a military manner does not mean looking up at the sky. Thus the guards did not see the dim shadow that glided noiselessly through the foliage of trees, high over their heads.

Leaves rattle and tree limbs bend easily under heavy weight. But so carefully did the shadow among them move that there was not a sound. Yet it moved fast. Only seconds elapsed until it had passed the line of guards, reached the security of darkness on the other side.

Then a big figure dropped to the ground as lightly as a cat. It drifted across the yard, blending with shadows behind stunted trees and bushes.

Before a window, the figure halted. The shades were drawn, but there was light behind those shades. Voices came clearly.

"I personally do not take pleasure in watching torture, but if that is your wish, Glassell, you have my permission," came cold, flat tones.

Breath was drawn in gustily. Lips smacked, as if Glassell were anticipating a pleasurable experience. "It has been long since I have enjoyed such a sight," the general said. His Spanish had become blurred. It was guttural and harsh.

"This Renny is a big fellow, is he not?" the cold, lifeless voice asked.

"Big enough to stand plenty before he dies," Glassell gloated. "In that I shall take extreme delight. The other"—his tone expressed supreme disgust— "this Johnny, as he is called, is a half-starved-appearing fellow. He probably will not last long, although we have ways of keeping life existing, even when the poor pigs want to die."

The huge figure outside the window stiffened.

There was sound of a chair being drawn back. "First I shall eat," Glassell said. "Then I shall go. When I return, two more of Doc Savage's aides will be dead."

A shadow appeared to drift up one side of the house. It moved lightly, fingers finding the slightest projection. Then a window swung up. The shadow disappeared inside.

Glassell ate heartily. His close-set eyes were half shut. Already he was planning the exquisite torture he would use. There was the rack now; but that was not so good, it had been used too often. Perhaps it would be better to start by filling the bodies of his victims with sharp toothpick-sized pieces of wood imbedded not too deeply in their bodies. By burning those pieces of wood, every nerve would suffer agony, but the torture would not kill. After that—

Still smiling, he rose from the table and left the house. Guards snapped to attention as the general walked from the building and headed toward the dungeon.

THE soldiers who guarded the dungeon torture chamber were brutal. It took men of instinctive brutality to serve in those posts. Right now they were filled with a sense of well-being. There were two captives below who should furnish lots of amusement.

A bottle had been passed around earlier. Now several were smoking cigarettes. But they were alert. They could afford to take no chances on those prisoners escaping.

A sentinel whistled softly. The men leaped up, stepped on their cigarettes. Ugly, loutish figures drew to attention.

The swaggering form of General Glassell came into view. The general walked jauntily. His air bespoke a man well pleased with himself.

"The soul of Doc Savage is no doubt lonesome," he purred. "We will send it company."

He laughed harshly at his own joke as he passed the first guard.

"Step lively!" he rapped. "I wish to see the dogs immediately. The day's work is incomplete."

Four of the guards stepped forward. Here was a leader to their liking. He was ruthless, vain and brutal.

Moving at a rapid pace, the guards led the way down through long stone corridors. Deeper and deeper they went into the ground. The air was dampish and foul.

As they reached a heavy door, three of the guards stood back. They lifted bayoneted rifles.

"These are desperate men," said the turnkey. He twisted a huge key in the lock. The door swung open.

Johnny and Renny stared out calmly. They looked at the big figure of the general.

"A one-way trip?" Renny asked pleasantly.

"And not a joyful one," the turnkey sneered.

"Bring them out!" the general rapped.

The turnkey laughed. Johnny and Renny moved out slowly. The guards backed up, the points of their bayonets touching the stomachs of Doc's aides.

Safe behind them, the turnkey smashed Renny hard in the neck, spat at him. He kicked Johnny in the shins.

"Travel," he rasped. "If you're nice, we'll shoot you after using the thumbscrews. Otherwise, we may show you some of our other playthings."

"Guard them carefully!" the general barked. "Take them up above. We'll see about the torture then."

"A pleasant executioner," Johnny commented.

"I believe I prefer dying to his company anyway," Renny agreed.

"Silence, dogs!" The turnkey kicked out viciously.

Renny bit his lip, his huge hands working as if they already felt a throat in their grip.

The general stood to one side, smiling slightly as the procession passed him.

THERE was a sudden commotion above them. The sound was that of running feet. The guards halted, startled.

"Get going! What are you waiting for?" barked the general. His lips lifted in a savage snarl.

The guards quickened their pace. Sharp points of the bayonets boosted Johnny and Renny along.

"Holy cow," Renny exploded, "we can't even walk; we've got to run to the closest exit—and the kind of exit that probably will be our last one!"

The sound of running feet was nearer now. Two more guards tore around the end of the corridor, rushed toward those with Renny and Johnny.

They looked as if they had been seeing ghosts. Their faces were pale. They swallowed hard as they tried to speak.

Then another figure came around the bend in the corridor. Breaths came in sharply. Then there was silence. A deep, ghastly silence.

That second figure also was General Glassell! There were two General Glassells!

One stood near the prisoners. The other stood almost before them. The two looked exactly alike. They were dressed exactly alike.

It was almost as if one of them was standing before a mirror. Or as if the soldiers were seeing double.

"Arrest that man! He's an impostor!" howled the second General Glassell.

## Chapter XII
## THE TORTURE ROOM

THE soldiers stood rooted. Eyes were bulging, hands were fingering guns nervously. The wrong word would have filled that corridor with a deadly hail of lead. Nerves keyed, the men were ready to shoot at anything or anybody.

The two General Glassells were glowering at each other. The face of each grew red. Their mannerisms were the same, the very lift of their lips was identical.

"You heard me! Arrest that man!" The roar came not from one man, but from two.

Guns came up in the hands of the soldiers. And about half covered the second General Glassell. The others covered the one who had arrived first.

Johnny and Renny stood fast. They were barely breathing, but their eyes were sparkling. They alone of all those in the corridor knew what had happened, knew that one of the two men wearing a general's uniform was really Doc Savage!

But even they did not know which one!

The bronze man had often fooled them by his skillful use of makeup. This time, he had excelled himself. So closely did the two men resemble each other that none could tell which was real and which was counterfeit.

More guards and soldiers poured into the corridor. And that broke the spell. For in the lead was a captain of the guards, carrying a submachine gun.

The captain's wits were quick. He took in the situation with one quick glance.

"Both of you, up with your hands!" he bellowed.

"But I'm General Glassell!" shouted the second general to appear.

"Obey my orders! Arrest that man!" countered the first.

"You'll both be corpses if you don't do as I say!" snapped the captain. "One of you is lying. I'll find out which. Up with your paws!"

Slowly, two pairs of hands went up. The guards moved closer, encircling both of the men dressed as

**All attention was centered on Doc Savage. For just a moment no eyes were on Renny. The big engineer went into action.**

generals. Bayonet points went out, jabbed a trifle harder than was necessary. It is seldom that buck privates get a chance at generals.

"I cannot understand this," the first General Glassell snarled. His Spanish was guttural and harsh. "I come here to take these prisoners to the torture room. Then this fake general appears. I do not understand why you do not arrest him. He must be a spy."

"Spy!" The second general fairly shouted the words. "Spy! Me, the general in command of all Hidalgo's troops? This man looks like me outwardly; he talks like I do. But he is not me. I can prove it!"

A sharp gasp came from Johnny. Renny's huge figure shifted uneasily.

"Then prove it!" bellowed the captain.

The second General Glassell pawed at his tunic, he tore his shirt open.

"You have all fought with me!" he screamed. "Look!"

With one quick motion, he bared his chest. A long, vivid scar ran from the center of that chest almost to the waistline.

"See if the impostor has such a scar!" Glassell shrilled.

"That will not be necessary," came the calm tones of Doc Savage. "I congratulate you. You have won, General Glassell."

RENNY moaned in disappointment. Johnny shook his head sadly.

The real General Glassell was jumping up and down in anger. He surged close to the man who looked like him, took one incredulous look into the other's eyes. Then anger faded; fear and something like awe crept into his face.

"Doc Savage!" he breathed. "But—but you are dead!"

The guards stepped back when they heard Glassell's words. One who had imbibed too heavily turned a pale, sickly color.

"A spirit!" he moaned.

With a visible effort, General Glassell regained control. The red rim of rage crept into his eyes.

"Not a spirit yet!" he blasted. "This bronze man is hard to kill. But he is in my hands now. And this time he will die. I myself shall watch him die. Shall see him die by inches."

All attention was centered on Doc Savage. For just a moment no eyes were on Renny. The big engineer went into action.

The bellow of rage he gave would have done credit to a bull-ape—or to Monk. His huge arms swept out, knocked over two guards as if they had been tenpins.

Then his huge monstrosities of fists knotted. He really went to town! Arms working like pistons, Renny slugged with the grim efficiency of a battering ram.

Fists that could break the panels of a stout door, snapped jaw bones just as easily. Howls of pain and rage resounded through the corridor.

Johnny, also, had started to go into action. He had been stopped almost before he started. One guard was standing behind him. That guard brought the butt of his gun down on the geologist's head with deadly force. General Glassell paid no attention to Renny. He didn't even turn his head when Johnny went down. He held a .45 automatic in one fist, and the muzzle of that automatic was aimed directly at Doc Savage's head.

"Call your man off, or I'll order my captain to sweep this hall with his submachine gun!" he rapped.

The threat was no idle one. The guard captain had stepped back as the fight had started. An amused grin was on his hard features. He held the submachine gun ready for instant action.

Doc could have fought. He undoubtedly could have disarmed Glassell. With Glassell's gun, he could have killed many. But the odds were too heavy against them.

Alone, Doc would have taken the chance. He could not take a chance now without sealing the fate of Johnny and Renny. And thought of his men always came first.

"Hold it, Renny," he said calmly.

The huge engineer's arms dropped to his sides instantly. A surprised look crossed his puritanical features, but he asked no questions. If Doc said stop, then stop it was.

A moment more, and he was pinned in by bayonets. Further struggle was useless.

"To the torture room," Glassell said. And his voice had hoarsened, had become thick and gloating.

The general was well pleased with himself. He had just recovered from a shock that had badly disturbed him. For, finishing his dinner, Glassell had left his room, to meet what, at first, he had thought was a ghost. That had been the last thing he had remembered. A bronze fist had rendered him unconscious.

But lady luck had been with Glassell. A guard had, by chance, heard the thud of the general's body falling to the floor. Investigating, he had almost fallen across the unconscious man. A few minutes had been necessary to revive him. Doc Savage hadn't pulled his punch. Cold water had brought the general to.

There was a gleam in Glassell's eyes as he marched with the prisoners toward the torture room. There was a smile on his face—a smile that spoke death for the bronze man and his aides.

JOHNNY swayed dizzily as he was led into the torture room. His head still ached from the terrific blow he had received. But he forgot that blow, forgot the pain, as he saw the implements for inflicting pain which were stored in the dimly lighted, stone-walled room.

As an archaeologist, Johnny had often studied instruments of torture. He knew the history of most of them, had seen many extensive collections.

But he had never seen a more complete collection than had been assembled here. Every fiendish device perfected during the Spanish Inquisition was there, as well as many used by pirates and savages.

The rack appeared almost gentle compared to the other instruments designed to inflict pain for hours without killing. There was an ironlike cage in the shape of a man.

A victim would be placed there, and the door closed. The inside of that door was of solid iron spikes. Whenever the victim grew tired and slumped, those spikes drove into his body and forced him erect.

Hours of mental and physical torture would pass before the poor wretch would finally fall forward, impale himself on those spikes and be unable to rise again. He would die a slow, horrible death.

Then there was the platform to which a victim

would be trussed by his thumbs, with a noose slack about his neck. Blocks of wood were placed under the feet and the arms pulled up high over the head.

Then those blocks of wood were removed, one at a time, until the victim hung by his thumbs, pulling himself up, until he could stand no more and dropped down to strangle.

Iron pinchers were there. Spots were on those pinchers and the spots were not from rust. Toenails and finger nails were extracted with those gentle instruments, while other devices cut away the eyelids.

But all these were given only a passing glance by Renny. His attention centered on a huge machine in the middle of the room. His eyes grew wide, and he gave a strangled cry as he saw that machine. For Doc Savage was being led toward it!

The bronze man appeared perfectly calm. Rusty handcuffs had been placed on his wrists, with those wrists behind him. Guards were all about him. And at his side was General Glassell.

"I will explain this little pet of mine to you," Glassell jeered. "I am sure you will enjoy it. You see, we attach cords to each of your arms and legs. We pull you into the air, spread-eagled.

"You are hoisted high, at first. Under you, you see, is this sharp sword. It will be aimed directly at your belly. You will be lowered slowly, oh so slowly. When that sword pricks your stomach, you will draw yourself up. You are a strong man. That is what will make this amusing.

"For long minutes, perhaps, you will hold yourself up; then you will sink down. The sword will cut you; it may drive just a little way into your belly. You will lift again, and again you will drop, until finally that sword will start cutting into you, half an inch at a time until at last—"

"Shall we start now?" Doc asked politely.

Renny half sobbed. Doc had been in many tough places. But none, the big engineer thought, had ever been as tough as this. And he was helpless. Johnny was helpless. They had to stand by and watch—

*Blam!*

There was a sudden explosion, it came near the door to the torture chamber.

Tense nerves jumped. Guards spun. Their guns roared even before they could look. Then blank looks of astonishment crossed their faces.

No one was there!

"Fools! Must we wait all night?"

Half abashed, but still wondering, the guards turned back to the scene in the center of the room. Their eyes grew wider still.

The general was swinging a gun in his hand. With his other arm, he was supporting his prisoner. A mark on the jaw showed where that gun had collided hard.

THE guard captain leaped forward. Two other men joined him. Quickly they took the rusty handcuffs from the unconscious man's wrists. As swiftly, they attached strong cords to ankles and arms. The limp figure was swung up in the air, to hang spread-eagled, directly above the sharp-pointed sword beneath.

Johnny kept back a cry with difficulty. He had hoped until the last that the bronze man would find some way to escape. Now it could not be done. Knocked unconscious by that blow to the jaw with the butt of the heavy .45, he would recover to find slow, certain death awaiting him.

An evil, coarse chuckle came from the general. Features contorted into a hideous grimace, he whirled on Renny and Johnny, studied them for a moment. The corners of his mouth lifted higher.

"Are all the guards here?" he snapped at the captain.

"*Si*, none wished to miss the treat," the man agreed.

"Give me two brave men who are not afraid to kill," the general ordered. "I have thought of an added delight. The bronze man is more worried about his aides than he is about himself. If he should revive and find them missing, his mental torment will equal the pain the sword will inflict"

"*Si, si*, it is so," the captain smirked.

"Then give me two men. I will take these two out and place them where they will be safe. Do not lower that poor pig up there, even if he regains consciousness, until I return."

"*Si*, my general."

Johnny and Renny were bound swiftly. Then they were marched from the room. The general followed them, an almost insane look on his features.

The heavy door of the torture room swung closed. Instantly the general seized the heavy lock, threw it in place and locked it.

"What—" began one of the guards.

STRONG fingers flicked out. They caught the man just at the base of the brain, pressed hidden nerves there. The man collapsed like a bag of flour.

The second guard brought his gun up. It seemed to him later that strength must have deserted him. The gun was taken from him so fast he did not know what had happened. A hand smacked down over his mouth, he was propelled toward the entrance to the dungeon at a fast pace.

A moment more and they had reached the night air. The guard was flung back up against a wall. He hit so hard he was stunned.

"Turn around," a quiet voice ordered Johnny and Renny. The bonds were torn from their wrists.

"Now get back down there, save that general of yours before he is impaled on his own pet device," rasped the terrible figure that stood over the guard.

The guard turned, ran as if demons were pursuing him.

"How did you do it?" gasped Johnny, using small words in his surprise.

"A nitro capsule. I had it in my mouth, shot it across the room. The handcuffs were already loose. When the explosion came, I merely knocked out Glassell and put the handcuffs on him."

"Holy cow," exclaimed Renny.

Doc did not seem to hear. He was already running through the darkness. His aides took after him.

As they ran, they heard renewed firing at the palace, firing so fierce that it could only mean disaster.

## Chapter XIII
### THE LEADER STRIKES

THE small band of palace defenders was hard-pressed. Not many soldiers remained. Some had deserted in fear of the hand of death. Enemy bullets had accounted for many more.

The attackers were staging a bitter assault. But it seemed concentrated at the front gates. With a stone wall and concealed firing pits to aid them, the defenders fought desperately on. Even though only comparatively few remained, they held back the khaki-clad legions.

Near one side of the palace, a sentry paced restlessly. He strained his eyes, trying to peer into the darkness. Upon his shoulders rested the task of protecting President Avispa. And he preferred the sounds of the battle in front to the ominous stillness of the shadows inside the palace grounds.

That sentry wasn't afraid of guns. But he had heard of the hand of death. And a death that could creep out of the darkness and leave him with a horrible red stain on his neck made sweat course down his backbone.

A weird, high-pitched scream pierced the night. It came even above the crack of rifles and the typewriter-like chatter of machine guns. The sentry gripped his gun tightly, found it wet and slippery with his own perspiration.

Victims of the hand of death were supposed to scream like that.

The sentry pivoted, retraced his steps along his post. And behind him, two furtive figures crept from the shadows. They drifted noiselessly toward the side of the palace.

"Wait for a moment. I will take care of the guard," came a low, flat voice.

One of the two furtive figures halted. The other slipped ahead, blended with the blackness of the palace wall.

The sentry whirled, started back toward where that lurking assassin waited. He saw a dim movement, and opened his mouth to yell. That yell never came.

A vagrant moonbeam flickered faintly on cold steel. A long knife plunged up to the hilt in the sentry's heart.

The sentry was already dead, he could not scream. But with his last flash of consciousness, he saw something that froze his brain, made him grateful for the merciful plunge of the knife.

A hand darted out for his throat. It was a strange-appearing hand, a dreadful monstrosity. That hand closed on soft flesh and squeezed hard. But the sentry was saved that horror. Life had already departed.

The killer moved into the open briefly. His companion sped to his side. That companion was breathing heavily, his own eyes were filled with fear. Teeth chattered, despite the warmth of the night.

"Stop it, fool!" hissed a cold, flat voice.

With quick steps the killer reached a window, pushed it open. A moment more and he was inside. His companion followed him. Light showed under the bottom of a door leading to an adjoining room. The killer crept forward. His hand was light as he turned the knob of the door, swung it open slowly.

Before them, but with his back turned, sat President Avispa. The white-haired president of Hidalgo was studying maps.

A sudden draft of air swept the back of his neck. Avispa did not look up. One of his hands moved toward a drawer at his side. Then that hand halted.

"Hands still, Avispa!" snapped a cold, quiet voice. "Turn around!"

Defiantly, the white-haired president's head snapped up, he whirled in his chair. Then the defiance went out of him as if he were a punctured balloon.

He knew death had called for him.

THE lifeless, expressionless face of The Leader was before President Avispa. Malevolent eyes swept scornfully over the white-haired man. A gun was steady in one fist.

But it was on the frozen-faced one's companion that Avispa's attention centered.

The other was removing a hat. He unwrapped a long muffler from about his neck. Casually he slipped from a light topcoat. As he stood revealed in the light, he also was white-haired, his features were lined.

"A double!" Avispa whispered.

The frozen-faced one nodded. "Exactly." His cold, flat voice was clipped. "Doc Savage is not the only one who knows something of the art of makeup."

"W-what do you want?" Avispa's tones were choked.

"Your abdication—in return for your life."

There was silence for a moment.

"If you will abdicate and name General Glassell your successor, you will be spared," those cold, flat tones went on.

"And if I don't?"

The malevolent eyes of the frozen-faced one sparkled. "If you don't, you will die! My companion here will take your place. He is made up to look just like you. His act will be sufficiently good to fool your guards."

"But will it fool Doc Savage?" Avsipa asked quietly.

The lifeless face of The Leader split. Teeth showed as the red flare of rage lighted his eyes. The hand that held the gun came up, the fingers showing white on the butt.

"Doc Savage! Doc Savage is dead!" he half shrieked. He jumped up and down, screaming curses of hate.

Avispa took a chance. His hand shot to the desk drawer, closed over the gun that was there.

*Blam!*

Two shots sounded as one. Avispa's weapon dropped from his fist. There was a red stain across his knuckles.

The makeup double leaped forward, he smashed the aged president squarely in the face with a fist. Avispa was slammed back into his chair. Crimson streamed from his nose.

"I could have killed you then." The Leader's voice had become low and merciless. "I *am* going to kill you, but that way would be too easy."

He moved forward, his lifeless face jutted out, his malevolent eyes staring. One hand still held his gun. The other hand came from a pocket. It was a peculiar-looking hand. It appeared like a club-foot at the end of an arm. Queer fingers opened and closed.

Avispa opened his mouth, but no sound came. His vocal cords appeared paralyzed.

"Think, as you are en route to hell, of what will happen to your people," the frozen-faced one gloated. "They are to become the accursed of the earth. *Nothing* can save them! Your double, here, will rule for a time. Then Glassell. And now—"

Those clutching fingers shot out. They gripped President Avispa firmly by the throat.

A thin, high-pitched scream—a dreadful scream—broke from the aged man's lips. The bloody imprint of a hand appeared on his neck.

DOC SAVAGE was easing over the palace wall when he heard that scream. Close behind him were Renny and Johnny. Both aides knew their only chance to get by the guards was to follow him.

"Holy cow, what was that?" exclaimed the big engineer.

The bronze man did not answer. It had seemed he was moving fast before. But his speed then was nothing as compared with the speed he now showed.

Before his aides could hit the ground, he had dropped over the wall, was racing across the grounds toward the palace. He could see the faint light through the shade at Avispa's office windows.

A peculiar trill sounded. At Doc's feet was stretched the body of the sentry. He stopped only for a second. That second was enough to show the sentry was dead.

The bronze man then vaulted through the open window, dived into Avispa's office.

The white-haired president was slumped back in his chair. The prints on his throat were rapidly growing more red, His heart had stopped, he had quit breathing.

Renny and Johnny pounded into the room.

"Well, I'll be superamalgamated!" boomed Johnny.

Doc Savage crouched over the body of Carlos Avispa. His hands darted to the secret pouch that was always strapped next to his skin. He took out a tiny hypodermic syringe and a small vial. In an instant, he jabbed the hypodermic into the reddening flesh and shot home the plunger.

"If the stain continues to deepen for more than a few seconds, there is no hope," the bronze man clipped.

Even as he spoke, he was drawing another syringe from the pouch. This one was as long as a darning needle. Renny gasped as Doc jerked loose Avispa's shirt. The bronze man placed the needle directly over the white-haired president's heart. Then he drove that needle in, deep through the flesh.

Silence gripped the room. But that silence was broken. A voice from somewhere outside ripped through the night, rasping metallically from a powerful amplifier.

"It grieves me to confess that I have been deceived," the voice cried. "I had thought Juan Glassell was our enemy. He is not. And I had thought Doc Savage and his aides were our friends. That, also, was a mistake."

Incredulous gasps came from Renny and Johnny. Even through an amplifier, an intimate would have sworn the voice was that of Carlos Avispa.

Doc Savage did not look up. He was still working over the stricken body of the white-haired president.

And slowly at first, the red hand of death was fading.

"Extraordinary phenomenon," Johnny muttered. The geologist felt Avispa's wrist. A pulsebeat came faintly.

"The adrenaline injection in the heart I understood," Renny said. "But the other?"

Doc did not appear to hear. Avispa's eyes opened. He stared about wildly for an instant, incredible horror still mirrored in the pupils of his eyes.

"—and so," the amplifier blared outside, "as president of Hidalgo, I call upon you to surrender."

RENNY'S mouth dropped open. He leaped toward the door that connected with other parts of the palace. That door was locked.

An expression, almost of glee, crossed the big engineer's face. He squared off before the door, drew back one huge fist. With an explosion like that of a minor bomb, his fist struck. Two-inch oaken panels split.

The white-haired president stirred.

"Those words! That man—" he gasped.

Doc nodded. He bent over, lifted the white-haired president in his arms.

As Renny reached through and unlocked the door, Doc pushed past him, darted into the hallway.

At the front of the palace, the impostor was smiling, but there was a worried look in his eyes. He had spoken well and persuasively. But still a sullen murmur came from the defenders.

"What I say is true," he repeated into the amplifier. "Doc Savage is really the man behind this revolt. He wants all the gold from the Valley of the Vanished. He intends to defraud Hidalgo. I was tricked. General Glassell argued with me, but I did not believe him. Now, I know the truth. We must surrender. I will let Glassell become—"

He broke off.

A bronze man, carrying the white-haired figure of President Avispa appeared at his side. Avispa was weak, clung to Doc's shoulder as he was set on his feet.

The impostor's face paled. He glanced desperately toward a dim and darkened corner of the parade ground. He couldn't see the half-concealed figure there. But he needed instructions.

Sounds of firing outside the palace walls had stopped. It was as if the attackers expected an immediate surrender.

The crowd of palace soldiers stood in stunned silence. What they saw they could not comprehend. The impostor was an actor. He thought he could bluff it out. He screamed into the amplifier:

"Doc Savage is here with an impostor! Kill them before they do us harm!"

A roar came from the crowd. Figures crowded close to the stand.

The bronze man did not attempt to speak. He leaped to the side of the fake Avispa, seized him by his hair. The wig came off.

The impostor then stood revealed as a black-haired, villainous fake. The mob went wild.

THE impostor wasted no time. He leaped from the platform with a scream. Palace guardsmen raced toward him.

Doc Savage stepped before the amplifier. "Do not kill him," he said quietly. "His master is the one we want. Save this man until we can find out what he knows."

Renny and Johnny leaped into the raging throng, tried to fight their way to its center, where the impostor had gone down under a struggling mass.

Doc might as well have shouted down a well. Even over the amplifier, his voice was drowned on the howls of mob rage.

And Renny and Johnny stood no chance at all. They could not even penetrate the outer fringes of the struggling mass. The guardsmen had caught a traitor. They knew how to deal with traitors.

The impostor was literally torn to pieces.

From a darkened corner, at the far edge of the palace grounds, a frozen-faced man with malevolent eyes stared in amazement. A plan that couldn't go wrong, had gone wrong! A man that should be dead, was not dead!

Silent as a wraith, The Leader vanished from the grounds. Grim orders were issued.

"Wipe the palace from the face of the earth! Kill every man inside!"

Guns went into action. And for the first time, artillery was brought up. That artillery would soon blast the palace into dust.

## Chapter XIV
## A VOICE FROM THE SKY

THERE was a small chemical laboratory in the presidential palace. Carlos Avispa paced nervously up and down. Doc worked quietly at a small vat with several chemicals. Renny and Johnny stared dolefully out a window.

A red glare showed dully against heavy, overhanging clouds. Part of Blanco Grande was in flames. The reprisal of The Leader had not been long in coming.

"He's a killer," Renny muttered. "We gotta get that guy, somehow."

"I thought, at first, Glassell was the archfiend," Avispa said. "But this is beyond his planning. Even for all the gold in the Valley of the Vanished."

"The Mayan gold is only the start of this," Doc's voice said quietly. "And Glassell is merely a cog."

"Holy cow," Renny boomed, "what more than gold would he want?"

"This man is a person of unlimited ambition," Doc said cryptically, "Also one of ability."

The shrill of the telephone in the laboratory interrupted him. Avispa answered. His haggard face grew even grayer as he listened to an excited voice on the other end of the wire. His lips grew into a tight line. When he hung up, he turned to Doc.

"It was a spy I have in their camp. I am afraid you must go, Doc Savage. I know your sworn pledge to the Mayans. Five thousand troops have left for the Valley of the Vanished."

He paused, seemed about to speak again, then changed his mind. Doc looked at him for a moment.

"That is not all the message you received," he said gently. "Tell me the rest of it."

Avispa hesitated.

"Another large group of troops has been left behind. Even now, they are bringing up artillery to shell the palace. When we are wiped out, Blanco Grande is to be burned."

"Astounding retributory determination," Johnny grumbled. "We should do something."

"I can do nothing but urge you to leave," Avispa said sadly. "My place is here. I must die with Blanco Grande, but you should do your best for the Mayans."

Doc walked to one corner of the room. Concealed in a wall was a small but powerful radio transmitter. The bronze man flicked on the switch. He twirled the dials, waiting briefly for the tubes to heat.

"Monk speaking," a voice bawled. It was startlingly clear as it boomed from a tiny loudspeaker.

"A large enemy force is on the way to the Valley of the Vanished," Doc's voice clipped. "I will endeavor to be there with Renny and Johnny before they arrive. But in the meantime, there is much to be done." He issued instructions in concise, swift sentences.

"I gotcha, Doc," Monk's voice said. The radio clicked off.

The bronze man sped back to the chemical vat. He poured a peculiar-colored liquid into several bottles. His flake gold eyes gleamed.

"Wait," he instructed briefly. Then he was gone.

THE rumble of heavy artillery, being towed through the streets, sounded ominously as the bronze man left the palace grounds.

Khaki-clad rebels were jubilant. When that artillery was fired at point-blank range, the battle would be over. Blanco Grande would be theirs.

A small, smartly-clad captain strutted down the street. He had served in wars all over the world. He had fought under a dozen flags. But none that afforded him as much pleasure as now. Here was an opportunity for just the sort of wild looting and killing that he liked.

Strolling easily, he went past a dark alleyway. Steel-strong fingers reached out, caught him back of the neck. He floated into the alleyway.

The captain was no coward. But he felt fear then. He tried to struggle. He could not seem to move a muscle. A low voice came to his ears, a vibrant, compelling voice.

"Where is the gold?"

"W-what gold?" he stammered.

A finger pressed on nerves at the back of his head.

"The gold is under guard in the bank building. It was taken from the Mayans," the captain said in a dull, colorless voice.

Pressure on that nerve had done something to the captain. He found that he could not think clearly enough to lie. He had to tell the truth.

A hand flicked across the back of his head. The captain dropped to the ground, unconscious. A shadowy, dimly-seen figure eased through the night. It headed toward the bank where the stolen gold was hidden.

The bank was brightly lighted. There was a reason for that. The rebel soldiers did not trust each other. They wanted to see anyone who went in or out. The structure itself was a severe, stout affair of stone.

There were five men on guard. They were villainous-looking criminals and well-armed. A voice came from around a corner. It was a feminine voice. It screamed in pain.

"Help! Help! Let me go! Please!"

The five khaki-clad men grinned evilly. They strolled down to the corner, peered around. There was nothing there. Grumbling, puzzled, and faintly worried, they hurried back to their posts.

Inside, a bronze figure was active.

Pile after pile of gold was there. That gold had cost the lives of many brave Mayans.

The bottles of chemicals came from the bronze man's pockets.

The guards were talking uneasily. The rumor had spread. Word had come that Doc Savage was not dead. And the mysterious call for help when there had been no one about, weighed on over-tensed nerves.

"I've heard that the bronze guy was an excellent ventriloquist; maybe he played a trick on us," one muttered.

Fear-shadowed eyes glanced into the bank. A voice howled hoarsely. Something was there.

Guns ready, the men darted to the door. That door was unlocked. It had been locked ten minutes before.

Frantically they rushed in, darted toward the back of the building. Then they halted, abashed. A dummy hung there. There was no sign of any living creature.

Tiptoeing, lips tight, the five guards crept out. Something had happened—something puzzling. But, without words, they decided what they would do: they would say nothing. To admit someone had entered the gold storeroom would be inviting the hand of death.

At the outskirts of Blanco Grande, the tall figure of Doc Savage moved swiftly to a small field. His plane was concealed there. The motor of that plane roared.

Outside the palace, artillerymen were swinging their guns into lines. Shells were piled by the guns. In the distance sounded the drone of a plane's motor.

The artillerymen glanced up curiously, then pushed shells home. In a moment the palace of Hidalgo would be no more.

"This is Doc Savage speaking," came a clear, vibrant voice. The voice came from the sky.

"SOLDIERS of General Glassell, listen!" The clipped tones of the bronze man won instant attention. Artillerymen halted their work, necks craning upward. Everywhere in the capital city, noise ceased. It was as if all were listening to that voice.

The plane loafed easily in the sky. A radio loudspeaker amplified the voice of Doc Savage thousands of times. Each word he said came clearly.

"You were promised gold for your fighting," Doc's voice went on. "For that gold, you must murder innocent people. But how do you know, even after you have committed your crimes, that you will receive the gold that is promised you?"

Jeering laughter rose from the khaki-clad men below.

"You have seen the gold, I know." It seemed almost as though Doc had heard those jeers, and was answering them. "When the Mayans were slaughtered and the gold they escorted brought here, that gold was exhibited. But were you given any of it?"

The jeers died suddenly. That was so. The men had seen the gold, but none had been paid with the precious metal. With closer attention, they listened to the next words from the sky.

"Early tonight, more than half your force was dispatched to the Valley of the Vanished. It is there that the real gold is. There is more of it there than could be carried by all of you. There is enough there to make every man a king. But again, how do you know you will receive your share?"

The khaki-clad men were silent. Hard faces bore wondering expressions.

"There is one way in which you might answer that question." Doc's voice seemed to rise slightly. His plane pivoted directly over the heart of the city.

"If those who led you are playing fairly with you, then what you think is gold now stored under guard, is really gold. But suppose it is not? Suppose the gold has been taken by your leaders, and only worthless metal remains?

"Then, in that case, you have been tricked. You have nothing. The men storming the Valley of the Vanished may get gold, but how do you know if you will get anything?

"I say to you then—investigate. Find out if that is really gold that is stored in the bank. If it is not, then go after those who are really on the way to a fortune. Do not be fooled!"

A moment of silence followed those last words. Then there was a yell from a thousand throats. Gold, not glory, was what these men fought for.

Artillery was forgotten. Machine guns were forgotten. Hundreds of yelling men smashed through the streets toward the bank.

THE five men guarding the bank did not know whether to join the rush or to fight. They lifted their guns, hesitantly.

That was a mistake.

They were cut down almost before they could move. Angered killers swarmed into the building.

The sacks of gold were at the rear. In an instant, those sacks had been ripped open.

Howls of disappointment and futile anger came from those who were close enough to see.

When the golden loot had first been brought back by the raiders, it had been shown to the soldiers. It had gleamed dully, as only gold can gleam.

What the khaki-clad men saw now did not gleam. There was no sign of gold. Only bars and ingots of lead lay before them.

The word passed swiftly. The leaden bars were hurled furiously aside. Men rushed from the building. In disordered streams, they poured down the street.

It was just as well they did not investigate too closely. One leaden bar struck a marble wall with such force that the bar broke in two pieces.

Had the ends of those pieces been examined carefully, they would have revealed much. The outer side of the bars appeared to be lead. For as much as a quarter of an inch from the surface, they also appeared lead.

But the centers were pure gold.

The chemical Doc had mixed, a combination chiefly of graphite, had done its work well. It had worked into the porous, precious metal, had seemingly worked alchemy in reverse, changing gold into lead.

Actually, it had done nothing of the sort. But the angered, charging troops did not know that.

They did not even recall Doc's actual words, did not know that he had not lied to them, but had merely tricked them. They believed the gold that was to have been paid them had been stolen, that their only hope of getting gold was to join the rush on the Valley of the Vanished.

Frantically, they streamed from Blanco Grande, following those who had left hours before.

High above them, Doc looked on, a peculiar expression in his flake gold eyes.

He had saved President Avispa. He had saved Blanco Grande from destruction.

But at what a cost! Now, hundreds more gold-hungry attackers were streaming toward the Mayans he was sworn to protect.

HALF an hour later, Doc was in the air again. This time, he pointed the nose of his plane toward the Valley of the Vanished. With him were Renny and Johnny.

They did not see the plane that left close after them. That plane carried General Glassell and a frozen-faced one whose eyes could only glare with rage.

But the evil brain behind that frozen face was working. A preliminary skirmish had been lost. But the main fight was still to come. And The Leader was confident.

For he knew the cards were stacked against Doc Savage.

## Chapter XV
### SHOT DOWN

THE sun was high when Doc eased the motor of his plane and headed downward.

Below lay a scene such as few have ever viewed. It was a big valley, shaped roughly like an egg. Most of the ground was sloping, far too steep upon which to land a plane. But there was one small, smooth lake.

In the center of the valley towered a pyramid. The sides were absolutely smooth, except for the center where steps had been carved. At the top, on a flat place, stood a temple, with a flat stone roof, supported by square pillars.

The entire pyramid glowed with a yellow, metallic aurora. It had been constructed of quartz literally filled with pure gold.

Doc had arrived at the Valley of the Vanished.

As the bronze man sat his plane down on the small lake, scores of figures raced toward him. The air was filled with strange cries of welcome.

In the lead was a tall, solid man, with snowy-white hair. His skin was golden-colored, he wore a broad girdle of red, with the ends forming an apron in front and back.

Close behind him was a young woman, nearly as tall as he, whose beauty caused a gasp from Renny and Johnny, even though they had seen her before.

"Greetings, King Chaac and Princess Monja," Doc said in perfect Mayan.

The lumbering figure of Monk and the tall, perfectly attired Ham, with Long Tom at his heels were approaching at a more dignified pace.

"Boy, I'm glad you got here!" Monk bellowed.

Renny's ordinarily tight-lipped face had relaxed in a huge grin. Johnny appeared just as pleased as Mayans rushed to the sides of the plane and hoisted them out, carrying them through the water on their shoulders.

King Chaac seemed almost speechless. He grasped Doc's hands and held them tightly in his own. His daughter had eyes only for the bronze man. She was looking at him in a way that showed clearly that she loved him, even though she knew that love was hopeless.

"It has been long, too long since you were here," Princess Monja said. Her voice was low and trembled slightly with emotion.

"Son of my old friend, I am happy," King Chaac said.

Others crowded about, chatting happily. Renny and Johnny were seized by old friends who talked as if they could never stop. Monk and Ham eased their way closer, moving slowly through the throng. Long Tom stood back, his eyes thoughtful.

No sign of the danger in which they all stood was marring the welcome to Doc. Young men and women, dressed in clothing that showed expert weaving and dyeing, some with fine wire-gold interwoven, were bubbling joyously.

A dozen were trying to talk to Doc at once. The bronze man was answering all as swiftly as he could. His features were as emotionless as usual.

But Long Tom wondered just what memories this reception brought back to the bronze man. King Chaac was still erect, but his hair was whiter, his shoulders more bowed than when last he and Doc had met.

And Long Tom knew that Doc must be thinking of that first meeting, must be recalling the sad events that had led up to it, even though he did not show that fact.

For the gold in the Valley of the Vanished, the gold that had provided Doc Savage with funds to fight wrongdoers and now was being sought by the worst criminal of them all, had been a legacy to the bronze man from his father.

Clark Savage, Sr., had discovered this lost valley with its strange inhabitants many years before. He had secured possession of the land inclosing the valley, and had made arrangements with King Chaac for Doc to have the gold when the bronze man came and proved himself worthy.

Then Clark Savage, Sr., had been murdered.

LONG TOM'S eyes darkened with pain as he thought of that, even though it was long in the past. Enemies had killed the elder Savage, had tried to prevent Doc from ever reaching or claiming his legacy.

Those enemies had been defeated. Doc had won out, but the loss of his father had been a severe blow.

And now the Valley of the Vanished was threatened again. It was threatened by modern, well-armed foes. Even Long Tom, with all his marvelous faith in the ability of the bronze man, did not see how the present peril could be defeated.

The happy, chatting Mayans were faced with extermination by relentless, merciless foes.

Still talking to King Chase, with Princess Monja clinging to one arm, the bronze man was led toward the Mayan village.

"I am glad you have come in our time of danger," Chaac said with simple dignity.

"Our enemies are many. Our task will be a difficult one," said Doc Savage.

"But with you here, I know we shall be safe," the Mayan king responded.

"The preparations you asked us to make are completed," Long Tom said, drawing nearer.

"Those bums are in for a surprise when they jump us," Monk put in.

"What I cannot understand is who could be behind this," said Ham. "You mentioned a General Glassell—"

"He is only a tool," Doc Savage said.

"And a renegade Mayan," King Chaac said, bitterly.

"I thought so," the bronze man agreed gravely. "His skin and features showed me he was of your race."

"He is a product of what you call civilization," Chaac continued, and his face was hard. "Also, he is the son of Morning Breeze."

Renny's puritanical face lighted. "Morning Breeze! The one who tried to kill us when we were here before?"

King Chaac nodded. "That is correct. And Glassell, as he calls himself, really is Son of the Moon, the child of Morning Breeze. After Morning Breeze was killed, Son of the Moon apparently reformed. He became very popular with our younger people."

"He is no good," Princess Monja said unexpectedly. Her beautiful face twisted scornfully. "He tried to make love to me!"

"Son of the Moon convinced a majority of my people that we were missing much that civilization could give us," King Chaac explained. "He persuaded me he should be sent to Blanco Grande. He said he would study, would bring back to us things that would help us."

"He didn't," Monja said angrily. "Instead—"

"Instead," Chaac continued, "he became a too apt pupil of civilization. We heard disgraceful stories about him. But President Avispa liked him, made him head of his army. Now he has betrayed that trust."

"And now he intends to kill his own people," Princess Monja said.

"Not if we can help it," growled Monk. The hairy chemist's gaze never left the face of the girl.

"Hero saves life of girl's father, wins her hand," whispered Ham maliciously.

Monk blushed.

THE council of war was held in King Chaac's quarters. Doc sat at the head of the table with the Mayan ruler. The others ranged themselves on either side.

"We have made a thorough study of the terrain," said Ham. His words were crisp, concise.

"Now we have Brigadier General Theodore Marley Brooks speaking," Monk put in slyly.

"With Major Thomas J. Roberts and Lieutenant Colonel Andrew Blodgett Mayfair, I reconnoitered the situation," Ham went on smoothly. "It is bad."

"The entrance to this valley is a narrow one," objected Renny.

"True. It could be held against a large number of men—provided we had sufficient modern weapons," Ham replied. "But while we have only our mercy pistols and a few other things, the foe is in possession of high-powered artillery."

"Did not your diligent preparations provide for such a contingency?" asked Johnny.

Ham grinned. "We followed out Doc's orders. That is the only reason we may hope for success."

"I think the invaders are in for a surprise," Long Tom agreed. He smiled with quiet pride.

King Chaac turned to Doc Savage. "What are your instructions for my people?" he asked simply.

The bronze man's flake gold eyes swept swiftly over his aides. "We do not wish to cause loss of life among your people," he said. "However, you have scouts out now, I presume?"

Chaac nodded. "They are watching all possible routes of approach."

"Then there is little more they can do," the bronze man said. "But we should not underestimate the foe who opposes us. He is clever. Above all, counsel your young men to take no unnecessary chances."

"They are filled with anger at the brutal murder of their friends," said Chaac. "When the invaders appear, they will want vengeance. They may be difficult to control."

"But they must be controlled," Doc Savage said quietly. "Against the modern weapons of the soldiers of fortune who are marching here, they would stand no chance."

"They have motorized battalions," Renny put in. "They have artillery, machine guns and rifles. When they attack—"

He broke off. A tall Mayan had suddenly raced into the room. Perspiration was pouring from his body. He spoke excitedly.

"They come! They come! An advance guard is even now entering the canyon only one removed from this!"

KING CHAAC started to speak. Doc Savage already was on his feet. The others leaped up.

"You remain here. I will see what is to be done," the bronze man clipped.

Without waiting for a reply, he vanished from the room. Johnny was close behind him. Monk and Ham exchanged one quick glance, then poured from the room, followed by Long Tom and Renny.

Doc was racing down the street of the village with long, quick strides. He did not appear to be moving fast, but a Mayan runner who attempted to keep up with him found himself quickly outdistanced.

"He's going for the plane!" Long Tom shouted. "We've got to stay here, but at least we can look!"

He turned the opposite way and sped toward a narrow, dangerous trail that led upward, toward the head of the canyon—the direction from which the invaders must come.

Princess Monja appeared from a nearby building. Without a word, she joined the group of running men.

"You go back!" Monk roared.

The girl shook her head. A strange look was on her face. "If Doc Savage goes into danger, I want to see," she argued.

Ham chuckled as Monk's jaw dropped. "Thought she was worried about you, you hairy ape, did you?" the dapper lawyer gibed.

Behind them, a plane's motor came to life with a sullen roar. As Renny glanced over one shoulder, he saw the plane move swiftly across the small lake, then take to the air.

The climb was steep, but Doc's aides were all in good condition. They mounted swiftly.

Princess Monja alone lagged slightly. Renny caught hold of one of her arms in a huge fist. Monk glowered, and grabbed her on the other side.

The plane was now far above them, moving over the end of the canyon.

"Lucky Doc destroyed most of their air fleet, or we'd be worse off than we are," Renny commented. "A few eggs from the air could sure make it tough."

*Br-r-r-r-r-r!*

The wicked snap of a machine gun came faintly to their ears.

Just as the group reached the top of the mountain, where they could look down into the adjoining valley, a puff of smoke appeared in the sky near Doc's plane.

"They've even brought antiaircraft guns along with them," Long Tom marveled.

It was impossible to see the men who were firing on Doc. They had taken shelter among trees and rocks several miles away. But the sound of shooting came clearly.

More and more puffs of smoke appeared near Doc's plane. The bronze man was swinging the ship around in lazy circles.

Princess Monja's dainty fingers gripped hard into Monk's arm.

"They won't—they can't—he'll be safe, won't he?" she asked anxiously.

"Sure," Monk comforted. "Doc can take care of himself. He won't take any unnecessary chances.

Why—"

A moan came from Johnny. The lean archaeologist looked sick suddenly. An exclamation of dismay came from Monk and Long Tom. Ham's hands clenched tightly, while Renny was banging one huge fist into an open palm as pain showed on his tight-lipped face.

Smoke was billowing from Doc's plane. Even as they watched, the plane faltered in mid-air. Slowly, its nose dropped; then it was falling over and over. Going down, down—

## Chapter XVI
### A NET CLOSES

"HE—he's lost!" sobbed Princess Monja.

"Don't be silly. Doc will be all right," said Monk, but his simian features were worried.

"Ah-ah, Doc has extricated himself from much more precarious situations than this," Johnny said hollowly. His glasses were bobbing up and down.

The plane was almost out of sight now, sinking behind a projecting corner of the canyon. Smoke had increased until huge billows were rolling from the stricken craft.

"Doc's got something up his sleeve. Don't you worry!" boomed Renny. But the huge engineer's mouth was compressed tightly, his features even more severe than usual.

"I—I'm glad we got the stuff rigged up in time," Long Tom said, desperately trying to change the subject.

His yellow complexion even more unhealthy-appearing than before, the electrical wizard glanced down the rim of the canyon where long, pipelike weapons had been rigged. Those weapons pointed downward, so that they covered the approach to the Valley of the Vanished.

A faint crash came to their ears. A cloud of dust rose far down in the canyon. Doc's plane had struck.

"Let's get back to the village," Monja pleaded brokenly. Tears were streaming from her face.

Had Monja not been present, Doc's aides probably would have delayed their departure. As it was, they followed the weeping princess.

Thus, they did not see the creeping, stealthily moving figures who were wiggling their way to where the pipelike weapons hung over the canyon's rim.

The safety of those in the Valley of the Vanished depended upon those weapons. They were supposed to be guarded at all times. Only chance left them vulnerable. The slinking figures were taking advantage of that chance.

DOC'S plane crashed almost at the spot where the advance guard of the soldiers of fortune had made their stand.

Khaki-clad figures, bayoneted guns ready, rushed forward as the ship came down. At the last moment the plane seemed to right itself, but still it struck with resounding force.

Smoke clouds rolled out on all sides. The soldiers plunged into the smoke and vanished from view. Others followed them. Some were shouting hoarsely as they charged.

Those shouts died suddenly. The smoke spread out in a thin cloud. Even those who had hung back were enveloped in it.

A huge captain, face scarred from some ancient encounter with a sabre, halted abruptly, a heavy automatic in one hand.

"Halt!" he roared. "Wait!"

The sound of his voice appeared to dwindle on the second word. A faint whiff of the smoke had reached his nostrils. A surprised expression crossed his battle-hardened features.

Slowly, he crumpled. His arms fell limply to his sides. His head landed on one of those arms. His eyes closed as in sleep. Around him, others were dropping. Those who had first darted toward the plane already were down.

Scarcely ten seconds after the plane had crashed, not a soldier in the advance guard was on his feet. The entire company was sprawled motionless, weapons still in hand.

Slowly, the smoke cloud lifted. Fresh currents of air swept through the canyon, rolling the mist away.

A soldier stirred, sat up to stare about stupidly. One by one others awakened. Their faces were dull and stupid. They pressed their hands to their heads as if unaware of what had happened.

The scarred-faced captain recovered more swiftly. Intelligence dawned in his eyes. He leaped up, snarling viciously as he raced to the side of the plane. Shock-absorbers on that plane had taken up most of the force of the crash landing. The ship was virtually undamaged.

And it was empty!

"Where did he go?" the captain roared angrily.

The soldiers glanced about with dull eyes. One, a huge fellow in khaki, moved over to the machine guns that had been trained on the plane, started to dismantle them.

"They—they ain't nobody here," a sergeant gasped. There was a note of awe in his voice. "Would a ghost 'a' been flying that plane?"

"Ghost, hell!" The captain's jaws worked furiously. "This is one of that Doc Savage's tricks!" His eyes widened suddenly, and he whipped a hand to one pocket. A relieved expression showed on his hard features as his fingers felt papers there.

"Form your men and call the roll!" he shouted.

The sergeant wet his lips uncertainly, "But—but, captain," he objected, "there had to be someone in that plane. There ain't now. Where did he go? And what happened to us?"

"Form the company!" the captain roared, his face livid with anger. "Doc Savage must have been flying that plane! I've always heard he was tricky. And that couldn't have been smoke that rolled from the ship; it was gas. A kind of gas that just put us to sleep."

The sergeant looked dazed for a moment, then snapped out commands. The huge fellow who had been dismounting the guns rose with a sigh and ambled toward the forming ranks. He stumbled as he neared the captain, threw out one hand to catch himself.

"Excuse me, captain," he mumbled.

The captain snarled, one fist dropped to the .45 at his hip, but the big soldier was already walking away. The sound of paper being crumpled came faintly.

THERE was uneasy murmuring in the ranks of the soldiers. Facing bullets was one thing; facing an enemy who dropped from the sky, overpowered an entire company and vanished, was something else. It smacked too much of the supernatural.

Corporals cursed bitterly as they swung their men into formation and checked off names. Two or three stepped out of ranks to confer with the first sergeant.

"All present and accounted for, sir," the first sergeant reported. "And, if the captain pleases—" he hesitated.

"Well?" snapped the scarred-faced man.

"The men are upset by what has occurred," the sergeant said hesitantly. "They are willing to take orders, but they want to remind you they are all in this just as much as you are. They are afraid we may run into a trap in canyons such as these, and respectfully ask your plans."

The scar flamed like a red gash on the captain's face. For a moment, he seemed too inflamed to speak, and the first words that rolled from his lips singed even the hardened hides of the men who faced him.

"We attack in just two hours!" he bellowed. His hands opened and closed on the butt of his .45.

"We want to know what we're runnin' into. Gold ain't no good to us if we're dead!" a voice shouted from the rear rank. It was the big soldier who had dismounted the machine guns who spoke.

Others yelled in assent.

"And if our company can be gassed, why couldn't all our army get it the same way?" the big soldier went on.

"I'll answer that question." There was a decisive ring in the captain's voice. His face had hardened, but he spoke with assurance. "First, I want to see the man who dares question me. Who is he? Bring him here."

Men in the ranks shifted uncertainly, then the big soldier was pushed to the front. He shuffled forward between two other khaki-clad veterans until he stood within a few feet of the captain.

"We knew of this gas. Preparations have been made to render it useless!" the captain snapped. He darted a quick glance at the big soldier, then again faced the company. "Doc Savage is clever, but The Leader is clever, also. He has known in advance every move this Doc Savage has made, and checkmated it. A plan has been devised to kill every Mayan without risk to ourselves. Why, right here in my pocket is—"

The captain's hand touched his pocket. A blank look crossed his features. For a moment, he was quite pale, standing as if stricken. His head turned slowly, his eyes bored into the face of the big soldier before him.

Slowly, his hand went to his hip, pulled out his .45. The muzzle of the .45 came up, pointed squarely at the head of the big soldier.

Flake gold eyes stared back calmly at the captain. The gold-flecked eyes of Doc Savage.

"Damn you!" shouted the captain, and pulled the trigger.

AN entire company of men was watching the scene. None could have told exactly what happened next. It came too fast.

A harmless *click* came from the .45 in the scarred-faced man's hand. In the same instant, the two men beside Doc Savage turned somersaults in the air. Powerful hands had snapped out, grabbed and hurled them as if they were weightless.

The body of one struck the captain. They crashed to the ground together.

In the same flash, the bronze man started running. As the company of soldiers stood stupefied, they saw the big soldier fairly fade across the ground, start up the side of the canyon.

The captain staggered to his feet.

"Fire! Get him!" he bellowed. "That's Doc Savage! A thousand in gold extra to the man who kills him!"

Rifles came up. Bolts clicked. Hammers fell.

But no shots came!

A squad rushed to one of the half-dismantled machine guns, assembled it swiftly, inserted a belt of bullets and swung the muzzle to cover Doc Savage's fast-disappearing figure. The gun would not work.

"The firing pin's been knocked off my rifle!" one of the soldiers yelled. Others took up the cry. Not a workable gun was left in the company. Doc Savage had worked swiftly in the few minutes the men had been unconscious.

Now he was traveling swiftly back toward the Valley of the Vanished.

As he ran, sure-footed as a mountain goat up the steep canyon side and over rocks, the bronze man examined the papers he had taken from the scarred-faced captain.

The papers were covered with orders. They were concise, detailed military orders. A map showed every canyon, every possible adit and exit to the Mayan kingdom.

And they revealed that even now huge forces of armed men were marching to bottle up both the upper and lower entrance to the huge canyon where the Mayans lived. The attack was to be launched simultaneously from each end.

The orders read:

> When the signal for the attack comes, move forward fearlessly. The canyon should be taken without loss of a life.

A faint, trilling sound filled the air, the sound of Doc Savage. The final notations on the orders read:

> We understand what Doc Savage intends to do. He will be rendered harmless.

The bronze man redoubled his speed, stripping off the khaki coat he wore. The original owner of that coat was trussed and gagged firmly. His bound form would be found when the advance guard started ahead.

Doc Savage was following no trail. Sometimes it seemed as if he literally were running on a thread, so narrow was the ledge of rock he traversed.

He mounted sharply, sped along the crest of the canyon. Two huge boulders loomed before him. There was a narrow passageway between.

The bronze man was moving almost soundlessly, despite his speed. As he neared the boulders, he traveled even faster. Like a high jumper, he leaped at one of the huge rocks.

With fingers that gripped like steel, he hurled himself upward, reached the summit.

On either side of the passageway, now below him, waited an armed man.

ONE of the soldiers thought he sensed the shadow of an eagle. He glanced up, tried to cry out.

He had no chance. Doc Savage flashed downward. One arm whipped out. The man went down without a sound. His companion turned, squeezed the trigger of his gun.

There was a streak of bronze as Doc's fingers went forward, lightning fast. One finger caught between the trigger and the trigger guard, preventing the ambusher from firing.

The bronze man's right hand flicked hard against the other's neck, struck the paralyzing nerves there.

Scarcely slowing, never hesitating to look back, Doc raced on. Behind him were two prone figures. Ahead were other boulders, but they were farther apart.

A shot rang out, close at hand. At the same instant, Doc Savage was whipped into the air.

One moment there had been firm footing beneath him. The next, and the ground seemed to rise swiftly.

A group of men rushed forward from all sides. At four corners, several men had hold of ropes. They were holding up a huge fishing net, of the type used by deep-sea fishers, and woven to withstand tremendous pressure. A thin layer of dirt had concealed that net.

Doc was being held up in the air, as the onrushing men seized the edges of the net, pulling it up, pinning him in the center.

The bronze man had nothing firm to get a grip on. The net beneath his feet gave him no leverage. But his giant muscles erupted. Men yelled with sudden fear.

Enmeshed as he was in the huge net, Doc went into action. His fists cracked on jaws. His skilled fingers brought quick oblivion to those who came within his reach.

Without the net, he would have stood a chance of victory. But that net was a handicap. Too big a handicap, combined with the number of attackers that now launched themselves upon him.

Pistol butts rose and fell, showering blows unmercifully on Doc's closely combed bronze hair. The avalanche of attackers swarmed over him, pulling the net tight, wrapping ropes about it.

Doc Savage resembled a mummy in a hempen cocoon as a broad-shouldered, powerful man strolled on the scene. The fellow wore the uniform of a general.

"Well done, men," smirked General Glassell. "The famous Doc Savage who escapes even torture rooms, is now harmless. Before we are through with him, he may regret he ever made that escape."

## Chapter XVII
### A KNIFE FALLS

DOC'S flake gold eyes moved briefly over Glassell, the son of Morning Breeze. They remained longer on the man who followed the renegade Mayan.

The newcomer was dressed in the uniform of a field marshal. But his appearance would not have been called commanding. Rather, it was fearsome. It affected even the hardboiled soldiers of fortune. They cleared a path for him, with awe and unbidden terror showing on their features.

The face of the field marshal showed nothing at all. It was lifeless. The nose, cheeks, lips and chin were devoid of all expression, as are those of a corpse. Only the eyes seemed alive. They were malevolent beyond description.

The Leader stood before Doc Savage!

The bronze man's gaze was steady. He appeared not to show the effects of the beating that had brought crimson through his light bronze hair. His attitude was that of a disinterested spectator surveying a freak.

The Leader's features did not move. They remained leaden and set. But hate sparkled deeper in his malevolent eyes.

"I am pleased to meet the so famous Doc Savage," he said in a flat, lifeless voice. "One of us had to go. Naturally, it had to be you."

General Glassell shifted uneasily. "We shall kill him now?" he asked anxiously.

The cold, lifeless face turned toward him. The burly Mayan took a step backward involuntarily. "I—I only thought—" he began.

A faint flicker of scorn came to The Leader's malevolent eyes. "Certainly we kill him, but in my own way—and in my own time." He whirled toward the soldiers. "Get blankets and more ropes."

The Leader's eyes blazed as he turned back to the bronze man. "Have you no curiosity?" he flared.

"Why should I be curious?" Doc Savage's voice was even and unruffled. "You probably arrived here soon after I went to visit your advance guard. You saw what I did there and laid a trap for me. The trap was well set."

The frozen-faced one bowed. "Thank you," he sneered. Then his voice returned to its usual cold, lifeless tone. "We did just that. The first two men you encountered were mere decoys. They served their purpose. But I didn't mean that. I meant, weren't you curious as to what my plans are, what I mean to do?"

"No." The bronze man's face did not change. "I am not curious. I know."

Lifeless lips drew back to show gleaming teeth. Eyes became thin slits. "And you shall die with that knowledge. You will not pass it on."

The Leader spun swiftly to the soldiers with the blankets and ropes. "Do as you were instructed!"

The soldiers moved forward. Even with Doc Savage trussed so that movement was impossible, they were cautious. A grin spread over Glassell's features. He seemed to anticipate some special amusement.

"You once caused the downfall of my father," he jeered. "I hope the gods permit him to watch his son aid in revenging that downfall."

Doc made no reply. Soldiers were wrapping blankets about his already-trussed figure. More ropes went about the blankets. Only his head was left free.

Then a rope cradle was fashioned. His helpless form was tossed into the cradle. A strong hempen strand was placed over an outjutting rock, and fastened to the cleverly fashioned support.

"Now!" rasped The Leader.

Three soldiers lifted Doc's bound form. With sure-footed steps, they walked to the edge of the cliff. A corporal barked a sharp order.

Without hesitation, the three soldiers threw Doc over the side. A sheer thousand-foot fall lay below!

THE rope snapped taut. Doc's body jerked viciously, struck the side of the canyon wall and bounded out again. Above him, the single rope that kept him from falling to destruction was stretched tight as a violin string.

The frozen-faced one peered over the edge. A sharp knife was in his hand.

"Anticipation is always half the enjoyment," he advised in that cold, lifeless voice. "You cannot see me. I can see you. Sooner or later, death will strike. Hang there, helpless. Meditate on the rocks that wait for your body far below. When you least expect it, this knife will do its work. You will die."

A battle-hardened corporal shivered slightly. It was ghastly, he reflected, to hang there, never knowing when you were to fall, with a horrifying, mangling death below you—one that would leave your body a smashed, pulpy mass.

And Doc Savage had been a great man. But, of course, The Leader was greater.

General Glassell was trying to express somewhat the same sentiments.

"You have genius," he said flatteringly. "No one but you could have defeated the bronze man. He even escaped me."

The Leader's lifeless face did not change, but his eyes showed pleasure. "I am a genius," he agreed.

"And is not now a good time to tell me what is to happen, now that the bronze man is through and victory within our grasp?" Glassell asked cunningly.

The frozen-faced one glanced at a wrist watch. "Ten minutes before we attack," he said coldly. "Where are the reports from your Mayan spies that you promised we would have?"

General Glassell squirmed as if suddenly stricken with a chill. "They will come, they will come in time," he said hastily. "None could fail you." He drew a deep breath. "But is it not time that I knew the plan?"

The Leader hesitated. Then his eyes glowed fanatically.

"Perhaps I should tell you a little," he conceded. "You called me a genius. And that is correct. For none but a genius could have devised this plan. For it is simple. Simple and yet so complex that no one but me could have thought or carried it out."

The wild light had left his eyes for a moment. Now they blazed with the lust for power that makes and wrecks kingdoms.

"Gold is the answer! Gold and gold alone!"

"But—but, I know," stammered Glassell. "But you are a wealthy man. You have far more of a fortune than you could ever use, or ever spend. I don't understand."

THE LEADER gazed at him scornfully. "Of course you don't. And certainly I have money—much money. But money isn't always gold. And it is gold I want. Gold to bring me power, power to rule the world.

"I have men in every nation of the world. They are trained men, trained agitators." The lifeless-faced man spoke as if to himself. "They have stirred up disorder. They can stir up much more. My money and their skill have done that.

"Some of them are leaders in their own fashion. They can cause revolts that might upset one or two nations where the people are none too well pleased with their present governments. But what is that?"

Glassell's eyes were large, his mouth half open.

"Nothing!" The frozen-faced one's lips came together tightly. "Money alone will not buy enough men to rule the world. Even gold as a purchasing power will not do that. You must strike in another way. And that can be done with gold."

"But I do not see!" Glassell objected blankly.

"Of course, you do not see. No one has, except me. That is where genius comes in. That is where a simple plan that suddenly becomes complex, baffles the average mind. But not mine."

"Doc Savage said he knew," Glassell put in suddenly.

For a moment, faint admiration appeared in the malevolent eyes of The Leader.

"Perhaps he does," he admitted. "But he is an extraordinary man. The knowledge, however, will do him no good. I will seize the gold in the Valley of the Vanished. I will use it as no one else has thought of using it."

He paused dramatically. "And I—I shall become the dictator of the world!"

Glassell's breath was coming fast. His features bore a strange look.

"And me. I'll run Hidalgo!" he breathed.

The words seemed to snap The Leader back to reality. His eyes swung about swiftly.

"Yes, you shall rule Hidalgo," he agreed, but there was a faint, underlying sarcasm in his words. "I shall rule you."

The Leader tested the edge of his knife on the ball of a thumb. A thin, crimson line showed. He nodded, walked toward the rope that alone held Doc Savage's helpless body suspended.

The knife blade pulled across the rope gently. A thread snapped up. General Glassell looked on, hypnotized. Conversation between the soldiers stopped. They stood frozen.

Again the knife caressed the taut rope. Another fragment of hemp unwound like a steel spring.

Glassell moistened lips that suddenly had become dry and parched. His eyes were burning feverishly. His own hand made unconscious, sweeping moves, as if it were he who wielded the knife.

The frozen-faced one lifted the knife high, tensed for a swift, sweeping blow that would cut entirely through the rope. Then he halted, his head came up quickly.

In the almost absolute silence, came the faint sound of running feet.

"The spies," Glassell said, his voice coarse and choking.

A TRAVESTY of a smile, a mere lifting of the corners of the mouth, unexpectedly marked The Leader's face.

"Savage has been where he could hear all we have said so far. He should live until he can hear this. Death will then be even more unbearable," his flat tones came.

Two men rounded a turn in the mountain wall, came racing toward the group of soldiers.

Glassell chuckled. "I told you they'd get here in time," he reminded.

The newcomers were not dressed in the khaki of Glassell's troops. They were dressed as Mayans dressed, their fingertips painted a brilliant red. Once that had been a sign of fighting men. Now it meant only those who were outcasts.

"We come, Son of the Moon," they said in Mayan.

Shifty-eyed, they stood in front of the renegade who once had won the respect of King Chaac in the Valley of the Vanished. These two, also, had been trusted. Friends of Glassell's father, they had appeared to reform. But when Glassell called, they had answered. They had turned traitors.

"You did your work?" Glassell asked harshly.

"Speak Spanish, French, English or anything else, but not that gibberish," the frozen-faced one ordered.

Glassell's eyes narrowed slightly, but he interpreted without hesitation.

"They say the task you sent them on has been completed," he reported.

"The fangs of Doc Savage's men have been drawn?"

"*Si*, completely. They found the big chambers of gas, with special projectors aiming in our direction, just as you had said they would. Using masks you provided, they succeeded in freeing that gas."

"And it must have been a good gas," the frozen-faced one said reflectively, "judging from how it tumbled over the advance guard when Savage used it from his plane. I am glad our radio experts heard his orders. That gas, released at the proper time, might have left our entire army helpless."

"But not now." Glassell was jubilant. "They think they are armed to receive us. They are not. They are without a weapon. They have nothing to fight with."

"Right." The Leader turned, looked over the edge of the canyon, down to where Doc Savage hung swaying on the end of the rope. The bronze man was trussed so thoroughly only his head was in view. He glanced up, his flake gold eyes emotionless as they saw the lifeless face of The Leader.

The knife made a quick circuit in the air. Sunlight glanced off its shiny surface as it cut cleanly through the rope.

Below—a thousand feet below—sharp-pointed rocks seemed to leap upward to receive Doc's body as his cocoon-bound figure hurtled downward.

Somewhere in the distance a bugle sounded.

## Chapter XVIII
## THE ATTACK

"I DON'T like it." Monk was frankly worried. Perspiration showed on his apelike features. He paced back and forth restlessly.

"Doc will win out somehow." Ham tried to speak with assurance, but he somehow failed.

Long Tom held a pair of field glasses to his eyes and peered down the canyon. "If we only hadn't gone down with Princess Monja, we might have been able to see something that would have given us a clue as to what happened," he worried.

"Female perversity predominates even antediluvian craniums," Johnny contributed, with a bitter look at Monk.

"You didn't have to go down with us just because I was taking Monja!" Monk flared. Red crept over his face.

"Quit speaking of girls." Renny's puritanical features became even more severe. "You said, I believe, that you have something rigged up that Doc suggested might halt the army that is to attack us. Perhaps we had better inspect that apparatus and see that it is in working order."

"Gladly." Ham brightened. He swung his sword cane back and forth. "Anything to be doing something, and anything to keep from having to look at the lovesick face of this ape."

Monk growled something unintelligible, but even he seemed glad of something to do.

With Long Tom leading the way, the five moved along the lip of the canyon to where the pipes extended over the edge.

Johnny and Renny examined them with frank interest.

"It was a tough job, but one that should work," Long Tom said, with pardonable pride.

"Unless attacks are launched from both ends of the canyon at the same time," objected Renny.

"We've got others just like this at the far end," Monk rumbled. "A couple of Chaac's men are down there to operate them."

"And the motivating principle behind these cylindrical protuberances?" asked Johnny.

"Compressed air and a gas Doc invented," Long Tom explained. "We will use masks so we won't be affected, then press this button"—he stepped forward to illustrate—"and gas, much heavier than air—"

His mouth dropped. His ordinarily yellow, unhealthy appearing features became ghastly. "It—it—" he choked.

Monk and Ham rushed forward, investigated swiftly.

The hairy chemist's mouth worked wordlessly. Ham straightened, spoke in strangled tones.

"Some one has tampered with them! The gas has been released!"

"And that kicks us into eternity," Monk rumbled thickly. "It took us hours to fix that gas. Doc might do it quicker. But he isn't here. And without it we're lost. The Valley of the Vanished is doomed!"

Renny spoke the thought of all of them.

"Perhaps it would be well if Doc hurried back," he said simply.

DOC was hurrying—downward.

When the rope was cut, his body fell as if it had been shot from a gun. Glassell yelled out gleefully. The malevolent eyes of The Leader were half shut, as if savoring a delectable joke.

Those eyes opened wide with startling quickness. Glassell's yell shut off in mid-breath.

The unbelievable had happened!

The blankets, cocoon-tied ropes and huge fishnet that bound the bronze man suddenly opened and fell away. Doc Savage appeared, free of any bonds.

In the same instant, his long arms and unbelievably strong fingers shot out. They caught a narrow crevice in the seemingly sheer face of the cliff.

His fall was halted.

A foot more, or a foot less, and the effort would have been in vain. He made his catch at the one place where the cliff bulged sufficiently that he could reach it.

Only years of training of eyes and muscles could have achieved the bronze man's purpose. The hours he spent daily in going through the most rigorous exercises, training every muscle, every faculty, had their reward.

For the space of a heartbeat, he hung motionless; then he was in action.

With the grace and ease of a human fly, but with a speed that no other human fly ever possessed, Doc moved across the face of that flat mass of rocks.

The unexpectedness of it all had caught Glassell and his frozen-faced companion flatfooted. For long moments they were as if drugged, eyes unbelieving.

The Leader was the first to recover. He whipped a heavy .45 from his pocket, fired hastily. That haste was his undoing. His bullets went wild. Even as Glassell drew his gun free, and before his companion could fire again, Doc reached shelter.

It wasn't much of a shelter. It was merely a wrinkle in the cliff. That wrinkle, like a glass-smooth wave, was above him. Lead struck it and whined away harmlessly. The bronze man moved along easily beneath it.

Glassell was raging. The frozen-faced one's thin mouth was set; he was firing clip after clip of bullets. Soldiers had raced forward, were adding their rifle fire to the din.

Doc Savage went on, swiftly.

The corporal who had heard much of Doc Savage surmised what had happened. In a way, he was almost glad. He held a reluctant admiration for the bronze man.

But he had no intention of reminding the others of what they must have forgotten.

Doc Savage had been tied, and tied tightly. But the bronze man had been tied before. Slipping his bonds had been simple enough. And in the kit he always carried around his body were razor-sharp knives. It had not been difficult to obtain one of those knives and cut through net, ropes and blankets.

The bronze man, had he desired, could have climbed back up the rope to the top of the cliff. But that would have meant facing bullets without a chance for defense.

Now he had rounded a corner of the canyon, reached a place where he could climb to the top and run.

With sure-footed speed, he tore toward the lip of the gorge where his aides awaited him.

Once more a bugle sounded. And as the shrill blast of the trumpet still echoed, artillery went into action.

The invaders launched screaming shells toward the Valley of the Vanished.

As Doc reached the place where his aides waited, the first of those shells tore overhead. At the other end of the canyon came the rumble of attacking forces there.

"WE can't hold out long." Renny's voice was as calm and conversational as if Doc had just returned from a pleasure jaunt.

"They freed that gas we had," Monk grumbled.

None of Doc's aides showed surprise at the bronze man's reappearance. They always pretended that they never worried when he was on dangerous errands.

"I know." The bronze man wasn't even breathing fast. He made no reference to his experiences.

"The mercy guns?" he asked.

"We got them as soon as we found the gas had been destroyed," said Long Tom.

Doc Savage nodded slightly. The roar of heavy artillery increased.

So far, the shells were overshooting. The gunners may deliberately have been intending to frighten, rather than kill.

"Two of you go to the other end of the canyon," Doc said swiftly. "The other three remain here. Use mercy bullets in your guns and delay the invaders as long as possible."

He turned, raced on down the canyonside toward the Mayan village.

Renny and Johnny picked up weapons and followed, headed toward the lower end of the gorge.

"So long, if we don't see you again." Renny said dryly.

The others nodded. Their plight was desperate, and they knew it, but their spirits were far from low. Doc Savage was back again.

Far down the canyon in front of them the first of a skirmish line could be seen advancing. It was moving slowly, the khaki-clad men taking care to stay behind rocks. The invaders were taking no chances.

The artillery fire had settled down now to a steady, thunderous roar.

A modern army, with all that civilization had developed in the way of death dealing, was moving relentlessly on the last remnant of an ancient race.

Only one man stood between that army and victory. And even his aides wore frowns as they wondered what one man, even Doc Savage, could do to stop a well-armed, well-disciplined mass of troops.

PRINCESS MONJA'S features lighted as she sighted the bronze man. Face still stained with tears, she rushed to him, threw her arms around his neck.

"I'm so glad, so happy you are back," she half sobbed.

An unaccustomed color mounted on Doc's face. There was no time in his busy life for love. He long ago had renounced any thought of marriage. And his unfailing attraction for women had often proved a source of embarrassment. He felt far more at ease in a desperate fight than he did when some beautiful girl showed affection for him.

Monja's arms were locked tightly around Doc's head, her well-molded form was close to his. Gently, he released her grip.

"You must never worry or be concerned ever about my fate," he told her gravely.

The deafening explosion of a big shell drowned out all lesser sounds. Princess Monja shuddered.

"I—I was afraid," she said. "I am not afraid now."

"But still there remains much to be done," Doc said softly. "Please tell your father I wish to see him."

The girl hurried to obey. Doc made haste to the building where Long Tom had taken temporary quarters. One room was filled with chemical supplies and strange equipment. Swiftly, he went to work.

Only the fact that the canyon walls were so high saved the Mayan village from destruction. The gunners were forced to elevate the muzzles of their weapons to such an angle that accurate fire was impossible.

But the troops with those guns were advancing.

King Chaac's face was worried as he entered the room where Doc worked. "Are—are we lost, Clark Savage?" he asked anxiously.

"The assault will be centered on the buildings here," the bronze man observed, ignoring the question. "Glassell, since he formerly lived here, knows of the gold caverns beneath us. I believe he expects you to run there for shelter, since you would be safe from shells if you were underground."

"An excellent idea," the aged king said. "I'll give instructions—"

"Such caverns also could prove to be a gigantic trap," Doc went on. "Openings could be blasted into them, and we would be caught. Therefore, take your people and seek shelter in the undergrowth and small caves along the walls of the gorge. There you will be safe."

"And you?" King Chaac asked.

"I shall be busy," the bronze man replied grimly.

"WE can't hold out much longer," Monk panted. The hairy chemist was perspiring feverishly. Much as he loved a fight, this one was becoming just a little too warm.

Ham and Long Tom were twenty paces on either side of him. Each had sought shelter behind large rocks, was making himself as small as possible.

And they needed all the protection they could get. Snipers were raining lead about them. Several times, bullets had smacked into various parts of their anatomy. Only the bulletproof armor they wore saved them.

Even so, Doc's aids knew they could not hold out much longer. Their rapid-fire pistols, loaded with bullets that brought unconsciousness but not death, sounded occasionally with bullfiddle roars. But they had no chance.

Had the situation not been so serious, they might have marveled at the scene beneath them.

Small baby tanks were creeping forward with machine guns spitting. Those tanks could never scale the cliff and descend on the Mayan village, but they could come close enough so that the men safe inside could drive defenders from the top of the canyon wall.

A stream of lead, fully a hundred feet in length, burst from one of the tanks, played up and down the side of the gorge, but fell short of the men crouched on the top.

Small trench mortars were throwing up bombs. Some of these exploded too close for comfort.

Heavy artillery, machine guns, flame-throwers, tanks and infantry—all were being used in one strong, desperate assault.

"Doc's running the Mayans to shelter," Long Tom observed. He pulled restlessly on the lobe of one oversized ear.

"And we'd better be getting out of here," Ham put in grimly. The lawyer's usually dapper appearance was far from that now. He was hot and tired, his clothes dirty. The barrel of his gun was almost white-hot.

"I hope Doc's got some trick figured out," Monk worried as they retreated cautiously. "If he hasn't, we're really goners this time."

PRINCESS MONJA hoped that the bronze man had some way of halting the invaders, too. But she did more than that.

A look of determination was on her beautiful features. When others of the Mayans slipped toward the sides of the canyon in obedience to Doc's order, she did not go with them. She hid in one of the buildings near Doc until the streets were clear.

Then she slipped out, began a cautious approach to the head of the canyon, circling to dodge Monk, Ham and Long Tom as they moved slowly back. At the rim of the gorge, she halted at a point where she could see all that was going on beneath her.

A strange glint entered her eyes as she made out a bulgy, heavy-set figure in the uniform of a general. One hand felt softly the hilt of a peculiar stone dagger.

Son of the Moon was a traitor. It was he who had brought this trouble on his people. She, as princess and heiress to the throne of her people, should kill Son of the Moon, and with his death remove the one who had forgotten those of his own blood. Thus reasoned Princess Monja.

Carefully, taking shelter where she could, she crept slowly down the side of the gorge, toward the point where that bulky, heavyset figure was.

At the bottom of the canyon, she halted briefly. No one was looking in her direction. General Glassell was only a hundred yards away. Earphones were on his head. He appeared to be talking into a black box. His back was toward the girl.

Whipping the stone dagger from her dress, Monja crept onward.

And it was then, with terrifying suddenness, that strong arms seized her from behind!

Monja kicked, scratched and fought with the fury of a trapped wildcat. Her mouth was open; she screamed frantically.

Words were being whispered into her ear. Too late, she realized their significance.

Monk, growling and muttering, pulled the still struggling girl back toward the side of the gorge.

Catching sight of her as she had started down the canyon wall, he had grasped the mad mission she was on, had set out in pursuit.

But he had reached her too late. Monja's scream had been heard. An entire platoon of khaki-clad figures descended upon them.

Monk fought. He fought as he had never fought before, mouthing defiance as his apelike arms bowled soldiers right and left. But he could not protect his rear.

A heavy weight crashed upon him, bore him to the ground. Still struggling, he was bound, a revolver butt smashed down on the back of his skull.

Dazed, but with belligerence undiminished, he was jerked to where General Glassell stood waiting. Princess Monja was held firmly between two of the invaders.

"This is a surprise," Glassell said, with mock politeness. "I'm glad to see you, Lieutenant Colonel Mayfair, and you, Princess." His eyes gleamed with a strange emotion as they looked upon the scornful features of the Mayan girl. He whipped around to the soldiers.

"Execute Colonel Mayfair at once!" he snapped. "As for the girl"—he paused, smirked slyly—"I had intended to get her anyhow. I am just as well pleased that she could not wait, but came to me. I will keep her."

## Chapter XIX
### A TRAIL OF GOLD

GLASSELL turned back to the radio he had been using. Monja, bound tightly, was propped against a rock near by. The soldiers led Monk away. The girl's eyes were soft as she watched the hairy chemist go to his doom. Monk glanced at her once. What he saw in her face made his heart beat swiftly.

"I'm sorry, Monja," he rumbled.

"You are a brave man, Monk," she said softly. "I shall always remember you."

Glassell was speaking excitedly. "I've captured the one they call Monk and King Chaac's daughter!" he reported.

"It is well." The cold, colorless tones of The Leader sounded in the earphones. "Save both of them in case Doc Savage offers unexpected resistance and it becomes necessary to bargain with him."

"I've ordered Monk shot!" Glassell half howled.

"Countermand that order at once!" The other's voice did not rise, but there was something in it that made Glassell's hands shake as he tore the earphones from his head and raced in the direction the soldiers had taken Monk.

Then he paused. A cunning look crossed his heavy features. The hand of death was terrible, but still—

Sharp orders sounded clearly. "Ready! Aim—"

Glassell motioned to a nearby soldier. "I have changed my mind," he said. "Tell Sergeant Audib he must not execute Colonel Mayfair."

"Fire!" A volley of rifle shots crashed out.

The soldier gaped stupidly. "But, señor general—"

"Fool! Idiot!" Glassell swore with seemingly genuine rage. He jerked out his .45, shot once. The soldier crumpled, a look of surprise still on his face.

"I am sorry," Glassell reported over the radio a moment later. "I gave a soldier orders to run and halt the execution. He did not move swiftly enough. Monk already had been executed. I shot the soldier myself."

At the opposite end of the canyon, the frozen-faced one listened without change of expression. Only his malevolent eyes turned a shade darker.

"Proceed with your advance," he instructed, in that flat, cold voice. "Do not move too swiftly. Doc Savage may have something up his sleeve, although I doubt it. We shall start moving here in five minutes and pinch the Mayans between us. We should have achieved our entire aim inside half an hour."

The Leader switched off his radio. For a moment, he stood silent. When he spoke, it was to himself.

"And I am afraid, General Glassell, that you have blundered once too often. Your usefulness, also, will have expired within the next half an hour."

SOLDIERS mounted to the canyon rim overlooking the Valley of the Vanished. Other khaki-clad figures appeared from the opposite end of the gorge. The men moved forward, cautiously.

Below them, they could see only the collection of queer-shaped buildings—and the huge, gold-built pyramid.

Eyes became feverish; a tenseness filled those advancing soldiers of fortune. Captains shouted orders harshly, delaying with difficulty the advance of troops that were muttering rebelliously.

"That's the gold we're after. What are we waiting for?" a gigantic, red-eyed invader snarled.

"There is no one in view. It might be a trap," a companion counseled.

"Trap, hell!" The big soldier spat contemptuously. "That bunch down there is licked, and they know it!"

The Mayans hidden at the sides of the canyon also felt that hope was gone. Peering through trees, they saw Doc's aides retreat to the building where the bronze man had been at work. Then they saw nothing more.

Glum features faced Doc. "Monk is gone," Ham said, softly. Sorrow showed on the lawyer's face.

Pain flashed for an instant in the bronze man's flake-gold eyes. "You are sure?"

Long Tom nodded slowly. "We saw him overcome and later executed. We were too far away to help him."

"He tried to save Princess Monja," Ham explained haltingly. "The big ape, I—I—"

"We understand," Renny said. His thin lips were tight. All felt a stunning loss, but all knew that Ham probably was the most affected, despite the continual bickering between the two that had marked their careers.

"Time is short," Doc Savage said. He stared straight ahead for a moment, then spoke crisply. "We have only a faint chance. The forces against us are overpowering. But we can try. The fate of the Mayans, the fate of the world, depends on us. Here is what must be done."

He spoke on, in short, clipped sentences. The others nodded. No need to tell them that their plight was desperate. They all knew they were faced with almost certain death. But it was not in their code to surrender.

Once Johnny opened his mouth to protest. Then his lips came together, the words unspoken. Doc Savage was taking the most dangerous, the most desperate chance of all in the one plan that offered the slightest hope of winning out. But that was the bronze man's way. Johnny knew protests would be useless.

One by one, the men turned to their allotted tasks.

Doc wheeled a small machine to the doorway. In appearance it was not unlike a miniature cannon, except that the barrel was solid steel, with no opening for a shell. Wires led from it to a small dynamo. At one side was a row of buttons and across the top, running parallel to the barrel, were two heavily-insulated wires, strung like a radio aerial.

Soldiers were moving over the edge of the canyon wall. Doc spun the point of his strange weapon in that direction. The dynamo hummed, its pitch gradually increasing.

The bronze man pressed one of the buttons beside the barrel.

*Blam!*

Rock and dirt exploded with a tremendous blast directly in the face of the onrushing force.

Again Doc pressed a button.

"HE'S pulled one out of his hat."

The speaker was clad in khaki. He was pressed close to the ground, where he could get a clear view of what was happening. Small, deep-set eyes peered from beneath layers of gristle. One long, crooked arm was tossed carelessly over the small form beside him.

"Yes, Monk, but I expected that," said Princess Monja.

The hairy chemist twisted his head, looked admiringly at his companion.

Explosions were blasting at the entire edge of the cliff where the attacking force had halted. The blasts came with the force of high-powered shells. The attackers were milling in confusion.

"Atomic blasts." Monk explained.

"At—at what?" asked Monja.

Monk blushed slightly. "Long Tom is the electrical guy; he could explain better than I can," he confessed. "But Doc's got an electrical dingbat rigged up that shoots bolts of juice, and when that juice hits the rocks it releases the atomic energy inside, causing an internal explosion, creating the illusion of artillery shells hitting."

"O—oh, yes. I—I understand perfectly." A dazed look was on Monja's face.

Monk grinned happily. He didn't understand perfectly either, but he was glad just to be alive, and to be with Monja.

He really should be dead, he conceded. In fact, he'd been left for dead by the firing squad. But the commander of that firing squad evidently hadn't heard of the bulletproof armor. None of the soldiers had fired at his head. All had shot at his body.

The tremendous striking power of the bullets had knocked Monk out, but they hadn't killed him. He'd recovered, just as the advance had started. Borrowing the uniform of an unconscious soldier, he'd found Monja, freed her and started back to rejoin Doc.

Slowly, the hairy chemist's grin faded. Additional hordes of khaki-clad troops were pouring up the canyon.

The gold-maddened reserves from Blanco Grande had arrived!

In the same instant, officers of the invaders saw through Doc's trick. The explosions were continuing. Rocks and dirt were being thrown high in the air, but casualties were few. Shouted orders came distinctly.

Troops dived through the dust clouds, started charging down the slope toward the Mayan village. From the opposite end of the gorge, the first of the attackers there came into view.

Streams of khaki-clad troops were swarming toward the golden pyramid from all directions. Literally thousands of men were staging a last, furious charge.

Below them, Doc Savage stood alone!

AS the charge started, Doc Savage abandoned the atomic gun. It had served its purpose. It had delayed the attack until the bronze man's aides had completed their tasks and disappeared.

But Monk did not know that. A groan burst from his lips.

Nothing could withstand the resistless force of that charging mass of gold-maddened, inflamed band of soldiers of fortune, an army composed of little better than bandits, whose sole aim was to kill and loot.

And then a strange thing occurred—a thing that not even Monk could understand.

Doc left the doorway of the building where he had been crouched. He raced into the open. He raced directly for the golden pyramid.

Order almost disappeared in the ranks of the invaders. They became little more than an unruly, senseless mob. Attempts of their officers to control them were unheeded.

All had heard of the extra reward offered to the man who killed Doc Savage. They raised guns, fired, and ran downward.

Doc apparently paid no attention to the bullets that sang about him. As Monk watched, the bronze man reached the front of the pyramid, started up.

Narrow paths, chiseled in the side of the gorge, offered the only route for one group of the advancing soldiers, but they were tumbling down that with little regard either for their own safety or the safety of their companions.

Some were pushed off, to fall to horrible deaths. The others did not even pause. Behind them came even more, as those who had left Blanco Grande last joined in that frantic rush.

All eyes were on the bronze man. The steps up the front of the pyramid were steep, but he was mounting them with apparent ease. His rapidly moving figure made a difficult target, but even so it seemed impossible that he could reach the top in safety.

But reach the top he did. A sigh of relief came from Monk, a sigh that was half a groan. For Doc had swung open the huge door at the top of the pyramid—the door that led to the enormous gold caverns beneath the ground.

"He's safe for a minute, but he'll be trapped! They'll get him sure!" the hairy chemist wailed.

But he found he was talking to himself. Monja had slipped from under his arm, was on her feet and running down another narrow trail.

"If Clark Savage dies, I want to be with him," she sobbed.

For a moment, a lugubrious expression was on Monk's homely face. It seemed he hadn't been making the progress with the pretty Mayan that he had thought.

But Monk's hesitation was only momentary. Then he, too, was on his feet, plunging after the girl. He also could die with Doc.

From the far end of the canyon, a fresh regiment of khaki-clad veterans streamed into view. The valley seemed filled with shouting, murderous invaders.

Then Doc reappeared. And at sight of him, Monk's breath came in with sudden comprehension.

The bronze man was running down the face of the pyramid now. He was carrying a huge load in his big arms. And as he ran, he dropped objects from that load.

The sun flashed briefly on the burden he carried. It was a dull, golden gleam. The objects that were being dropped were golden ingots, goblets and golden vessels.

The bronze man was leaving a golden trail leading straight to the enormous storehouse underground—the storehouse where thousands upon thousands of similar ingots and immense stores of beautiful golden images and vessels lay hidden.

## Chapter XX
### WHEN PLANS MISFIRE

THE tumult that followed was almost indescribable. No such desperate, hideous stampede had ever been seen before.

The sight of those golden objects, the clear intimation that they led to a storehouse where an almost inexhaustible supply was hidden, released passions that long had been hidden. The thin veneer that civilization had stamped on the murderous troops intent on a bloody errand was stripped away.

They became savages. Only one thought filled them; only one desire impelled them.

Each wanted to be the first to get the gold. Each wanted to seize all the gleaming metal that he could carry, to paw over it, to revel in wealth, to steal and loot and kill.

Officers tried desperately to stem the tide. Automatics cracked as those officers shot the men in the leading ranks, striving to restore sanity.

They might just as well have tried to reason with a hurricane, and they stood as little chance of stopping the rush.

More guns roared. But those guns were in the hands of the gold-maddened soldiers. The officers dropped. Some were trampled to death, others were shot down, still others were run through by bayonets. None lived.

The race up the front of the pyramid resembled the rushing onslaught of warrior ants, who climb over the bodies of their fellows to surmount any obstacle, and who leave nothing behind them.

So it was with the khaki-clad invaders. Those who slipped, those who paused for an instant to draw a breath, were knocked to the steps, were ground under hobnailed boots.

Screams of pain and torture filled the air, mingling with other yells from those who did not even know they were making a sound, but knew only

they intended to go on, and that nothing could stop them.

The bronze man had disappeared. Even had he been in plain view, it is doubtful that he would have been noticed. Every eye was focused on that yawning opening near the top of the pyramid, the opening that led to the gold vaults.

THE LEADER had been thrust aside by the first rush of his troops. And he had realized at once what had happened.

The anger that filled him against Doc Savage made his malevolent eyes gleam like red balls of fire. His expressionless face was even more lifeless and frozen.

He alone made no attempt to try and halt the soldiers. That, he saw, was useless. The very reason that had impelled him to enlist such men as his warriors was now working against him.

He had wanted only those to whom killing is just another job, who were outside the law and ready for any desperate venture. Now those qualities had broken out in a way that would be impossible to control.

Doc Savage had outwitted him.

But the frozen-faced one had no intention of giving up. He still had one desperate play he could make. His eyes narrowed with cunning thought. Cautiously, he started toward the pyramid.

Thunderous noise of fighting men came from under the ground now. The stream of struggling bandits climbing up the pyramid had dwindled. In a few minutes all would be in the deep, hidden caverns.

There was huge chamber after huge chamber in that underground vault. Every chamber was filled with gold. Pile upon pile of it was there for the taking. But the frozen features of The Leader betrayed no interest, now, in that fact.

The soldiers, he knew, could still be taken care of. They could be taken care of in a way that was hideous beyond all human reason.

But The Leader was scarcely reasonable. And now he was hunting and stalking. He wanted to find Doc Savage. If he could find him—

AT one side of the village was a peculiar-appearing structure. Once it had housed the sacrificial well. At the bottom of that well had hissed vicious snakes. It had been used by the Mayans for executions.

The snakes were no longer there. It had been long since the sacrificial well had been used. But if the snakes were gone, the well did hold other queer creatures.

As the din and tumult quieted, those strange creatures appeared, pulling themselves awkwardly over the edge of the well.

There were four of them. They were huge, and far from human in appearance, although each did appear to have two legs and two other appendages that might have been arms.

But where the heads should have been, were bucket-shaped objects, something like divers' helmets. Shoulders and torsos were hidden in bulky jackets that joined the helmets at the top, and overall-shaped trousers below.

Each of the four was carrying a large cylinder. A bellowslike arrangement was at one end of each cylinder, while a hose was attached to the other end.

The cylinders were heavy. The four, big as each was, grunted inaudibly as they hoisted their burdens and started slowly toward the pyramid.

And as they moved forward, another figure came into view. Doc Savage glided from a nearby building, took up a position in front of the strange-appearing figures.

He did not appear surprised, nor did the four seem to notice him.

But another did. The frozen features of The Leader peered cautiously around a corner, two hundred yards away. A gun came up in his hand, then dropped. The distance was too great.

The Leader was not superstitious. He saw nothing awesome in the four creatures that trailed Doc Savage. He did see deadly peril there to his plans.

He did not know, but he felt with fierce certainty that he knew what was in the cylinders those four carried, and felt he knew why they were dressed as they were.

Men about to use an overpowering gas would be dressed that way. Men who planned an attack on a large force where their only hope lay in rendering their opponents helpless, would be dressed that way.

If such a gas were loosed in the gold caverns, the soldiers there would be helpless. Even if the gas did not kill, it would leave the bandits easy prey, so that they might be disarmed and bound.

Under the direction of the Mayans, terrible when aroused, an army could be marched, powerless, back to Blanco Grande to face the summary justice of military rule.

The Leader darted forward with fierce strides.

GENERAL GLASSELL, also, was stalking prey. Unlike the commander, the Mayan renegade had not been in the front ranks of the attackers. He had arrived behind the fierce rush of the maddened men.

But bringing up the rear, he had seen something that at first made him believe in ghosts.

Speeding along ahead of him had been a beautiful girl, closely pursued by an apelike form, whose long, dangling arms almost touched the ground.

Glassell's .45 had appeared in his hand; he had slipped along rapidly behind them.

The Mayan, also, saw that all was lost. There had been one instant of fierce regret, then he had reverted to type. With the fatalism of his race, he had accepted defeat. But all his fierce hatred had centered on Monk.

As the roar of underground fighting increased in volume, Doc led his four aids to the base of the pyramid. He held a mercy pistol in one hand.

The scramble of running feet came to his keen ears. He whirled. A strange trilling filled the air, a trilling low, yet penetrating. It was heard by his four aides, even inside the huge helmets they wore.

From one side of the pyramid had appeared Princess Monja, with Monk close behind her. And in the rear, pistol raised, was General Glassell.

At another corner, almost behind Doc, came the frozen, expressionless features of The Leader. His gun was aimed directly at the bronze man's head.

THERE was an instant of perfect silence among those at the base of the golden pyramid.

The fate of the world hung on that one breathless moment. Victory for either side could be decided in the space of a heartbeat.

The Leader saw that victory in his hands. A single pressure on the trigger, and lead would drill the bronze-haired head of Doc Savage.

Monk saw the danger to Doc. He let out a hoarse bellow of rage and leaped forward with the clumsy, gangling, yet tremendous speed of the bull-ape he resembled. Four men in queer costumes also leaped to shield the bronze man.

But even quicker than his aides, even faster than the finger squeeze of The Leader, was Doc Savage.

A gun cracked. Lead whistled through the space Doc's head had occupied a moment before. But the bronze man was no longer there.

With a coordination of muscles that would have appeared unbelievable unless it had been seen, Doc had jumped to one side. In that same flash, he had turned in mid-air. He landed facing the horrible features and malevolent eyes of the frozen-faced one.

It was then that the man who had wanted to rule the world knew he had lost. It was then he knew that the golden trail he had followed could have but one ending.

With a shrill scream, he vanished behind the side of the pyramid. He ran frantically along the wall toward a small niche.

General Glassell saw that move. He understood what it meant. Some deep, hidden remnant of manliness came to the surface. With frantic steps, he charged desperately to intercept the man he had so long obeyed.

They came face to face, directly before the niche.

Insane rage gleamed from the frozen-faced one's eyes. Glassell was yelling, was shouting frantic words. What those words were, The Leader never knew.

He squeezed the trigger of his gun, again and again.

The renegade Mayan went to the ground, his head almost shot from his body. The Leader clawed frantically at a small spot on the side of the pyramid.

Doc Savage shot around a corner. Lead tugged the side of his coat as the frozen-faced one fired at him.

Mouth drawn back in a terrible grimace, eyes almost popping from his head, The Leader's clawing hand found what it sought. It was a small key.

Doc Savage's keen eyes saw that key. His lips tightened. He fired his mercy pistol at the other's hand.

That mercy bullet struck even as the key was pushed home.

THERE was a tremendous, earth-shaking roar. The ground trembled and rocked beneath their feet. Even Doc was shaken off balance, while his aides were thrown to the earth bodily by the force of that explosion. The pyramid rocked and teetered, seemed almost about to collapse entirely.

While ears still rang, while bodies still were stunned by the force of that overpowering blast, other sounds rose from the depths of the earth. The sounds were such that none who heard them ever could forget.

They made tame by comparison the worst nightmare ever experienced. They were animal cries of unendurable pain and torment. They were wrung from hundreds of throats—the throats of gold-maddened bandits, trapped and dying.

The simple pressure of a hidden key had exploded tons of dynamite planted by spies at either entrance to the gold cavern. That explosion had been planned to trap and kill Mayans who had been expected to seek refuge there from the artillery bombardment.

Instead, it had trapped and killed those who had sought to destroy the Mayans. And they had been killed by their own commander. Hidden caches of deadly gas, designed to wipe out any Mayan who might survive the explosion, had been released with the blast. That poison was now killing the last of the bandit horde.

Doc Savage ran forward, firing once more with his mercy pistol.

The Leader had fallen. He made no attempt to rise. One fist made feeble swipes at his throat.

As the bronze man reached his side, the other fell back. On his throat was the crimson-soaked hand of death.

## Chapter XXI
## FRIENDS PART

DOC SAVAGE reached quickly for the kit inside his coat. His hand came out. It held only a broken hypodermic. The Leader's last shot at the bronze man had sealed his own doom. It had broken the only vial of antidote Doc had had for the hand of death.

The bronze man's aides gathered swiftly. The metal helmets came off, to reveal Renny, Johnny, Long Tom and Ham. Monk stood close to Princess Monja.

A peculiar-shaped glove was on one hand of the frozen-faced one. It was literally covered with hundreds of tiny needles.

"The hand of death," Monk said solemnly.

"Be careful when you touch it," Doc cautioned. "The point of each of those needles has been covered with a very swift-action poison. It was only by analyzing some of the blood of the slain messenger boy that I was able to develop an antidote. Now that antidote has been destroyed."

Ham nodded. Mayans were streaming down from the hills. The noise underground had ceased. There was only the silence of the tomb—a tomb that enfolded all those who had come to murder and loot.

Renny glanced at the body on the ground curiously. "But who is he, Doc?"

"Yeah, I never saw that mug before," Long Tom muttered.

Doc Savage smiled slightly. He reached down, his hands worked about the fallen one's face.

A gasp of astonishment came from the lanky chemist as Doc Savage rose. In his hands, he held a cleverly-fashioned mask. That mask had fitted closely over the real features of The Leader.

The man who lay dead was Baron Vardon.

"BUT he's the one who wanted us to go to Switzerland. We saw him dead in the hotel room in New York!" Monk exploded.

"He is the one who wanted us to go to Switzerland, but we did not see him dead," Doc corrected quietly.

"You mean—"

"I mean he tried to decoy us abroad, so he might have a clear field here," the bronze man went on. "He realized he might fail, so he pretended to be a victim of the hand of death. When we first entered the hotel room, his acting was realistic.

"Before we left, I knew he was not dead, but there was no time to do anything, or any reason to then. I didn't want to make him a prisoner then. It would have meant letting the rest of his men know that fact and disperse before I could trap them all. But, unfortunately, I failed."

"The pulse on his throat?" Johnny asked. "Is that how you knew he wasn't dead?"

"Exactly. The pulsebeat there showed he was alive."

"But his purpose?" Ham asked. "From Long Tom's investigation, Baron Vardon was an exceedingly wealthy man in his own right. Why did he want the gold here?"

"Baron Vardon was wealthy," Doc agreed, "but he wanted power. Through his League of Nations connections, he learned of the Valley of the Vanished. And he saw a way to use the gold.

"Gold is almost a forbidden metal on a majority of the world's leading money markets, yet those money markets are based on it. And the peace and prosperity of the world depends on the money markets.

"Should the financial centers of the world suddenly be disrupted, the entire financial structure of the world would be toppled; and nations, even the strongest, would fall."

"Then he—"

"He intended to throw the billions of dollars' worth of gold of the Valley of the Vanished on the world market in one big sweep. Financial security of nations would have been overthrown. His agitators would have stirred up trouble where stirring was necessary. Gold would have made him dictator of the world."

"A golden peril!" Ham breathed.

THE MAYANS did not want to see Doc and his men go. But the bronze man's errand was over. Hidalgo and the Valley of the Vanished had been saved.

The plane Long Tom had purchased in Havana, virtually undamaged, was flown from the nearby canyon to the small lake in the Valley of the Vanished. Equipment was placed aboard.

No attempt had been made to open the underground tombs where murderers and thieves lay buried. The Mayans would wait for months, until all poison gas was gone, before they did that.

Princess Monja stood silent and forlorn at the edge of the lake as the six men started for the plane.

Monk paused beside her. His homely face worked with emotion. It seemed he had words to say, but he could not say them.

The Mayan princess had eyes only for Doc. Face lengthening, Monk walked on.

The plane's motor roared. The ship began to move slowly across the water. Cries of farewell, mingled with sadness, filled the air. It might be long before they saw Doc Savage again.

Monk's eyes were glued to Monja. Under the full sweep of the Central American sun, her skin was golden, her face beautiful.

Ham's face screwed up mischievously; then he sobered. The look on Monk's face showed only too well where his heart was.

"Skip it," the dapper lawyer advised affectionately. "She's beautiful, and she's a princess. But you have no more chance there than she has of winning Doc. Women are dangerous, too."

"Yeah," Monk sighed deeply. "A golden peril."

THE END

# Postscript

*The Golden Peril* is one of the many Doc Savage collaborations between Lester Dent and his old Tulsa *World* crony, Harold A. Davis. Born in Lamar, Colorado in 1902, Davis worked as a newspaperman in California and Texas, ending up at the Tulsa *World* in the late 1920s, where he ran the telegraph desk. Dent was an Associated Press telegrapher working at the *World.* The two became fast friends.

In 1932, Davis landed a job on the New York *News-American,* moving over to the *Daily News* three years later. Along with a third Tulsa transplant, western radio commentator and newspaper columnist Cal Tinney, who was famous for his "Oklahoma" parties, the trio formed a tight-knit circle.

Dent considered himself a Westerner to the bone. Although born in La Plata, Missouri, and graduating from high school there, in the years between Dent lived in Wyoming, Nebraska and Oklahoma. He once said, "I guess I'm more Oklahoman than anything else, having lived there longer than anywhere else by about five years." Not until World War II, when he built his remarkable "House of Gadgets" in La Plata, did Lester reconnect with his roots and become an unalloyed son of Missouri.

Late in 1933, Dent hired Davis to ghost *The King Maker.* Dent had to revise it heavily, as he did subsequent Davis Docs. But over time, the red-headed newsman got the hang of writing Doc Savage. He became Dent's most reliable collaborator, and a frequent contributor of short stories to John Nanovic's titles. His blinding speed at the typewriter helped. Davis often wrote his fiction between duties at his newspaper job.

Early in 1937, Lester Dent returned from a six-month hiatus to resume writing Doc Savage. He had spent much of the prior year breaking into prestigious pulp markets like *Argosy* and *Black Mask.*

But now Street & Smith called him again.

Dent began the new year writing *Devil on the Moon.* Then apparently someone at Street & Smith decided it was high time Doc Savage revisited his origins. Over at *The Shadow,* Walter Gibson had just written *Crime, Insured,* following it with the equally electrifying *The Shadow Unmasks.* Editor John L. Nanovic no doubt suggested that it was time Doc Savage had an adventure just as momentous.

But Dent was busy revising *Hocus Pocus,* a serial for *Argosy,* and handed the chore off to Davis. Evidently, Dent was not sentimental about his first Doc Savage effort, leaving it to Davis to sequel *The Man of Bronze.* Or perhaps having adapted it several times for radio, he felt a fresh approach was needed.

Davis reread that first adventure and produced an outline entitled "The Throne Maker." Dent realized Doc fans wouldn't be likely to buy a story about a royal furniture builder, so the title was the first thing he changed.

Unlike Dent, Harold Davis wrote lengthy outlines which he followed the way a carpenter adheres to blueprints. Few are the variations between the prepared plot and the finished story. The only differences worth noting are the fact that Baron Vardon's first name, Weille, never made it into the tale; the villain originally went by the alias, "the Throne Maker"; and the renegade Mayan, Juan Glassell, intended to marry Princess Monja. Since Monja was as close to a girlfriend as the Man of Bronze ever had, even as a threat that simply wouldn't do.

The published novel shows the unmistakable signs of Lester Dent's canny hand. Clearly, he took a pen to Davis's first draft, and inserted distinctive Lester Dent touches that help make this novel so very special. Dent missed one mistake Davis often made—Johnny Littlejohn had stopped wearing glasses back in 1934, but in every Harold Davis Doc Savage, they're back. Davis abandoned fiction writing in 1940 to become *Newsday*'s first managing editor, and was succeeded in 1944 by another Doc Savage ghost, Alan Hathway.

*Doc Savage* editor John Nanovic considered *The Golden Peril* to be one of the most important stories of the entire series. In 1943, he assembled a *Doc Savage Annual* that was to have reprinted the three most-requested Doc novels. Only a severe cutback in war-rationed paper prevented it from going to press. The contents were to be: *The Man of Bronze, The Monsters* and—*The Golden Peril.*

—Will Murray

**Harold A. Davis**

**Lester Dent at the Tulsa *World***